" I will take it upstairs and find out what it is worth "

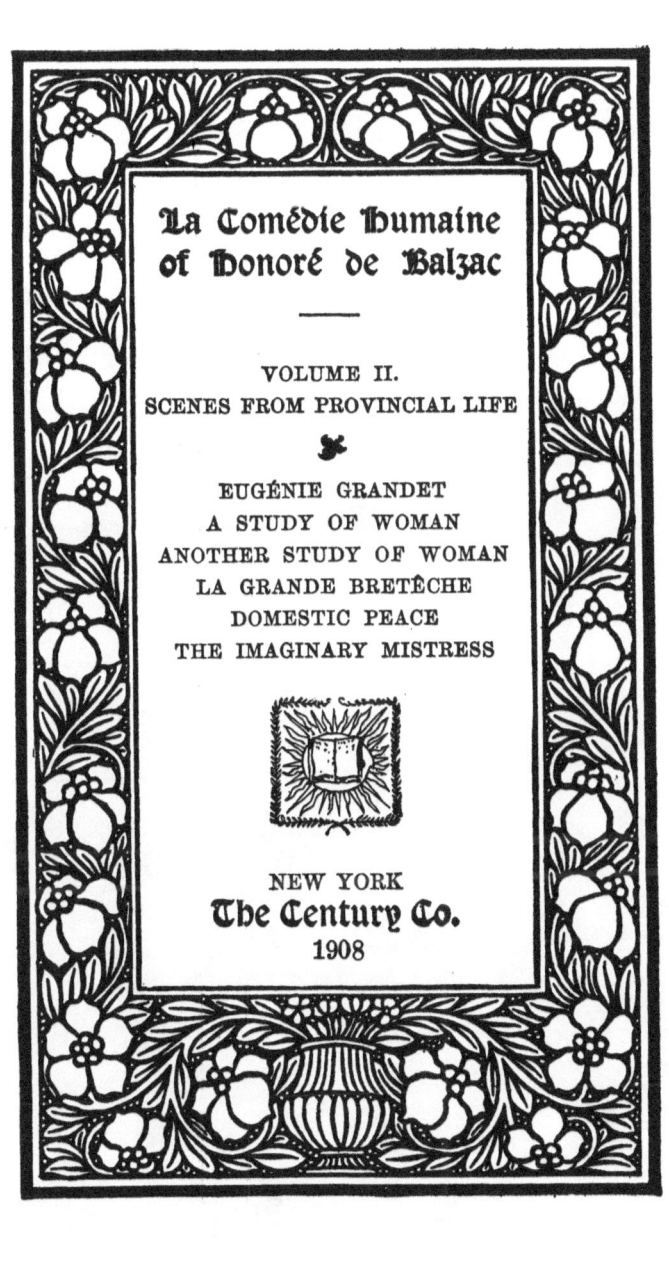

La Comédie Humaine of Honoré de Balzac

VOLUME II.
SCENES FROM PROVINCIAL LIFE

EUGÉNIE GRANDET
A STUDY OF WOMAN
ANOTHER STUDY OF WOMAN
LA GRANDE BRETÊCHE
DOMESTIC PEACE
THE IMAGINARY MISTRESS

NEW YORK
The Century Co.
1908

CONTENTS

INTRODUCTION*

Readers have long since formed their judgment of "Eugénie Grandet." With the exception of "Père Goriot," it is probably the most widely read and most thoroughly admired of all Balzac's works. He himself, during its composition, wrote to Mme. Hanska that it was "ravishing," but later, when he found that the public was disposed to compare with it unfavorably subsequent works that he liked, he complained rather testily of its popularity. Except perhaps in " Père Goriot," he never touched the hearts of his readers so profoundly as in "Eugénie Grandet," he never elsewhere gave to his work that *cachet* of the genius who can deal adequately with almost infinite powers and passions. In "Eugénie Grandet" he showed himself to be practically a faultless artist and but little less than a great poet. The public, recognizing these facts, has been within its rights in choosing the book for special admiration, the " Comédie Humaine" being quite too large to be appreciated in its entirety by many persons. The "Comedy" must be appreciated as a whole before Balzac can be fairly judged; but pending this consummation, the master does not suffer greatly in being judged by "Eugénie Grandet."

To unfold adequately the merits of the story would require a volume. Think of the description of Grandet's house at Saumur, think of the vivid portraiture of the great miser himself, of the faithful Nanon, of patient Mme. Grandet, of the incomparable Eugénie. Think of the absorbing interest lent even to the least of Grandet's business transactions as well as to the least of the strategic moves of the Cruchots and the des Grassins. As for the imperishable scenes such as that in which Grandet discovers the sugar intended for Charles, they are literally too numerous to mention. But, after all, the dominant notes of the book are the pathetic sufferings of the two women and the infinite egotism of the miser. No one will forget the imprisonment of Eugénie, or Mme. Grandet's uncomplaining death, or the old man gazing his last upon, his precious gold, or Eugénie's reception of Charles' dastardly letter. The story may not end quite as English readers would have it, but it is probably as full of inevitable touches as any other novel of the century. What more inevitable, for example, what more Shakespearian, than Eugénie's exclamation when the coach is carrying her lover away:—"Mother, I should like to have for a moment the power of God." The whole pious, filial, enamored, pure maiden is in that exclamation.

But "Eugénie Grandet" has not escaped criticism. People have wondered why its heroine did not rebel more thoroughly, which has caused other persons to wonder why these critical individuals do not know more about French life. Others have thought that Charles plays a part altogether too foolish and villainous, yet it is not clear that his training and his adventurous career fitted him for acting otherwise than as he did. But the most vital criticism has been directed at Eugénie herself. English and American readers have doubted whether she is altogether natural, and have proceeded to descant upon Balzac's inability to depict a girl's character— a matter which some Frenchmen also lay up against him. On this point, which bears on other stories, we may say a few words once for all.

Balzac's pure girls—or young women—seem unnatural and unattractive to some readers and very natural and attractive to others. The safe conclusion is, not that he did not understand young girls, but that he drew certain types of girl well and did not, save occasionally, attempt to draw others—probably because he knew little or nothing about them. Most English novel readers seem to keep a lively, free, attractive female in their mind's eye whom they label "girl" and with whom they instinctively compare all the fair young creatures they read about. Perhaps some Frenchmen of reactionary temperaments do this also. But it is quite certain that there are many English and American girls who are far from conforming to this established type, and it seems to be certain that a majority of European girls are still farther from doing so. The sweet, submissive, innocent type of girl that Balzac loved to draw, such as Ursule Mirouët, is the more or less natural product of European training; she has her own charm, and she ought to appeal to a catholic-minded reader. This is not saying that Balzac's young women equal Shakespeare's, but only that it is foolish to write about them as if they were hardly superior to Cooper's. The Frenchman's knowledge of matured women is conceded; is it not safer to infer that he knew French females from the cradle to the grave and that many of his critics know only the English girl? And after all we have very definite proof that he was not without opportunities to study young girls. He was devoted to his sisters and his nieces, and to think that he did not study them is to think that he completely changed his nature when he entered his family circle. Some of us cannot believe this, and we shall continue to regard Eugénie Grandet as a creation worthy of Balzac. There can scarcely be higher praise.

Little space is left for discussing the other stories contained in this volume, but with the exception of "La Grande Bretèche" they need little comment. "Étude de Femme" is clever but slight. The second "study" is forced in places, and but for Blondet's subtle description of a woman of the world and Montcornet's and Bianchon's stories—all previously utilized—it would be regarded as a comparatively unimportant Parisian sketch. "La Paix du Ménage" gives a good picture of high life during the Napoleonic régime, but is perhaps written on a scale disproportionate to the interest if not to the importance of its general theme.

"La Fausse Maîtresse" is much more interesting and important, containing as it does in Paz one of Balzac's finest if somewhat grandiose characters. Paz is in many respects the Balzac anxious to be loved—the Balzac who was dreaming of doing mighty things for a countrywoman of Paz's—the fair Mme. Hanska. The story is not without sensational touches, but it has also marked psychological strength. Like the three sketches just commented on, it brings one face to face with the often mooted question whether Balzac was successful in describing high life.

Yet must an introduction that begins with "Eugénie Grandet" end with such qualified praise as is given in the preceding paragraph? Fortunately this is not necessary. "La Grande Bretèche" still demands a word, and for this tragic tale no praise is too high. The honors of the "short story"—and great honors they are—have generally gone, for this century at least, to another Frenchman, Maupassant, who has been pushed hard by a Russian, Turgenev, and an American, Poe. Yet it seems scarcely too much to say that none of these masters has surpassed Balzac in this tale in which he has given proof that if his genius had not called him to higher work he might have made himself the greatest short-story writer since Boccaccio.

W. P. TRENT.

EUGÉNIE GRANDET

To Maria.

Your portrait is the fairest ornament of this book, and here
it is fitting that your name should be set, like the branch of box
taken from some unknown garden to lie for a while in the holy
water, and afterwards set by pious hands above the threshold,
where the green spray, ever renewed, is a sacred talisman to
ward off all evil from the house.

In some country towns there are houses more depressing to
the sight than the dimmest cloister, the most melancholy
ruins, or the dreariest stretch of sandy waste. Perhaps such
houses as these combine the characteristics of all the three,
and to the dumb silence of the monastery they unite the
gauntness and grimness of the ruin, and the arid desolation
of the waste. So little sign is there of life or of movement
about them, that a stranger might take them for uninhabited
dwellings; but the sound of an unfamiliar footstep brings
some one to the window, a passive face suddenly appears
above the sill, and the traveler receives a listless and indifferent glance—it is almost as if a monk leaned out to look for a
moment on the world.

There is one particular house front in Saumur which possesses all these melancholy characteristics; the house is still
standing at the end of the steep street which leads to the castle,
at the upper end of the town. The street is very quiet nowadays; it is hot in summer and cold in winter, and very dark
in places; besides this, it is remarkably narrow and crooked,
there is a peculiarly formal and sedate air about its houses,

and it is curious how every sound reverberates through it—
the cobble stones (always clean and dry) ring with every
passing footfall.

This is the oldest part of the town, the ramparts rise immediately above it. The houses of the quarter have stood
for three centuries; and albeit they are built of wood, they
are strong and sound yet. Each house has a certain character
of its own, so that for the artist and antiquary this is the most
attractive part of the town of Saumur. Indeed, it would
hardly be possible to go past the house without a wondering
glance at the grotesque figures carved on the projecting ends
of the huge beams, set like a black bas-relief above the ground
floor of almost every dwelling. Sometimes, where these
beams have been protected from the weather by slates, a strip
of dull blue runs across the crumbling walls, and crowning
the whole is a high-pitched roof oddly curved and bent with
age; the shingle boards that cover it are all warped and
twisted by the alternate sun and rain of many a year. There
are bits of delicate carving too, here and there, though you
can scarcely make them out, on the worn and blackened window sills that seem scarcely strong enough to bear the weight
of the red flower-pot in which some poor workwoman has set
her tree carnation or her monthly rose.

Still further along the street there are more pretentious
house doors studded with huge nails. On these our forefathers exercised their ingenuity, tracing hieroglyphs and
mysterious signs which were once understood in every household, but all clues to their meaning are forgotten now—they
will be understood no more of any mortal. In such wise
would a Protestant make his profession of faith, there also
would a Leaguer curse Henry IV. in graven symbols. A
burgher would commemorate his civic dignities, the glory of
his long-forgotten tenure of office as alderman or sheriff.
On those old houses, if we could but read it, the history of
France is chronicled.

Beside the rickety little tenement built of wood, with masonry of the roughest, upon the wall of which the craftsman

has set the glorified image of his trade—his plane—stands the mansion of some noble, with its massive round arched gateway; you can still see some traces above it of the arms borne by the owner, though they have been torn down in one of the many revolutions which have convulsed the country since 1789.

You will find no imposing shop windows in the streets; strictly speaking indeed, there are no shops at all, for the rooms on the ground floor in which articles are exposed for sale are neither more nor less than the workshops of the times of our forefathers; lovers of the Middle Ages will find here the primitive simplicity of an older world. The low-ceiled rooms are dark, cavernous, and guiltless alike of plate glass windows or of show cases; there is no attempt at decoration either within or without, no effort is made to display the wares. The door as a rule is heavily barred with iron and divided into two parts; the upper half is thrown back during the day, admitting fresh air and daylight into the damp little cave; while the lower portion, to which a bell is attached, is seldom still. The shop front consists of a low wall of about elbow height, which fills half the space between floor and ceiling; there is no window sash, but heavy shutters fastened with iron bolts fit into a groove in the top of the wall, and are set up at night and taken down in the morning. The same wall serves as a counter on which to set out goods for the customer's inspection. There is no sort of charlatanism about the proceeding. The samples submitted to the public vary according to the nature of the trade. You behold a keg or two of salt or of salted fish, two or three bales of sail-cloth or coils of rope, some copper wire hanging from the rafters, a few cooper's hoops on the walls, or a length or two of cloth upon the shelves.

You go in. A neat and tidy damsel with a pair of bare red arms, the fresh good looks of youth, and a white handkerchief pinned about her throat, lays down her knitting and goes to summon a father or mother, who appears and sells goods to you as you desire, be it a matter of two sous or of

twenty thousand francs; the manner of the transaction varying as the humor of the vendor is surly, obliging or independent. You will see a dealer in barrel-staves sitting in his
doorway, twirling his thumbs as he chats with a neighbor;
judging from appearances, he might possess nothing in this
world but the bottles on his few rickety shelves, and two or
three bundles of laths; but his well-stocked timber yard on
the quay supplies all the coopers in Anjou, he knows to a
barrel-stave how many casks he can "turn out," as he says, if
the vines do well and the vintage is good; a few scorching
days and his fortune is made, a rainy summer is a ruinous
thing for him; in a single morning the price of puncheons
will rise as high as eleven francs or drop to six.

Here, as in Touraine, the whole trade of the district depends upon an atmospherical depression. Landowners, vine-
growers, timber merchants, coopers, innkeepers, and lighter-
men, one and all are on the watch for a ray of sunlight. Not
a man of them but goes to bed in fear and trembling lest
he should hear in the morning that there has been a frost in
the night. If it is not rain that they dread, it is wind or
drought; they must have cloudy weather or heat, and the
rainfall and the weather generally all arranged to suit their
peculiar notions.

Between the clerk of the weather and the vine-growing
interest there is a duel which never ceases. Faces visibly
lengthen or shorten, grow bright or gloomy, with the ups and
downs of the barometer. Sometimes you hear from one end
to the other of the old High Street of Saumur the words,
"This is golden weather!" or again, in language which likewise is no mere figure of speech, "It is raining gold louis!"
and they all know the exact value of sun or rain at the right
moment.

After twelve o'clock or so on a Saturday in the summer
time, you will not do a pennyworth of business among the
worthy townsmen of Saumur. Each has his little farm and
his bit of vineyard, and goes to spend the "week end" in the
country. As everybody knows this beforehand, just as every-

body knows everybody else's business, his goings and comings, his buyings and sellings, and profits to boot, the good folk are free to spend ten hours out of the twelve in making up pleasant little parties, in taking notes and making comments and keeping sharp look-out on their neighbors' affairs. The mistress of a house cannot buy a partridge but the neighbors will inquire of her husband whether the bird was done to a turn; no damsel can put her head out of the window without being observed by every group of unoccupied observers.

Impenetrable, dark, and silent as the houses may seem, they contain no mysteries hidden from public scrutiny, and in the same way every one knows what is passing in every one else's mind. To begin with, the good folk spend most of their lives out of doors, they sit on the steps of their houses, breakfast there and dine there, and adjust any little family differences in the doorway. Every passer-by is scanned with the most minute and diligent attention; hence, any stranger who may happen to arrive in such a country town has, in a manner, to run the gauntlet, and is severely quizzed from every doorstep. By dint of perseverance in the methods thus indicated a quantity of droll stories may be collected; and, indeed, the people of Angers, who are of an ingenious turn, and quick at repartee, have been nicknamed "the tattlers" on these very grounds.

The largest houses of the old quarter in which the nobles once dwelt are all at the upper end of the street, and in one of these the events took place which are about to be narrated in the course of this story. As has been already said, it was a melancholy house, a venerable relic of a bygone age, built for the men and women of an older and simpler world, from which our modern France is further and further removed day by day. After you have followed for some distance the windings of the picturesque street, where memories of the past are called up by every detail at every turn, till at length you fall unconsciously to musing, you come upon a sufficiently gloomy recess in which a doorway is dimly visible, the door of *M. Grandet's house.* Of all the pride and glory of proprietorship conveyed to the provincial mind by those three words, it is impossible to give any idea, except by giving the biography of the owner—M. Grandet.

M. Grandet enjoyed a certain reputation in Saumur. Its causes and effects can scarcely be properly estimated by out-siders who have not lived in a country town for a longer or shorter time. There were still old people in existence who could remember former times, and called M. Grandet "Good-man Grandet," but there were not many of them left, and they were rapidly disappearing year by year.

In 1789 Grandet was a master cooper, in a very good way of business, who could read and write and cast accounts. When the French Republic, having confiscated the lands of the Church in the district of Saumur, proceeded to sell them by auction, the cooper was forty years of age, and had just married the daughter of a wealthy timber merchant. As Grandet possessed at that moment his wife's dowry as well as some considerable amount of ready money of his own, he repaired to the bureau of the *district;* and making due allow-ance for two hundred double louis offered by his father-in-law to that man of stern morals, the Republican who conducted the sale, the cooper acquired some of the best vineland in the neighborhood, an old abbey, and a few little farms, for an old song, to all of which property, though it might be ill-gotten, the law gave him a clear title.

There was little sympathy felt with the Revolution in Sau-mur. Goodman Grandet was looked upon as a bold spirit, a Republican, a patriot, an "advanced thinker," and what not; but all the "thinking" the cooper ever did turned simply and solely on the subject of his vines. He was nominated as a member of the administration of the district of Saumur, and exercised a pacific influence both in politics and in com-merce. Politically, he befriended the ci-devants, and did all that he could to prevent the sale of their property; com-mercially, he contracted to supply two thousand hogsheads of white wine to the Republican armies, taking his payment for the aforesaid hogsheads in the shape of certain broad acres of rich meadow land belonging to a convent, the property of the nuns having been reserved till the last.

In the days of the Consulate, Master Grandet became mayor; did prudently in his public capacity, and did very well for himself. Times changed, the Empire was established, and he became *Monsieur* Grandet. But M. Grandet had been looked upon as a red Republican, and Napoleon had no liking for Republicans, so the mayor was replaced by a large landowner, a man with a *de* before his name, and a prospect of one day becoming a baron of the Empire. M. Grandet turned his back upon municipal honors without a shadow of regret. He had looked well after the interests of the town during his term of office, excellent roads had been made, passing in every case by his own domains. His house and land had been assessed very moderately, the burden of the taxes did not fall too grievously upon him; since the assessment moreover he had given ceaseless attention and care to the cultivation of his vines, so that they had become the *tête du pays*, the technical term for those vineyards which produce wine of the finest quality. He had a fair claim to the Cross of the Legion of Honor, and he received it in 1806.

By this time M. Grandet was fifty-seven years old, and his wife about thirty-six. The one child of the marriage was a daughter, a little girl ten years of age. Providence doubtless sought to console M. Grandet for his official downfall; for in this year he succeeded to three fortunes; the total value was matter for conjecture, no certain information being forthcoming. The first fell in on the death of Mme. de la Guadinière, Mme. Grandet's mother; the deceased lady had been a de la Bertellière, and her father, old M. de la Bertellière, soon followed her; the third in order was Mme. Gentillet, M. Grandet's grandmother on the mother's side. Old M. de la Bertellière used to call an investment "throwing money away;" the sight of his hoards of gold repaid him better than any rate of interest upon it. The town of Saumur, therefore, roughly calculated the value of the amount that the late de la Bertellière was likely to have saved out of his yearly takings; and M. Grandet received a new distinction which none of our manias for equality can efface—he paid more taxes than any one else in the country round.

He now cultivated a hundred acres of vineyard; in a good year they would yield seven or eight hundred puncheons. He had thirteen little farms, an old abbey (motives of economy had led him to wall up the windows, and so preserve the traceries and stained glass), and a hundred and twenty-seven acres of grazing land, in which three thousand poplars, planted in 1793, were growing taller and larger every year. Finally, he owned the house in which he lived.

In these visible ways his prosperity had increased. As to his capital, there were only two people in a position to make a guess at its probable amount. One of these was the notary, M. Cruchot, who transacted all the necessary business whenever M. Grandet made an investment; and the other was M. des Grassins, the wealthiest banker in the town, who did Grandet many good offices which were unknown to Saumur. Secrets of this nature, involving extensive business transactions, are usually well kept; but the discreet caution of MM. Cruchot and des Grassins did not prevent them from addressing M. Grandet in public with such profound deference that close observers might draw their own conclusions. Clearly the wealth of their late mayor must be prodigious indeed that he should receive such obsequious attention.

There was no one in Saumur who did not fully believe the report which told how, in a secret hiding-place, M. Grandet had a hoard of louis, and how every night he went to look at it and gave himself up to the inexpressible delight of gazing at the huge heap of gold. He was not the only money-lover in Saumur. Sympathetic observers looked at his eyes and felt that the story was true, for they seemed to have the yellow metallic glitter of the coin over which it was said they had brooded. Nor was this the only sign. Certain small indefinable habits, furtive movements, slight mysterious promptings of greed did not escape the keen observation of fellow-worshipers. There is something vulpine about the eyes of a man who lends money at an exorbitant rate of interest; they gradually and surely contract like those of the gambler, the sensualist, or the courtier; and there is, so to speak, a sort of freemasonry among the passions, a written language of hieroglyphs and signs for those who can read them.

M. Grandet therefore inspired in all around him the respectful esteem which is but the due of a man who has never owed any one a farthing in his life; a just and legitimate tribute to an astute old cooper and vinegrower who knew beforehand with the certainty of an astronomer when five hundred casks would serve for the vintage, and when to have a thousand in readiness; a man who had never lost on any speculation, who had always a stock of empty barrels whenever casks were so dear that they fetched more than the contents were worth; who could store his vintage in his own cellars, and afford to bide his time, so that his puncheons would bring him in a couple of hundred francs, while many a little proprietor who could not wait had to be content with half that amount. His famous vintage in the year 1811 discreetly held, and sold only as good opportunities offered, had been worth two hundred and forty thousand livres to him.

In matters financial M. Grandet might be described as combining the characteristics of the Bengal tiger and the boa constrictor. He could lie low and wait, crouching, watching for his prey, and make his spring, unerringly at last; then the jaws of his purse would unclose, a torrent of coin would be swallowed down, and, as in the case of the gorged reptile, there would be a period of inaction; like the serpent, moreover, he was cold, apathetic, methodical, keeping to his own mysterious times and seasons.

No one could see the man pass without feeling a certain kind of admiration, which was half dread, half respect. The tiger's clutch was like steel, his claws were sharp and swift; was there any one in Saumur who had not felt them? Such an one, for instance, wanted to borrow money to buy that piece of land which he had set his heart upon; M. Cruchot had found the money for him—at eleven per cent. And there was So-and-so yonder; M. des Grassins had discounted his bills, but it was at a ruinous rate.

There were not many days when M. Grandet's name did not come up in conversation, in familiar talk in the evenings, or in the gossip of the town. There were people who took a kind of patriotic pride in the old vinegrower's wealth. More than one innkeeper or merchant had found occasion to remark to a stranger with a certain complacency, "There are millionaires in two or three of our firms here, sir; but as for M. Grandet, he himself could hardly tell you how much he was worth!"

In 1816 the shrewdest heads in Saumur set down the value of the cooper's landed property at about four millions; but as, to strike a fair average, he must have drawn something like a hundred thousand francs (they thought) from his property between the years 1793 and 1817, the amount of money he possessed must nearly equal the value of the land. So when M. Grandet's name was mentioned over a game at boston, or a chat about the prospects of the vines, these folk would look wise and remark, "Who is that you are talking of? Old Grandet? . . . Old Grandet must have five or six millions, there is no doubt about it."

"Then you are cleverer than I am; I have never been able to find out how much he has," M. Cruchot or M. des Grassins would put in, if they overheard the speech.

If any one from Paris mentioned the Rothschilds or M. Laffitte, the good people in Saumur would ask if any of those persons were as rich as M. Grandet? And if the Parisian should answer in the affirmative with a pitying smile, they looked at one another incredulously and flung up their heads. So great a fortune was like a golden mantle; it covered its owner and all that he did. At one time some of the eccentricities of his mode of life gave rise to laughter at his expense; but the satire and the laughter had died out, and M. Grandet still went his way, till at last even his slightest actions came to be taken as precedents, and every trifling thing he said or did carried weight. His remarks, his clothing, his gestures, the way he blinked his eyes, had all been studied with the care with which a naturalist studies the workings of instinct in some wild creature; and no one failed to discern the taciturn and profound wisdom that underlay all these manifestations.

"We shall have a hard winter," they would say; "old Grandet has put on his fur gloves, we must gather the grapes." Or, "Goodman Grandet is laying in a lot of cask staves; there will be plenty of wine this year."

M. Grandet never bought either meat or bread. Part of his rents were paid in kind, and every week his tenants brought in poultry, eggs, butter, and wheat sufficient for the needs of his household. Moreover, he owned a mill, and the miller, besides paying rent, came over to fetch a certain quantity of corn, and brought him back both the bran and the flour. Big Nanon, the one maid-servant, baked all the bread once a week on Saturday mornings (though she was not so young as she had been). Others of the tenants were market gardeners, and M. Grandet had arranged that these were to keep him supplied with fresh vegetables. Of fruit there was no lack; indeed, he sold a great deal of it in the market. Firewood was gathered from his own hedges, or taken from old stumps of trees that grew by the sides of his fields. His tenants chopped up the wood, carted it into the town, and obligingly stacked his fagots for him, receiving in return—his thanks. So he seldom had occasion to spend money. His only known items of expenditure were for sacramental bread, for sittings in the church for his wife and daughter, their dress, Nanon's wages, renewals of the linings of Nanon's saucepans, repairs about the house, candles, rates and taxes, and the necessary outlays of money for improvements. He had recently acquired six hundred acres of woodland, and, being unable to look after it himself, had induced a keeper belonging to a neighbor to attend to it, promising to repay the man for his trouble. After this purchase had been made, and not before, game appeared on the Grandets' table.

Grandet's manners were distinctly homely. He did not say very much. He expressed his ideas, as a rule, in brief, sententious phrases, uttered in a low voice. Since the time of the Revolution, when for a while he had attracted some attention, the worthy man had contracted a tiresome habit of stammering as soon as he took part in a discussion or began to speak at any length. He had other peculiarities. He habitually drowned his ideas in a flood of words more or less incoherent; his singular inaptitude for reasoning logically was usually set down to a defective education; but this, like his unwelcome fluency, the trick of stammering, and various other mannerisms, was assumed, and for reasons which, in the course of the story, will be made sufficiently clear. In conversation, moreover, he had other resources: four phrases, like algebraical formulæ, which fitted every case, were always forthcoming to solve every knotty problem in business or domestic life—"I do not know," "I cannot do it," "I will have nothing to do with it," and "We shall see." He never committed himself. He never said Yes or No; he never put anything down in writing. He listened with apparent indifference when he was spoken to, caressing his chin with his right hand, while the back of his left supported his elbow. When once he had formed his opinion in any matter of business, he never changed it; but he pondered long even over the smallest transactions. When in the course of deep and weighty converse he had managed to fathom the intentions of an antagonist, who meanwhile flattered himself that *he* at least knew where to have Grandet, the latter was wont to say, "I must talk it over with my wife before I can give a definite answer." In business matters the wife, whom he had reduced to the most abject submission, was unquestionably a most convenient support and screen.

He never paid visits, never dined away from home, nor asked any one to dinner; his movements were almost noiseless; he seemed to carry out his principles of economy in everything; to make no useless sound, to be chary of spending even physical energy. His respect for the rights of ownership was so habitual that he never displaced nor disturbed anything belonging to another. And yet, in spite of the low tones of his voice, in spite of his discretion and cautious bearing, the cooper's real character showed itself in his language and manners, and this was more especially the case in his own house, where he was less on his guard than elsewhere.

As to Grandet's exterior. He was a broad, square-shouldered, thick-set man, about five feet high; his legs were thin (he measured perhaps twelve inches round the calves), his knee joints large and prominent. He had a bullet-shaped head, a sun-burned face, scarred with the smallpox, and a narrow chin; there was no trace of a curve about the lines of his mouth. He possessed a set of white teeth, eyes with the expression of stony avidity in them with which the basilisk is credited, a deeply-furrowed brow on which there were prominences not lacking in significance, hair that had once been of a sandy hue, but which was now fast turning gray; so that thoughtless youngsters, rash enough to make jokes on so serious a subject, would say that M. Grandet's very hair was "gold and silver." On his nose, which was broad and blunt at the tip, was a variegated wen; gossip affirmed, not without some appearance of truth, that spite and rancor was the cause of this affection. There was a dangerous cunning about this face, although the man, indeed, was honest according to the letter of the law; it was a selfish face; there were but two things in the world for which its owner cared—the delights of hoarding wealth in the first place, and in the second, the only being who counted for anything in his estimation, his daughter Eugénie, his only child, who one day should inherit that wealth. His attitude, manner, bearing, and everything about him plainly showed that he had the belief in himself which is the natural outcome of an unbroken record of successful business speculations. Pliant and smooth-spoken though he might appear to be, M. Grandet was a man of bronze. He was always dressed after the same fashion; in

1819 he looked in this respect exactly as he had looked at any time since 1791. His heavy shoes were secured by leather laces; he wore thick woolen stockings all the year round, knee breeches of chestnut brown homespun, silver buckles, a brown velvet waistcoat adorned with yellow stripes and buttoned up to the throat, a loosely-fitting coat with ample skirts, a black cravat, and a broad-brimmed Quaker-like hat. His gloves, like those of the gendarmerie, were chosen with a view to hard wear; a pair lasted him nearly two years. In order to keep them clean, he always laid them down on the same place on the brim of his hat, till the action had come to be mechanical with him. So much, and no more, Saumur knew of this her citizen.

A few fellow-townspeople, six in all, had the right of entry to Grandet's house and society. First among these in order of importance was M. Cruchot's nephew. Ever since his appointment as president of the court of first instance, this young man had added the appellation "de Bonfons" to his original name of Cruchot; in time he hoped that the Bonfons would efface the Cruchot, when he meant to drop the Cruchot altogether, and was at no little pains to compass this end. Already he styled himself C. de Bonfons. Any litigant who was so ill inspired as to address him in court as "M. Cruchot," was soon made painfully aware that he had blundered. The magistrate was about thirty-three years of age, and the owner of the estate of Bonfons (*Boni Fontis*), which brought in annually seven thousand livres. In addition to this he had prospects; he would succeed some day to the property of his uncle the notary, and there was yet another uncle besides, the Abbé Cruchot, a dignitary of the chapter of Saint Martin of Tours; both relatives were commonly reported to be men of substance. The three Cruchots, with a goodly number of kinsfolk, connected too by marriage with a score of other houses, formed a sort of party in the town, like the family of the Medicis in Florence long ago; and, like the Medicis, the Cruchots had their rivals—their Pazzi.

Mme. des Grassins, the mother of a son of twenty-three

years of age, came assiduously to take a hand at cards with
Mme. Grandet, hoping to marry her own dear Adolphe to
Mademoiselle Eugénie. She had a powerful ally in her husband the banker, who had secretly rendered the old miser
many a service, and who could give opportune aid on her
field of battle. The three des Grassins had likewise their
host of adherents, their cousins, and trusty auxiliaries.

The Abbé (the Talleyrand of the Cruchot faction), well
supported by his brother the notary, closely disputed the
ground with the banker's wife; they meant to carry off the
wealthy heiress for their nephew the president. The struggle
between the two parties for the prize of the hand of Eugénie
Grandet was an open secret; all Saumur watched it with the
keenest interest.   Which would Mlle. Grandet marry?
Would it be M. le Président or M. Adolphe des Grassins?
Some solved the problem by saying that M. Grandet would
give his daughter to neither. The old cooper (said they) was
consumed with an ambition to have a peer of France for his
son-in-law, and he was on the look-out for a peer of France,
who for the consideration of an income of three hundred
thousand livres would find all the past, present, and future
barrels of the Grandets no obstacle to a match. Others de-
murred to this, and urged that both M. and Mme. des Grassins came of a good family, that they had wealth enough for
anything, that Adolphe was a very good-looking, pretty behaved young man, and that unless the Grandets had a Pope's
nephew somewhere in the background, they ought to be satisfied with a match in every way so suitable; for they were
nobodies after all; all Saumur had seen Grandet going about
with an adze in his hands, and moreover he had worn the red
cap of Liberty in his time.

The more astute observers remarked that M. Cruchot de
Bonfons was free of the house in the High Street, while his
rival only visited there on Sundays. Some maintained that
Mme. des Grassins, being on more intimate terms with the
women of the house, had opportunities of inculcating certain ideas which sooner or later must conduce to her success.

Others retorted that the Abbé Cruchot had the most insinuating manner in the world, and that with a churchman on one side and a woman on the other the chances were about even.

"It is gown against cassock," said a local wit.

Those whose memories went further back, said that the Grandets were too prudent to let all that property go out of the family. Mlle. Eugénie Grandet of Saumur would be married one of these days to the son of the other M. Grandet of Paris, a rich wholesale wine merchant. To these both Cruchotins and Grassinistes were wont to reply as follows:—

"In the first place, the brothers have not met twice in thirty years. Then M. Grandet of Paris is ambitious for that son of his. He himself is mayor of his division of the department, a deputy, a colonel of the National Guard, and a judge of the tribunal of commerce. He does not own to any relationship with the Grandets of Saumur, and is seeking to connect himself with one of Napoleon's dukes."

What will not people say of an heiress? Eugénie Grandet was a stock subject of conversation for twenty leagues round; nay, in public conveyances, even as far as Angers on the one hand and Blois on the other!

In the beginning of the year 1811 the Cruchotins gained a signal victory over the Grassinistes. The young Marquis de Froidfond being compelled to realize his capital, the estate of Froidfond, celebrated for its park and its handsome château, was for sale; together with its dependent farms, rivers, fishponds, and forest; altogether it was worth three million francs. M. Cruchot, President Cruchot, and the Abbé Cruchot by uniting their forces had managed to prevent a proposed division into small lots. The notary made an uncommonly good bargain for his client, representing to the young marquis that the purchase money of the small lots could only be collected after endless trouble and expense, and that he would have to sue a large proportion of the purchasers for it; while here was M. Grandet, a man whose credit stood high, and who was moreover ready to pay for the land at once in hard coin, it would be better to take M. Grandet's

offer. In this way the fair marquisate of Froidfond was swallowed down by M. Grandet, who, to the amazement of Saumur, paid for it in ready money (deducting discount of
course) as soon as the required formalities were completed.
The news of this transaction traveled far and wide; it
reached Orleans; it was spoken of at Nantes.

M. Grandet went to see his château, and on this wise: a
cart happened to be returning thither, so he embraced this
opportunity of visiting his newly acquired property, and took
a look round in the capacity of owner. Then he returned to
Saumur, well convinced that this investment would bring
him in a clear five per cent, and fired with a magnificent ambition; he would add his own bits of land to the marquisate
of Froidfond, and everything should lie within a ring fence.
For the present he would set himself to replenish his almost
exhausted coffers; he would cut down every stick of timber in
his copses and forests, and fell the poplars in his meadows.

It is easy after this explanation to understand all that was
conveyed by the words, "M. Grandet's house"—the cold,
dreary, and silent house at the upper end of the town, under
the shadow of the ruined ramparts.

Two pillars supported the arch above the doorway, and for
these, as also for the building of the house itself, a porous
crumbling stone peculiar to the district along the banks of
the Loire had been employed, a kind of tufa so soft that at
most it scarcely lasts for two hundred years. Rain and frost
had gnawed numerous irregular holes in the surface, with a
curious effect; the piers and the voussoirs looked as though
they were composed of the vermicular stones often met with
in French architecture. The doorway might have been the
portal of a jail. Above the arch there was a long sculptured
bas-relief of harder stone, representing the four Seasons, four
forlorn figures, aged, blackened, and weather worn. Above
the bas-relief there was a projecting ledge of masonry where
some chance-sown plants had taken root; yellow pellitory,
bindweed, a plantain or two, and a little cherry-tree, that
even now had reached a fair height.

2

The massive door itself was of dark oak, shrunk and warped, and full of cracks; but, feeble as it looked, it was firmly held together by a series of iron nails with huge heads, driven into the wood in a symmetrical design. In the middle there was a small square grating covered with rusty iron bars, which served as an excuse for a door knocker which hung there from a ring, and struck upon the menacing head a great iron bolt. The knocker itself, oblong in shape, was of the kind that our ancestors used to call a "Jaquemart," and not unlike a huge note of admiration. If an antiquary had examined it carefully, he might have found some traces of the grotesque human head that it once represented, but the features of the typical clown had long since been effaced by constant wear. The little grating had been made in past times of civil war, so that the household might recognize their friends without before admitting them, but now it afforded to inquisitive eyes a view of a dank and gloomy archway, and a flight of broken steps leading to a not unpicturesque garden shut in by thick walls through which the damp was oozing, and a hedge of sickly-looking shrubs. The walls were part of the old fortifications, and up above upon the ramparts there were yet other gardens belonging to some of the neighboring houses.

A door beneath the arch of the gateway opened into a large parlor, the principal room on the ground floor. Few people comprehend the importance of this apartment in little towns in Anjou, Berri, and Touraine. The parlor is also the hall, drawing-room, study, and boudoir all in one; it is the stage on which the drama of domestic life is played, the very heart and centre of the home. Hither the hairdresser repaired once in six months to cut M. Grandet's hair. The tenants and the curé, the sous-préfet and the miller's lad, were all alike shown into this room. There were two windows which looked out upon the street, the floor was boarded, the walls were paneled from floor to ceiling, covered with old carvings, and painted gray. The rafters were left visible, and were likewise painted gray, the plaster in intervening spaces was yellow with age.

'An old brass clock case inlaid with arabesques in tortoise-shell stood on the chimney-piece, which was of white stone, and adorned with rude carvings. Above it stood a mirror of a greenish hue, the edges were beveled in order to display the thickness of the glass, and reflected a thin streak of colored light into the room, which was caught again by the polished surface of another mirror of Damascus steel, which hung upon the wall.

Two branched sconces of gilded copper which adorned either end of the chimney-piece answered a double purpose. The branch roses which served as candle-sockets were removable, and the main stem, fitted into an antique copper contrivance on a bluish marble pedestal, did duty as a candlestick for ordinary days.

The old-fashioned chairs were covered with tapestry, on which the fables of La Fontaine were depicted; but a thorough knowledge of the author was required in order to make out the subjects, for the colors had faded badly, and the outlines of the figures were hardly visible through a multitude of darns. Four sideboards occupied the four corners of the room, each of these articles of furniture terminating in a tier of very dirty shelves. An old inlaid card-table with a chess-board marked out upon its surface stood in the space between the two windows, and on the wall, above the table, hung an oval barometer in a dark wooden setting, adorned by a carved bunch of ribbons; they had been gilt ribbons once upon a time, but generations of flies had wantonly obscured the gilding, till its existence had become problematical. Two portraits in pastel hung on the wall opposite the fireplace. One was believed to represent Mme. Grandet's grandfather, old M. de la Bertellière, as a lieutenant in the Guards, and the other the late Mme. Gentillet as a shepherdess.

Crimson curtains of *gros de Tours* were hung in the windows and fastened back with silk cords and huge tassels. This luxurious upholstery, so little in harmony with the manners and customs of the Grandets, had been included in the purchase of the house, like the pier-glass, the brass timepiece,

the tapestry-covered chairs, and the rosewood corner sideboards. In the further window stood a straw-bottomed chair,
raised on blocks of wood, so that Mme. Grandet could watch
the passers-by as she sat. A work-table of cherry wood,
bleached and faded by the light, filled the other window space,
and close beside it Eugénie Grandet's little armchair was set.

The lives of mother and daughter had flowed on tranquilly
for fifteen years. Day after day, from April to November,
they sat at work in the windows; but the first day of the latter month found them beside the fire, where they took up
their positions for the winter. Grandet would not allow a
fire to be lighted in the room before that date, nor again
after the 31st of March, let the early days of spring or of
autumn be cold as they might. Big Nanon managed by
stealth to fill a little brazier with glowing ashes from the
kitchen fire, and in this way the chilly evenings of April and
October were rendered tolerable for Mme. and Mlle. Grandet.
All the household linen was kept in repair by the mother and
daughter; and so conscientiously did they devote their days
to this duty (no light task in truth), that if Eugénie wanted
to embroider a collarette for her mother she was obliged to
steal the time from her hours of slumber, and to resort to a
deception to obtain from her father the candle by which she
worked. For a long while past it had been the miser's wont
to dole out the candles to his daughter and big Nanon in the
same way that he gave out the bread and the other matters
daily required by the household.

Perhaps big Nanon was the one servant in existence who
could and would have endured her master's tyrannous rule.
Every one in the town used to envy M. and Mme. Grandet.
"Big Nanon," so called on account of her height of five feet
eight inches, had been a part of the Grandet household for
thirty-five years. She was held to be one of the richest servants in Saumur, and this on a yearly wage of seventy
livres! The seventy livres had accumulated for thirty-
five years, and quite recently Nanon had deposited four thousand livres with M. Cruchot for the purchase of an annuity.

This result of a long and persevering course of thrift appealed to the imagination—it seemed tremendous. There was not a maid-servant in Saumur but was envious of the poor woman, who by the time she had reached her sixtieth year would have scraped together enough to keep herself from want in her old age; but no one thought of the hard life and all the toil which had gone to the making of that little hoard.

Thirty-five years ago, when Nanon had been a homely, hard-featured girl of two and twenty, she had not been able to find a place because her appearance had been so much against her. Poor Nanon! it was really very hard. If her head had been set on the shoulders of a grenadier it would have been greatly admired, but there is a fitness in things, and Nanon's style of beauty was inappropriate. She had been a herdswoman on a farm for a time, till the farmhouse had been burnt down, and then it was, that, full of the robust courage that shrinks from nothing, she came to seek service in Saumur.

At that time M. Grandet was thinking of marriage, and already determined to set up housekeeping. The girl, who had been rebuffed from door to door, came under his notice. He was a cooper, and therefore a good judge of physical strength; he foresaw at once how useful this feminine Hercules could be, a strongly-made woman who stood planted as firmly on her feet as an oak tree rooted in the soil where it has grown for two generations, a woman with square shoulders, large hips, and hands like a ploughman's, and whose honesty was as unquestionable as her virtue. He was not dismayed by a martial countenance, a disfiguring wart or two, a complexion like burnt clay, and a pair of sinewy arms; neither did Nanon's rags alarm the cooper, whose heart was not yet hardened against misery. He took the poor girl into his service, gave her food, clothes, shoes and wages. Nanon found her hard life not intolerably hard. Nay, she secretly shed tears of joy at being so treated; she felt a sincere attachment for this master, who expected as much from her as ever feudal lord required of a serf.

Nanon did all the work of the house. She did the cooking and the washing, carrying all the linen down to the Loire and bringing it back on her shoulders. She rose at daybreak and went to bed late. It was she who, without any assistance, cooked for the vintagers in the autumn, and looked sharply after the market-folk. She watched over her master's property like a faithful dog, and with a blind belief in him; she obeyed his most arbitrary commands without a murmur—his whims were law to her.

After twenty years of service, in the famous year 1811, when the vintage had been gathered in after unheard-of toil and trouble, Grandet made up his mind to present Nanon with his old watch, the only gift she had ever received from him. She certainly had the reversion of his old shoes (which happened to fit her), but as a rule they were so far seen into already that they were of little use to any one else, and could not be looked upon as a present. Sheer necessity had made the poor girl so penurious that Grandet grew quite fond of her at last, and regarded her with the same sort of affection that a man gives to his dog; and as for Nanon, she cheerfully wore the collar of servitude set round with spikes that she had ceased to feel. Grandet might stint the day's allowance of bread, but she did not grumble. The fare might be scanty and poor, but Nanon's spirits did not suffer, and her health appeared to benefit; there was never any illness in that house.

And then Nanon was one of the family. She shared every mood of Grandet's, laughed when he laughed, was depressed when he was out of spirits, took her views of the weather or of the temperature from him, and worked with him and for him. This equality was an element of sweetness which made up for many hardships in her lot. Out in the vineyards her master had never said a word about the small peaches, plums, or nectarines eaten under the trees that are planted between the rows of vines.

"Come, Nanon, take as much as you like," he would say, in years when the branches were bending beneath their load, and fruit was so abundant that the farmers round about were forced to give it to the pigs.

For the peasant girl, for the outdoor farm servant, who had known nothing but harsh treatment from childhood, for the girl who had been rescued from starvation by charity, old Grandet's equivocal laughter was like a ray of sunshine. Besides, Nanon's simple nature and limited intelligence could only entertain one idea at a time; and during those thirty-five years of service one picture was constantly present to her mind—she saw herself a barefooted girl in rags standing at the gate of M. Grandet's timber yard, and heard the sound of the cooper's voice, saying, "What is it, lassie?" and the warmth of gratitude filled her heart to-day as it did then. Sometimes, as he watched her, the thought came up in Grandet's mind how that no syllable of praise or admiration had ever been breathed in her ears, that all the tender feelings that a woman inspires had no existence for her, and that she might well appear before God one day as chaste as the Virgin Mary herself. At such times, prompted by a sudden impulse of pity, he would exclaim, "Poor Nanon!"

The remark was always followed by an indescribable look from the old servant. The words so spoken from time to time were separate links in a long and unbroken chain of friendship. But in this pity in the miser's soul, which gave a thrill of pleasure to the lonely woman, there was something indescribably revolting; it was a cold-blooded pity that stirred the cooper's heart; it was a luxury that cost him nothing. But for Nanon it meant the height of happiness! Who will not likewise say, "Poor Nanon!" God will one day know His angels by the tones of their voices and by the sorrow hidden in their hearts.

There were plenty of households in Saumur where servants were better treated, but where their employers, nevertheless, enjoyed small comfort in return. Wherefore people asked, "What have the Grandets done to that big Nanon of theirs that she should be so attached to them? She would go through fire and water to serve them!"

Her kitchen, with its barred windows that looked out into the yard, was always clean, cold, and tidy, a thorough miser's

kitchen, in which nothing was allowed to be wasted. When
Nanon had washed her plates and dishes, put the remains
of the dinner into the safe, and raked out the fire, she left
her kitchen (which was only separated from the dining-room
by the breadth of a passage), and sat down to spin hemp in
the company of her employers, for a single candle must suffice for the whole family in the evening. The serving-maid
slept in a little dark closet at the end of the passage, lit only
by a borrowed light. Nanon had an iron constitution and
sound health, which enabled her to sleep with impunity year
after year in this hole, where she could hear the slightest
sound that broke the heavy silence brooding day and night
over the house; she lay like a watch-dog, with one ear open;
she was never off duty, not even while she slept.   ,

Some description of the rest of the house will be necessary
in the course of the story in connection with later events;
but the parlor, wherein all the splendor and luxury of the
house was concentrated, has been sketched already, and the
emptiness and bareness of the upper rooms can be surmised
for the present.

It was in the middle of November, in the year 1819, twilight was coming on, and big Nanon was lighting a fire in
the parlor for the first time. It was a festival day in the
calendar of the Cruchotins and Grassinistes, wherefore the
six antagonists were preparing to set forth, all armed cap-à-
pie, for a contest in which each side meant to outdo the other
in proofs of friendship. The Grandets' parlor was to be the
scene of action. That morning Mme. and Mlle. Grandet,
duly attended by Nanon, had repaired to the parish church
to hear mass. All Saumur had seen them go, and every one
had been put in mind of the fact that it was Eugénie's birthday. M. Cruchot, the Abbé Cruchot, and M. C. de Bonfons,
therefore, having calculated the hour when dinner would be
over, were eager to be first in the field, and to arrive
before the Grassinistes to congratulate Mlle. Grandet. All
three carried huge bunches of flowers, gathered in their little

ADD

ADD

garden plots, but the stalks of the magistrate's bouquet were ingeniously bound round by a white satin ribbon with a tinsel fringe at the ends.

In the morning M. Grandet had gone to Eugénie's room before she had left her bed, and had solemnly presented her with a rare gold coin. It was her father's wont to surprise her in this way twice every year—once on her birthday, once on the equally memorable day of her patron saint. Mme. Grandet usually gave her daughter a winter or a summer dress, according to circumstances. The two dresses and two gold coins, which she received on her father's birthday and on New Year's Day, altogether amounted to an annual income of nearly a hundred crowns; Grandet loved to watch the money accumulating in her hands. He did not part with his money; he felt that it was only like taking it out of one box and putting it into another; and besides, was it not, so to speak, fostering a proper regard for gold in his heiress? she was being trained in the way in which she should go. Now and then he asked for an account of her wealth (formerly swelled by gifts from the La Bertellières), and each time he did so he used to tell her, "This will be your *dozen* when you are married."

The *dozen* is an old-world custom which has lost none of its force, and is still religiously adhered to in several midland districts in France. In Berri or Anjou when a daughter is married, it is incumbent upon her parents, or upon her bridegroom's family, to give her a purse containing either a dozen, or twelve dozen, or twelve hundred gold or silver coins, the amount varying with the means of the family. The poorest herd-girl would not be content without her *dozen* when she married, even if she could only bring twelve pence as a dower. They talk even yet at Issoudun of a fabulous dozen once given to a rich heiress, which consisted of a hundred and forty-four Portuguese moidores; and when Catherine de Medicis was married to Henry II., her uncle, Clement VII., gave the bride a dozen antique gold medals of priceless value.

Eugénie wore her new dress at dinner, and looked prettier than usual in it; her father was in high good humor.

"Let us have a fire," he cried, "as it is Eugénie's birth-day! It will be a good omen!"

"Mademoiselle will be married within the year, that's certain," said big Nanon, as she removed the remains of a goose, that pheasant of the coopers of Saumur.

"There is no one that I know of in Saumur who would do for Eugénie," said Mme. Grandet, with a timid glance at her husband, a glance that revealed how completely her husband's tyranny had broken the poor woman's spirit.

Grandet looked at his daughter, and said merrily, "We must really begin to think about her; the little girl is twenty-three years old to-day."

Neither Eugénie nor her mother said a word, but they exchanged glances; they understood each other.

Mme. Grandet's face was thin and wrinkled and yellow as saffron; she was awkward and slow in her movements, one of those beings who seem born to be tyrannized over. She was a large-boned woman, with a large nose, large eyes, and a prominent forehead; there seemed to be, at first sight, some dim suggestion of a resemblance between her and some shriveled, spongy, dried-up fruit. The few teeth that remained to her were dark and discolored; there were deep lines fretted about her mouth, and her chin was something after the "nut-cracker" pattern. She was a good sort of woman, and a La Bertellière to the backbone. The Abbé Cruchot had more than once found occasion to tell her that she had not been so bad looking when she was young, and she did not disagree with him. An angelic sweetness of disposition, the helpless meekness of an insect in the hands of cruel children, a sincere piety, a kindly heart, and an even temper that nothing could ruffle or sour, had gained universal respect and pity for her.

Her appearance might provoke a smile, but she had brought her husband more than three hundred thousand francs, partly as her dowry, partly through bequests. Yet Grandet never gave his wife more than six francs at a time for pocket money, and she always regarded herself as dependent upon her husband. The meek gentleness of her nature forbade any revolt against his tyranny; but so deeply did she feel the humiliation of her position, that she had never asked him for a sou, and when M. Cruchot demanded her signature to any document, she always gave it without a word. This foolish sensitive pride, which Grandet constantly and unwittingly hurt, this magnanimity which he was quite incapable of understanding, were Mme. Grandet's dominant characteristics.

Her dress never varied. Her gown was always of the same dull, greenish shade of laventine, and usually lasted her nearly a twelvemonth; the large handkerchief at her throat was of some kind of cotton material; she wore a straw bonnet, and was seldom seen without a black silk apron. She left the house so rarely that her walking shoes were seldom worn out; indeed, her requirements were very few, she never wanted anything for herself. Sometimes it would occur to Grandet that it was a long while since he had given the last six francs to his wife, and his conscience would prick him a little; and after the vintage, when he sold his wine, he always demanded pin-money for his wife over and above the bargain. These four or five louis out of the pockets of the Dutch or Belgian merchants were Mme. Grandet's only certain source of yearly income. But although she received her five louis, her husband would often say to her, as if they had had one common purse, "Have you a few sous that you can lend me?" and she, poor woman, glad that it was in her power to do anything for the man whom her confessor always taught her to regard as her lord and master, used to return to him more than one crown out of her little store in the course of the winter. Every month, when Grandet disbursed the five-franc piece which he allowed his daughter for needles, thread, and small expenses of dress, he remarked to his wife (after he had buttoned up his pocket), "And how about you, mother; do you want anything?" And with a mother's dignity Mme. Grandet would answer, "We will talk about that by-and-by, dear."

Her magnanimity was entirely lost upon Grandet; he considered that he did very handsomely by his wife. The philosophic mind contemplating the Nanons, the Mme. Grandets, the Eugénies of this life, holds that the Author of the universe is a profound satirist, and who will quarrel with the conclusion of the philosophic mind? After the dinner, when the question of Eugénie's marriage had been raised for the first time, Nanon went up to M. Grandet's room to fetch a bottle of black currant cordial, and very nearly lost her footing on the staircase as she came down.

"Great stupid! Are *you* going to take to tumbling about?" inquired her master.

"It is all along of the step, sir; it gave way. The staircase isn't safe."

"She is quite right," said Mme. Grandet. "You ought to have had it mended long ago. Eugénie all but sprained her foot on it yesterday."

"Here," said Grandet, who saw that Nanon looked very pale, "as to-day is Eugénie's birthday, and you have nearly fallen downstairs, take a drop of black currant cordial; that will put you right again."

"I deserve it, too, upon my word," said Nanon. "Many a one would have broken the bottle in my place; I should have broken my elbow first, holding it up to save it."

"Poor Nanon!" muttered Grandet, pouring out the black currant cordial for her.

"Did you hurt yourself?" asked Eugénie, looking at her in concern.

"No, I managed to break the fall; I came down on my side."

"Well," said Grandet, "as to-day is Eugénie's birthday, I will mend your step for you. Somehow you women folk cannot manage to put your foot down in the corner, where it is still solid and safe."

Grandet took up the candle, left the three women without any other illumination in the room than the bright dancing firelight, and went to the bakehouse, where tools, nails, and odd pieces of wood were kept.

"Do you want any help?" Nanon called to him, when the first blow sounded on the staircase.

"No! no! I am an old hand at it," answered the cooper.

At this very moment, while Grandet was doing the repairs himself to his worm-eaten staircase, and whistling with all his might as memories of his young days came up in his mind, the three Cruchots knocked at the house door.

"Oh, it's you, is it, M. Cruchot?" asked Nanon, as she took a look through the small square grating.

"Yes," answered the magistrate.

Nanon opened the door, and the glow of the firelight shone on the three Cruchots, who were groping in the archway.

"Oh! you have come to help us keep her birthday," Nanon said, as the scent of flowers reached her.

"Excuse me a moment, gentlemen," cried Grandet, who recognized the voices of his acquaintances; "I am your very humble servant! There is no pride about me; I am patching up a broken stair here myself."

"Go on, go on, M. Grandet! The charcoal burner is mayor in his own house," said the magistrate sententiously. Nobody saw the allusion, and he had his laugh all to himself.

Mme. and Mlle. Grandet rose to greet them. The magistrate took advantage of the darkness to speak to Eugénie.

"Will you permit me, mademoiselle, on the anniversary of your birthday, to wish you a long succession of prosperous years, and may you for long preserve the health with which you are blessed at present."

He then offered her such a bouquet of flowers as was seldom seen in Saumur; and taking the heiress by both arms, gave her a kiss on either side of the throat, a fervent salute which brought the color into Eugénie's face. The magistrate was tall and thin, somewhat resembling a rusty nail; this was his notion of paying court.

"Do not disturb yourselves," said Grandet, coming back into the room. "Fine doings these of yours, M. le Président, on high days and holidays!"

"With mademoiselle beside him, every day would be a holiday for my nephew," answered the Abbé Cruchot, also armed with a bouquet; and with that the Abbé kissed Eugénie's hand. As for M. Cruchot, he kissed her unceremoniously on both cheeks, saying, "This sort of thing makes us feel older, eh? A whole year older every twelve months."

Grandet set down the candle in front of the brass clock on the chimney-piece; whenever a joke amused him he kept on repeating it till it was worn threadbare; he did so now.

"As to-day is Eugénie's birthday," he said, " let us have an illumination."

He carefully removed the branches from the two sconces, fitted the sockets into either pedestal, took from Nanon's hands a whole new candle wrapped in a scrap of paper, fixed it firmly in the socket, and lighted it. Then he went over to his wife and took up his position beside her, looking by turns at his daughter, his friends, and the two lighted candles.

The Abbé Cruchot was a fat, dumpy little man with a well-worn, sandy peruke. His peculiar type of face might have belonged to some old lady whose life is spent at the card table. At this moment he was stretching out his feet and displaying a very neat and strong pair of shoes with silver buckles on them.

"The des Grassins have not come round?" he asked.

"Not yet," answered Grandet.

"Are they sure to come?" put in the old notary, with various contortions of a countenance as full of holes as a colander.

"Oh! yes, I think they will come," said Mme. Grandet.

"Is the vintage over?" asked President de Bonfons, addressing Grandet, "are all your grapes gathered?"

"Yes, everywhere!" answered the old vinegrower, rising and walking up and down the length of the room; he straightened himself up as he spoke with a conscious pride that appeared in that word "everywhere."

As he passed by the door that opened into the passage, Grandet caught a glimpse of the kitchen; the fire was still alight, a candle was burning there, and big Nanon was about to begin her spinning by the hearth; she did not wish to intrude upon the birthday party.

"Nanon!" he called, stepping out into the passage, "Nanon! why ever don't you rake out the fire; put out the candle and come in here! *Pardieu!* the room is large enough to hold us all."

"But you are expecting grand visitors, sir."

"Have you any objection to them? They are all descended from Adam just as much as you are."

Grandet went back to the president.

"Have you sold your wine?" he inquired.

"Not I; I am holding it. If the wine is good now, it will be better still in two years' time. The growers, as you know, of course, are in a ring, and mean to keep prices up. The Belgians shall not have it all their own way this year. And if they go away, well and good, let them go; they will come back again."

"Yes; but we must hold firm," said Grandet in a tone that made the magistrate shudder.

"Suppose he should sell his wine behind our backs?" he thought.

At that moment another knock at the door announced the des Grassins, and interrupted a quiet talk between Mme. Grandet and the Abbé Cruchot.

Mme. des Grassins was a dumpy, lively little person with a pink-and-white complexion, one of those women for whom the course of life in a country town has flowed on with almost claustral tranquillity, and who, thanks to this regular and virtuous existence, are still youthful at the age of forty. They are something like the late roses in autumn, which are fair and pleasant to the sight, but the almost scentless petals have a pinched look, there is a vague suggestion of coming winter about them. She dressed tolerably well, her gowns came from Paris, she was a leader of society in Saumur, and received on certain evenings. Her husband had been a quartermaster in the Imperial Guard, but he had retired from the army with a pension, after being badly wounded at Austerlitz. In spite of his consideration for Grandet, he still retained, or affected to retain, the bluff manners of a soldier.

"Good day, Grandet," he said, holding out his hand to the cooper with that wonted air of superiority with which he eclipsed the Cruchot faction. "Mademoiselle," he added, addressing Eugénie, after a bow to Mme. Grandet, "you are always charming, ever good and fair, and what more can one wish you?"

With that he presented her with a small box, which a servant was carrying, and which contained a Cape heath, a plant only recently introduced into Europe, and very rare.

Mme. des Grassins embraced Eugénie very affectionately; squeezed her hand, and said, "I have commissioned Adolphe to give you my little birthday gift."

A tall, fair-haired young man, somewhat pallid and weakly in appearance, came forward at this; his manners were passably good, although he seemed to be shy. He had just completed his law studies in Paris, where he had managed to spend eight or ten thousand francs over and above his allowance. He now kissed Eugénie on both cheeks, and laid a workbox with gilded silver fittings before her; it was a showy, trumpery thing enough, in spite of the little shield on the lid, on which an E. G. had been engraved in Gothic characters, a detail which gave an imposing air to the whole. Eugénie raised the lid with a little thrill of pleasure, the happiness was as complete as it was unlooked for—the happiness that brings bright color into a young girl's face and makes her tremble with delight. Her eyes turned to her father as if to ask whether she might accept the gift; M. Grandet answered the mute inquiry with a "Take it, my daughter!" in tones which would have made the reputation of an actor. The three Cruchots stood dumfounded when they saw the bright, delighted glance that Adolphe des Grassins received from the heiress, who seemed to be dazzled by such undreamed-of splendors.

M. des Grassins offered his snuff-box to Grandet, took a pinch himself, brushed off a few stray specks from his blue coat and from the ribbon of the Legion of Honor at his button-hole, and looked at the Cruchots, as who should say, "Parry that thrust if you can!" Mme. des Grassins' eyes fell on the blue glass jars in which the Cruchots' bouquets had been set. She looked at their gifts with the innocent air of pretended interest which a satirical woman knows how to assume upon occasion. It was a delicate crisis. The Abbé got up and left the others, who were forming a circle round the fire, and joined Grandet in his promenade up and down the room. When the two elders had reached the embrasure of the window at the further end, away from the group by the fire, the priest said in the miser's ear; "Those people yonder are throwing their money out of the windows."

"What does that matter to me, so long as it comes my way?" the old vinegrower answered.

"If you had a mind to give your daughter golden scissors, you could very well afford it," said the Abbé.

"I shall give her something better than scissors," Grandet answered.

"What an idiot my nephew is!" thought the Abbé, as he looked at the magistrate, whose dark, ill-favored countenance was set off to perfection at that moment by a shock head of hair. "Why couldn't *he* have hit on some expensive piece of foolery?"

"We will take a hand at cards, Mme. Grandet," said Mme. des Grassins.

"But as we are all here, there are enough of us for two tables. . . ."

"As to-day is Eugénie's birthday, why not all play together at loto?" said old Grandet; "these two children could join in the game."

The old cooper, who never played at any game whatever, pointed to his daughter and Adolphe.

"Here, Nanon, move the tables out."

"We will help you, Mademoiselle Nanon," said Mme. des Grassins cheerfully; she was thoroughly pleased because she had pleased Eugénie.

"I have never seen anything so pretty anywhere," the heiress had said to her. "I have never been so happy in my life before."

3

"It was Adolphe who chose it," said Mme. des Grassins in the girl's ear; "he brought it from Paris."

"Go your ways, accursed scheming woman," muttered the magistrate to himself. "If you or your husband ever find yourselves in a court of law, you shall be hard put to it to gain the day."

The notary, calmly seated in his corner, watched the Abbé, and said to himself, "The des Grassins may do what they like; my fortune and my brother's and my nephew's fortunes altogether mount up to eleven hundred thousand francs. The des Grassins, at the very most, have only half as much, and they have a daughter. Let them give whatever they like, all will be ours some day—the heiress and her presents too."

Two tables were in readiness by half-past eight o'clock. Mme. des Grassins, with her winning ways, had succeeded in placing her son next to Eugénie. The actors in the scene, so commonplace in appearance, so full of interest beneath the surface, each provided with slips of pasteboard of various colors and blue glass counters, seemed to be listening to the little jokes made by the old notary, who never drew a number without making some remark upon it, but they were all thinking of M. Grandet's millions. The old cooper himself eyed the group with a certain self-complacency; he looked at Mme. des Grassins with her pink feathers and fresh toilette, at the banker's soldierly face, at Adolphe, at the magistrate, at the Abbé and the notary, and within himself he said: "They are all after my crowns; that is what they are here for. It is for my daughter that they come to be bored here. Aha! and my daughter is for none of them, and all these people are so many harpoons to be used in my fishing."

The merriment of this family party, the laughter, only sincere when it came from Eugénie or her mother, and to which the low whirring of Nanon's spinning-wheel made an accompaniment, the sordid meanness playing for high stakes, the young girl herself, like some rare bird, the innocent victim of its high value, tracked down and snared by specious pretences of friendship; taken altogether, it was a sorry comedy that was being played in the old gray-painted parlor, by the dim light of the two candles. Was it not, however, a drama of all time, played out everywhere all over the world, but here reduced to its simplest expression? Old Grandet towered above the other actors, turning all this sham affection to his own account, and reaping a rich harvest from this simulated friendship. His face hovered above the scene like the interpretation of an evil dream. He was like the incarnation of the one god who yet finds worshipers in modern times, of Money and the power of wealth.

With him the gentler and sweeter impulses of human life only occupied the second place; but they so filled three purer hearts there, that there was no room in them for other thoughts—the hearts of Nanon, and of Eugénie and her mother. And yet, how much ignorance mingled with their innocent simplicity! Eugénie and her mother knew nothing of Grandet's wealth; they saw everything through a medium of dim ideas peculiar to their own narrow world, and neither desired nor despised money, accustomed as they were to do without it. Nor were they conscious of an uncongenial atmosphere; the strength of their feelings, their inner life, made of them a strange exception in this gathering, wholly intent upon material interests. Appalling is the condition of man; there is no drop of happiness in his lot but has its source in ignorance.

Just as Mme. Grandet had won sixteen sous, the largest amount that had ever been punted beneath that roof, and big Nanon was beaming with delight at the sight of Madame pocketing that splendid sum, there was a knock at the house-door, so sudden and so loud that the women started on their chairs.

"No one in Saumur would knock in that way," said the notary.

"What do they thump like that for?" said Nanon. "Do they want to break our door down?"

"Who the devil is it?" cried Grandet.

Nanon took up one of the candles and went to open the door. Grandet followed her.

"Grandet! Grandet!" cried his wife; a vague terror seized her, and she hurried to the door of the room.

The players all looked at each other.

"Suppose we go too?" said M. des Grassins. "That knock meant no good, it seemed to me."

But M. des Grassins scarcely caught a glimpse of a young man's face and of a porter who was carrying two huge trunks and an assortment of carpet bags, before Grandet turned sharply on his wife and said—

"Go back to your loto, Mme. Grandet, and leave me to settle with this gentleman here."

With that he slammed the parlor door, and the loto players sat down again, but they were too much excited to go on with the game.

"Is it any one who lives in Saumur, M. des Grassins?" his wife inquired.

"No, a traveler."

"Then he must have come from Paris."

"As a matter of fact," said the notary, drawing out a heavy antique watch, a couple of fingers' breadth in thickness, and not unlike a Dutch punt in shape, "as a matter of fact, it is nine o'clock. *Peste!* the mail coach is not often behind time."

"Is he young looking?" put in the Abbé Cruchot.

"Yes," answered M. des Grassins. "The luggage he has with him must weigh three hundred kilos at least."

"Nanon does not come back," said Eugénie.

"It must be some relation of yours," the President remarked.

"Let us put down our stakes," said Mme. Grandet gently. "M. Grandet was vexed, I could tell that by the sound of his voice, and perhaps he would be displeased if he came in and found us all discussing his affairs."

"Mademoiselle," Adolphe addressed his neighbor, "it will be your cousin Grandet no doubt, a very nice looking young fellow whom I once met at a ball at M. de Nucingen's."

Adolphe went no further, his mother stamped on his foot

under the table. Aloud, she asked him for two sous for his stake, adding in an undertone, meant only for his ears, "Will you hold your tongue, you great silly?"

They could hear the footsteps of Nanon and the porter on the staircase, but Grandet returned to the room almost immediately, and just behind him came the traveler who had excited so much curiosity, and loomed so large in the imaginations of those assembled; indeed, his sudden descent into their midst might be compared to the arrival of a snail in a beehive, or the entrance of a peacock into some humdrum village poultry-yard.

"Take a seat near the fire," said Grandet, addressing the stranger.

The young man looked around the room and bowed very gracefully before seating himself. The men rose and bowed politely in return, the women curtseyed rather ceremoniously.

"You are feeling cold, I expect, sir," said Mme. Grandet; "you have no doubt come from——"

"Just like the women!" broke in the goodman, looking up from the letter which he held in his hand. "Do let the gentleman have a little peace."

"But, father, perhaps the gentleman wants something after his journey," said Eugénie.

"He has a tongue in his head," the vinegrower answered severely.

The stranger alone felt any surprise at this scene, the rest were quite used to the worthy man and his arbitrary behavior. But after the two inquiries had received these summary answers, the stranger rose and stood with his back to the fire, held out a foot to the blaze, so as to warm the soles of his boots, and said to Eugénie, "Thank you, cousin, I dined at Tours. And I do not require anything," he added, glancing at Grandet; "I am not in the least tired."

"Do you come from Paris?" (it was Mme. des Grassins who now put the inquiry).

M. Charles (for this was the name borne by the son of M. Grandet of Paris), hearing some one question him, took out an eyeglass that hung suspended from his neck by a cord, fixed it in his eye, and made a deliberate survey of the objects upon the table and of the people sitting round it, eyed Mme. des Grassins very coolly, and said (when he had completed his survey), "Yes, madame.—You are playing at loto, aunt," he added; "pray go on with your game, it is too amusing to be broken off . . ."

"I knew it was the cousin," thought Mme. des Grassins, and she gave him a side-glance from time to time.

"Forty-seven," cried the old Abbé. "Keep count. Mme. des Grassins, that is your number, is it not?"

M. des Grassins put down a counter on his wife's card; the lady herself was not thinking of loto, her mind was full of melancholy forebodings; she was watching Eugénie and the cousin from Paris. She saw how the heiress now and then stole a glance at her cousin, and the banker's wife could easily discover in those glances a *crescendo* of amazement or of curiosity.

There was certainly a strange contrast between M. Charles Grandet, a handsome young man of two-and-twenty, and the worthy provincials, who, tolerably disgusted already with his aristocratic airs, were scornfully studying the stranger with a view to making game of him. This requires some explanation.

At two-and-twenty childhood is not so very far away, and youth, on the borderland, has not finally and forever put away childish things; Charles Grandet's vanity was childish, but perhaps ninety-nine young men out of a hundred would have been carried away by it and behaved exactly as he did.

Some days previously his father had bidden him to go on a visit of several months to his uncle in Saumur; perhaps M. Grandet (of Paris) had Eugénie in his mind. Charles, launched in this way into a country town for the first time in his life, had his own ideas. He would make his appearance in provincial society with all the superiority of a young man of fashion; he would reduce the neighborhood to despair by his splendor; he would inaugurate a new epoch, and introduce all the latest and most ingenious refinement of Parisian luxury. To be brief, he meant to devote more time at Saumur than in Paris to the care of his nails, and to carry out schemes of elaborate and studied refinements in dress at his leisure; there should be none of the not ungrace-- ful negligence of attire which a young man of fashion some- times affects.

So Charles took with him into the country the most charm- ing of shooting costumes, the sweetest thing in hunting- knives and sheaths, and a perfect beauty of a rifle. He packed up a most tasteful collection of waistcoats; gray, white, black, beetle-green shot with gold, speckled and spangled; double waistcoats, waistcoats with rolled collars, stand-up collars, turned-down collars, open at the throat, buttoned up to the chin with a row of gold buttons. He took examples of all the ties and cravats in favor at that epoch. He took two of Buisson's coats. He took his finest linen, and the dressing- case with gold fittings that his mother had given him. He took all his dandy's paraphernalia, not forgetting an enchant- ing little writing-case, the gift of the most amiable of women (for him at least), a great lady whom he called Annette, and who at that moment was traveling with her husband in Scot- land, a victim to suspicions which demanded the temporary sacrifice of her happiness.

In short, his cargo of Parisian frivolities was as complete as it was possible to make it; nothing had been omitted, from the horse-whip, useful as a preliminary, to the pair of richly chased and mounted pistols that terminate a duel. There was all the ploughing gear required by a young idler in the field of life.

His father had told him to travel alone and modestly, and he had obeyed. He had come in the coupé of the diligence, which he secured all to himself; and was not ill-satisfied to save wear, in this way, to a smart and comfortable traveling carriage which he had ordered, and in which he meant to go to meet his Annette, the aforesaid great lady who . . . etc., and whom he was to rejoin next June at Baden-Baden.

Charles expected to meet scores of people during his visit to his uncle; he expected to have some shooting on his uncle's land; he expected, in short, to find a large house on a large estate; he had not thought to find his relatives in Saumur at all; he had only found out that they lived there by asking the way to Froidfond, and even after this discovery he expected to see them in a large mansion. But whether his uncle lived in Saumur or at Froidfond, he was determined to make his first appearance properly, so he had assumed a most fascinating traveling costume, made with the simplicity that is the perfection of art, a most *adorable* creation, to use the word which in those days expressed superlative praise of the special qualities of a thing or of a man. At Tours he had summoned a hairdresser, and his handsome chestnut hair was curled afresh. He had changed his linen and put on a black satin cravat, which, in combination with a round collar, made a very becoming setting for a pale and satirical face. A long overcoat, fitting tightly at the waist, gave glimpses of a cashmere waistcoat with a rolled collar, and beneath this again a second waistcoat of some white material. His watch was carelessly thrust into a side pocket, and save in so far as a gold chain secured it to a buttonhole, its continuance there appeared to be purely accidental. His gray trousers were buttoned at the sides, and the seams were adorned with designs embroidered in black silk. A pair of gray gloves had nothing to dread from contact with a gold-headed cane, which he managed to admiration. A discriminating taste was evinced throughout the costume, and shone conspicuous in the traveling cap. Only a Parisian, and a Parisian moreover from some remote and lofty sphere, could trick himself out in such attire, and bring all its absurd details into harmony by coxcombry carried to such a pitch that it ceased to be ridiculous; this young man carried it off, moreover, with a swaggering air befitting a dead shot, conscious of the possession of a handsome pair of pistols and the good graces of an Annette.

If, moreover, you wish to thoroughly understand the surprise with which the Saumurois and the young Parisian mutually regarded each other, you must behold, as did the former, the radiant vision of this elegant traveler shining in the gloomy old room, as well as the figures that composed the family picture that met the stranger's eyes. There sat the Cruchots; try to imagine them.

To begin with, all three took snuff, with utter disregard of personal cleanliness or of the black deposit with which their shirt frills were encrusted. Their limp silk handkerchiefs were twisted into a thick rope, and wound tightly about their necks. Their collars were crumpled and soiled, their linen was dingy; there was such a vast accumulation of underwear in their presses, that it was only necessary to wash twice in the year, and the linen acquired a bad color with lying by. Age and ugliness might have wrought together to produce a masterpiece in them. Their hard-featured, furrowed, and wrinkled faces were in keeping with their creased and thread-bare clothing, and both they and their garments were worn, shrunken, twisted out of shape. Dwellers in country places are apt to grow more or less slovenly and careless in their appearance; they cease by degrees to dress for others; the career of a pair of gloves is indefinitely prolonged, there is a general want of freshness and a decided neglect of detail. The slovenliness of the Cruchots, therefore, was not conspicuous; they were in harmony with the rest of the company, for there was one point on which both Cruchotins and Grassinistes were agreed for the most part—they held the fashions in horror.

The Parisian assumed his eyeglass again in order to study the curious accessories of the room; his eyes traveled over the rafters in the ceiling, over the dingy panels covered with fly-spots in sufficient abundance to punctuate the whole of the *Encyclopédie méthodique* and the *Moniteur* besides. The loto-players looked up at this and stared at him; if a giraffe had been in their midst they could hardly have gazed with more eager curiosity. Even M. des Grassins and his son, who had beheld a man of fashion before in the course of their

lives, shared in the general amazement; perhaps they felt
the indefinable influence of the general feeling about the
stranger, perhaps they regarded him not unapprovingly.
"You see how they dress in Paris," their satirical glances
seemed to say to their neighbors.

One and all were at liberty to watch Charles at their leisure,
without any fear of offending the master of the house, for by
this time Grandet was deep in a long letter which he held in
his hand. He had taken the only candle from the table beside him, without any regard for the convenience of his
guests or for their pleasure.

It seemed to Eugénie, who had never in her life beheld
such a paragon, that her cousin was some seraphic vision,
some creature fallen from the skies. The perfume exhaled
by those shining locks, so gracefully curled, was delightful to
her. She would fain have passed her fingers over the delicate, smooth surface of those wonderful gloves. She envied
Charles his little hands, his complexion, the youthful refinement of his features. In fact, the sight of her cousin gave
her the same sensations of exquisite pleasure that might be
aroused in a young man by the contemplation of the fanciful
portraits of ladies in English *Keepsakes,* portraits drawn by
Westall and engraved by Finden, with a burin so skilful that
you fear to breathe upon the vellum surface lest the celestial
vision should disappear. And yet—how should the impression produced by a young exquisite upon an ignorant girl
whose life was spent in darning stockings and mending her
father's clothes, in the dirty wainscoted window embrasure
whence, in an hour, she saw scarcely one passer-by in the
silent street, how should her dim impressions be conveyed by
such an image as this?

Charles drew from his pocket a handkerchief embroidered
by the great lady who was traveling in Scotland. It was a
dainty piece of work wrought by love, in hours that were lost
to love; Eugénie gazed at her cousin, and wondered, was he
really going to use it? Charles' manners, his way of ad-
justing his eyeglass, his superciliousness, his affectations,

his manifest contempt for the little box which had but lately given so much pleasure to the wealthy heiress, and which in his eyes seemed to be a very absurd piece of rubbish; everything, in short, which had given offence to the Cruchots and the Grassinistes pleased Eugénie so much that she lay awake for long that night thinking about this phœnix of a cousin.

Meanwhile the numbers were drawn but languidly, and very soon the loto came to an end altogether. Big Nanon came into the room and said aloud, "Madame, you will have to give me some sheets to make the gentleman's bed."

Mme. Grandet disappeared with Nanon, and Mme. des Grassins said in a low voice, "Let us keep our sous, and give up the game."

Each player took back his coin from the chipped saucer which held the stakes. Then there was a general stir, and a wheeling movement in the direction of the fire.

"Is the game over?" inquired Grandet, still reading his letter.

"Yes, yes," answered Mme. des Grassins, seating herself next to Charles.

Eugénie left the room to help her mother and Nanon, moved by a thought that came with the vague feeling that stirred her heart for the first time. If she had been questioned by a skilful confessor, she would have no doubt admitted that her thought was neither for Nanon nor for her mother, but that she was seized with a restless and urgent desire to see that all was right in her cousin's room, to busy herself on her cousin's account, to see that nothing was forgotten, to think of everything he might require, and to make sure that it was there, to make certain that everything was as neat and pretty as might be. She alone, so Eugénie thought already, could enter into her cousin's ideas and understand his tastes.

As a matter of fact, she came just at the right moment. Her mother and Nanon were about to leave the room in the belief that it was all in readiness; Eugénie convinced them in a moment that everything was yet to do. She filled

4

EUGENIE GRANDET

Nanon's head with these ideas: the sheets had not been aired. Nanon must bring the warming-pan, there were ashes, there was a fire downstairs. She herself covered the old table with a clean white cloth, and told Nanon to mind and be sure to change it every morning. There must be a good fire in the room; she overcame her mother's objections; she induced Nanon to put a good supply of firewood outside in the passage, and to say nothing about it to her father. She ran downstairs into the parlor, sought in one of the sideboards for an old japanned tray which had belonged to the late M. de la Bertellière, and from the same source she procured a hexagonal crystal glass, a little gilt spoon with almost all the gilding rubbed off, and an old slender-necked glass bottle with Cupids engraved upon it; these she deposited in triumph on a corner of the chimney-piece. More ideas had crowded up in her mind during that one quarter of an hour than in all the years since she had come into the world.

"Mamma," she began, "he will never be able to bear the smell of a tallow candle. Suppose that we buy a wax candle?"

She fled, lightly as a bird, to find her purse, and drew thence the five francs which she had received for the month's expenses.

"Here, Nanon, be quick."

"But what will your father say?"

This dreadful objection was raised by Mme. Grandet when she saw her daughter with an old Sèvres china sugar-basin which Grandet had brought back with him from the château at Froidfond.

"And where is the sugar to come from?" she went on. "Are you mad?"

"Nanon can easily buy the sugar when she goes for the candle, mamma."

"But how about your father?"

"Is it a right thing that his nephew should not have a glass of *eau sucrée* to drink if he happens to want it? Besides, he will not notice it."

"Your father always notices things," said Mme. Grandet, shaking her head.

Nanon hesitated; she knew her master.

"Do go, Nanon; it is my birthday to-day, you know!"

Nanon burst out laughing in spite of herself at the first joke her young mistress had ever been known to make, and did her bidding.

While Eugénie and her mother were doing their best to adorn the room which M. Grandet had allotted to his nephew, Mme. des Grassins was bestowing her attention on Charles, and making abundant use of her eyes as she did so.

"You are very brave," she said, "to leave the pleasures of the capital in winter in order to come to stay in Saumur. But if you are not frightened away at first sight of us, you shall see that even here we can amuse ourselves." And she gave him a languishing glance, in true provincial style.

Women in the provinces are wont to affect a demure and staid demeanor, which gives a furtive and eager eloquence to their eyes, a peculiarity which may be noted in ecclesiastics, for whom every pleasure is stolen or forbidden. Charles was so thoroughly out of his element in this room, it was all so far removed from the great château and the splendid surroundings in which he had thought to find his uncle, that, on paying closer attention to Mme. des Grassins, she almost reminded him of Parisian faces half obliterated already by these strange new impressions. He responded graciously to the advances which had been made to him, and naturally they fell into conversation.

Mme. des Grassins gradually lowered her voice to tones suited to the nature of her confidences. Both she and Charles Grandet felt a need of mutual confidence, of explanations and an understanding; so after a few minutes spent in coquettish chatter and jests that covered a serious purpose, the wily provincial dame felt free to converse without fear of being overheard, under cover of a conversation on the sale of the vintage, the one all-absorbing topic at that moment in Saumur.

"If you will honor us with a visit," she said, "you will

certainly do us a pleasure; my husband and I shall be very glad to see you. Our salon is the only one in Saumur where you will meet both the wealthy merchant society and the noblesse. We ourselves belong in a manner to both; they do not mix with each other at all except at our house; they come to us because they find it amusing. My husband, I am proud to say, is very highly thought of in both circles. So we will do our best to beguile the tedium of your stay. If you are going to remain with the Grandets, what will become of you! *Bon Dieu!* Your uncle is a miser, his mind runs on nothing but his vine cuttings; your aunt is a saint who cannot put two ideas together; and your cousin is a silly little thing, a common sort of a girl, with no breeding and no money, who spends her life in mending dish-cloths."

" 'Tis a very pretty woman," said Charles to himself; Mme. des Grassins' coquettish glances had not been thrown away upon him.

"It seems to me that you mean to monopolize the gentleman," said the big banker, laughing, to his wife, an unlucky observation, followed by remarks more or less spiteful from the notary and the president; but the Abbé gave them a shrewd glance, took a pinch of snuff, and handed his snuff-box to the company, while he gave expression to their thoughts, "Where could the gentleman have found any one better qualified to do the honors of Saumur?" he said.

"Come, Abbé, what do you mean by that?" asked M. des Grassins.

"It is meant, sir, in the most flattering sense, for you, for madame, for the town of Saumur, and for this gentleman," added the shrewd ecclesiastic, turning toward Charles. Without appearing to pay the slightest heed to their talk, he had managed to guess the drift of it.

Adolphe des Grassins spoke at last, with what was meant to be an offhand manner. "I do not know," he said, addressing Charles, "whether you have any recollection of me; I once had the pleasure of dancing in the same quadrille at a ball given by M. le Baron de Nucingen, and . . ."

"I remember it perfectly," answered Charles, surprised to find himself the object of general attention.

"Is this gentleman your son?" he asked of Mme. des Grassins.

The Abbé gave her a spiteful glance.

"Yes, I am his mother," she answered.

"You must have been very young when you came to Paris?" Charles went on, speaking to Adolphe.

"We cannot help ourselves, sir," said the Abbé. "Our babes are scarcely weaned before we send them to Babylon."

Mme. des Grassins gave the Abbé a strangely penetrating glance; she seemed to be seeking the meaning of those words.

"You must go into the country," the Abbé went on, "if you want to find women not much on the other side of thirty, with a grown-up son a licentiate of law, who look as fresh and youthful as Mme. des Grassins. It only seems like the other day when the young men and the ladies stood on chairs to see you dance, madame," the Abbé added, turning towards his fair antagonist; "your triumphs are as fresh in my memory as if they had happened yesterday."

"Oh! the old wretch!" said Mme. des Grassins to herself, "is it possible that he has guessed?"

"It looks as though I should have a great success in Saumur," thought Charles. He unbuttoned his overcoat and stood with his hand in his waistcoat pocket, gazing into space, striking the attitude which Chantrey thought fit to give to Byron in his statue of that poet.

Meanwhile Grandet's inattention, or rather his preoccupation, during the reading of his letter, had escaped neither the notary nor the magistrate. Both of them tried to guess at the contents by watching the almost imperceptible changes in the worthy man's face, on which all the light of a candle was concentrated. The vinegrower was hard put to it to preserve his wonted composure. His expression must be left to the imagination, but here is the fatal letter:—

"MY BROTHER,—It is nearly twenty-three years now since we saw each other. The last time we met it was to make arrangements for my marriage, and we parted in high spirits. Little did I then think, when you were congratulating yourself on our prosperity, that one day you would be the sole hope and stay of our family. By the time that this letter reaches your hands, I shall be no more. In my position, I could not survive the disgrace of bankruptcy; I have held up my head above the surface till the last moment, hoping to weather the storm; it is all of no use, I must sink now. Just after the failure of my stockbroker came the failure of Roguin (my notary); my last resources have been swept away, and I have nothing left. It is my heavy misfortune to owe nearly four millions; my assets only amount to twenty-five per cent of my debts. I hold heavy stocks of wine, and owing to the abundance and good quality of your vintages, they have fallen ruinously in value. In three days time all Paris will say, 'M. Grandet was a rogue!' and I, honest though I am, shall lie wrapped in a winding sheet of infamy. I have despoiled my own son of his mother's fortune and of the spotless name on which I have brought disgrace. He knows nothing of all this—the unhappy child whom I have idolized. Happily for him, he did not know when we bade each other good-bye, and my heart overflowed with tenderness for him, how soon it should cease to beat. Will he not curse me some day? Oh! my brother, my brother, a child's curse is an awful thing! If we curse the children, they may appeal against us, but their curses cling to us forever! Grandet, you are my older brother, you must shield me from this; do not let Charles say bitter things of me when I am lying in my grave. Oh! my brother, if every word in this letter were written in my tears, in my blood, it would not cost me such bitter anguish, for then I should be weeping, bleeding, dying, and the agony would be ended; but now I am still suffering—I see the death before me with dry eyes. You therefore are Charles' father, now! He has no relations on his mother's side for reasons which you know. Why did I not defer to social prejudices? Why did I yield to love? Why did I marry the natural daughter of a noble? Charles is the

last of his family; he is alone in the world. Oh! my unhappy
boy! my son! . . . Listen, Grandet, I am asking nothing for myself, and you could scarcely satisfy my creditors
if you would; your fortune cannot be sufficient to meet a demand of three millions; it is for my son's sake that I write.
You must know, my brother, that as I think of you, my petition is made with clasped hands; that this is my dying prayer
to you. Grandet, I know that you will be a father to him;
I know that I shall not ask in vain, and the sight of my pistols does not cause me a pang.

"And then Charles is very fond of me; I was kind to him,
I never said him nay; he will not curse me! For the rest,
you will see how sweet-tempered and obedient he is; he takes
after his mother; he will never give you any trouble, poor
boy! He is accustomed to luxurious ways; he knows nothing
of the hardships that you and I experienced in the early days
when we were poor. . . . And now he has not a penny,
and he is alone in the world, for all his friends are sure to
leave him, and it is I who have brought these humiliations
upon him. Ah! if I had only the power to send him straight
to heaven now, where his mother is! This is madness! To
go back to my misfortunes and Charles' share in them. I
have sent him to you so that you may break the news of my
death and explain to him what his future must be. Be a
father to him; ah! more than that, be an indulgent father!
Do not expect him to give up his idle ways all at once; it
would kill him. On my knees I beg him to renounce all
claims to his mother's fortune; but I need not ask that of
him, his sense of honor will prevent him from adding himself to the list of my creditors; see that he resigns his claims
when the right time comes. And you must lay everything before him, Grandet—the struggle and the hardships that he
will have to face in the life that I have spoiled for him; and
then if he has any tenderness still left for me, tell him from
me that all is not lost for him—be sure you tell him that.
Work, which was our salvation, can restore the fortune which
I have lost; and if he will listen to his father's voice, which

4

would fain make itself heard yet a little while from the grave, let him leave this country and go to the Indies! And, brother, Charles is honest and energetic; you will help him with his first trading venture, I know you will; he would die sooner than not repay you; you will do as much as that for him, Grandet, or you will lay up regrets for yourself. Ah! if my boy finds no kindness and no help in you, I shall forever pray God to punish your hard-heartedness. If I could have withheld a few payments, I might have saved a little sum for him—he surely has a right to some of his mother's fortune—but the payments at the end of the month taxed all my resources, and I could not manage it. I would fain have died with my mind at rest about his future; I wish I could have received your solemn promise, coming straight from your hand it would have brought warmth with it for me; but time presses. Even while Charles is on his way, I am compelled to file my schedule. My affairs are all in order; I am endeavoring so to arrange everything that it will be evident that my failure is due neither to carelessness nor to dishonesty, but simply to disasters which I could not help. Is it not for Charles' sake that I take these pains? Farewell, my brother. May God bless you in every way for the generosity with which you (as I cannot doubt) will accept and fulfil this trust. There will be one voice that will never cease to pray for you in the world whither we must all go sooner or later, and where I am even now.

"VICTOR-ANGE-GUILLAUME GRANDET."

"So you are having a chat?" said old Grandet, folding up the letter carefully in the original creases, and putting it into his waistcoat pocket.

He looked at his nephew in a shy and embarrassed way, seeking to dissemble his feelings and his calculations.

"Do you feel warmer?"

"I am very comfortable, my dear uncle."

"Well, what ever are the women after?" his uncle went on; the fact that his nephew would sleep in the house had by that time slipped from his memory. Eugénie and Mme. Grandet came into the room as he spoke.

"Is everything ready upstairs?" the goodman inquired. He had now quite recovered himself, and recollected the facts of the case.

"Yes, father."

"Very well then, nephew, if you are feeling tired, Nanon will show you to your room. Lord! there is nothing very smart about it, but you will overlook that here among poor vinegrowers, who never have a penny to bless themselves with. The taxes swallow up everything we have."

"We don't want to be intrusive, Grandet," said the banker. "You and your nephew may have some things to talk over; we will wish you good evening. Good-bye till to-morrow."

Every one rose at this, and took leave after their several fashions. The old notary went out under the archway to look for his lantern, lighted it, and offered to see the des Grassins to their house. Mme. des Grassins had not been prepared for the event which had brought the evening so early to a close, and her maid had not appeared.

"Will you honor me by taking my arm, madame?" said the Abbé Cruchot, addressing Mme. des Grassins.

"Thank you, M. l'Abbé," said the lady dryly; "my son is with me."

"I am not a compromising acquaintance for a lady," the Abbé continued.

"Take M. Cruchot's arm," said her husband.

The Abbé, with the fair lady on his arm, walked on quickly for several paces, so as to put a distance between them and the rest of the party.

"That young man is very good-looking, madame," he said, with a pressure on her arm to give emphasis to the remark. "'Tis good-bye to the baskets, the vintage is over! You must give up Mlle. Grandet; Eugénie is meant for her cousin. Unless he happens to be smitten with some fair face in Paris, your son Adolphe will have yet another rival——"

"Nonsense, M. l'Abbé."

"It will not be long before the young man will find out that Eugénie is a girl who has nothing to say for herself; and she has gone off in looks. Did you notice her? She was as yellow as a quince this evening."

"Which, possibly, you have already pointed out to her cousin?"

"Indeed, I have not taken the trouble——"

"If you always sit beside Eugénie, madame," interrupted the Abbé, "you will not need to tell the young man much about his cousin; he can make his own comparisons."

"He promised me at once to come to dine with us the day after to-morrow."

"Ah! madame," said the Abbé, "if you would only . . ."

"Would only what, M. l'Abbé? Do you mean to put evil suggestions into my mind? I have not come to the age of thirty-nine with a spotless reputation (Heaven be thanked) to compromise myself now—not for the Empire of the Great Mogul! We are both of us old enough to know what that kind of talk means; and I must say that your ideas do not square very well with your sacred calling. For shame! this is worthy of *Faublas.*"

"So you have read *Faublas?*"

"No, M. l'Abbé; *Les Liaisons dangereuses* is what I meant to say."

"Oh! that book is infinitely more moral," said the Abbé, laughing. "But you would make me out to be as depraved as young men are nowadays. I only meant that you——"

"Do you dare to tell me that you meant no harm? The thing is plain enough. If that young fellow (who certainly is good-looking, that I grant you) paid court to me, it would not be for the sake of my interest with that cousin of his. In Paris, I know, there are tender mothers who sacrifice themselves thus for their children's happiness and welfare, but we are not in Paris, M. l'Abbé."

"No, madame."

"And," continued she, "neither Adolphe nor I would purchase a hundred millions at such a price."

"Madame, I said nothing about a hundred millions. Perhaps such a temptation might have been too much for either of us. Still, in my opinion, an honest woman may indulge in a little harmless coquetry, in the strictest propriety; it is a part of her social duties, and——"

"You think so?"

"Do we not owe it to ourselves, madame, to endeavor to be as agreeable as possible to others? . . . Permit me to blow my nose. Take my word for it, madame," resumed the Abbé, "that he certainly regarded you with rather more admiration than he saw fit to bestow on me, but I can forgive him for honoring beauty rather than gray hairs——"

"It is perfectly clear," said the President in his thick voice, "why M. Grandet of Paris is sending his son to Saumur; he has made up his mind to make a match——"

"Then why should the cousin have dropped from the skies like this?" answered the notary.

"There is nothing in that," remarked M. des Grassins, "old Grandet is so close."

"Des Grassins," said his wife, "I have asked that young man to come and dine with us. So you must go to M. and Mme. de Larsonnière, dear, and ask them to come, and the du Hautoys; and they must bring that pretty girl of theirs, of course; I hope she will dress herself properly for once. Her mother is jealous of her, and makes her look such a figure. I hope that you gentlemen will do us the honor of coming too?" she added, stopping the procession in order to turn to the two Cruchots, who had fallen behind.

"Here we are at your door, madame," said the notary. The three Cruchots took leave of the three des Grassins, and on their way home the talent for pulling each other to pieces, which provincials possess in perfection, was fully called into play; the great event of the evening was exhaustively discussed, and all its bearings upon the respective positions of Cruchotins and Grassinistes were duly considered. Clearly it behooved both alike to prevent Eugénie from falling in love with her cousin, and to hinder Charles from thinking

of Eugénie. Sly hints, plausible insinuations, faint praise,
vindications undertaken with an air of candid friendliness—
what resistance could the Parisian offer when the air hurtled
with deceptive weapons such as these?

As soon as the four relatives were left alone in the great
room, M. Grandet spoke to his nephew.

"We must go to bed. It is too late to begin to talk to-night
of the business that brought you here; to-morrow will be
time enough for that. We have breakfast here at eight
o'clock. At noon we take a snatch of something, a little
fruit, a morsel of bread, and a glass of white wine, and, like
Parisians, we dine at five o'clock. That is the way of it. If
you care to take a look at the town, or to go into the country
round about, you are quite free to do so. You will excuse me
if, for business reasons, I cannot always accompany you.
Very likely you will be told hereabouts that I am rich: 'tis
always M. Grandet here and M. Grandet there. I let them
talk. Their babble does not injure my credit in any way.
But I have not a penny to bless myself with; and, old as I
am, I work like any young journeyman who has nothing in
the world but his plane and a pair of stout arms. Perhaps
you will find out for yourself some of these days what a lot
of work it takes to earn a crown when you have to toil and
moil for it yourself. Here, Nanon, bring the candles."

"I hope you will find everything you want, nephew," said
Mme. Grandet; "but if anything has been forgotten, you will
call Nanon."

"It would be difficult to want anything, my dear aunt, for
I believe I have brought all my things with me. Permit me
to wish you and my young cousin good night."

Charles took a lighted wax-candle from Nanon; it was a
commodity of local manufacture, which had grown old in the
shop, very dingy, very yellow, and so like the ordinary tallow variety that M. Grandet had no suspicion of the article
of luxury before him; indeed, it never entered into his head
to imagine that there could be such a thing in the house.

"I will show you the way," said the goodman.

One of the doors in the dining-room gave immediate access to the archway and to the staircase; but to-night, out of compliment to his guest, Grandet went by way of the passage which separated the kitchen from the dining-room. A folding-door, with a large oval pane of glass let into it, closed in the passage at the end nearest the staircase, an arrangement intended to keep out the blasts of cold air that rushed through the archway. With a like end in view, strips of list had been nailed to the doors; but in winter the east wind found its way in, and whistled none the less shrewdly about the house, and the dining-room was seldom even tolerably warm.

Nanon went out, drew the bolts on the entrance gate, fastened the door of the dining-room, went across to the stable to let loose a great wolf-dog with a cracked voice; it sounded as though the animal was suffering from laryngitis. His savage temper was well known, and Nanon was the only human being who could manage him. There was some wild strain in both these children of the fields; they understood each other.

Charles glanced round at the dingy yellow walls and smoke-begrimed ceiling, and saw how the crazy, worm-eaten stairs shook beneath his uncle's heavy tread; he was fast coming to his senses, this was sober reality indeed! The place looked like a hen-roost. He looked round questioningly at the faces of his aunt and cousin, but they were so thoroughly accustomed to the staircase and its peculiarities that it never occurred to them that it could cause any astonishment; they took his signal of distress for a simple expression of friendliness, and smiled back at him in the most amiable way. That smile was the last straw; the young man was at his wits' end.

"What the devil made my father send me here?" said he to himself.

Arrived on the first landing, he saw before him three doors painted a dull red-brown color; there were no moldings round any of them, so that they would have been scarcely

visible in the dust surface of the wall if it had not been for
the very apparent heavy bars of iron with which they were
embellished, and which terminated in a sort of rough orna-
mental design, as did the ends of the iron scutcheons which
surrounded the keyholes. A door at the head of the stairs,
which had once given entrance into the room over the kitchen,
was evidently blocked up. As a matter of fact, the only entrance was through Grandet's own room, and this room over
the kitchen was the vinegrower's sanctum.

Daylight was admitted into it by a single window which
looked out upon the yard, and which, for greater security,
was protected by a grating of massive iron bars. The master of the house allowed no one, not even Mme. Grandet, to
set foot in this chamber; he kept the right of entry to himself, and sat there, undisturbed and alone, like an alchemist
in the midst of his crucibles. Here, no doubt, there was
some cunningly contrived and secret hiding-place; for here
he stored up the title-deeds of his estates; here, too, he kept
the delicately adjusted scales in which he weighed his gold
louis; and here every night he made out receipts, wrote ac-
knowledgments of sums received, and laid his schemes, so
that other business men, seeing Grandet never busy, and
always prepared for every emergency, might have been excused for imagining that he had a fairy or familiar spirit at
his beck and call. Here, no doubt, when Nanon's snoring
shook the rafters, when the savage watch-dog bayed and
prowled about the yard, when Mme. Grandet and Eugénie
were fast asleep, the old cooper would come to be with his
gold, and hug himself upon it, and toy with it, and fondle it,
and brood over it, and so, with the intoxication of the gold
upon him, at last to sleep. The walls were thick, the closed
shutters kept their secret. He alone had the key of this
laboratory, where, if reports spoke truly, he pored over plans
on which every fruit tree belonging to him was mapped out,
so that he could reckon out his crops, so much to every vine
stem; and his yield of timber, to a fagot.

The door of Eugénie's room was opposite this closed-up

portal, the room occupied by M. and Mme. Grandet was at
the end of the landing, and consisted of the entire front of
the house. It was divided within by a partition. Mme. Grandet's chamber was next to Eugénie's, with which it communicated by a glass door; the other half of the room, separated
from the mysterious cabinet by a thick wall, belonged to the
master of the house. Goodman Grandet had cunningly
lodged his nephew on the second story, in an airy garret immediately above his own room, so that he could hear every
sound and inform himself of the young man's goings and
comings, if the latter should take it into his head to leave
his quarters.

Eugénie and her mother, arrived on the first landing, kissed
each other, and said good night; they took leave of Charles
in a few formal words, spoken with an apparent indifference,
which in her heart the girl was far from feeling, and went
to their rooms.

"This is your room, nephew," said Grandet, addressing
Charles as he opened the door. "If you should wish to go out,
you will have to call Nanon; for if you don't, it will be 'no
more at present from your most obedient,' the dog will gobble
you down before you know where you are. Good night, sleep
well. Ha! ha! the ladies have lighted a fire in your room,"
he went on.

Just at that moment big Nanon appeared, armed with a
warming-pan.

"Did any one ever see the like?" said M. Grandet. "Do
you take my nephew for a sick woman? he is not an invalid.
Just be off, Nanon! you and your hot ashes."

"But the sheets are damp, sir, and the gentleman looks as
delicate as a woman."

"All right, go through with it, since you have taken it into
your head," said Grandet, shrugging his shoulders, "but
mind you don't set the place on fire," and the miser groped
his way downstairs, muttering vaguely to himself.

Charles, breathless with astonishment, was left among his
trunks. He looked round about him, at the sloping roof of

the attic, at the wallpaper of a pattern peculiar to little
country inns, bunches of flowers symmetrically arranged on
a buff-colored background; he looked at the rough stone
chimney-piece full of rifts and cracks (the mere sight of it
sent a chill through him, in spite of the fire in the grate),
at the ramshackle cane-seated chairs, at the open night-table
large enough to hold a fair-sized sergeant-at-arms, at the
strip of worn rag-carpet beside the canopied bedstead, at the
curtains which shook every moment as if the whole worm-
eaten structure would fall to pieces; finally, he turned his attention to big Nanon, and said earnestly—

"Look here, my good girl, am I really in M. Grandet's
house? M. Grandet, formerly Mayor of Saumur, and brother
of M. Grandet of Paris?"

"Yes, sir, you are; and you are staying with a very kind,
a very amiable and excellent gentleman. Am I to help you
to unpack those trunks of yours?"

"Faith, yes, old soldier, I wish you would. Did you serve
in the horse marines?"

"Oh! oh! oh!" chuckled Nanon. "What may they be?
What are the horse marines? Are they old salts? Do they
go to sea?"

"Here, look out my dressing-gown; it is in that portman-.
teau, and this is the key."

Nanon was overcome with astonishment at the sight of a
green silk dressing-gown, embroidered with gold flowers after
an antique pattern.

"Are you going to sleep in *that*?" she inquired.

"Yes."

"Holy Virgin! What a beautiful altar cloth it would make
for the parish church! Oh, my dear young gentleman, you
should give it to the Church, and you will save your soul
which you are like to lose for that thing. Oh! how nice you
look in it. I will go and call mademoiselle to look at you."

"Come now, Nanon, since that is your name, will you hold
your tongue, and let me go to bed. I will set my things
straight to-morrow, and as you have taken such a fancy to

my gown, you shall have a chance to save your soul. I am too good a Christian to take it away with me when I go; you shall have it, and you can do whatever you like with it."

Nanon stood stock still, staring at Charles; she could not bring herself to believe that he really meant what he said.

"You are going to give that grand dressing-gown to *me!*" she said, as she turned to go. "The gentleman is dreaming already. Good night."

"Good night, Nanon.—What ever am I doing here?" said Charles to himself, as he dropped off to sleep. "My father is no fool; I have not been sent here for nothing. Pooh! 'serious business to-morrow,' as some old Greek wiseacre used to say."

"*Sainte Vierge!* how nice he is!" said Eugénie to herself in the middle of her prayers, and that night they remained unfinished.

Mme. Grandet alone lay down to rest, with no thought in her quiet mind. Through the door in the thin partition she could hear her husband pacing to and fro in his room. Like all sensitive and timid women, she had thoroughly studied the character of her lord and master. Just as the sea-mew foresees the coming storm, she knew by almost imperceptible signs that a tempest was raging in Grandet's mind, and, to use her own expression, she "lay like one dead" at such seasons. Grandet's eyes turned towards his sanctum; he looked at the door, which was lined with sheet iron on the inner side (he himself had seen to that), and muttered, "What a preposterous notion this is of my brother's, to leave his child to me! A pretty legacy! I haven't twenty crowns to spare, and what would twenty crowns be to a popinjay like that, who looked at my weather-glass as if it wasn't fit to light the fire with?"

And Grandet, meditating on the probable outcome of this mournful dying request, was perhaps more perturbed in spirit than the brother who had made it.

"Shall I really have that golden gown?" Nanon said, and she fell asleep wrapped around in her altar cloth, dreaming

for the first time in her life of shining embroideries and
flowered brocade, just as Eugénie dreamed of love.

In a girl's innocent and uneventful life there comes a mysterious hour of joy when the sunlight spreads through the
soul, and it seems to her that the flowers express the thoughts
that rise within her, thoughts that are quickened by every
heart beat, only to blend in a vague feeling of longing, when
the days are filled with innocent melancholy and delicious
happiness. Children smile when they see the light for the
first time, and when a girl dimly divines the presence of
love in the world she smiles as she smiled in her babyhood.
If light is the first thing that we learn to love, is not love
like light in the heart? This moment had come for Eugénie;
she saw the things of life clearly for the first time.

Early rising is the rule in the country, so, like most other
girls, Eugénie was up betimes in the morning; this morning
she rose earlier than usual, said her prayers, and began to
dress; her toilette was henceforth to possess an interest unknown before. She began by brushing her chestnut hair, and
wound the heavy plaits about her head, careful that no loose
ends should escape from the braided coronet which made
an appropriate setting for a face both frank and shy, a simple coiffure which harmonized with the girlish outlines.

As she washed her hands again and again in the cold
spring water that roughened and reddened the skin, she
looked down at her pretty rounded arms and wondered what
her cousin did to have hands so soft and so white, and nails
so shapely. She put on a pair of new stockings, and her best
shoes, and laced herself carefully, without passing over a
single eyelet-hole. For the first time in her life, in fact, she
wished to look her best, and felt that it was pleasant to have
a pretty new dress to wear, a becoming dress which was nicely
made.

The church clock struck just as she had finished dressing;
she counted the strokes, and was surprised to find that it was
still only seven o'clock. She had been so anxious to have
plenty of time for her toilette, that she had risen too early.

and now there was nothing left to do. Eugénie, in her ignorance, never thought of studying the position of a tress of hair, and of altering it a dozen times to criticise its effect; she simply folded her arms, sat down by the window, and looked out upon the yard, the long strip of garden, and the terraced gardens up above upon the ramparts.

It was a somewhat dreary outlook thus shut in by the grim rock walls, but not without a charm of its own, the mysterious beauty of quiet over-shaded gardens, or of wild and solitary places. Under the kitchen window there was a well with a stone coping round it; a pulley was suspended above the water from an iron bracket overgrown by a vine; the vine-leaves were red and faded now that the autumn was nearly at an end, and the crooked stem was plainly visible as it wound its way to the house wall, and crept along the house till it came to an end by the wood stack, where the fagots were arranged with as much neatness and precision as the volumes on some book-lover's shelves. The flag-stones in the yard were dark with age and mosses, and dank with the stagnant air of the place; weeds grew here and there among the chinks. The massive outworks of the old fortifications were green with moss, with here and there a long dark brown streak where water dripped, and the eight tumble-down steps, which gave access to the garden at the further end of the yard, were almost hidden by a tall growth of plants; the general effect of the crumbling stones had a vague resemblance to some crusader's tomb erected by his widow in the days of yore and long since fallen into ruin.

Along the low mouldering stone wall there was a fence of open lattice-work, rotten with age, and fast falling to pieces; overrun by various creeping plants that clambered over it at their own sweet will. A couple of stunted apple trees spread out their gnarled and twisted branches on either side of the wicket gate that led into the garden—three straight gravel walks with strips of border in between, and a line of box-edging on either side; and, at the further end, underneath the ramparts, a sort of arbor of lime trees, and a row of rasp-

berry canes. A huge walnut tree grew at the end nearest
to the house, and almost overshadowed the cooper's strong
room with its spreading branches.

It was one of those soft, bright, autumn mornings peculiar
to the districts along the Loire; there was not a trace of mist;
the light frosty rime of the previous night was rapidly disappearing as the mild rays of the autumn sun shone on the
picturesque surroundings, the old walls, the green tangled
growth in the yard and garden.

All these things had been long familiar to Eugénie's eyes,
but to-day it seemed to her that there was a new beauty about
them. A throng of confused thoughts filled her mind as the
sunbeams overflowed the world without. A vague, inexplicable new happiness stirred within her, and enveloped her
soul, as a bright cloud might cling about some object in the
material world. The quaint garden, the old walls, every detail in her little world seemed to be living through this new
experience with her; the nature without her was in harmony
with her inmost thoughts. The sunlight crept along the wall
till it reached a maiden-hair fern; the changing hues of a
pigeon's breast shone from the thick fronds and glossy stems,
and all Eugénie's future grew bright with radiant hopes.
Henceforward the bit of wall, its pale flowers, its blue hare-
bells and bleached grasses, was a pleasant sight for her; it
called up associations which had all the charm of the memories of childhood.

The rustling sound made by the leaves as they fell to the
earth, the echoes that came up from the court, seemed like
answers to the girl's secret questionings as she sat and mused;
she might have stayed there by the window all day and never
have noticed how the hours went by, but other thoughts
surged up within her soul. Again and again she rose and
stood before the glass, and looked at herself, as a conscientious writer scrutinizes his work, criticises it, and says hard
things about it to himself.

"I am not pretty enough for him!"

This was what Eugénie thought, in her humility, and the

thought was fertile in suffering. The poor child did not do herself justice; but humility, or more truly, fear, is born with love. Eugénie's beauty was of a robust type often found among the lower middle classes, a type which may seem somewhat wanting in refinement, but in her the beauty of the Venus of Milo was ennobled and purified by the beauty of Christian sentiment, which invests woman with a dignity unknown to ancient sculptors. Her head was very large; the masculine but delicate outlines of her forehead recalled the Jupiter of Phidias; all the radiance of her pure life seemed to shine from the clear gray eyes. An attack of smallpox, so mild that it had left no scars on the oval face or features, had yet somewhat blurred their fresh, fair coloring, and coarsened the smooth and delicate surface, still so fine and soft that her mother's gentle kiss left a passing trace of faint red on her cheek. Perhaps her nose was a little too large, but it did not contradict the kindly and affectionate expression of the mouth, and the red lips covered with finely-etched lines. Her throat was daintily rounded. There was something that attracted attention and stirred the imagination in the curving lines of her figure, covered to the throat by her high-necked dress; no doubt she possessed little of the grace that is due to the toilette, and her tall frame was strong rather than lissome, but this was not without its charm for judges of beauty.

For Eugénie was both tall and strongly built. She had nothing of the prettiness that ordinary people admire; but her beauty was unmistakable, and of a kind in which artists alone delight. A painter in quest of an exalted and spiritual type, searching women's faces for the beauty which Raphael dreamed of and conjured into being, the eyes full of proud humility, the pure outlines, often due to some chance inspiration of the artist, but which a virtuous and Christian life can alone acquire or preserve,—a painter haunted by this ideal would have seen at once in Eugénie Grandet's face her unconscious and innate nobility of soul, a world of love behind the quiet brow, and in the way she had with her eyelids and in her eyes that divine something which baffles description. There was a serene tranquillity about her features, unspoiled and unwearied by the expression of pleasure; it was as if you watched, across some placid lake, the shadowy outlines of hills far off against the sky. The beauty of Eugénie's face, so quiet and so softly colored, was like that of some fair, half-opened flower about which the light seems to hover; in its quality of restfulness, its subtle revelation of a beautiful nature, lay the charm that attracted beholders. Eugénie was still on the daisied brink of life, where illusions blossom and joys are gathered which are not known in later days. So she looked in the glass, and with no thought of love as yet in her mind, she said, "He will not give me a thought; I am too ugly!"

Then she opened her door, went out on to the landing, and bent over the staircase to hear the sounds in the house.

"He is not getting up yet," she thought. She heard Nanon's morning cough as the good woman went to and fro, swept out the dining-room, lit the kitchen fire, chained up the dog, and talked to her friends the brutes in the stable.

Eugénie fled down the staircase, and ran over to Nanon, who was milking the cow.

"Nanon," she cried, "do let us have some cream for my cousin's coffee, there's a dear."

"But, mademoiselle, you can't have cream off this morning's milk," said Nanon, as she burst out laughing. "I can't make cream for you. Your cousin is as charming as charming can be, that he is! You haven't seen him in that silk night rail of his, all flowers and gold! I did though! The linen he wears is every bit as fine as M. le Curé's surplice."

"Nanon, make some cake for us."

"And who is to find the wood to heat the oven, and the flour and the butter?" asked Nanon, who in her capacity of Grandet's prime minister was a person of immense importance in Eugénie's eyes, and even in Eugénie's mother's. "Is *he* to be robbed to make a feast for your cousin? Ask for the butter and the flour and the firewood; he is your father, go and ask him, he may give them to *you*. There! there he is, just coming downstairs to see after the provisions——"

But Eugénie had escaped into the garden; the sound of her father's footstep on the creaking staircase terrified her. She was conscious of a happiness that shrank from the observation of others, a happiness which, as we are apt to think, and perhaps not without reason, shines from our eyes, and is written at large upon our foreheads. And not only so, she was conscious of other thoughts. The bleak discomfort of her father's house had struck her for the first time, and, with a dim feeling of vexation, the poor child wished that she could alter it all, and bring it more into harmony with her cousin's elegance. She felt a passionate longing to do something for him, without the slightest idea what that something should be. The womanly instinct awakened in her at the first sight of her cousin was only the stronger because she had reached her three-and-twentieth year, and mind and heart were fully developed; and she was so natural and simple that she acted on the promptings of her angelic nature without submitting herself, her impressions, or her feelings to any introspective process.

For the first time in her life the sight of her father struck a sort of terror into her heart; she felt that he was the master of her fate, and that she was guiltily hiding some of her thoughts from him. She began to walk hurriedly up and down, wondering how it was that the air was so fresh; there was a reviving force in the sunlight, it seemed to be within her as well as without, it was as if a new life had begun.

While she was still thinking how to gain her end concerning the cake, a quarrel came to pass between Nanon and Grandet, a thing as rare as a winter swallow. The goodman had just taken his keys, and was about to dole out the provisions required for the day.

"Is there any bread left over from yesterday?" he asked of Nanon.

"Not a crumb, sir."

Grandet took up a large loaf, round in form and close in

5

consistence, shaped in one of the flat baskets which they use for baking in Anjou, and was about to cut it, when Nanon broke in upon him with—

"There are five of us to-day, sir."

"True," answered Grandet; "but these loaves of yours weigh six pounds apiece; there will be some left over. Besides, these young fellows from Paris never touch bread, as you will soon see."

"Then do they eat *'kitchen?'*" asked Nanon.

This word *kitchen* in the Angevin dictionary signifies anything which is spread upon bread; from butter, the commonest variety, to preserved peaches, the most distinguished of all *kitchens;* and those who, as small children, have nibbled off the *kitchen* and left the bread, will readily understand the bearing of Nanon's remark.

"No," replied Grandet with much gravity, "they eat neither bread nor *kitchen;* they are like a girl in love, as you may say."

Having at length cut down the day's rations to the lowest possible point, the miser was about to go to his fruit-loft, first carefully locking up the cupboards of his storeroom, when Nanon stopped him.

"Just give me some flour and butter, sir," she said, "and I will make a cake for the children."

"Are you going to turn the house upside down because my nephew is here?"

"Your nephew was no more in my mind than your dog, no more than he was in yours. . . . There, now! you have only put out six lumps of sugar, and I want eight."

"Come, come, Nanon; I have never seen you like this before. What has come over you? Are you mistress here? You will have six lumps of sugar and no more."

"Oh, very well; and what is your nephew to sweeten his coffee with?"

"He can have two lumps; I shall go without it myself."

"*You* go without sugar! and at your age! I would sooner pay for it out of my own pocket."

"Mind your own business."

In spite of the low price of sugar, it was, in Grandet's eyes, the most precious of all colonial products. For him it was always something to be used sparingly; it was still worth six francs a pound, as in the time of the Empire, and this petty economy had become an inveterate habit with him. But every woman, no matter how simple she may be, can devise some shift to gain her ends; and Nanon allowed the question of the sugar to drop, in order to have her way about the cake.

"Mademoiselle," she called through the window, "wouldn't you like some cake?"

"No, no," answered Eugénie.

"Stay, Nanon," said Grandet as he heard his daughter's voice; "there!"

He opened the flour-bin, measured out some flour, and added a few ounces of butter to the piece which he had already cut.

"And firewood; I shall want firewood to heat the oven," said the inexorable Nanon.

"Ah! well, you can take what you want," he answered ruefully; "but you will make a fruit tart at the same time, and you must bake the dinner in the oven, that will save lighting another fire."

"*Quien!*" cried Nanon; "there is no need to tell me that!"

Grandet gave his trusty prime minister a glance that was almost paternal.

"Mademoiselle," cried the cook, "we are going to have a cake."

Grandet came back again with the fruit, and began by setting down a plateful on the kitchen table.

"Just look here, sir," said Nanon, "what lovely boots your nephew has! What leather, how nice it smells! What are they to be cleaned with? Am I to put your egg-blacking on them?"

"No, Nanon," said Eugénie; "I expect the egg would spoil the leather. You had better tell him that you have no idea how to clean black morocco. . . . Yes, it is morocco, and he himself will buy you something in Saumur to clean his boots with. I have heard it said that they put sugar into their blacking, and that is what makes it so shiny."

"Then is it good to eat?" asked the maid, as she picked up the boots and smelt them. "*Quien, quien!* they smell of madame's eau-de-Cologne! Oh, how funny!"

"*Funny!*" said her master; "people spend more money on their boots than they are worth that stand in them, and you think it funny!" He had just returned from a second and final expedition to the fruit loft, carefully locking the door after him.

"You will have soup once or twice a week while your nephew is here, sir, will you not?"

"Yes."

"Shall I go round to the butcher's?"

"You will do nothing of the kind. You can make some chicken-broth; the tenants will keep you going. But I shall tell Cornoiller to kill some ravens for me. That kind of game makes the best broth in the world."

"Is it true, sir, that they live on dead things?"

"You are a fool, Nanon! They live, like everybody else, on anything that they can pick up. Don't we all live on dead things? What about legacies?" And Goodman Grandet, having no further order to give, drew out his watch, and finding that there was yet half an hour to spare before breakfast, took up his hat, gave his daughter a kiss, and said, "Would you like to take a walk along the Loire? I have something to see after in the meadows down there."

Eugénie put on her straw hat lined with rose-colored silk; and then father and daughter went down the crooked street towards the market-place.

"Where are you off to so early this morning?" said the notary Cruchot, as he met the Grandets.

"We are going to take a look at something," responded his friend, in no wise deceived by this early move on the notary's part.

Whenever Grandet was about to "take a look at something," the notary knew by experience that there was something to be gained by going with him. With him, therefore, he went.

"Come along, Cruchot," said Grandet, addressing the notary. "You are one of my friends; I am going to show you what a piece of folly it is to plant poplars in good soil——"

"Then the sixty thousand francs that you fingered for those poplars of yours in the meadows by the Loire are a mere trifle to you?" said Cruchot, opening his eyes wide in his bewilderment. "And such luck as you had too! . . . Felling your timber just when there was no white wood to be had in Nantes, so that every trunk fetched thirty francs!"

Eugénie heard and did not hear, utterly unconscious that the most critical moment of her life was rapidly approaching, that a paternal and sovereign decree was about to be pronounced, and that the old notary was to bring this all about. Grandet had reached the magnificent meadow-land by the Loire, which had come into his hands in his Republican days. Some thirty laborers were busy digging out the roots of the poplars that once stood there, filling up the holes that were left, and leveling the ground.

"Now, M. Cruchot, see how much space a poplar takes up," said he, addressing the notary. "Jean," he called to a workman, "m—m—measure r—round the sides with your rule."

"Eight feet four times over," said the workman when he had finished.

"Thirty-two feet of loss," said Grandet to Cruchot. "Now along that line there were three hundred poplars, weren't there? Well, then, three hundred t—t—times thirty-two f—feet will eat up five hundredweight of hay. Allow twice as much again for the space on either side, and you get fifteen hundredweight; then there is the intervening space—say a thousand t—t—trusses of hay altogether."

"Well," said Cruchot, helping his friend out, "and a thousand trusses of that hay would fetch something like six hundred francs."

"S—s—say t—twelve hundred, because the s—second crop is worth three or four hundred francs. Good, then reckon up what t—t—twelve hundred francs per annum d—d—during f—forty years comes to, at compound interest of course."

"Sixty thousand francs, or thereabouts," said the notary.

"That is what I make it! Sixty thousand f—f—francs. Well," the vinegrower went on without stammering, "two thousand poplars will not bring in fifty thousand francs in forty years. So you lose on them. That *I* found out," said Grandet, who was vastly pleased with himself. "Jean," he continued, turning to the laborer, "fill up all the holes except those along the riverside, where you can plant those poplar saplings that I bought. If you set them along by the Loire, they will grow there finely at the expense of the Government," he added, and as he looked round at Cruchot the wen on his nose twitched slightly; the most sardonic smile could not have said more.

"Yes, it is clear enough, poplars should only be planted in poor soil," said Cruchot, quite overcome with amazement at Grandet's astuteness.

"Y—e—s, sir," said the cooper ironically.

Eugénie was looking out over the glorious landscape and along the Loire, without heeding her father's arithmetic; but Cruchot's talk with his client took another turn, and her attention was suddenly aroused.

"So you have a son-in-law come from Paris; they are talking about nothing but your nephew in all Saumur. I shall soon have settlements to draw up; eh, père Grandet?"

"Did you come out early to t—t—tell me that?" inquired Grandet, and again the wen twitched. "Very well, you are an old crony of mine; I will be p—plain with you, and t—t—tell you what you w—want to know. I would rather fling my d—d—daughter into the Loire, look you, than g—give her to her cousin. You can give that out. But, no; l—l—let people gossip."

Everything swam before Eugénie's eyes. Her vague hopes of distant happiness had suddenly taken definite shape, had sprung up and blossomed, and then her harvest of flowers had been as suddenly cut down and lay on the earth. Since yesterday she had woven the bonds of happiness that unite two souls, and henceforward sorrow, it seemed, was to strengthen them. Is it not written in the noble destiny of woman that the grandeur of sorrow should touch her more closely than all the pomp and splendor of fortune?

How came it that a father's feelings had been extinguished (as it seemed) in her father's heart? What crime could be laid at Charles' door? Mysterious questions! Mysterious and sad forebodings already surrounded her growing love, that mystery within her soul. When they turned to go home again, she trembled in every limb; and as they went up the shady street, along which she had lately gone so joyously, the shadows looked gloomy, the air she breathed seemed full of the melancholy of autumn, everything about her was sad. Love, that had brought these keener perceptions, was quick to interpret every boding sign. As they neared home, she walked on ahead of her father, knocked at the house door, and stood waiting beside it. But Grandet, seeing that the notary carried a newspaper still in its wrapper, asked, "How are consols?"

"I know you will not take my advice, Grandet," Cruchot replied. "You should buy at once; the chance of making twenty per cent on them in two years is still open to you, and they pay a very fair rate of interest besides, five thousand livres is not a bad return on eighty thousand francs. You can buy now at eighty francs fifty centimes."

"We shall see," remarked Grandet pensively, rubbing his chin.

"*Mon Dieu!*" exclaimed the notary, who by this time had unfolded his newspaper.

"Well, what is it?" cried Grandet as Cruchot put the paper in his hands and said—

"Read that paragraph."

"M. Grandet, one of the most highly respected merchants in Paris, shot himself through the head yesterday afternoon, after putting in an appearance on 'Change as usual. He had

previously sent in his resignation to the President of the
Chamber of Deputies, resigning his position as Judge of the
Tribunal of Commerce at the same time. His affairs had become involved through the failures of his stockbroker and
notary, MM. Roguin and Souchet. M. Grandet, whose character was very greatly esteemed, and whose credit stood high,
would no doubt have found temporary assistance on the market which would have enabled him to tide over his difficulties.
It is to be regretted that a man of such high character
should have given way to the first impulse of despair"—and
so forth, and so forth.

"I knew it," the old vinegrower said.

Phlegmatic though Cruchot was, he felt a horrible shudder
run through him at the words; perhaps Grandet of Paris had
stretched imploring hands in vain to the millions of Grandet of Saumur; the blood ran cold in his veins.

"And his son?" he asked presently; "he was in such spirits
yesterday evening."

"His son knows nothing as yet," Grandet answered, im-
perturbable as ever.

"Good morning, M. Grandet," said Cruchot. He understood the position now, and went to reassure the President de
Bonfons.

Grandet found breakfast ready. Mme. Grandet was already seated in her chair, mounted on the wooden blocks,
and was knitting woolen cuffs for the winter. Eugénie ran
to her mother and put her arms about her, with the eager
hunger for affection that comes of a hidden trouble.

"You can get your breakfast," said Nanon, bustling downstairs in a hurry; "he is sleeping like a cherub. He looks so
nice with his eyes shut! I went in and called him, but it was
all one, he never heard me."

"Let him sleep," said Grandet; "he will wake soon enough
to hear bad news, in any case."

"What is the matter?" asked Eugénie. She was putting
into her cup the two smallest lumps of sugar, weighing good-

ness knows how many grains; her worthy parent was wont to amuse himself by cutting up sugar whenever he had nothing better to do.

Mme. Grandet, who had not dared to put the question herself, looked at her husband.

"His father has blown his brains out."

"*My uncle?*" said Eugénie.

"Oh! that poor boy!" cried Mme. Grandet.

"Poor indeed!" said Grandet; "he has not a penny."

"Ah! well, he is sleeping as if he were the king of all the world," said Nanon pityingly.

Eugénie could not eat. Her heart was wrung as a woman's heart can be when for the first time her whole soul is filled with sorrow and compassion for the sorrow of one she loves. She burst into tears.

"You did not know your uncle, so what is there to cry about?" said her father with a glance like a hungry tiger's; just such a glance as he would give, no doubt, to his heaps of gold.

"But who wouldn't feel sorry for the poor young man, sir?" said the serving-maid; "sleeping there like a log, and knowing nothing of his fate."

"I did not speak to you, Nanon! Hold your tongue."

In that moment Eugénie learned that a woman who loves must dissemble her feelings. She was silent.

"Until I come back, Mme. Grandet, you will say nothing about this to him, I hope," the old cooper continued. "They are making a ditch in my meadows along the road, and I must go and see after it. I shall come back for the second breakfast at noon, and then my nephew and I will have a talk about his affairs. As for you, Mademoiselle Eugénie, if you are crying over that popinjay, let us have no more of it, child. He will be off posthaste to the Indies directly, and you will never set eyes on *him* any more."

Her father took up his gloves, which were lying on the rim of his hat, put them on in his cool, deliberate way, inserting the fingers of one hand between those of the other, dovetail fashion, so as to thrust them down well into the tips of the gloves, and then he went out.

"Oh! mamma, I can scarcely breathe!" cried Eugénie when she was alone with her mother; "I have never suffered like this!"

Mme. Grandet, seeing her daughter's white face, opened the window and let fresh air into the room.

"I feel better now," said Eugénie after a little.

This nervous excitement in one who was usually so quiet and self-possessed produced an effect on Mme. Grandet. She looked at her daughter, and her mother's love and sympathetic instinct told her everything. But, in truth, the celebrated Hungarian twin-sisters, united to each other by one of Nature's errors, could scarcely have lived in closer sympathy than Eugénie and her mother. Were they not always together; together in the window where they sat the livelong day, together at church? Did they not breathe the same air even when they slept?

"My poor little girl!" said Mme. Grandet, drawing Eugénie's head down till it rested upon her bosom.

Her daughter lifted her face, and gave her mother a questioning look which seemed to read her inmost thoughts.

"Why must he be sent to the Indies?" said the girl. "If he is in trouble, ought he not to stay here with us? Is he not our nearest relation?"

"Yes, dear child, that would only be natural; but your father has reasons for what he does, and we must respect them."

Mother and daughter sat in silence, the one on her chair mounted on the wooden blocks, the other in her little armchair. Both women took up their needlework. Eugénie felt that her mother understood her, and her heart was full of gratitude for such tender sympathy.

"How kind you are, dear mamma!" she said as she took her mother's hand and kissed it.

The worn, patient face, aged with many sorrows, lighted up at the words.

"Do you like him?" asked Eugénie.

For all answer, Mme. Grandet smiled. Then after a moment's pause she murmured, "You cannot surely love him already? That would be a pity."

"Why would it be a pity?" asked Eugénie. "You like him, Nanon likes him, why should I not like him too? Now then, mamma, let us set the table for his breakfast."

She threw down her work, and her mother followed her example, saying as she did so, "You are a mad girl!"

But none the less she did sanction her daughter's freak by assisting in it.

Eugénie called Nanon.

"Haven't you all you want yet, mamselle?"

"Nanon, surely you will have some cream by twelve o'clock?"

"By twelve o'clock? Oh! yes," answered the old servant.

"Very well, then, let the coffee be very strong. I have heard M. des Grassins say that they drink their coffee very strong in Paris. Put in plenty."

"And where is it to come from?"

"You must buy some."

"And suppose the master meets me?"

"He is down by the river."

"I will just slip out then. But M. Fessard asked me when I went about the candle if the Three Holy Kings were paying us a visit. Our goings on will be all over the town."

"Your father would be quite capable of beating us," said Mme. Grandet, "if he suspected anything of all this."

"Oh! well, then, never mind; he will beat us, we will take the beating on our knees."

At this Mme. Grandet raised her eyes to heaven, and said no more. Nanon put on her sun-bonnet and went out. Eugénie spread a clean linen tablecloth, then she went upstairs in quest of some bunches of grapes which she had amused herself by hanging from some strings up in the attic. She tripped lightly along the corridor, so as not to disturb her cousin, and could not resist the temptation to stop a moment before the door to listen to his even breathing.

"Trouble wakes while he is sleeping," she said to herself.

She arranged her grapes on the few last green vine leaves as daintily as any experienced *chef d'office,* and set them on the table in triumph. She levied contributions on the pears which her father had counted out, and piled them up pyramid fashion, with autumn leaves among them. She came and went, and danced in and out. She might have ransacked the house; the will was in nowise lacking, but her father kept everything under lock and key, and the keys were in his pocket. Nanon came back with two new-laid eggs. Eugénie could have flung her arms round the girl's neck.

"The farmer from La Lande had eggs in his basket; I asked him for some, and to please me he let me have these, the nice man."

After two hours of industrious application, Eugénie succeeded in preparing a very simple meal; it cost but little, it is true, but it was a terrible infringement of the immemorial laws and customs of the house. No one sat down to the midday meal, which consisted of a little bread, some fruit or butter, and a glass of wine. Twenty times in those two hours Eugénie had left her work to watch the coffee boil, or to listen for any sound announcing that her cousin was getting up; now looking round on the table drawn up to the fire, with one of the armchairs set beside it for her cousin, on the two plates of fruit, the egg-cups, the bottle of white wine, the bread, and the little pyramid of white sugar in a saucer; Eugénie trembled from head to foot at the mere thought of the glance her father would give her if he should happen to come in at that moment. Often, therefore, did she look at the clock, to see if there was yet time for her cousin to finish his breakfast before her parent's return.

"Never mind, Eugénie, if your father comes in, I will take all the blame," said Mme. Grandet.

Eugénie could not keep back the tears. "Oh! my kind mother," she cried; "I have not loved you enough!"

Charles, after making innumerable pirouettes around his room, came down at last, singing gay little snatches of song.

Luckily it was only eleven o'clock after all. He had taken as much pains with his appearance (the Parisian!) as if he had been staying in the château belonging to the high-born fair one who was traveling in Scotland; and now he came in with that gracious air of condescension which sits not ill on youth, and which gave Eugénie a melancholy pleasure. He had come to regard the collapse of his castles in Anjou as a very good joke, and went up to his aunt quite gaily.

"I hope you slept well, dear aunt? And you too, cousin?"

"Very well, sir; how did you sleep?"

"Soundly."

"Cousin, you must be hungry," said Eugénie; "sit down."

"Oh! I never breakfast before twelve o'clock, just after I rise. But I have fared so badly on my journey, that I will yield to persuasion. Besides——" he drew out the daintiest little watch that ever issued from Bréguet's workshop. "Dear me, it is only eleven o'clock; I have been up betimes."

"Up betimes?" asked Mme. Grandet.

"Yes, but I wanted to set my things straight. Well, I am quite ready for something, something not very substantial, a fowl or a partridge."

"Holy Virgin!" exclaimed Nanon, hearing these words.

"A partridge," Eugénie said to herself. She would, willingly have given all she had for one.

"Come and take your seat," said Mme. Grandet, addressing her nephew.

The dandy sank into the armchair in a graceful attitude, much as a pretty woman might recline on her sofa. Eugénie and her mother drew their chairs to the fire and sat near him.

"Do you always live here?" Charles inquired, thinking that the room looked even more hideous by daylight than by candle light.

"Always," Eugénie answered, watching him as she spoke. "Always, except during the vintage. Then we go to help Nanon, and we all stay at the Abbey at Noyers."

"Do you never take a walk?"

"Sometimes, on Sundays after vespers, when it is fine, we

walk down as far as the bridge," said Mme. Grandet, "or we sometimes go to see them cutting the hay."

"Have you a theatre here?"

"Go to the play!" cried Mme. Grandet; "go to see play-actors! Why, sir, do you not know that that is a mortal sin?"

"There, sir," said Nanon, bringing in the eggs, "we will give you chickens in the shell."

"Oh! new-laid eggs," said Charles, who, after the manner of those accustomed to luxury, had quite forgotten all about his partridge. "Delicious! Do you happen to have any butter, eh, my good girl?"

"Butter? If you have butter now, you will have no cake by-and-by," said the handmaid.

"Yes, of course, Nanon; bring some butter," cried Eugénie.

The young girl watched her cousin while he cut his bread and butter into strips, and felt happy. The most romantic shop-girl in Paris could not more thoroughly enjoy the spectacle of innocence triumphant in a melodrama. It must be conceded that Charles, who had been brought up by a graceful and charming mother, and had received his "finishing education" from an accomplished woman of the world, was as dainty, neat and elegant in his ways as any coxcomb of the gentler sex. The girl's quiet sympathy produced an almost magnetic effect. Charles, finding himself thus waited upon by his cousin and aunt, could not resist the influence of their overflowing kindness. He was radiant with good-humor, and the look he gave Eugénie was almost a smile. As he looked at her more closely he noticed her pure, regular features, her unconscious attitude, the wonderful clearness of her eyes, in which love sparkled, though she as yet knew nothing of love but its pain and a wistful longing.

"Really, my dear cousin," he said, "if you were in a box at the opera and in evening dress, and I would answer for it, my aunt's remark about deadly sin would be justified; all the men would be envious, and all the women jealous."

Eugénie's heart beat fast with joy at this compliment, though it conveyed no meaning whatever to her mind.

"You are laughing at a poor little country cousin," she said.

"If you knew me better, cousin, you would know that I detest banter; it sears the heart and deadens the feelings." And he swallowed down a strip of bread and butter with perfect satisfaction.

"No," he continued, "I never make fun of others, very likely because I have not wit enough, a defect which puts me at a great disadvantage. They have a deadly trick in Paris of saying, 'He is *so* good-natured,' which, being interpreted, means—'the poor youth is as stupid as a rhinoceros.' But as I happen to be rich, and it is known that I can hit the bull's eye straight off at thirty paces with any kind of pistol anywhere, these witticisms are not leveled at me."

"It is evident from what you say, nephew," said Mme. Grandet gravely, "that you have a kind heart."

"That is a very pretty ring of yours," said Eugénie; "is there any harm in asking to see it?"

Charles took off the ring and held it out; Eugénie reddened as her cousin's rose-pink nails came in contact with her finger-tips.

"Mother, only see how fine the work is!"

"Oh, what a lot of gold there is in it!" said Nanon, who brought in the coffee.

"What is that?" asked Charles, laughing, as he pointed to an oval pipkin, made of glazed brown earthenware, ornamented without by a circular fringe of ashes. It was full of a brown boiling liquid, in which coffee grounds were visible as they rose to the surface and fell again.

"Coffee; boiling hot!" answered Nanon.

"Oh! my dear aunt, I must at least leave some beneficent trace of my stay here. You are a long way behind the times! I will show you how to make decent coffee in a *cafetière à la Chaptal.*" Forthwith he endeavored to explain the principles on which this utensil is constructed.

"Bless me! if there is all that to-do about it," said Nanon, "you would have to give your whole time to it. I'll never make coffee that way, I know. Who is to cut the grass for our cow while I am looking after the coffee pot?"

"I would do it," said Eugénie.

"Child!" said Mme. Grandet, with a look at her daughter; and at the word came a swift recollection of the misery about to overwhelm the unconscious young man, and the three women were suddenly silent, and gazed pityingly at him. He could not understand it.

"What is it, cousin?" he asked Eugénie.

"Hush!" said Mme. Grandet, seeing that the girl was about to reply. "You know that your father means to speak to the gentleman——"

"Say, 'Charles,' " said young Grandet.

"Oh, is your name Charles?" said Eugénie. "It is a nice name."

Evil forebodings are seldom vain.

Just at that moment Mme. Grandet, Eugénie, and Nanon, who could not think of the cooper's return without shuddering, heard the familiar knock at the door.

"That is papa!" cried Eugénie.

She took away the saucer full of sugar, leaving one or two lumps on the tablecloth. Nanon hurried away with the egg-cups. Mme. Grandet started up like a frightened fawn. There was a sudden panic of terror, which amazed Charles, who was quite at a loss to account for it.

"Why, what is the matter?" he asked.

"My father is coming in," explained Eugénie.

"Well, and what then?"

M. Grandet entered the room, gave one sharp glance at the table, and another at Charles. He saw how it was at once.

"Aha! you are making a fête for your nephew. Good, very good, oh! very good, indeed!" he said, without stammering. "When the cat is away, the mice may play."

"Fête?" thought Charles, who had not the remotest conception of the state of affairs in the Grandet household.

"Bring me my glass, Nanon," said the goodman.

Eugénie went for the glass. Grandet drew from his waist-coat pocket a large clasp-knife with a stag's horn handle, cut a slice of bread, buttered it slowly and sparingly, and began to eat as he stood. Just then Charles put some sugar into his coffee; this called Grandet's attention to the pieces of sugar on the table; he looked hard at his wife, who turned pale, and came a step or two towards him; he bent down and said in the poor woman's ear—

"Where did all that sugar come from?"

"Nanon went out to Fessard's for some; there was none in the house."

It is impossible to describe the painful interest that this dumb show possessed for the three women; Nanon had left her kitchen, and was looking into the dining-room to see how things went there. Charles meanwhile tasted his coffee, found it rather strong, and looked round for another piece of sugar, but Grandet had already pounced upon it and taken it away.

"What do you want, nephew?" the old man inquired.

"The sugar."

"Pour in some more milk if your coffee is too strong," answered the master of the house.

Eugénie took up the saucer, of which Grandet had previously taken possession, and set it on the table, looking quietly at her father the while. Truly, the fair Parisian who exerts all the strength of her weak arms to help her lover to escape by a ladder of silken cords, displays less courage than Eugénie showed when she put the sugar upon the table. The Parisian will have her reward. She will proudly exhibit the bruises on a round white arm, her lover will bathe them with tears and cover them with kisses, and pain will be extinguished in bliss; but Charles had not the remotest conception of what his cousin endured for him, or of the horrible dismay that filled her heart as she met her father's angry eyes; he would never even know of her sacrifice.

"You are eating nothing, wife?"

6

The poor bond-slave went to the table, cut a piece of bread in fear and trembling, and took a pear. Eugénie, grown reckless, offered the grapes to her father, saying as she did so—

"Just try some of my fruit, papa! You will take some, will you not, cousin? I brought those pretty grapes down on purpose for you."

"Oh! if they could have their way, they would turn Saumur upside down for you, nephew! As soon as you have finished we will take a turn in the garden together; I have some things to tell you that would take a deal of sugar to sweeten them."

Eugénie and her mother both gave Charles a look, which the young man could not mistake.

"What do you mean by that, uncle? Since my mother died . . . (here his voice softened a little) there is no misfortune possible for me. . . ."

"Who can know what afflictions God may send to make trial of us, nephew," said his aunt.

"Tut, tut, tut," muttered Grandet, "here you are beginning with your folly already! I am sorry to see that you have such white hands, nephew."

He displayed the fists, like shoulders of mutton, with which nature had terminated his own arms.

"That is the sort of hand to rake the crowns together! You put the kind of leather on your feet that we used to make pocket-books of to keep bills in. That is the way you have been brought up. That's bad! That's bad!"

"What do you mean, uncle? I'll be hanged if I understand one word of this."

"Come along," said Grandet.

The miser shut his knife with a snap, drained his glass, and opened the door.

"Oh! keep up your courage, cousin!"

Something in the girl's voice sent a sudden chill through Charles; he followed his formidable relative with dreadful misgivings. Eugénie and her mother and Nanon went into the kitchen; an uncontrollable anxiety led them to watch the two actors in the scene which was about to take place in the damp little garden.

Uncle and nephew walked together in silence at first. Grandet felt the situation to be a somewhat awkward one; not that he shrank at all from telling Charles of his father's death, but he felt a kind of pity for a young man left in this way without a penny in the world, and he cast about for phrases that should break this cruel news as gently as might be. "You have lost your father!" he could say that; there was nothing in that; fathers usually predecease their children. But, "You have not a penny!" All the woes of the world were summed up in those words, so for the third time the worthy man walked the whole length of the path in the centre of the garden, crunching the gravel beneath his heavy boots, and no word was said.

At all great crises in our lives, any sudden joy or great sorrow, there comes a vivid consciousness of our surroundings that stamps them on the memory forever; and Charles, with every faculty strained and intent, saw the box-edging to the borders, the falling autumn leaves, the mouldering walls, the gnarled and twisted boughs of the fruit-trees, and till his dying day every picturesque detail of the little garden came back with the memory of the supreme hour of that early sorrow.

"It is very fine, very warm," said Grandet, drawing in a deep breath of air.

"Yes, uncle, but why——"

"Well, my boy," his uncle resumed, "I have some bad news for you. Your father is very ill . . ."

"What am I doing here?" cried Charles. "Nanon!" he shouted, "order post horses! I shall be sure to find a carriage of some sort in the place, I suppose," he added, turning to his uncle, who had not stirred from where he stood.

"Horses and a carriage are of no use," Grandet answered, looking at Charles, who immediately stared straight before him in silence. "Yes, my poor boy, you guess what has happened; he is dead. But that is nothing; there is something worse; he has shot himself through the head——"

"My father?"

"Yes, but that is nothing either. The newspapers are discussing it, as if it were any business of theirs. There, read for yourself."

Grandet had borrowed Cruchot's paper, and now he laid the fatal paragraph before Charles. The poor young fellow—he was only a lad as yet—made no attempt to hide his emotion, and burst into tears.

"Come, that is better," said Grandet to himself. "That look in his eyes frightened me. He is crying; he will pull through.—Never mind, my poor nephew," Grandet resumed aloud, not knowing whether Charles heard him or not, "that is nothing, you will get over it, but——"

"Never! never! My father! my father!"

"He has ruined you; you are penniless."

"What is that to me. Where is my father? . . . my father!" The sound of his sobbing filled the little garden, reverberated in ghastly echoes from the walls. Tears are as infectious as laughter; the three women wept with pity for him. Charles broke from his uncle without waiting to hear more, and sprang into the yard, found the staircase, and fled to his own room, where he flung himself across the bed and buried his face in the bedclothes, that he might give way to his grief in solitude as far as possible from these relations.

"Let him alone till the first shower is over," said Grandet, going back to the parlor. Eugénie and her mother had hastily returned to their places, had dried their eyes, and were sewing with cold, trembling fingers.

"But that fellow is good for nothing," went on Grandet; "he is so taken up with dead folk that he doesn't even think about the money."

Eugénie shuddered to hear the most sacred of sorrows spoken of in such a way; from that moment she began to criticise her father. Charles' sobs, smothered though they were, rang through that house of echoes; the sounds seemed to come from under the earth, a heart-rending wail that grew fainter towards the end of the day, and only ceased as night drew on.

"Poor boy!" said Mme. Grandet.

It was an unfortunate remark! Goodman Grandet looked at his wife, then at Eugénie, then at the sugar basin; he recollected the sumptuous breakfast prepared that morning for their unhappy kinsman, and planted himself in the middle of the room.

"Oh! by the bye," he said, in his usual cool, deliberate way, "I hope you will not carry your extravagance any further, Mme. Grandet; I do not give you MY money for you to squander it on sugar for that young rogue."

"Mother had nothing whatever to do with it," said Eugénie. "It was I——"

"Because you are come of age," Grandet interrupted his daughter, "you think you can set yourself to thwart me, I suppose? Mind what you are about, Eugénie——"

"But, father, your own brother's son ought not to have to go without sugar in your house."

"Tut, tut, tut, tut!" came from the cooper in a cadence of four semitones. "'Tis 'my nephew' here, and 'my brother's son' there; Charles is nothing to us, he has not a brass farthing. His father is a bankrupt, and when the young sprig has cried as much as he wishes, he shall clear out of this; I will not have my house turned topsy-turvy for him."

"What is a bankrupt, father?" asked Eugénie.

"A bankrupt," replied her father, "is guilty of the most dishonorable action that can dishonor a man."

"It must be a very great sin," said Mme. Grandet, "and our brother will perhaps be eternally lost."

"There you are with your preachments," her husband retorted, shrugging his shoulders. "A bankrupt, Eugénie," her father continued, "is a thief whom the law unfortunately takes under its protection. People trusted Guillaume Grandet with their goods, confiding in his character for fair-dealing and honesty; he has taken all they have, and left them nothing but the eyes in their heads to cry over their losses with. A bankrupt is worse than a highwayman; a highwayman sets upon you, and you have a chance to defend yourself;

he risks his life besides, while the other—Charles is dis-
graced in fact."

The words filled the poor girl's heart; they weighed upon
her with all their weight; she herself was so scrupulously
conscientious; no flower in the depths of a forest had grown
more delicately free from spot or stain; she knew none of the
maxims of worldly wisdom, and nothing of its quibbles and
its sophistries. So she accepted her father's cruel definition
and sweeping statements as to bankrupts; he drew no distinction between a fraudulent bankruptcy and a failure from un-
avoidable causes, and how should she?

"But, father, could you not have prevented this misfortune?"

"My brother did not ask my advice; besides, his liabilities
amount to four millions."

"How much is a million, father?" asked Eugénie, with the
simplicity of a child who would fain have its wish ful-
filled at once.

"A million?" queried Grandet. "Why, it is a million
francs, two hundred thousand five-franc pieces; there are
twenty sous in a franc, and it takes five francs of twenty sous
each to make a five-franc piece."

"Mon Dieu! Mon Dieu!" cried Eugénie, "how came my
uncle to have four millions of his own? Is there really anybody in France who has so many millions as that?"

Grandet stroked his daughter's chin and smiled. The wen
seemed to grow larger.

"What will become of cousin Charles?"

"He will set out for the East Indies, and try to make a
fortune. That is his father's wish."

"But has he any money to go with?"

"I shall pay his passage out as far as . . . yes . . .
as far as Nantes."

Eugénie sprang up and flung her arms about her father's
neck.

"Oh! father," she said, "you are good!"

Her warm embrace embarrassed Grandet somewhat; perhaps, too, his conscience was not quite at ease.

"Does it take a long while to make a million?" she asked.

"Lord! yes," said the cooper; "you know what a Napoleon is; well, then, it takes fifty thousand of them to make a million."

"Mamma, we will have a *neuvaine* said for him."

"That was what I was thinking," her mother replied.

"Just like you! always thinking how to spend money. Really, one might suppose that we had any amount of money to throw away!"

As he spoke a sound of low, hoarse sobbing, more ominous than any which had preceded it, came from the garret. Eugénie and her mother shuddered.

"Nanon," called Grandet, "go up and see that he is not killing himself."

"Look here! you two," he continued, turning to his wife and daughter, whose cheeks grew white at his tones, "there is to be no nonsense, mind! I am leaving the house. I am going round to see the Dutchmen who are going to-day. Then I shall go to Cruchot's, and have a talk with him about all this."

He went out. As soon as the door closed upon Grandet, Eugénie and her mother breathed more freely. The girl had never felt constraint in her father's presence until that morning; but a few hours had wrought rapid changes in her ideas and feelings.

"Mamma, how many louis is a hogshead of wine worth?"

"Your father gets something between a hundred and a hundred and fifty francs for his; sometimes two hundred I believe, from what I have heard him say."

"And would there be fourteen hundred hogsheads in a vintage?"

"I don't know how many there are, child, upon my word; your father never talks about business to me."

"But, anyhow, papa must be rich."

"Maybe. But M. Cruchot told me that your father bought Froidfond two years ago. That would be a heavy pull on him."

Eugénie, now at a loss as to her father's wealth, went no further with her arithmetic.

"He did not even so much as see me, the poor dear!" said
Nanon on her return. "He is lying there on his bed like a
calf, crying like a Magdalen, you never saw the like! Poor
young man, what can be the matter with him?"

"Let us go up at once and comfort him, mamma; if we
hear a knock, we will come downstairs."

There was something in the musical tones of her daughter's voice which Mme. Grandet could not resist. Eugénie
was sublime; she was a girl no longer, she was a woman.
With beating hearts they climbed the stairs and went together to Charles' room. The door was open. The young
man saw nothing, and heard nothing; he was absorbed in
his grief, an inarticulate cry broke from him now and again.

"How he loves his father!" said Eugénie in a low voice,
and in her tone there was an unmistakable accent which betrayed the passion in her heart, and hopes of which herself
was unaware. Mme. Grandet, with the quick instinct of a
mother's love, glanced at her daughter and spoke in a low
voice in her ear.

"Take care," she said, "or you may love him."

"Love him!" said Eugénie. "Ah! if you only knew what
my father said."

Charles moved slightly as he lay, and saw his aunt and
cousin.

"I have lost my father," he cried; "my poor father! If
he had only trusted me and told me about his losses, we
might have worked together to repair them. *Mon Dieu!* my
kind father! I was so sure that I should see him again, and
I said good-bye so carelessly, I am afraid, never thinking . . ."

His words were interrupted by sobs.

"We will surely pray for him," said Mme. Grandet. "Submit yourself to the will of God."

"Take courage, cousin," said Eugénie, gently; "nothing
can give your father back to you; you must now think how to
save your honor . . ."

A woman always has her wits about her, even in her ca-

pacity of comforter, and with instinctive tact Eugénie sought
to divert her cousin's mind from his sorrow by leading him
to think about himself.

"My honor?" cried the young man, hastily pushing back
the hair from his eyes. He sat upright upon the bed, and
folded his arms. "Ah! true. My uncle said that my father
had failed."

He hid his face in his hands with a heartrending cry of
pain.

"Leave me! leave me! cousin Eugénie," he entreated. "Oh!
God forgive my father, for he must have been terribly unhappy!"

There was something in the sight of this young sorrow,
this utter abandonment of grief, that was horribly engaging.
It was a sorrow that shrank from the gaze of others, and
Charles' gesture of entreaty that they should leave him to
himself was understood by Eugénie and her mother. They
went silently downstairs again, took their places by the great
window, and sewed on for nearly an hour without a word to
each other.

Eugénie had looked round the room; it was a stolen glance.
In one of those hasty surveys by which a girl sees everything
in a moment, she had noticed the pretty trifles on the toilette-
table—the scissors, the razors mounted with gold. The
gleams of splendor and luxury, seen amidst all this misery,
made Charles still more interesting in her eyes, perhaps by
the very force of the contrast. Their life had been so lonely
and so quiet; such an event as this, with its painful interest,
had never broken the monotony of their lives; little had occurred to stir their imaginations, and now this tragical drama
was being enacted under their eyes.

"Mamma," said Eugénie, "shall we wear mourning?"

"Your father will decide that," replied Mme. Grandet, and
once more they sewed in silence. Eugénie's needle moved
with a mechanical regularity which betrayed her preoccupation of mind. The first wish of this adorable girl was to
share her cousin's mourning. About four o'clock a sharp

knock at the door sent a sudden thrill of terror through Mme. Grandet.

"What can have brought your father back?" she said to her daughter.

The vinegrower came in in high good humor. He rubbed his hands so energetically that nothing but a skin like leather could have borne it, and indeed his hands were tanned like Russia leather, though the fragrant pine-rosin and incense had been omitted in the process. For a time he walked up and down and looked at the weather, but at last his secret escaped him.

"I have hooked them, wife," he said, without stammering; "I have them safe. Our wine is sold! The Dutchmen and Belgians were setting out this morning; I hung about in the market-place in front of their inn, looking as simple as I could. What's-his-name—you know the man—came up to me. All the best growers are hanging off and holding their vintages; they wanted to wait, and so they can, I have not hindered them. Our Belgian was at his wits' end, I saw that. So the bargain was struck; he is taking the whole of our vintage at two hundred francs the hogshead, half of it paid down at once in gold, and I have promissory notes for the rest. There are six louis for you. In three months' time prices will go down."

The last words came out quietly enough, but there was something so sardonic in the tone that if the little knots of growers, then standing in the twilight in the market-place of Saumur, in dismay at the news of Grandet's sale, had heard him speak, they would have shuddered; there would have been a panic on the market—wines would have fallen fifty per cent.

"You have a thousand hogsheads this year, father, have you not?" asked Eugénie.

"Yes, little girl."

These words indicated that the cooper's joy had indeed reached high-water mark.

"That will mean two hundred thousand francs?"

"Yes, Mademoiselle Grandet."

"Well, then, father, you can easily help Charles."

The surprise, the wrath and bewilderment with which Belshazzar beheld *Mene Mene Tekel Upharsin* written upon his palace wall were as nothing compared with Grandet's cold fury; he had forgotten all about Charles, and now he found that all his daughter's inmost thoughts were of his nephew, and that this arithmetic of hers referred to him. It was exasperating.

"Look here!" he thundered; "ever since that scapegrace set foot in *my* house everything has gone askew. You take it upon yourselves to buy sugar-plums, and make a great set-out for him. I will not have these doings. I should think, at my age, I ought to know what is right and proper to do. At any rate, I have no need to take lessons from my daughter, nor from any one else. I shall do for my nephew whatever it is right and proper for me to do; it is no business of yours, you need not meddle in it.—And now, as for you, Eugénie," he added, turning towards her, "if you say another word about it, I will send you and Nanon off to the Abbey at Noyers, see if I don't. Where is that boy? has he come downstairs yet?"

"No, dear," answered Mme. Grandet.

"Why, what is he doing then?"

"He is crying for his father," Eugénie said.

Grandet looked at his daughter, and found nothing to say. There was some touch of the father even in him. He took one or two turns up and down, and then went straight to his strong-room to think over possible investments. He had thoughts of buying consols. Those two thousand acres of woodland had brought him in six hundred thousand francs; then there was the money from the sale of the poplars, there was last year's income from various sources, and this year's savings, to say nothing of the bargain which he had just concluded; so that, leaving those two hundred thousand francs out of the question, he possessed a lump sum of nine hundred thousand livres. That twenty per cent, to be made in so short a time upon his outlay, tempted him. Consols stood at seventy. He jotted down his calculations on the margin of the paper that had brought the news of his brother's death; the moans of his nephew sounded in his ears the while, but he did not hear them; he went on with his work till Nanon thumped vigorously on the thick wall to summon her master to dinner. On the last step of the staircase beneath the archway, Grandet paused and thought.

"There is the interest beside the eight per cent.—I will do it. Fifteen hundred thousand francs in two years' time, in gold from Paris too, full weight.—Well, what has become of my nephew?"

"He said he did not want anything," replied Nanon. "He ought to eat, or he will fall ill."

"It is so much saved," was her master's comment.

"Lord! yes," she replied.

"Pooh! he will not keep on crying forever. Hunger drives the wolf from the wood."

Dinner was a strangely silent meal. When the cloth had been removed, Mme. Grandet spoke to her husband.

"We ought to go into mourning, dear."

"Really, Mme. Grandet, you must be hard up for ways of getting rid of money. Mourning is in the heart; it is not put on with clothes."

"But for a brother, mourning is indispensable, and the Church bids us——"

"Then buy mourning out of your six louis; a band of crape will do for me; you can get me a band of crape."

Eugénie said nothing, and raised her eyes to heaven. Her generous instincts, so long repressed and dormant, had been suddenly awakened, and every kindly thought had been harshly checked as it had arisen. Outwardly this evening passed just as thousands of others had passed in their monotonous lives, but for the two women it was the most painful that they had ever spent. Eugénie sewed without raising her head; she took no notice of the workbox which Charles had looked at so scornfully yesterday evening. Mme. Grandet knitted away at her cuffs. Grandet sat twirling his thumbs, absorbed in schemes which should one day bring about results that would startle Saumur. Four hours went by. Nobody dropped in to see them. As a matter of fact, the whole town was ringing with the news of Grandet's sharp practice, following on the news of his brother's failure and his nephew's arrival. So imperatively did Saumur feel the need to thrash these matters thoroughly out, that all the vine-growers, great or small, were assembled beneath the des Grassins' roof, and frightful were the imprecations which were launched at the head of their late Mayor.

Nanon was spinning; the whir of her wheel was the only sound in the great room beneath the gray-painted rafters.

"Our tongues don't go very fast," she said, showing her large teeth, white as blanched almonds.

"There is no call for them to go," answered Grandet, roused from his calculations.

He beheld a vision of the future—he saw eight millions in three years' time—he had set forth on a long voyage upon a golden sea.

"Let us go to bed. I will go up and wish my nephew a good night from you all, and see if he wants anything."

Mme. Grandet stayed on the landing outside her room door to hear what her worthy husband might say to Charles. Eugénie, bolder than her mother, went a step or two up the second flight.

"Well, nephew, you are feeling unhappy? Yes, cry, it is only natural, a father is a father. But we must bear our troubles patiently. Whilst you have been crying, I have been thinking for you; I am a kind uncle, you see. Come, don't lose heart. Will you take a little wine? Wine costs nothing at Saumur; it is common here; they offer it as they might offer you a cup of tea in the Indies.—But you are all in the dark," Grandet went on. "That's bad, that's bad; one ought to see what one is doing."

Grandet went to the chimney-piece.

"What!" he cried, "a wax candle! Where the devil have

they fished that from? I believe the wenches would pull up the floor of my house to cook eggs for that boy."

Mother and daughter, hearing these words, fled to their rooms, and crept into their beds like frightened mice.

"Mme. Grandet, you have a lot of money somewhere, it seems," said the vinegrower, walking into his wife's rooms.

"I am saying my prayers, dear; wait a little," faltered the poor mother.

"The devil take your pious notions!" growled Grandet.

Misers have no belief in a life to come, the present is all in all to them. But if this thought gives an insight into the miser's springs of action, it possesses a wider application, it throws a pitiless light upon our own era—for money is the one all-powerful force, ours is pre-eminently the epoch when money is the lawgiver, socially and politically. Books and institutions, theories and practice, all alike combine to weaken the belief in a future life, the foundation on which the social edifice has been slowly reared for eighteen hundred years. The grave has almost lost its terrors for us. That Future which awaited us beyond the *Requiem* has been transported into the present, and one hope and one ambition possesses us all—to pass *per fas et nefas* into this earthly paradise of luxury, vanity, and pleasure, to deaden the soul and mortify the body for a brief possession of this promised land, just as in other days men were found willing to lay down their lives and to suffer martyrdom for the hope of eternal bliss. This thought can be read at large; it is stamped upon our age, which asks of the voter—the man who makes the laws—not "What do you think?" but "What can you pay?" —And what will become of us when this doctrine has been handed down from the bourgeoisie to the people?

"Mme. Grandet, have you finished?" asked the cooper.

"I am praying for you, dear."

"Very well, good night. To-morrow morning I shall have something to say to you."

Poor woman! she betook herself to sleep like a schoolboy who has not learned his lessons, and sees before him the

angry face of the master when he wakes. Sheer terror led her
to wrap the sheets about her head to shut out all sounds, but
just at that moment she felt a kiss on her forehead; it was
Eugénie who had slipped into the room in the darkness, and
stood there barefooted in her nightdress.

"Oh! mother, my kind mother," she said, "I shall tell him
to-morrow morning that it was all my doing."

"No, don't; if you do, he will send you away to Noyers.
Let me manage it; he will not eat me, after all."

"Oh! mamma, do you hear?"

"What?"

"*He* is crying still."

"Go back to bed, dear. The floor is damp, it will strike
cold to your feet."

So ended the solemn day, which had brought for the poor
wealthy heiress a lifelong burden of sorrow; never again
would Eugénie Grandet sleep as soundly or as lightly as
heretofore. It not seldom happens that at some time in
their lives this or that human being will act literally "unlike
himself," and yet in very truth in accordance with his nature. Is it not rather that we form our hasty conclusions of
him without the aid of such light as psychology affords, without attempting to trace the mysterious birth and growth of
the causes which led to these unforeseen results? And this
passion, which had its roots in the depths of Eugénie's nature,
should perhaps be studied as if it were the delicate fibre of
some living organism to discover the secret of its growth.
It was a passion that would influence her whole life, so that
one day it would be sneeringly called a malady. Plenty of
people would prefer to consider a catastrophe improbable
rather than undertake the task of tracing the sequence of
the events that led to it, to discovering how the links of the
chain were forged one by one in the mind of the actor. In
this case Eugénie's past life will suffice to keen observers of
human nature; her artless impulsiveness, her sudden outburst of tenderness will be no surprise to them. Womanly
pity, that treacherous feeling, had filled her soul but the more

completely because her life had been so uneventful that it
had never been so called forth before.

So the trouble and excitement of the day disturbed her
rest; she woke again and again to listen for any sound from
her cousin's room, thinking that she still heard the moans
that all day long had vibrated through her heart. Sometimes she seemed to see him lying up there, dying of grief;
sometimes she dreamed that he was being starved to death.
Towards morning she distinctly heard a terrible cry. She
dressed herself at once, and in the dim light of the dawn fled
noiselessly up the stairs to her cousin's room. The door stood
open, the wax candle had burned itself down to the socket.
Nature had asserted herself; Charles, still dressed, was sleeping in the armchair, with his head fallen forward on the bed;
he had been dreaming as famished people dream. Eugénie
admired the fair young face. It was flushed and tear-stained;
the eyelids were swollen with weeping; he seemed to be still
crying in his sleep, and Eugénie's own tears fell fast. Some
dim feeling that his cousin was present awakened Charles;
he opened his eyes, and saw her distress.

"Pardon me, cousin," he said dreamily. Evidently he had
lost all reckoning of time, and did not know where he was.

"There are hearts here that feel for you, cousin, and *we*
thought that you might perhaps want something. You should
go to bed; you will tire yourself out if you sleep like that."

"Yes," he said, "that is true."

"Good-bye," she said, and fled, half in confusion, half glad
that she had come. Innocence alone dares to be thus bold,
and virtue armed with knowledge weighs its actions as carefully as vice.

Eugénie had not trembled in her cousin's presence, but
when she reached her own room again she could scarcely
stand. Her ignorant life had suddenly come to an end; she
remonstrated with herself, and blamed herself again and
again. "What will he think of me? He will believe that
I love him." Yet she knew that this was exactly what she
wished him to believe. Love spoke plainly within her, know-

ing by instinct how love calls forth love. The moment when she stole into her cousin's room became a memorable event in the girl's lonely life. Are there not thoughts and deeds which, in love, are for some souls like a solemn betrothal?

An hour later she went to her mother's room, to help her to dress, as she always did. Then the two women went downstairs and took their places by the window, and waited for Grandet's coming in the anxiety which freezes or burns. Some natures cower, and others grow reckless, when a scene or painful agitation is in prospect; the feeling of dread is so widely felt that domestic animals will cry out when the slightest pain is inflicted on them as a punishment, while the same creature if hurt inadvertently will not utter a sound.

The cooper came downstairs, spoke in an absent-minded way to his wife, kissed Eugénie, and sat down to table. He seemed to have forgotten last night's threats.

"What has become of my nephew? The child is not much in the way."

˙ "He is asleep, sir," said Nanon.

"So much the better, he won't want a wax candle for that," said Grandet facetiously.

His extraordinary mildness and satirical humor puzzled Mme. Grandet; she looked earnestly at her husband. The goodman—here perhaps it may be observed that in Touraine, Anjou, Poitou, and Brittany the designation *goodman* (*bonhomme*), which has been so often applied to Grandet, conveys no idea of merit; it is allowed to people of the worst temper as well as to good-natured idiots, and is applied without distinction to any man of a certain age—the goodman, therefore, took up his hat and gloves with the remark—

"I am going to have a look round in the market-place; I want to meet the Cruchots."

"Eugénie, your father certainly has something on his mind."

As a matter of fact, Grandet always slept but little, and was wont to spend half the night in revolving and maturing schemes, a process by which his views, observations, and

7

plans gained amazingly in clearness and precision; indeed, this was the secret of that constant success which was the admiration of Saumur. Time and patience combined will effect most things, and the man who accomplishes much is the man with the strong will who can wait. The miser's life is a constant exercise of every human faculty in the service of a personality. He believes in self-love and interest, and in no other motives of action, but interest is in some sort another form of self-love, to wit, a practical form dealing with the tangible and the concrete, and both forms are comprised in one master-passion, for self-love and interest are but two manifestations of egoism. Hence perhaps the prodigious interest which a miser excites when cleverly put upon the stage. What man is utterly without ambition? And what social ambition can be obtained without money? Every one has something in common with this being; he is a personification of humanity, and yet is revolting to all the feelings of humanity.

Grandet really "had something on his mind," as his wife used to say. In Grandet, as in every miser, there was a keen relish for the game, a constant craving to play men off one against another for his own benefit, to mulct them of their crowns without breaking the law. And did not every victim who fell into his clutches renew his sense of power, his just contempt for the weak of the earth who let themselves fall such an easy prey? Ah! who has understood the meaning of the lamb that lies in peace at the feet of God, that most touching symbol of meek victims who are doomed to suffer here below, and of the future that awaits them hereafter, of weakness and suffering glorified at last? But here on earth it is quite otherwise; the lamb is the miser's legitimate prey, and by him (when it is fat enough) it is contemptuously penned, killed, cooked, and eaten. On money and on this feeling of contemptuous superiority the miser thrives.

During the night this excellent man's ideas had taken an entirely new turn; hence his unusual mildness. He had been weaving a web to entangle them in Paris; he would envelop them in its toils, they should be as clay in his hands; they should hope and tremble, come and go, toil and sweat, and all for his amusement, all for the old cooper in the dingy room at the head of the worm-eaten staircase in the old house at Saumur; it tickled his sense of humor.

He had been thinking about his nephew. He wanted to save his dead brother's name from dishonor in a way that should not cost a penny either to his nephew or to himself. He was about to invest his money for three years, his mind was quite at leisure from his own affairs; he really needed some outlet for his malicious energy, and here was an opportunity supplied by his brother's failure. The claws were idle, he had nothing to squeeze between them, so he would pound the Parisians for Charles' benefit, and exhibit himself in the light of an excellent brother at a very cheap rate. As a matter of fact, the honor of the family name counted for very little with him in this matter; he looked at it from the purely impersonal point of view of the gambler, who likes to see a game well played although it is no affair of his. The Cruchots were necessary to him, but he did not mean to go in search of them; they should come to him. That very evening the comedy should begin, the main outlines were decided upon already, to-morrow he would be held up as an object of admiration all over the town, and his generosity should not cost him a farthing!

Eugénie, in her father's absence, was free to busy herself openly for her cousin, to feel the pleasure of pouring out for him in many ways the wealth of pity that filled her heart; for in pity alone women are content that we should feel their superiority, and the sublimity of devotion is the one height which they can pardon us for leaving to them.

Three or four times Eugénie went to listen to her cousin's breathing, that she might know whether he was awake or still sleeping; and when she was sure that he was rising, she turned her attention to his breakfast, and cream, coffee, fruit, eggs, plates, and glasses were all in turn the objects of her especial care. She softly climbed the rickety stairs to listen

again. Was he dressing? Was he still sobbing? She went
to the door at last and spoke—

"Cousin!"

"Yes, cousin."

"Would you rather have breakfast downstairs or up here
in your room?"

"Whichever you please."

"How do you feel?"

"I am ashamed to say that I am hungry."

This talk through the closed door was like an episode in
a romance for Eugénie.

"Very well then, we will bring your breakfast up to your
room, so that my father may not be vexed about it."

She sprang downstairs, and ran into the kitchen with the
swiftness of a bird.

"Nanon, just go and set his room straight."

The familiar staircase which she had gone up and down so
often, and which echoed with every sound, seemed no longer
old in Eugénie's eyes; it was radiant with light, it seemed to
speak in a language which she understood, it was young again
as she herself was, young like the love in her heart. And
the mother, the kind, indulgent mother, was ready to lend
herself to her daughter's whims, and as soon as Charles'
room was ready they both went thither to sit with him. Does
not Christian charity bid us comfort the mourner? Little
religious sophistries were not wanting by which the women
justified themselves.

Charles Grandet received the most tender and affectionate
care. Such delicate tact and sweet kindness touched him very
closely in his desolation; and for these two souls, they found
a moment's freedom from the restraint under which they
lived; they were at home in an atmosphere of sorrow; they
could give him the quick sympathy of fellowship in misfortune. Eugénie could avail herself of the privilege of relationship to set his linen in order, and to arrange the trifles
that lay on the dressing-table; she could admire the wonderful knick-knacks at her leisure; all the paraphernalia of

luxury, the delicately-wrought gold and silver passed through her hands, her fingers dwelt lingeringly on them under the pretext of looking closely at the workmanship.

Charles was deeply touched by the generous interest which his aunt and cousin took in him. He knew Parisian life quite sufficiently to know that under these circumstances his old acquaintances and friends would have grown cold and distant at once. But his trouble had brought out all the peculiar beauty of Eugénie's character, and he began to admire the simplicity of manner which had provoked his amusement but yesterday. So when Eugénie waited on her cousin with such frank goodwill, taking from Nanon the earthenware bowl full of coffee and cream to set it before him herself, the Parisian's eyes filled with tears; and when he met her kind glance he took her hand in his and kissed it.

"Well, what is the matter now?" she asked.

"Oh! they are tears of gratitude," he answered.

Eugénie turned hastily away, took the candles from the chimney-piece and held them out to Nanon.

"Here," she said, "take these away."

When she could look at her cousin again, the flush was still on her face, but her eyes at least did not betray her, and gave no sign of the excess of joy that flooded her heart; yet the same thought was dawning in both their souls, and could be read in the eyes of either, and they knew that the future was theirs. This thrill of happiness was all the sweeter to Charles in his great sorrow, because it was so little expected.

There was a knock at the door, and both the women hurried down to their places by the window. It was lucky for them that their flight downstairs was sufficiently precipitate, and that they were at their work when Grandet came in, for if he had met them beneath the archway, all his suspicions would be aroused at once. After the mid-day meal, which he took standing, the keeper, who had not yet received his promised reward, appeared from Froidfond, bringing with him a hare, some partridges shot in the park, a few eels, and a couple of pike sent by him from the miller's.

"Aha! so here is old Cornoiller; you come just when you are wanted, like salt fish in Lent. Is all that fit to eat?"

"Yes, sir; all killed the day before yesterday."

"Come, Nanon, look alive! Just take this, it will do for dinner to-day; the two Cruchots are coming."

Nanon opened her eyes with amazement, and stared first at one and then at another.

"Oh! indeed," she said; "and where are the herbs and the bacon to come from?"

"Wife," said Grandet, "let Nanon have six francs, and remind me to go down into the cellar to look out a bottle of good wine."

"Well, then, M. Grandet," the gamekeeper began (he wished to see the question of his salary properly settled, and was duly primed with a speech), "M. Grandet——"

"Tut, tut, tut," said Grandet, "I know what you are going to say; you are a good fellow, we will see about that to-morrow, I am very busy to-day. Give him five francs, wife," he added, looking at Mme. Grandet, and with that he beat a retreat. The poor woman was only too happy to purchase peace at the price of eleven francs. She knew by experience that Grandet usually kept quiet for a fortnight after he had made her disburse coin by coin the money which he had given her.

"There, Cornoiller," she said, as she slipped ten francs into his hand; "we will repay you for your services one of these days."

Cornoiller had no answer ready, so he went.

"Madame," said Nanon, who had by this time put on her black bonnet and had a basket on her arm, "three francs will be quite enough; keep the rest. I shall manage just as well with three."

"Let us have a good dinner, Nanon; my cousin is coming downstairs," said Eugénie.

"There is something very extraordinary going on, I am sure," said Mme. Grandet. "This makes the third time since we were married that your father has asked any one here to dinner."

It was nearly four o'clock in the afternoon; Eugénie and her mother had laid the cloth and set the table for six persons, and the master of the house had brought up two or three bottles of the exquisite wines, which are jealously hoarded in the cellars of the vinegrowing district.

Charles came into the dining-room looking white and sad; there was a pathetic charm about his gestures, his face, his looks, the tones of his voice; his sorrow had given him the interesting look that women like so well, and Eugénie only loved him the more because his features were worn with pain. Perhaps, too, this trouble had brought them nearer in other ways. Charles was no longer the rich and handsome young man who lived in a sphere far beyond her ken; he was a kinsman in deep and terrible distress, and sorrow is a great leveler. Woman has this in common with the angels—all suffering creatures are under her protection.

Charles and Eugénie understood each other without a word being spoken on either side. The poor dandy of yesterday, fallen from his high estate, to-day was an orphan, who sat in a corner of the room, quiet, composed, and proud; but from time to time he met his cousin's eyes, her kind and affectionate glance rested on him, and compelled him to shake off his dark and sombre forebodings, and to look forward with her to a future full of hope, in which she loved to think that she might share.

The news of Grandet's dinner-party caused even greater excitement in Saumur than the sale of his vintage, although this latter proceeding had been a crime of the blackest dye, an act of high treason against the vinegrowing interest. If Grandet's banquet to the Cruchots has been prompted by the same idea which on a memorable occasion cost Alcibiades' dog its tail, history might perhaps have heard of the miser; but he felt himself to be above public opinion in this town which he exploited; he held Saumur too cheap.

It was not long before the des Grassins heard of Guillaume Grandet's violent end and impending bankruptcy. They determined to pay a visit to their client that evening, to con-

dole with him in his affliction, and to show a friendly interest; while they endeavored to discover the motives which
could have led Grandet to invite the Cruchots to dinner at
such a time.

Precisely at five o'clock President C. de Bonfons and his
uncle the notary arrived, dressed up to the nines this time.
The guests seated themselves at table, and began by attack-
ing their dinner with remarkably good appetites. Grandet
was solemn, Charles was silent, Eugénie was dumb, and Mme.
Grandet said no more than usual; if it had been a funeral
repast, it could not well have been less lively. When they rose
from the table, Charles addressed his aunt and uncle—

"Will you permit me to withdraw? I have some long and
difficult letters to write."

"By all means, nephew."

When Charles had left the room, and his amiable relative
could fairly assume that he was out of earshot and deep in
his correspondence, Grandet gave his wife a sinister glance.

"Mme. Grandet, what we are going to say will be Greek
to you; it is half-past seven o'clock, you ought to be off
to bed by this time. Good night, my daughter." He kissed
Eugénie, and mother and daughter left the room.

Then the drama began. Now, if ever in his life, Grandet
displayed all the shrewdness which he had acquired in the
course of his long experience of men and business, and all
the cunning which had gained him the nickname of "old
fox" among those who had felt his teeth a little too sharply.
Had the ambition of the late Mayor of Saumur soared a
little higher; if he had had the luck to rise to a higher social
sphere, and destiny had sent him to mingle in some congress
in which the fate of nations is at stake, the genius which he
was now devoting to his own narrow ends would doubtless
have done France glorious service. And yet, after all, the
probability is that once away from Saumur the worthy cooper
would have cut but a poor figure, and that minds, like certain
plants and animals, are sterile when removed to a distant
climate and an alien soil.

"M-m-monsieur le P-p-président, you were s-s-saying that b-b-bankruptcy——"

Here the trick of stammering which it had pleased the vinegrower to assume so long ago that every one believed it to be natural to him (like the deafness of which he was wont to complain in rainy weather), grew so unbearably tedious for the Cruchot pair, that as they strove to catch the syllables, they made unconscious grimaces, moving their lips as if they would fain finish the words in which the cooper entangled both himself and them at his pleasure.

And here, perhaps, is the fitting place to record the history of Grandet's deafness and the impediment in his speech. No one in Anjou had better hearing or could speak Angevin French more clearly and distinctly than the wily vinegrower —when he chose. Once upon a time, in spite of all his shrewdness, a Jew had got the better of him. In the course of their discussion the Israelite had applied his hand to his ear, in the manner of an ear-trumpet, the better to catch what was said, and had gibbered to such purpose in his search for a word, that Grandet, a victim to his own humanity, felt constrained to suggest to that crafty Hebrew the words and ideas of which the Israelite appeared to be in search, to finish himself the reasonings of the said Hebrew, to say for that accursed alien all that he ought to have said for himself, till Grandet ended by fairly changing places with the Jew.

From this curious contest of wits the vinegrower did not emerge triumphant; indeed, for the first and last time in his business career he made a bad bargain. But loser though he was from a money point of view, he had received a great practical lesson, and later on he reaped the fruits of it. Wherefore in the end he blessed the Jew who had shown him how to wear out the patience of an opponent, and to keep him so closely employed in expressing his adversary's ideas that he completely lost sight of his own. The present business required more deafness, more stammering, more of the mazy circumlocutions in which Grandet was wont to involve himself, than any previous transaction in his life; for, in the first place, he wished to throw the responsibility of his ideas on some one else; some one else was to suggest his own schemes to him, while he was to keep himself to himself, and leave every one in the dark as to his real intentions.

"Mon-sieur de B-B-Bonfons." (This was the second time in three years that he had called the younger Cruchot "M. de Bonfons," and the president might well consider that this was almost tantamount to being acknowledged as the crafty cooper's son-in-law.)

"You were s-s-s-saying that in certain cases, p-p-p-proceedings in b-b-bankruptcy might be s-s-s-stopped b-b-by——"

"At the instance of a Tribunal of Commerce. That is done every day of the year," said M. C. de Bonfons, guessing, as he thought, at old Grandet's idea, and running away with it. "Listen!" he said, and in the most amiable way he prepared to explain himself.

"I am l-listening," replied the older man meekly, and his face assumed a demure expression; he looked like some small boy who is laughing in his sleeve at his schoolmaster while appearing to pay the most respectful attention to every word.

"When anybody who is in a large way of business and is much looked up to, like your late brother in Paris, for instance——"

"My b-b-brother, yes."

"When any one in that position is likely to find himself insolvent——"

"Ins-s-solvent, do they call it?"

"Yes. When his failure is imminent, the Tribunal of Commerce, to which he is amenable (do you follow me?) has power by a judgment to appoint liquidators to wind up the business. Liquidation is not bankruptcy, do you understand? It is a disgraceful thing to be a bankrupt, but a *liquidation* reflects no discredit on a man."

"It is quite a d-d-d-different thing, if only it d-d-does not cost any more," said Grandet.

"Yes. But a liquidation can be privately arranged without having recourse to the Tribunal of Commerce," said the president as he took a pinch of snuff. "How is a man declared bankrupt?"

"Yes, how?" inquired Grandet. "I have n-n-never thought about it."

"In the first place, he may himself file a petition and leave his schedule with the clerk of the court, the debtor himself draws it up or authorizes some one else to do so, and it is duly registered. Or, in the second place, his creditors may make him a bankrupt. But supposing the debtor does not file a petition, and none of his creditors make application to the court for a judgment declaring him bankrupt; now let us see what happens then!"

"Yes, let us s-s-see."

"In that case, the family of the deceased, or his representatives, or his residuary legatee, or the man himself (if he is not dead), or his friends for him (if he has absconded), liquidate his affairs. Now, possibly, *you* may intend to do this in your brother's case?" inquired the president.

"Oh! Grandet," exclaimed the notary, "that would be acting very handsomely. We in the provinces have our notions of honor. If you saved your name from dishonor, for it is your name, you would be——"

"Sublime!" cried the president, interrupting his uncle.

"Of course, my b-b-brother's n-n-name was Grandet, th-that is certain sure, I d-d-don't deny it, and anyhow this l-l-l-l-liquidation would be a very g-good thing for my n-n-nephew in every way, and I am very f-f-fond of him. But we shall see. I know n-n-nothing of those sharpers in P-Paris, and their t-tricks. And here am I at S-Saumur, you see! There are my vine-cuttings, m-my d-d-draining; in sh-sh-short, there are my own af-f-affairs, to s-s-see after. *I* have n-n-never accepted a bill. What is a bill? I have t-t-taken many a one, b-b-but I have n-n-never put my n-n-name to a piece of p-paper. You t-t-take 'em, and you can d-d-d-discount 'em, and that is all I know. I have heard s-s-say that you can b-b-b-buy them——"

"Yes," assented the president. "You can buy bills on the market, less so much per cent. Do you understand?"

Grandet held his hand to his ear, and the president repeated his remark.

"But it s-s-seems there are t-t-two s-sides to all this?" replied the vinegrower. "At my age, I know n-n-n-nothing about this s-s-s-sort of thing. I must st-top here to l-look after the g-g-grapes, the vines d-d-don't stand still, and the g-g-grapes have to p-pay for everything. The vintage m-must be l-l-looked after before anything else. Then I have a g-great d-d-deal on my hands at Froidfond that I can't p-p-possibly l-l-l-leave to any one else. I don't underst-t-tand a word of all this; it is a p-p-pretty kettle of fish, confound it; I can't l-l-leave home to s-see after it. You s-s-s-say that to bring about a l-l-liquidation I ought to be in Paris. Now you can't be in t-t-two p-places at once unless you are a b-b-bird."

"*I* see what you mean," cried the notary. "Well, my old friend, you have friends, friends of long standing ready to do a great deal for you."

"Come, now!" said the vinegrower to himself, "so you are making up your minds, are you?"

"And if some one were to go to Paris, and find up your brother Guillaume's largest creditor, and say to him——"

"Here, just l-l-listen to me a moment," the cooper struck in. "Say to him ——what? S-s-something like this: 'M. Grandet of Saumur th-this, M. Grandet of Saumur th-th-that. He l-l-loves his brother, he has a r-r-regard for his n-nephew; Grandet thinks a l-l-lot of his f-family, he means to d-do well by them. He has just s-s-sold his vintage uncommonly well. Don't drive the thing into b-b-b-bankruptcy, call a meeting of the creditors, and ap-p-point l-l-liquidators. Then s-see what Grandet will do. You will do a great d-deal b-b-better for yourselves by coming to an arrangement than by l-l-letting the l-l-l-lawyers poke their noses into it.' That is how it is, eh?"

"Quite so!" said the president.

"Because, look you here, Monsieur de Bon-Bon-Bonfons, you must l-l-look before you l-l-l-leap. And you can't d-do more than you can. A big af-f-fair like this wants l-l-l-looking into, or you may ru-ru-ruin yourself. That is so, isn't it? eh?"

"Certainly," said the president. "I myself am of the opinion that in a few months' time you could buy up the debts for a fixed sum and pay by instalments. Aha! you can trail a dog a long way with a bit of bacon. When a man has not been declared bankrupt, as soon as the bills are in your hands, you will be as white as snow."

"As s-s-s-snow?" said Grandet, holding his hand to his ear. "S-s-s-snow? I don't underst-t-tand."

"Why, then, just listen to me!" cried the president.

"I am l-l-listening——"

"A bill of exchange is a commodity subject to fluctuations in value. This is a deduction from Jeremy Bentham's theory of interest. He was a publicist who showed conclusively that the prejudices entertained against money-lenders were irrational."

"Bless me!" put in Grandet.

"And seeing that, according to Bentham, money itself is a commodity, and that that which money represents is no less a commodity," the president went on; "and since it is obvious that the commodity called a bill of exchange is subject to the same laws of supply and demand that control production of all kinds, a bill of exchange bearing this or that signature, like this or that article of commerce, is scarce or plentiful in the market, commands a high premium or is worth nothing at all. Wherefore the decision of this Court—— There! how stupid I am, I beg your pardon; I mean I am of the opinion that you could easily buy up your brother's debts for twenty-five per cent. of their value."

"You m-m-m-mentioned Je-je-je-jeremy Ben——"

"Bentham, an Englishman."

"That is a Jeremiah who will save us many lamentations in business matters," said the notary, laughing.

"The English s-s-sometimes have s-s-s-sensible notions," said Grandet. "Then, according to B-Bentham, how if my b-b-brother's b-bills are worth n-n-n-nothing? If I am right, it looks to me as if . . . the creditors would . . . n-no, they wouldn't . . . I underst-t-tand."

"Let me explain all this to you," said the president. "In law, if you hold all the outstanding bills of the firm of Grandet, your brother, his heirs and assigns, would owe no one a penny. So far, so good."

"Good," echoed Grandet.

"And in equity; suppose that your brother's bills were negotiated upon the market (negotiated, do you understand the meaning of that term?) at a loss of so much per cent; and suppose one of your friends happened to be passing, and bought up the bills; there would have been no physical force brought to bear upon the creditors, they gave them up of their own free-will, and the estate of the late Grandet of Paris would be clear in the eye of the law."

"True," stuttered the cooper, "b-b-business is business. So that is s-s-s-settled. But, for all that, you underst-t-tand that it is a d-d-difficult matter. I have not the m-m-money, nor have I the t-t-t-time, nor——"

"Yes, yes; you cannot be at the trouble. Well, now, I will go to Paris for you if you like (you must stand the expenses of the journey, that is a mere trifle). I will see the creditors, and talk to them, and put them off; it can all be arranged; you will be prepared to add something to the amount realized by the liquidation so as to get the bills into your hands."

"We shall s-see about that; I cannot and *will* not under-t-t-take anything unless I know . . . You can't d-d-do more than you can, you know."

"Quite so, quite so."

"And I am quite. bewildered with all these head-splitting ideas that you have sp-prung upon me. Th-this is the f-f-f-first t-time in my l-l-life that I have had to th-th-think about such th——"

"Yes, yes, you are not a consulting barrister."

"I am a p-p-poor vinegrower, and I know n-n-nothing about what you have just t-t-told me; I m-m-must th-think it all out."

"Well! then," began the president, as if he meant to reopen the discussion.

"Nephew!" interrupted the notary reproachfully.

"Well, uncle?" answered the president.

"Let M. Grandet explain what he means to do. It is a very important question, and you are to receive his instructions. Our dear friend might now very pertinently state——"

A knock at the door announced the arrival of the des Grassins; their coming and exchange of greetings prevented Cruchot senior from finishing his sentence. Nor was he ill-pleased with this diversion; Grandet was looking askance at him already, and there was that about the wen on the cooper's face which indicated that a storm was brewing within. And on sober reflection it seemed to the cautious notary that a president of a court of first instance was not exactly the person to dispatch to Paris, there to open negotiations with creditors, and to lend himself to a more than dubious transaction which, however you looked at it, hardly squared with notions of strict honesty; and not only so, but he had particularly noticed that Goodman Grandet had shown not the slightest inclination to disburse anything whatever, and he trembled instinctively at the thought of his nephew becoming involved in such a business. He took advantage of the entrance of the des Grassins, took his nephew by the arm, and drew him into the embrasure of the window.

"You have gone quite as far as there is any need," he said, "that is quite enough of such zeal; you are overreaching yourself in your eagerness to marry the girl. The devil! You should not rush into a thing open-mouthed, like a crow at a walnut. Leave the steering of the ship to me for a bit, and just shift your sails according to the wind. Now, is it a part you ought to play, compromising your dignity as magistrate in such a——"

He broke off suddenly, for he heard M. des Grassins saying to the old cooper, as he held out his hand—

"Grandet, we have heard of the dreadful misfortunes which have befallen your family—the ruin of the firm of Guillaume Grandet and your brother's death; we have come to express our sympathy with you in this sad calamity."

"There is only one misfortune," the notary interrupted at this point—"the death of the younger M. Grandet; and if he had thought to ask his brother for assistance, he would not have taken his own life. Our old friend here, who is a man of honor to his finger tips, is prepared to discharge the debts contracted by the firm of Grandet in Paris. In order to spare our friend the worry of what is, after all, a piece of lawyer's business, my nephew the president offers to start immediately for Paris, so as to arrange with the creditors, and duly satisfy their claims."

The three des Grassins were thoroughly taken aback by these words; Grandet appeared to acquiesce in what had been said, for he was pensively stroking his chin. On their way to the house the family had commented very freely upon Grandet's niggardliness, and indeed had almost gone so far as to accuse him of fratricide.

"Ah! just what I expected!" cried the banker, looking at his wife. "What was I saying to you only just now as we came along, Mme. des Grassins? Grandet, I said, is a man who will never swerve a hair's-breadth from the strict course of honor; he will not endure the thought of the slightest spot on his name! Money without honor is a disease. Oh! we have a keen sense of honor in the provinces! This is noble—really noble of you, Grandet. I am an old soldier, and I do not mince matters, I say what I think straight out; and *mille tonnerres!* this is sublime!"

"Then the s-s-sub-sublime costs a great d-d-deal," stuttered the cooper, as the banker shook him warmly by the hand.

"But this, my good Grandet (no offence to you, M. le Président), is simply a matter of business," des Grassins went on, "and requires an experienced man of business to deal with it. Thére will have to be accounts kept of sales and outgoing expenses; you ought to have tables of interest at

your finger ends. I must go to Paris on business of my own,
and I could undertake——"

"Then we must s-s-see about it, and t-t-t-try to arrange
between us to p-p-provide for anything that m-may t-t-turn
up, but I d-d-don't want to be d-d-drawn into anything that
I would rather not d-d-d-do," continued Grandet, "because,
you see, M. le Président naturally wants me to pay his expenses." The good man did not stammer over these last
words.

"Eh?" said Mme. des Grassins. "Why, it is a pleasure
to stay in Paris! For my part, I should be glad to go there
at my own expense."

She made a sign to her husband, urging him to seize this
opportunity of discomfiting their enemies and cheat them of
their mission. Then she flung a withering glance at the now
crestfallen and miserable Cruchots. Grandet seized the
banker by the buttonhole and drew him aside.

"I should feel far more confidence in you than in the president," he remarked; "and besides that," he added (and the
wen twitched a little), "there are other fish to fry. I want to
make an investment. I have several thousand francs to put
into consols, and I don't mean to pay more than eighty for
them. Now, from all I can hear, that machine always runs
down at the end of the month. You know all about these
things, I expect?"

"*Pardieu!* I should think I did. Well, then, I shall have
to buy several thousand livres worth of consols for you?"

"Just by way of a beginning. But mum, I want to play
at this game without letting any one know about it. You
will buy them for me at the end of the month, and say nothing to the Cruchots; it would only annoy them. Since you
are going to Paris, we might as well see at the same time
what trumps are for my poor nephew's sake."

"That is an understood thing. I shall travel post to Paris
to-morrow," said des Grassins aloud, "and I will come round
to take your final instructions at—when shall we say?"

8

"At five o'clock, before dinner," said the vinegrower, rubbing his hands.

The two factions for a little while remained facing each other. Des Grassins broke the silence again, clapping Grandet on the shoulder, and saying—

"It is a fine thing to have a good uncle like——"

"Yes, yes," returned Grandet, falling into the stammer again, "without m-making any p-p-parade about it; I am a good uncle; I l-l-loved my brother; I will give p-p-p-proof of it, if-if-if it d-doesn't cost——"

Luckily the banker interrupted him at this point.

"We must go, Grandet. If I am to set out sooner than I intended, I shall have to see after some business at once before I go."

"Right, quite right. I myself, in connection with you know what, must p-p-put on my cons-s-sidering cap, as P-President Cruchot s-s-says."

"Plague take it! I am no longer M. de Bonfons," thought the magistrate moodily, and his face fell; he looked like a judge who is bored by the cause before him.

The heads of the rival clans went out together. Both had completely forgotten Grandet's treacherous crime of that morning; his disloyal behavior had faded from their minds. They sounded each other, but to no purpose, as to the goodman's real intentions (if intentions he had) in this new turn that matters had taken.

"Are you coming with us to Mme. Dorsonval's?" des Grassins asked the notary.

"We are going there later on," replied the president. "With my uncle's permission, we will go first to see Mlle. de Gribeaucourt; I promised just to look in on her to say goodnight."

"We shall meet again, then," smiled Mme. des Grassins.

But when the des Grassins were at some distance from the two Cruchots, Adolphe said to his father, "They are in a pretty stew, eh?"

"Hush!" returned his mother, "they can very likely hear

what we are saying, and besides, that remark of yours was not in good taste; it sounds like one of your law school phrases."

"Well, uncle!" cried the magistrate, when he saw the des Grassins were out of earshot, "I began by being President de Bonfons, and ended as plain Cruchot."

"I saw myself that you were rather put out about it; and the des Grassins took the wind out of our sails. How stupid you are, for all your sharpness! Let *them* set sail, on the strength of a 'We shall see'· from Grandet; be easy, my boy, Eugénie shall marry you for all that."

A few moments later, and the news of Grandet's magnanimity was set circulating in three houses at once; the whole town talked of nothing but Grandet's devotion to his brother. The sale of his vintage in utter disregard of the agreement made among the vinegrowers was forgotten; every one fell to praising his scrupulous integrity, and to lauding his generosity, a quality which no one had suspected him of possessing. There is that in the French character which is readily excited to fury or to passionate enthusiasm by any meteor that appears above their horizon, that is captivated by the bravery of a blatant fact. Can it be that collectively men have no memories?

As soon as Grandet had bolted the house door he called to Nanon.

"Don't go to bed," he said, "and don't unchain the dog; there is something to be done, and we must do it together. Cornoiller will be round with the carriage from Froidfond at eleven o'clock. You must sit up for him, and let him in quietly; don't let him rap at the door, and tell him not to make a noise. You get into trouble with the police if you raise a racket at night. And besides, there is no need to let all the quarter know that I am going out."

Having thus delivered himself, Grandet went up to his laboratory, and Nanon heard him stirring about, rummaging, going and coming, all with great caution. Clearly he had no wish to waken his wife or daughter, and above all things he desired in nowise to excite any suspicion in the mind of his nephew; he had seen that a light was burning in the young man's room, and had cursed his relative forthwith.

In the middle of the night Eugénie heard a sound like the groan of a dying man; her cousin was always in her thoughts, and for her the dying man was Charles. How white and despairing he had looked when he wished her good-night; perhaps he had killed himself. She hastily wrapped herself in her capuchine, a sort of long cloak with a hood to it, and determined to go to see for herself. Some rays of bright light streaming through the cracks of her door frightened her not a little at first, perhaps the house was on fire; but she was soon reassured. She could hear Nanon's heavy footsteps outside, and the sounds of the old servant's voice mingled with the neighing of several horses.

"Can my father be taking Charles away?" she asked herself, as she set her door ajar cautiously, for fear the hinges should creak, so that she could watch all that was going on in the corridor.

All at once her eyes met those of her father, and, absent and indifferent as they looked, a cold shudder ran through her. The cooper and Nanon were coming along carrying something which hung by a chain from a stout cudgel, one end of which rested on the right shoulder of either; the something was a little barrel such as Grandet sometimes amused himself by making in the bakehouse, when he had nothing better to do.

"Holy Virgin! how heavy it is, sir!" said Nanon in a whisper.

"What a pity it is only full of pence!" replied the cooper. "Look out! or you will knock down the candlestick."

The scene was lighted by a single candle set between two balusters.

"Cornoiller," said Grandet to his gamekeeper *in partibus,* "have you your pistols with you?"

"No, sir. Lord, love you! What can there be to fear for a keg of coppers?"

"Oh! nothing, nothing," said Goodman Grandet.

"Besides, we shall get over the ground quickly," the keeper went on; "your tenants have picked out their best horses for you."

"Well, well. You did not let them know where I was going?"

"I did not know that myself."

"Right. Is the carriage strongly built?"

"That's all right, mister. Why, what is the weight of a few paltry barrels like those of yours? It would carry two or three thousand of the like of them."

"Well," said Nanon, "I know there's pretty well eighteen hundred weight *there,* that there is!"

"Will you hold your tongue, Nanon! You tell my wife that I have gone into the country, and that I shall be back to dinner.—Hurry up, Cornoiller; we must be in Angers before nine o'clock."

The carriage started. Nanon bolted the gateway, let the dog loose, and lay down and slept in spite of her bruised shoulder; and no one in the quarter had any suspicion of Grandet's journey or of its object. The worthy man was a miracle of circumspection. Nobody ever saw a penny lying about in that house full of gold. He had learned that morning from the gossip on the quay that some vessels were being fitted out at Nantes, and that in consequence gold was so scarce there that it was worth double its ordinary value, and speculators were buying it in Angers. The old cooper, by the simple device of borrowing his tenants' horses, was prepared to sell his gold at Angers, receiving in return an order upon the Treasury from the Receiver-General for the sum destined for the purchase of his consols, and an addition in the shape of the premium paid on his gold.

"My father is going out," said Eugénie to herself. She had heard all that had passed from the head of the staircase.

Silence reigned once more in the house. The rattle of the wheels in the streets of sleeping Saumur grew more and more distant, and at last died away. Then it was that a sound seemed to reach Eugénie's heart before it fell on her ears, a wailing sound that rang through the thin walls above—it came from her cousin's room. There was a thin line of light, scarcely wider than a knife edge, beneath his door; the rays slanted through the darkness and left a bright gleaming bar along the balusters of the crazy staircase.

"He is unhappy," she said, as she went up a little further. A second moan brought her to the landing above. The door stood ajar; she thrust it open. Charles was sleeping in the rickety old armchair, his head drooped over to one side, his hand hung down and nearly touched the floor, the pen that he had let fall lay beneath his fingers. Lying in this position, his breath came in quick, sharp jerks that startled Eugénie. She entered hastily.

"He must be very tired," she said to herself, as she saw a dozen sealed letters lying on the table. She read the addresses—*MM. Farry, Breilman and Co., carriage builders; M. Buisson, tailor;* and so forth.

"Of course, he has been settling his affairs, so that he may leave France as soon as possible," she thought.

Her eyes fell upon two unsealed letters. One of them began—"My dear Annette . . ." she felt dazed, and could see nothing more for a moment. Her heart beat fast, her feet seemed glued to the floor.

"His dear Annette! He loves, he is beloved! . . . Then there is no more hope! . . . What does he say to her?" These thoughts flashed through her heart and brain. She read the words everywhere: on the walls, on the very floor, in letters of fire.

"Must I give him up already? No, I will not read the letter. I ought not to stay . . . And yet, even if I did read it?"

She looked at Charles, gently took his head in her hands, and propped it against the back of the chair. He submitted like a child, who even while he is sleeping knows that it is his mother who is bending over him, and, without waking, feels his mother's kisses. Like a mother, Eugénie raised the drooping hand, and, like a mother, laid a soft kiss on his hair. *"Dear Annette!"* A mocking voice shrieked the words in her ear.

"I know that perhaps I may be doing wrong, but I will read that letter," she said.

Eugénie turned her eyes away; her high sense of honor reproached her. For the first time in her life there was a struggle between good and evil in her soul. Hitherto she had never done anything for which she needed to blush. Love and curiosity silenced her scruples. Her heart swelled higher with every phrase as she read; her quickened pulses seemed to send a sharp, tingling glow through her veins, and to heighten the vivid emotions of her first love.

"MY DEAR ANNETTE,—Nothing should have power to separate us save this overwhelming calamity that has befallen me, a calamity that no human foresight could have predicted. My father has died by his own hand; his fortune and mine are both irretrievably lost. I am left an orphan at an age when, with the kind of education I have received, I am almost a child; and, nevertheless, I must now endeavor to show myself a man, and to rise from the dark depths into which I have been hurled. I have been spending part of my time to-night in revolving plans for my future. If I am to leave France as an honest man, as of course I mean to do, I have not a hundred francs that I can call my own with which to tempt fate in the Indies or in America. Yes, my poor Anna, I am going in quest of fortune to the most deadly foreign climes. Beneath such skies, they say, fortunes are rapidly and surely made. As for living on in Paris, I could not bring myself to do it. I could not face the coldness, the contempt, and the affronts that a ruined man, the son of a bankrupt, is sure to receive. Great heaven! to owe two millions! . . . I should fall in a duel before a week had passed. So I shall not return to Paris. Your love—the tenderest, the most devoted love that ever ennobled the heart of man—would not seek to draw me back. Alas! my darling, I have

not money enough to take me to you, that I might give and
receive one last kiss, a kiss that should put strength into me
for the task that lies before me . . ."

"Poor Charles, I did well to read this. I have money, and
he shall have it," said Eugénie. She went on with the letter
when she could see for her tears.

"I have not even begun to think of the hardships of poverty. Supposing that I find I have the hundred louis to pay
for my passage out, I have not a sou to lay out on a trading
venture. Yet, no; I shall not have a hundred louis, nor yet
a hundred sous; I have no idea whether anything will be left
when I have settled all my debts in Paris. If there is nothing, I shall simply go to Nantes and work my passage out.
I will begin at the bottom of the ladder, like many another
man of energy who has gone out to the Indies as a penniless
youth, to return thence a rich man. This morning I began
to look my future steadily in the face. It is far harder for
me than for others; I have been the petted child of a mother
who idolized me, indulged by the best and kindest of fathers;
and at my very entrance into the world I met with the love
of an Anna! As yet I have only known the primrose paths
of life; such happiness could not last. Yet, dear Annette,
I have more fortitude than could be looked for from a
thoughtless youth; above all, from a young man thus lapped
round in happiness from the cradle, spoiled and flattered by
the most delightful woman in Paris, the darling of Fortune,
whose wishes were as law to a father who . . . Oh! my
father!   He is dead, Annette! . . . Well, I have
thought seriously over my position, and I have likewise
thought over yours. I have grown much older in the last
twenty-four hours. Dear Anna, even if, to keep me beside
you, you were to give up all the luxuries that you enjoy, your
box at the opera, and your toilette, we should not have nearly
sufficient for the necessary expenses of the extravagant life
that I am accustomed to; and besides, I could not think of

allowing you to make such sacrifices for me. To-day, therefore, we part forever."

"Then this is to take leave of her! *Sainte Vierge!* what
happiness!"

Eugénie started and trembled for joy. Charles stirred in
his chair, and Eugénie felt a chill of dread. Luckily, however, he did not wake. She went on reading.

"When shall I come back? I cannot tell. Europeans grow
old before their time in those tropical countries, especially
Europeans who work hard. Let us look forward and try to
see ourselves in ten years' time. In ten years from now your
little girl will be eighteen years old; she will be your constant
companion; that is, she will be a spy upon you. If the world
will judge you very harshly, your daughter will probably
judge more harshly still; such ingratitude on a young girl's
part is common enough, and we know how the world regards
these things. Let us take warning and be wise. Only keep
the memory of those four years of happiness in the depths
of your soul, as I shall keep them buried in mine; and be
faithful, if you can, to your poor friend. I shall not be too
exacting, dear Annette; for, as you can see, I must submit
to my altered lot; I am compelled to look at life in a business-
like way, and to base my calculations on dull, prosaic fact.
So I ought to think of marriage as a necessary step in my
new existence; and I will confess to you that here, in my
uncle's house in Saumur, there is a cousin whose manners,
face, character, and heart you would approve; and who,
moreover, has, it appears——"

"How tired he must have been to break off like this when
he was writing to *her!*" said Eugénie to herself, as the letter
ended abruptly in the middle of a sentence. She was ready
with excuses for him.

How was it possible that an inexperienced girl should discover the coldness and selfishness of this letter? For young

girls, religiously brought up as she had been, are innocent and unsuspecting, and can see nothing but love when they have set foot in love's enchanted kingdom. It is as if a light from heaven shone in their own souls, shedding its beams upon their path; their lover shines transfigured before them in reflected glory, radiant with fair colors from love's magic fires, and endowed with noble thoughts which perhaps in truth are none of his. Women's errors spring, for the most part, from a belief in goodness, and a confidence in truth. In Eugénie's heart the words, "My dear Annette—my beloved," echoed like the fairest language of love; they stirred her soul like organ music—like the divine notes of the *Venite adoremus* falling upon her ears in childhood.

Surely the tears, not dry even yet upon her cousin's eyelids, betokened the innate nobility of nature that never fails to attract a young girl. How could she know that Charles' love and grief for his father, albeit genuine, was due rather to the fact that his father had loved him than to a deeply-rooted affection on his own part for his father? M. and Mme. Guillaume Grandet had indulged their son's every whim; every pleasure that wealth could bestow had been his; and thus it followed that he had never been tempted to make the hideous calculations that are only too common among the younger members of a family in Paris, when they see around them all the delights of Parisian life, and reflect with disgust that, so long as their parents are alive, all these enjoyments are not for them. The strange result of the father's lavish kindness had been a strong affection on the part of his son, an affection unalloyed by any after thought. But, for all that, Charles was a thorough child of Paris, with the Parisian's habit of mind; Annette herself had impressed upon him the importance of thinking out all the consequences of every step; he was not youthful, despite the mask of youth.

He had received the detestable education of a world in which more crimes (in thought and word at least) are committed in one evening than come before a court of justice in the course of a whole session; a world in which great ideas perish, done to death by a witticism, and where it is reckoned a weakness not to see things as they are. To see things as they are—that means, believe in nothing, put faith in nothing and in no man, for there is no such thing as sincerity in opinion or affection; mistrust events, for even events at times have been known to be manufactured. To see things as they are you must weigh your friend's purse morning by morning; you must know by instinct the right moment to interfere for your own profit in every matter that turns up; you must keep your judgment rigorously suspended, be in no hurry to admire a work of art or a noble deed, and give every one credit for interested motives on every possible occasion.

After many follies, the great lady, the fair Annette, compelled Charles to think seriously; she talked to him of his future, passing a fragrant hand through his hair, and imparted counsel to him on the art of getting on in the world, while she twisted a stray curl about her fingers. She had made him effeminate, and now she set herself to make a materialist of him, a twofold work of demoralization, a corruption none the less deadly because it never offended against the canons of good society, good manners, and good taste.

"You are a simpleton, Charles," she would say; "I see that it will be no easy task to teach you the ways of the world. You were very naughty about M. des Lupeaulx. Oh! he is not over-fastidious, I grant you, but you should wait until he falls from power, and then you may despise him as much as you like. Do you know what Mme. Campan used to say to us? 'My children, so long as a man is a Minister, adore him; if he falls, help to drag him to the shambles. He is a kind of deity so long as he is in power, but after he is fallen and ruined he is viler than Marat himself, for he is still alive, while Marat is dead and out of sight. Life is nothing but a series of combinations, which must be studied and followed very carefully if a good position is to be successfully maintained.'"

Charles had no very exalted aims; he was too much of a

worldling; he had been too much spoiled by his father and
mother, too much flattered by the society in which he moved,
to be stirred by any lofty enthusiasm. In the clay of his
nature there was a grain of gold, due to his mother's teaching; but it had been passed through the Parisian draw-plate,
and beaten out into a thin surface gilding which must soon
be worn away by contact with the world.

At this time Charles, however, was only one-and-twenty.
and it is taken for granted that freshness of heart accom-
panies the freshness of youth; it seems so unlikely that the
mind within should be at variance with the young face, and
the young voice, and the candid glance. Even the hardest
judge, the most sceptical attorney, the flintiest-hearted
money-lender will hesitate to believe that a wizened heart and
a warped and corrupted nature can dwell beneath a young
exterior, when the forehead is smooth and tears come so
readily to the eyes. Hitherto Charles had never had occasion
to put his Parisian maxims in practice; his character had not
been tried, and consequently had not been found wanting;
but, all unknown to him, egoism had taken deep root in his
nature. The seeds of this baneful political economy had been
sown in his heart; it was only a question of time, they would
spring up and flower as soon as the soil was stirred, as soon
as he ceased to be an idle spectator and became an actor in
the drama of real life.

A young girl is nearly always ready to believe unquestioningly in the promise of a fair exterior; but even if Eugénie
had been as keenly observant and as cautious as girls in the
provinces sometimes are, how could she have brought herself
to mistrust her cousin, when all he did and said, and everything about him, seemed to be the spontaneous outcome of a
noble nature? This was the last outburst of real feeling, the
last reproachful sigh of conscience in Charles' life; fate had
thrown them together at that moment, and, unfortunately
for her, all her sympathies had been aroused for him.

So she laid down the letter that seemed to her so full of
love, and gave herself up to the pleasure of watching her

sleeping cousin; the dreams and hopes of youth seemed to hover over his face; and then and there she vowed to herself that she would love him always. She glanced over the other letter; there could be no harm in reading it, she thought; she should only receive fresh proofs of the noble qualities with which, womanlike, she had invested the man whom she had idealized.

"MY DEAR ALPHONSE," so it began, "by the time this letter is in your hands I shall have no friends left; but I will confess that though I put no faith in the worldly-minded people who use the word so freely, I have no doubts of your friendship for me. So I am commissioning you to settle some matters of business. I look to you to do the best you can for me in this, for all I have in the world is involved in it. By this time you must know how I am situated. I have nothing, and have made up my mind to go out to the Indies. I have just written to all the people to whom any money is owing, and the enclosed list is as accurate as I can make it from memory. I think the sale of my books, furniture, carriages, horses, and so forth ought to bring in sufficient to pay my debts. I only mean to keep back a few trinkets of little value, which will go some way towards a trading venture. I will send you a power of attorney in due form for this sale, my dear Alphonse, in case any difficulty should arise. You might send my guns and everything of that sort to me here. And you must take 'Briton;' no one would ever give me anything like as much as the splendid animal is worth; I would rather give him to you, you must regard him as the mourning ring which a dying man leaves in his will to his executor. Farry, Breilman and Co. have been building a very comfortable traveling carriage for me, but they have not sent it home yet; get them to keep it if you can, and if they decline to have it left on their hands, make the best arrangement you can for me, and do all you can to save my honor in the position in which I am placed. I lost six louis at play to that fellow from the British Isles, mind that he is . . ."

"Dear cousin," murmured Eugénie, letting the sheet fall, and, seizing one of the lighted candles, she hastened on tiptoe to her own room.

Once there, it was not without a keen feeling of pleasure that she opened one of the drawers in an old oak chest—a most beautiful specimen of the skill of the craftsmen of the Renaissance, you could still make out the half-effaced royal salamander upon it. From this drawer she took a large red velvet money-bag, with gold tassels, and the remains of a golden fringe about it, a bit of faded splendor that had belonged to her grandmother. In the pride of her heart she felt its weight, and joyously set to work to reckon up the value of her little hoard, sorting out the different coins. *Imprimis,* twenty Portuguese moidores as new and fresh as when they were struck in 1725, in the reign of John V.; each was nominally worth five lisbonines, or a hundred and sixty-five francs, but actually they were worth a hundred and eighty francs (so her father used to tell her), a fancy value on account of the rarity and beauty of the aforesaid coins, which shone like the sun. *Item,* five genovines, rare Genoese coins of a hundred livres each, their current value was perhaps about eighty francs, but collectors would give a hundred for them. These had come to her from old M. de la Bertellière. *Item,* three Spanish quadruples of the time of Philip V., bearing the date 1729. Mme. Gentillet had given them to her, one by one, always with the same little speech: "There's a little yellow bird, there's a buttercup for you, worth ninety-eight livres! Take great care of it, darling; it will be the flower of your flock." *Item* (and those were the coins that her father thought most of, for the gold was a fraction over the twenty-three carats), a hundred Dutch ducats, struck at the Hague in 1756, and each worth about thirteen francs. *Item,* a great curiosity! . . . a few coins dear to a miser's heart, three rupees bearing the sign of the Balance, and five with the sign of the Virgin stamped upon them, all pure gold of twenty-four carats—the magnificent coins of the Great Mogul. The weight of metal in them alone was worth thirty-seven francs forty centimes, but amateurs who love to finger gold would give fifty francs for such coins as those. *Item,* the double napoleon that had been given to her the day before, and which she had carelessly slipped into the red velvet bag.

There were new gold pieces fresh from the mint among her treasures, real works of art, which old Grandet liked to look at from time to time, so that he might count them over and tell his daughter of their intrinsic value, expatiating also upon the beauty of the bordering, the sparkling field, the ornate lettering with its sharp, clean, flawless outlines. But now she gave not a thought to their beauty and rarity; her father's mania, and the risks she ran by despoiling herself of a hoard so precious in his eyes, were all forgotten. She thought of nothing but her cousin, and managed at last to discover, after many mistakes in calculation, that she was the owner of eighteen hundred francs all told, or of nearly two thousand francs if the coins were sold for their actual value as curiosities.

She clapped her hands in exultation at the sight of her riches, like a child who is compelled to find some outlet for his overflowing glee and dances for joy. Father and daughter had both counted their wealth that night; he in order to sell his gold; she that she might cast it abroad on the waters of love. She put the money back into the old purse, took it up, and went upstairs with it without a moment's hesitation. Her cousin's distress was the one thought in her mind; she did not even remember that it was night, conventionalities were utterly forgotten; her conscience did not reproach her, she was strong in her happiness and her love.

As she stood upon the threshold with the candle in one hand and the velvet bag in the other, Charles awoke, saw his cousin, and was struck dumb with astonishment. Eugénie came forward, set the light on the table, and said with an unsteady voice—

"Cousin Charles, I have to ask your forgiveness for something I have done; it was very wrong, but if you will overlook it, God will forgive me."

"What can it be?" asked Charles, rubbing his eyes.

"I have been reading those two letters."

Charles reddened.

"Do you ask how I came to do it?" she went on, "and why I came up here? Indeed, I do not know now; and I am almost tempted to feel glad that I read the letters, for through reading them I have come to know your heart, your soul, and . . ."

"And what?" asked Charles.

"And your plans—the difficulty that you are in for want of money——"

"My *dear* cousin——"

"Hush! hush! do not speak so loud, do not let us wake anybody. Here are the savings of a poor girl who has no wants," she went on, opening the purse. "You must take them, Charles. This morning I did not know what money was; you have taught me that it is simply a means to an end, that is all. A cousin is almost a brother; surely you may borrow from your sister."

Eugénie, almost as much a woman as a girl, had not foreseen a refusal, but her cousin was silent.

"Why, are you going to refuse me?" asked Eugénie. The silence was so deep that the beating of her heart was audible. Her pride was wounded by her cousin's hesitation, but the thought of his dire need came vividly before her, and she fell on her knees.

"I will not rise," she said, "until you have taken that money. Oh! cousin, say something, for pity's sake! . . . so that I may know that you respect me, that you are generous, that . . ."

This cry, wrung from her by a noble despair, brought tears to Charles' eyes; he would not let her kneel, she felt his hot tears on her hands, and sprang to her purse, which she emptied out upon the table.

"Well, then, it is 'Yes,' is it not?" she said, crying for joy. "Do not scruple to take it, cousin; you will be quite rich. That gold will bring you luck, you know. Some day you shall pay it back to me, or, if you like, we will be partners; I will submit to any conditions that you may impose. But you ought not to make so much of this gift."

Charles found words at last.

"Yes, Eugénie, I should have a little soul indeed if I would not take it. But nothing for nothing, confidence for confidence."

"What do you mean?" she asked, startled.

"Listen, dear cousin, I have there——"

He interrupted himself for a moment to show her a square box in a leather case, which stood on the chest of drawers.

"There is something there that is dearer to me than life. That box was a present from my mother. Since this morning I have thought that if she could rise from her tomb she herself would sell the gold that in her tenderness she lavished on this dressing-case, but I cannot do it—it would seem like sacrilege."

Eugénie grasped her cousin's hand tightly in hers at these last words.

"No," he went on after a brief pause, during which they looked at each other with tearful eyes, "I do not want to pull it to pieces, nor to risk taking it with me on my wanderings. I will leave it in your keeping, dear Eugénie. Never did one friend confide a more sacred trust to another; but you shall judge for yourself."

He drew the box from its leather case, opened it, and displayed before his cousin's astonished eyes a dressing-case resplendent with gold—the curious skill of the craftsman had only added to the value of the metal.

"All that you are admiring is nothing," he said, pressing the spring of a secret drawer. "There is something which is worth more than all the world to me," he added sadly.

He took out two portraits, two of Mme. de Mirbel's masterpieces, handsomely set in pearls.

"How lovely she is! Is not this the lady to whom you were writing?"

"No," he said, with a little smile; "that is my mother, and

Q

this is my father—your aunt and uncle. Eugénie, I could beg and pray of you on my knees to keep this treasure safe for me. If I should die, and lose your little fortune, the gold will make good your loss; and to you alone can I leave those two portraits, for you alone are worthy to take charge of them, but do not let them pass into other hands, rather destroy them . . ."

Eugénie was silent.

"Well, 'it is *Yes,* is it not?' " he said, and there was a winning charm in his manner.

As the last words were spoken, she gave him for the first time such a glance as a loving woman can, a bright glance that reveals a depth of feeling within her. He took her hand and kissed it.

"Angel of purity! what is money henceforward between us two? It is nothing, is it not? but the feeling, which alone gave it worth, will be everything."

"You are like your mother. Was her voice as musical as yours, I wonder?"

"Oh! far more sweet . . ."

"Yes, for you," she said, lowering her eyelids. "Come, Charles, you must go to bed; I wish it. You are very tired. Good-night."

Her cousin had caught her hand in both of his; she drew it gently away, and went down to her room, her cousin lighting the way. In the doorway of her room they both paused.

"Oh! why am I a ruined man?" he said.

"Pshaw! my father is rich, I believe," she returned.

"My poor child," said Charles, as he set one foot in her room, and propped himself against the wall by the doorway, "if your father had been rich, he would not have let my father die, and you would not be lodged in such a poor place as this; he would live altogether in quite a different style."

"But he has Froidfond."

"And what may Froidfond be worth?"

"I do not know; but there is Noyers too."

"Some miserable farmhouse!"

"He has vineyards and meadows——"

"They are not worth talking about," said Charles scornfully. "If your father had even twenty-four thousand livres a year, do you suppose that you would sleep in a bare, cold room like this?" he added, as he made a step forward with his left foot. "That is where my treasures will be," he went on, nodding towards the old chest, a device by which he tried to conceal his thoughts from her.

"Go," she said, "and try to sleep," and she barred his entrance into an untidy room. Charles drew back; and the cousins bade each other a smiling good-night.

They fell asleep, to dream the same dream; and from that time forward Charles found that there were still roses to be gathered in the world in spite of his mourning. The next morning Mme. Grandet saw her daughter walking with Charles before breakfast. He was still sad and subdued; how, indeed, should he be otherwise than sad? He had been brought very low in his distress; he was gradually finding out how deep the abyss was into which he had fallen, and the thought of the future weighed heavily upon him.

"My father will not be back before dinner," said Eugénie, in reply to an anxious look in her mother's eyes.

The tones of Eugénie's voice had grown strangely sweet; it was easy to see from her face and manner that the cousins had some thought in common. Their souls had rushed together, while perhaps as yet they scarcely knew the power or the nature of this force which was binding them each to each.

Charles sat in the dining-room; no one intruded upon his sorrow. Indeed, the three women had plenty to do. Grandet had gone without any warning, and his work-people were at a standstill. The slater came, the plumber, the bricklayer, and the carpenter followed; so did laborers, tenants, and vinedressers, some came to pay their dues, and others to receive them, and yet others to make bargains for the repairs which were being done. Mme. Grandet and Eugénie, therefore, were continually coming and going; they had to listen to interminable histories from laborers and country people.

Everything that came into the house Nanon promptly and securely stowed away in her kitchen. She always waited for her master's instructions as to what should be kept, and what should be sold in the market. The worthy cooper, like many little country squires, was wont to drink his worst wine, and to reserve his spoiled or wind-fallen orchard fruit for home consumption.

Towards five o'clock that evening Grandet came back from Angers. He had made fourteen thousand francs on his gold, and carried a Government certificate bearing interest until the day when it should be transferred into *rentes*. He had left Cornoiller also in Angers to look after the horses, which had been nearly foundered by the night journey, and had given instructions to bring them back leisurely after they had had a thorough rest.

"I have been to Angers, wife," he said; "and I am hungry."

"Have you had nothing to eat since yesterday?" called Nanon from her kitchen.

"Nothing whatever," said the worthy man.

Nanon brought in the soup. Des Grassins came to take his client's instructions just as the family were sitting down to dinner. Grandet had not so much as seen his nephew all this time.

"Go on with your dinner, Grandet," said the banker. "We can have a little chat. Have you heard what gold is fetching in Angers, and that people from Nantes are buying it there? I am going to send some over."

"You need not trouble yourself," answered his worthy client; "they have quite enough there by this time. I don't like you to lose your labor when I can prevent it; we are too good friends for that."

"But gold is at thirteen francs fifty centimes premium."

"Say *was* at a premium."

"How the deuce did you get to know that?"

"I vent over to Angers myself last night," Grandet told him in a low voice.

The banker started, and a whispered conversation followed; both des Grassins and Grandet looked at Charles from time to time, and once more a gesture of surprise escaped the banker, doubtless at the point where the old cooper commissioned him to purchase *rentes* to bring in a hundred thousand livres.

"M. Grandet," said des Grassins, addressing Charles, "I am going to Paris, and if there is anything I can do for you ——"

"Thank you, sir, there is nothing," Charles replied.

"You must thank him more heartily than that, nephew. This gentleman is going to wind up your father's business and settle with his creditors."

"Then is there any hope of coming to an arrangement?" asked Charles.

"Why, are you not my nephew?" cried the cooper, with a fine assumption of pride. "Our honor is involved; is not your name Grandet?"

Charles rose from his chair, impulsively flung his arms about his uncle, turned pale, and left the room. Eugénie looked at her father with affection and pride in her eyes.

"Well, let us say good-bye, my good friend," said Grandet. "I am very much at your service. Try to get round those fellows over yonder."

The two diplomatists shook hands, and the cooper went to the door with his neighbor; he came back to the room again when he had closed the door on des Grassins, flung himself down in his easy chair, and said to Nanon: "Bring me some cordial."

But he was too much excited to keep still; he rose and looked at old M. de la Bertellière's portrait, and began to "dance a jig," in Nanon's phrase, singing to himself—

> Once in the *Gardes francaises*
> I had a grandpapa . . .

Nanon, Mme. Grandet, and Eugénie all looked at each other in silent dismay. The vinegrower's ecstasies never boded any good.

The evening was soon over. Old Grandet went off early to bed, and no one was allowed to stay up after that; when he slept, every one else must likewise sleep, much as in Poland, in the days of Augustus the Strong, whenever the king drank all his subjects were loyally tipsy. Wherefore, Nanon, Charles, and Eugénie were no less tired than the master of the house; and as for Mme. Grandet, she slept or woke, ate or drank, as her husband bade her. Yet during the two hours allotted to the digestion of his dinner the cooper was more facetious than he had ever been in his life before, and uttered not a few of his favorite aphorisms; one example will serve to plumb the depths of the cooper's mind. When he had finished his cordial, he looked pensively at the glass, and thus delivered himself—

"You have no sooner set your lips to a glass than it is empty! Such is life. You cannot have your cake and eat it too, and you can't turn over your money and keep it in your purse; if you could only do that, life would be too glorious."

He was not only jocose, he was good-natured, so that when Nanon came in with her spinning-wheel—"You must be tired," he said; "let the hemp alone."

"And if I did," the servant answered, *"Quien,* I should have to sit with my hands before me."

"Poor Nanon! would you like some cordial?"

"Cordial? Oh! I don't say no. Madame makes it much better than the apothecaries do. The stuff they sell is like physic."

"They spoil the flavor with putting too much sugar in it," said the goodman.

The next morning, at the eight o'clock breakfast, the party seemed, for the first time, almost like one family. Mme. Grandet, Eugénie, and Charles had been drawn together by these troubles, and Nanon herself unconsciously felt with them. As for the old vinegrower, he scarcely noticed his nephew's presence in the house, his greed of gold had been satisfied, and he was very shortly to be quit of this young sprig by the cheap and easy expedient of paying his nephew's traveling expenses as far as Nantes.

Charles and Eugénie meanwhile were free to do what seemed to them good. They were under Mme. Grandet's eyes, and Grandet reposed complete faith in his wife in all matters of conduct and religion. Moreover, he had other things to think of; his meadows were to be drained, and a row of poplars was to be planted along the Loire, and there was all the ordinary winter work at Froidfond and elsewhere; in fact, he was exceedingly busy.

And now began the springtime of love for Eugénie. Since that hour in the night when she had given her gold to her cousin, her heart had followed the gift. They shared a secret between them; they were conscious of this understanding whenever they looked at each other; and this knowledge, that brought them more and more closely together, drew them in a manner out of the current of everyday life. And did not relationship justify a certain tenderness in the voice and kindness in the eyes? Eugénie therefore set herself to make her cousin forget his grief in the childish joys of growing love.

For the beginnings of love and the beginnings of life are not unlike. Is not the child soothed by smiles and cradle-songs, and fairy tales of a golden future that lies before him? Above him, too, the bright wings of hope are always spread, and does he not shed tears of joy or of sorrow, wax petulant over trifles and quarrelsome over the pebbles with which he builds a tottering palace, or the flowers that are no sooner gathered than forgotten? Is he not also eager to outstrip Time, and to live in the future? Love is the soul's second transformation.

Love and childhood were almost the same thing for Charles and Eugénie; the dawn of love and its childish beginnings were all the sweeter because their hearts were full of gloom; and this love, that from its birth had been enveloped in crape, was in keeping with their homely surroundings in the melancholy old house. As the cousins interchanged a few words by the well in the silent courtyard, or sat out in the little garden towards sunset time, wholly absorbed by the momentous nothings that each said to each, or wrapped in the stillness that always brooded over the space between the ramparts and the house, Charles learned to think of love as something sacred. Hitherto, with his great lady, his "dear Annette," he had experienced little but its perils and storms; but that episode in Paris was over, with its coquetry and passion, its vanity and emptiness, and he turned to this love in its purity and truth.

He came to feel a certain fondness for the old house, and their way of life no longer seemed absurd to him. He would come downstairs early in the morning so as to snatch a few words with Eugénie before her father gave out the stores; and when the sound of Grandet's heavy footstep echoed on the staircase, he fled into the garden. Even Eugénie's mother did not know of this morning tryst of theirs, and Nanon made as though she did not see it; it was a small piece of audacity that gave the keen relish of a stolen pleasure to their innocent love. Then when breakfast was over, and Goodman Grandet had gone to see after his business and his improvements, Charles sat in the gray parlor between the mother and daughter, finding a pleasure unknown before in holding skeins of thread for them to wind, in listening to their talk, and watching them sew. There was something that appealed to him strongly in the almost monastic simplicity of the life, which had led him to discover the nobleness of the natures of these two unworldly women. He had not believed that such lives as these were possible in France; in Germany he admitted that old-world manners lingered still, but in France they were only to be found in fiction and in Auguste Lafontaine's novels. It was not long before Eugénie became an embodiment of his ideal, Goethe's Marguerite without her error.

Day after day, in short, the poor girl hung on his words and looks, and drifted further along the stream of love. She snatched at every happiness as some swimmer might catch at an overhanging willow branch, that so he might reach the bank and rest there for a little while.

Was not the time of parting very near now? The shadow of that parting seemed to fall across the brightest hours of those days that fled so fast; and not one of them went by but something happened to remind her how soon it would be upon them.

For instance, three days after des Grassins had started for Paris, Grandet had taken Charles before a magistrate with the funereal solemnity with which such acts are performed by provincials, and in the presence of that functionary the young man had had to sign a declaration that he renounced all claim to his father's property. Dreadful repudiation! An impiety amounting to apostasy! He went to M. Cruchot to procure two powers of attorney, one for des Grassins, the other for the friend who was commissioned to sell his own personal effects. There were also some necessary formalities in connection with his passport; and finally, on the arrival of the plain suit of mourning which Charles had ordered from Paris, he sent for a clothier in Saumur, and disposed of his now useless wardrobe. This transaction was peculiarly pleasing to old Grandet.

"Ah! *Now* you look like a man who is ready to set out, and means to make his way in the world," he said, as he saw his nephew in a plain, black overcoat of rough cloth. "Good, very good!"

"I beg you to believe, sir," Charles replied, "that I shall face my position with proper spirit."

"What does this mean?" asked his worthy relative; there was an eager look in the goodman's eyes at the sight of a handful of gold which Charles held out to him.

"I have gathered together my studs and rings and everything of any value that I have; I am not likely to want them now; but I know of nobody in Saumur, and this morning I thought I would ask you——"

"To buy it?" Grandet broke in upon him.

"No, uncle, to give me the name of some honest man who
———"

"Give it to me, nephew; I will take it upstairs and find out
what it is worth, and let you know the value to a centime.
Jeweler's gold," he commented, after an examination of a
long chain, "jeweler's gold, eighteen to nineteen carats, I
should say."

The worthy soul held out his huge hand for it, and carried
off the whole collection.

"Cousin Eugénie," said Charles, "permit me to offer you
these two clasps; you might use them to fasten ribbons
around your wrists, that sort of bracelet is all the rage just
now."

"I do not hesitate to take it, cousin," she said, with a look
of intelligence.

"And, aunt, this is my mother's thimble; I have treasured it up till now in my dressing-case," and he gave a pretty
gold thimble to Mme. Grandet, who for the past ten years
had longed for one.

"It is impossible to thank you in words, dear nephew," said
the old mother, as her eyes filled with tears. "But morning
and evening I shall repeat the prayer for travelers, and pray
most fervently for you. If anything should happen to me,
Eugénie shall take care of it for you."

"It is worth nine hundred and eighty-nine francs seventy-
five centimes, nephew," said Grandet, as he came in at the
door. "But to save you the trouble of selling it, I will let you
have the money in livres."

This expression "in livres" means, in the districts along
the Loire, that a crown of six livres is to be considered worth
six francs, without deduction.

"I did not venture to suggest such a thing," Charles answered, "but I shrank from hawking my trinkets about in
the town where you are living. Dirty linen ought not to be
washed in public, as Napoleon used to say. Thank you for
obliging me."

Grandet scratched his ear, and there was a moment's silence in the room.

"And, dear uncle," Charles went on, somewhat nervously,
and as though he feared to wound his uncle's susceptibilities,
"my cousin and aunt have consented to receive trifling me-
mentoes from me; will you not in your turn accept these
sleeve-links, which are useless to me now; they may perhaps
recall to your memory a poor boy, in a far-off country, whose
thought will certainly often turn to those who are all that
remain to him now of his family."

"Oh! my boy, my boy, you must not strip yourself like that
for us——"

"What have you there, wife?" said the cooper, turning
eagerly towards her. "Ah! a gold thimble? And you, little
girl? Diamond clasps; what next! Come, I will accept
your studs, my boy," he continued, squeezing Charles' hand.
"But . . . you must let me pay . . . your . . .
yes, your passage out to the Indies. Yes, I mean to pay your
passage. Besides, my boy, when I estimated your jewelry I
only took it at its value as metal, you see, without reckoning
the workmanship, and it may be worth a trifle more on that
account. So that is settled. I will pay you fifteen hundred
francs . . . in livres; Cruchot will lend it me, for I
have not a brass farthing in the house; unless Perrotet, who
is getting behindhand with his dues, will pay me in coin.
There! there! I will go and see about it," and he took up his
hat, put on his gloves, and went forthwith.

"Then you are going?" said Eugénie, with sad, admiring
eyes.

"I cannot help myself," he answered, with his head bent
down.

For several days Charles looked, spoke, and behaved like a
man who is in deep trouble, but who feels the weight of such
heavy obligations, that his misfortunes only brace him for
greater effort. He had ceased to pity himself; he had become
a man. Never had Eugénie augured better of her cousin's
character than she did on the day when she watched him

come downstairs in his plain, black mourning suit, which set
off his pale, sad face to such advantage. The two women had
also gone into mourning, and went with Charles to the
Requiem mass celebrated in the parish church for the soul of
the late Guillaume Grandet.

Charles received letters from Paris as they took the mid-
day meal; he opened and read them.

"Well, cousin," said Eugénie, in a low voice, "are your
affairs going on satisfactorily?"

"Never put questions of that sort, my girl," remarked
Grandet. "I never talk to you about my affairs, and why the
devil should you meddle in your cousin's? Just let the boy
alone."

"Oh! I have no secrets of any sort," said Charles.

"Tut, tut, tut. You will find out that you must bridle
your tongue in business, nephew."

When the two lovers were alone in the garden, Charles
drew Eugénie to the old bench under the walnut tree where
they so often sat of late.

"I felt sure of Alphonse, and I was right," he said; "he
has done wonders, and has settled my affairs prudently and
loyally. All my debts in Paris are paid, my furniture sold
well, and he tells me that he has acted on the advice of an old
sea captain who had made the voyage to the Indies, and has
invested the surplus money in ornaments and odds and ends
for which there is a great demand out there. He has sent my
packages to Nantes, where an East Indiaman is taking freight
for Java, and so, Eugénie, in five days we must bid each other
farewell, for a long while at any rate, and perhaps forever.
My trading venture and the ten thousand francs which two
of my friends have sent me, are a very poor start; I cannot
expect to return for many years. Dear cousin, let us not consider ourselves bound in any way; I may die, and very likely
some good opportunity for settling yourself——"

"You love me? . . ." she asked.

"Oh! yes, indeed," he replied, with an earnestness of manner that betokened a like earnestness in his feelings.

The two lovers were alone in the garden

"Then I will wait for you, Charles. *Dieu!* my father is looking out of his window," she exclaimed, evading her cousin, who had drawn closer to embrace her.

She fled to the archway; and seeing that Charles followed her thither, she retreated further, flung back the folding door at the foot of the staircase, and with no very clear idea, save that of flight, she rushed towards the darkest corner of the passage, outside Nanon's sleeping hole; and there Charles, who was close beside her, grasped both hands in his and pressed her to his heart; his arms went round her waist, Eugénie resisted no longer, and leaning against her lover she received and gave the purest, sweetest, and most perfect of all kisses.

"Dear Eugénie, a cousin is better than a brother; he can marry you," said Charles.

"Amen, so be it!" cried Nanon, opening the door behind them, and emerging from her den. Her voice startled the two lovers, who fled into the dining-room, where Eugénie took up her sewing, and Charles seized on Mme. Grandet's prayer book, opened it at the litanies of the Virgin, and began to read industriously.

"*Quien!*" said Nanon, "so we are all saying our prayers!"

As soon as Charles fixed the day for his departure, Grandet bustled about and affected to take the greatest interest in the whole matter. He was liberal with advice, and with anything else that cost him nothing, first seeking out a packer for Charles, and then, saying that the man wanted too much for his cases, setting to work with all his might to make them himself, using odd planks for the purpose. He was up betimes every morning planing, fitting, nailing deal boards together, squaring and shaping; and, in fact, he made some strong cases, packed all Charles' property in them, and undertook to send them by steamer down the Loire to Nantes in time to go by the merchant ship, and to insure them during the voyage.

Since that kiss given and taken in the passage, the hours

sped with terrible rapidity for Eugénie. At times she
thought of following her cousin; for of all ties that bind one
human being to another, this passion of love is the closest
and strongest, and those who know this, and know how every
day shortens love's allotted span, and how not time alone but
age and mortal sickness and all the untoward accidents of life
combine to menace it,—these will know the agony that Eugénie suffered. She shed many tears as she walked up and
down the little garden; it had grown so narrow for her now;
the courtyard, the old house, and the town had all grown narrow, and her thoughts fared forth already across vast spaces
of sea.

It was the day before the day of departure. That morning,
while Grandet and Nanon were out of the house, the precious
casket that held the two portraits was solemnly deposited in
Eugénie's chest, beside the now empty velvet bag in the only
drawer that could be locked, an installation which was not
effected without many tears and kisses. When Eugénie
locked the drawer and hid the key in her bosom, she had not
the courage to forbid the kiss by which Charles sealed the
act.

"The key shall always stay there, dear."

"Ah! well, my heart will always be there with it too."

"Oh! Charles, you should not say that," she said a little
reproachfully.

"Are we not married?" he replied. "I have your word;
take mine."

"Thine forever!" they said together, and repeated it a
second time. No holier vow was ever made on earth; for
Charles' love had received a moment's consecration in the
presence of Eugénie's simple sincerity.

It was a melancholy group round the breakfast-table next
morning. Even Nanon herself, in spite of Charles' gift of a
new gown and a gilt cross, had a tear in her eye; but she was
free to express her feelings and did so.

"Oh! that poor, delicate young gentleman who is going to
sea," was the burden of her discourse.

At half-past ten the whole family left the house to see Charles start for Nantes in the diligence. Nanon had let the dog loose, and locked the door, and meant to carry Charles' handbag. Every shopkeeper in the ancient street was in the doorway to watch the little procession pass. M. Cruchot joined them in the market-place.

"Eugénie," whispered her mother, "mind you do not cry!"

They reached the gateway of the inn, and there Grandet kissed Charles on both cheeks. "Well! nephew," he said, "set out poor and come back rich; you leave your father's honor in safe keeping. I—Grandet—will answer to you for that; you will only have to do your part——"

"Oh! uncle, this sweetens the bitterness of parting. Is not this the greatest gift you could possibly give me?"

Charles had broken in upon the old cooper's remarks before he quite understood their drift; he put his arms round his uncle's neck, and let fall tears of gratitude on the vine-grower's sunburned cheeks; Eugénie clasped her cousin's hand in one of hers, and her father's in the other, and held them tightly. Only the notary smiled to himself; he alone understood the worthy man, and he could not help admiring his astute cunning. The four Saumurois and a little group of onlookers hung about the diligence till the last moment; and looked after it until it disappeared across the bridge, and the sound of the wheels grew faint and distant.

"A good riddance!" said the cooper.

Luckily, no one but M. Cruchot heard this ejaculation; Eugénie and her mother had walked along the quay to a point of view whence they could still see the diligence, and stood there waving their handkerchiefs and watching Charles' answering signal till he was out of sight; then Eugénie turned.

"Oh! mother, mother, if I had God's power for one moment," she said.

To save further interruption to the course of the story, it is necessary to glance a little ahead, and give a brief account of the course of events in Paris, of Grandet's calculations, and the action taken by his worthy lieutenant the banker in the matter of Guillaume Grandet's affairs. A month after des Grassins had gone, Grandet received a certificate for a hundred thousand livres per annum of *rentes,* purchased at eighty francs. No information was ever forthcoming as to how and when the actual coin had been paid, or the receipt taken, which in due course had been exchanged for the certificate. The inventory and statement of his affairs which the miser left at his death threw no light upon the mystery, and Cruchot fancied that in some way or other Nanon must have been the unconscious instrument employed; for about that time the faithful serving-maid was away from home for four or five days, ostensibly to see after matters at Froidfond, as if its worthy owner were likely to forget anything there that required looking after! As for Guillaume Grandet's creditors, everything had happened as the cooper had intended and foreseen.

At the Bank of France (as everybody knows) they keep accurate lists of all the great fortunes in Paris or in the departments. The names of des Grassins and of Felix Grandet of Saumur were duly to be found inscribed therein; indeed, they shone conspicuous there as well-known names in the business world, as men who were not only financially sound, but owners of broad acres unencumbered by mortgages. And now it was said that des Grassins of Saumur had come to Paris with intent to call a meeting of the creditors of the firm of Guillaume Grandet; the shade of the wine merchant was to be spared the disgrace of protested bills. The seals were broken in the presence of the creditors, and the family notary proceeded to make out an inventory in due form.

Before very long, in fact, des Grassins called a meeting of the creditors, who with one voice appointed the banker of Saumur as trustee conjointly with François Keller, the head of a large business house, and one of the principal creditors, empowering them to take such measures as they thought fit, in order to save the family name (and the bills) from being dishonored. The fact that des Grassins was acting as his agent produced a hopeful tone in the meeting, and things went smoothly from the first; the banker did not find a single dissentient voice. No one thought of passing his bill to his profit and loss account, and each one said to himself— "Grandet of Saumur is going to pay!"

Six months went by. The Parisian merchants had withdrawn the bills from circulation, and had consigned them to the depths of their portfolios. The cooper had gained his first point. Nine months after the first meeting the two trustees paid the creditors a dividend of forty-seven per cent. This sum had been raised by the sale of the late Guillaume Grandet's property, goods, chattels and general effects; the most scrupulous integrity characterized these proceedings; indeed, the whole affair was conducted with the most conscientious honesty, and the delighted creditors fell to admiring Grandet's wonderful, indubitable and high-minded probity. When these praises had duly circulated for a sufficient length of time, the creditors began to ask themselves when the remainder of their money would be forthcoming, and bethought them of collectively writing a letter to Grandet.

"Here we are!" was the old cooper's comment, as he flung the letter in the fire. "Patience, patience, my dear friends."

By way of a reply to the propositions contained in the letter, Grandet of Saumur required them to deposit with a notary all the bills and claims against the estate of his deceased brother, accompanying each with receipts for the payments already made. The accounts were to be audited, and the exact condition of affairs was to be ascertained. Innumerable difficulties were cleared away by this notion of the deposit.

A creditor, generally speaking, is a sort of maniac; there is no saying what a creditor will do. One day he is in a hurry to bring the thing to an end, the next he is all for fire and sword, a little later and he is sweetness and benignity itself. To-day, very probably, his wife is in a good humor, his youngest hope has just cut a tooth, everything is going on comfortably at home, he has no mind to abate his claims

10

one jot; but to-morrow comes, and it rains, and he cannot go out; he feels low in his mind, and agrees hastily to anything and everything that is likely to settle the affair; the next morning brings counsel; he requires a guarantee, and by the end of the month he talks about an execution, the inhuman, bloodthirsty wretch! The creditor is not unlike that common or house sparrow on whose tail small children are encouraged to try to put a grain of salt—a pleasing simile which the creditor may twist to his own uses, and apply to his bills, from which he fondly hopes to derive some benefit at last. Grandet had observed these atmospheric variations among creditors; and his forecasts in the present case were correct, his brother's creditors were behaving in every respect exactly as he wished. Some waxed wroth, and flatly declined to have anything to do with the deposit, or to give up the vouchers.

"Good!" said Grandet; "that is all right!" He rubbed his hands as he read the letters which des Grassins wrote to him on the subject.

Yet others refused to consent to the aforesaid deposit unless their position was clearly defined in the first place; it was to be made without prejudice, and they reserved the right to declare the estate bankrupt should they deem it advisable. This opened a fresh correspondence, and occasioned a further delay, after which Grandet finally agreed to all the conditions, and as a consequence the more tractable creditors brought the recalcitrant to hear reason, and the deposit was made, not, however, without some grumbling.

"That old fellow is laughing in his sleeve at you and at us too," said they to des Grassins.

Twenty-three months after Guillaume Grandet's death, many of the merchants had forgotten all about their claims in the course of events in a business life in Paris, or they only thought of them to say to themselves—

"It begins to look as though the forty-seven per cent is about all I shall get out of that business."

The cooper had reckoned on the aid of Time, who, so he was wont to say, is a good fellow. By the end of the third

year, des Grassins wrote to Grandet saying that he had induced most of the creditors to give up their bills, and that
the amount now owing was only about ten per cent of the
outstanding two million four hundred thousand francs.
Grandet replied that there yet remained the notary and the
stockbroker, whose failures had been the death of his brother;
they were still alive. They might be solvent again by this
time, and proceedings ought to be taken against them;
something might be recovered in this way which would still
further reduce the sum-total of the deficit.

When the fourth year drew to a close the deficit had been
duly brought down to the sum of twelve hundred thousand
francs; the limit appeared to have been reached. Six months
were further spent in parleyings between the trustees and the
creditors, and between Grandet and the trustees. In short,
strong pressure being brought to bear upon Grandet of Saumur, he announced, somewhere about the ninth month of the
same year, that his nephew, who had made a fortune in the
East Indies, had signified his intention of settling in full all
claims on his father's estate; and that meantime he could not
take it upon himself to act, nor to defraud the creditors by
winding up the affair before he had consulted his nephew; he
added that he had written to him, and was now awaiting an
answer.

The middle of the fifth year had been reached, and still the
creditors were held in check by the magic words *in full,* let
fall judiciously from time to time by the sublime cooper, who
was laughing at them in his sleeve; "those PARISIANS," he
would say to himself, with a mild oath, and a cunning smile
would steal across his features.

In fact, a martyrdom unknown to the calendars of commerce was in store for the creditors. When next they appear
in the course of this story, they will be found in exactly the
same position that they were in now when Grandet had done
with them. Consols went up to a hundred and fifteen, old
Grandet sold out, and received from Paris about two million
four hundred thousand francs in gold, which went into his

wooden kegs to keep company with the six hundred thousand
francs of interest which his investment had brought in.

Des Grassins stayed on in Paris, and for the following
reasons. In the first place, he had been appointed a deputy;
and in the second, he, the father of a family, bored by the
exceeding dullness of existence in Saumur, was smitten with
the charms of Mlle. Florine, one of the prettiest actresses of
the Théâtre de Madame, and there was a recrudescence of the
quarter-master in the banker. It is useless to discuss his conduct; at Saumur it was pronounced to be profoundly im-
moral. It was very lucky for his wife that she had brains
enough to carry on the concern at Saumur in her own name,
and could extricate the remains of her fortune, which had
suffered not a little from M. des Grassins' extravagance and
folly. But the quasi-widow was in a false position, and the
Cruchotins did all that in them lay to make matters worse;
she had to give up all hope of a match between her son and
Eugénie Grandet, and married her daughter very badly.
Adolphe des Grassins went to join his father in Paris, and
there acquired, so it was said, an unenviable reputation. The
triumph of the Cruchotins was complete.

"Your husband has taken leave of his senses," Grandet
took occasion to remark as he accommodated Mme. des Grassins with a loan (on good security). "I am very sorry for
you; you are a nice little woman."

"Ah!" sighed the poor lady, "who could have believed that
day when he set out for Paris to see after that business of
yours that he was hurrying to his own ruin?"

"Heaven is my witness, madame, that to the very last I did
all I could to prevent him, and M. le Président was dying to
go; but we know now why your husband was so set upon it."

Clearly, therefore, Grandet lay under no obligation to des
Grassins.

In every situation a woman is bound to suffer in many
ways that a man does not, and to feel her troubles more
acutely than he can; for a man's vigor and energy is con-

stantly brought into play; he acts and thinks, comes and goes, busies himself in the present, and looks to the future for consolation. This was what Charles was doing. But a woman cannot help herself—hers is a passive part; she is left face to face with her trouble, and has nothing to divert her mind from it; she sounds the depths of the abyss of sorrow, and its dark places are filled with her prayers and tears. So it was with Eugénie. She was beginning to understand that the web of a woman's life will always be woven of love and sorrow and hope and fear and self-sacrifice; hers was to be a woman's lot in all things without a woman's consolations and her moments of happiness (to make use of Bossuet's wonderful illustration) were to be like the scattered nails driven into the wall, when all collected together they scarcely filled the hollow of the hand. Troubles seldom keep us waiting for them, and for Eugénie they were gathering thick and fast.

The day after Charles had gone, the Grandet household fell back into the old ways of life; there was no difference for any one but Eugénie—for her the house had grown very empty all on a sudden. Charles' room should remain just as he had left it; Mme. Grandet and Nanon lent themselves to this whim of hers, willingly maintained the *statu quo*, and said nothing to her father.

"Who knows?" Eugénie said. "He may come back to us sooner than we think."

"Ah! I wish I could see him here again," replied Nanon. "I could get on with him well enough! He was very nice, and an excellent gentleman; and he was pretty-like, his hair curled over his head just like a girl's."

Eugénie gazed at Nanon.

"Holy Virgin! mademoiselle, with such eyes, you are like to lose your soul. You shouldn't look at people in that way."

From that day Mlle. Grandet's beauty took a new character. The grave thoughts of love that slowly enveloped her soul, the dignity of a woman who is beloved, gave to her face the sort of radiance that early painters expressed by the au-

reole. Before her cousin came into her life, Eugénie might
have been compared to the Virgin as yet unconscious of her
destiny; and now that he had passed out of it, she seemed
like the Virgin Mother; she, too, bore love in her heart.
Spanish art has depicted these two Marys, so different each
from each—Christianity, with its many symbols, knows no
more glorious types than these.

The day after Charles had left them, Eugénie went to mass
(as she had resolved to do daily), and on her way back
bought a map of the world from the only bookseller in the
town. This she pinned to the wall beside her glass, so that she
might follow the course of her cousin's voyage to the Indies;
and night and morning might be beside him for a little while
on that far-off vessel, and see him and ask all the endless
questions she longed to ask.

"Are you well? Are you not sad? Am I in your thoughts
when you see the star that you told me about? You made
me see how beautiful it was."

In the morning she used to sit like one in a dream under
the great walnut tree, on the old gray, lichen-covered, worm-
eaten bench where they had talked so kindly and so foolishly,
where they had built such fair castles in the air in which to
live. She thought of the future as she watched the little strip
of sky shut in by the high walls on every side, then her eyes
wandered over the old buttressed wall and the roof—Charles'
room lay beneath it. In short, this solitary persistent love
mingling with all her thoughts became the substance, or, as
our forefathers would have said, the "stuff" of her life.

If Grandet's self-styled friends came in of an evening, she
would seem to be in high spirits, but the liveliness was only
assumed; she used to talk about Charles with her mother and
Nanon the whole morning through, and Nanon—who was of
the opinion that without faltering in her duty to her master
she might yet feel for her young mistress' troubles—Nanon
spoke on this wise—

"If I had had a sweetheart, I would have . . . I
would have gone with him to hell. I would have . . .

well, then, I would just have laid down my life for him, but
. . . no such chance! I shall die without knowing what
it is to live. Would you believe it, mam'selle, there is that
old Cornoiller, who is a good man all the same, dangling
about after my savings, just like the others who come here
paying court to you and sniffing after the master's money. I
see through it; I may be as big as a hay stack, but I am as
sharp as a needle yet. Well! and yet do you know, mam'selle,
it may not be love, but I rather like it."

In this way two months went by. The secret that bound
the three women so closely together had brought a new interest into the household life hitherto so monotonous. For them
Charles still dwelt in the house, and came and went beneath
the old gray rafters of the parlor. Every morning and evening Eugénie opened the dressing-case and looked at her
aunt's portrait. Her mother, suddenly coming into her room
one Sunday morning, found her absorbed in tracing out a
likeness to Charles in the lady of the miniature, and Mme.
Grandet learned for the first time a terrible secret, how that
Eugénie had parted with her treasures and had taken the
case in exchange.

"You have let him have it all!" cried the terrified mother.
"What will you say to your father on New Year's Day when
he asks to see your gold?"

Eugénie's eyes were set in a fixed stare; the horror of this
thought so filled the women that half the morning went by,
and they were distressed to find themselves too late for high
mass, and were only in time for the military mass. The year
1819 was almost over; there were only three more days left.
In three days a terrible drama would begin, a drama un-
dignified by poison, dagger or bloodshed, but fate dealt
scarcely more cruelly with the princely house of Atreus than
with the actors in this bourgeois tragedy.

"What is to become of us?" said Mme. Grandet, laying
down her knitting on her knee.

Poor mother! all the events of the past two months had
sadly hindered the knitting, the woolen cuffs for winter wear

were not finished yet, a homely and apparently insignificant fact which was to work trouble enough for her. For want of the warm cuffs she caught a chill after a violent perspiration brought on by one of her husband's fearful outbursts of rage.

"My poor child, I have been thinking, that if you had only told me about this, we should have had time to write to M. des Grassins in Paris. He might have managed to send us some gold pieces like those of yours; and although Grandet knows the look of them so well, still perhaps . . ."

"But where could we have found so much money?"

"I would have raised it on my property. Besides, M. des Grassins would have befriended us . . ."

"There is not time enough now," faltered Eugénie in a smothered voice. "To-morrow morning we shall have to go to his room to wish him a happy New Year, shall we not?"

"Oh! Eugénie, why not go and see the Cruchots about it?"

"No, no, that would be putting ourselves in their power; I should be entirely in their hands then. Besides, I have made up my mind. I have acted quite rightly, and I repent of nothing; God will protect me. May His holy will be done! Ah! if you had read that letter, mother, you would have thought of nothing but him."

The next morning, January 1, 1820, the mother and daughter were in an agony of distress that they could not hide; sheer terror suggested the simple expedient of omitting the solemn visit to Grandet's room. The bitter weather served as an excuse; the winter of 1819-20 was the coldest that had been known for years, and snow lay deep on the roofs.

Mme. Grandet called to her husband as soon as she heard him stirring, "Grandet, just let Nanon light a bit of fire in here for me, the air is so sharp that I am shivering under the bedclothes, and at my time of life I must take care of myself. And then," she went on after a little pause, "Eu-

génie shall come in here to dress. The poor girl may do herself a mischief if she dresses in her own room in such cold.
We will come downstairs into the sitting-room and wish you
a happy New Year there by the fire."

"Tut, tut, tut, what a tongue! What a way to begin the
year, Mme. Grandet! You have never said so much in your
life before. You have not had a sop of bread in wine, I suppose?"

There was a moment's pause. Doubtless his wife's pro-
posal suited his notions, for he said, "Very well, I will do as
you wish, Mme. Grandet. You really are a good sort of
woman, it would be a pity for you to expire before you are
due, though as a rule, the La Bertellières make old bones,
don't they, hey?" he cried, after a pause. "Well, their money
has fallen in at last; I forgive them," and he coughed.

"You are in spirits this morning," said the poor wife.

"I always am in spirits."

> Hey! hey! cooper gay,
> Mend your tub and take your pay.

He had quite finished dressing and came into his wife's room.
"Yes, *nom d'un petit bonhomme!* it is a mighty hard frost,
all the same. We shall have a good breakfast to-day, wife.
Des Grassins has sent me a pâté de foies gras, truffled! I am
going round to the coach office to see after it. He should
have sent a double napoleon for Eugénie along with it," said
the cooper, coming closer, and lowering his voice. "I have
no gold, I certainly had a few old coins still left, I may tell
you that in confidence, but I had to let them go in the course
of business," and by way of celebrating the first day of the
year he kissed his wife on the forehead.

"Eugénie," cried the kind mother, as soon as Grandet had
gone, "I don't know which side of the bed your father got
out on, but he is in a good humor this morning. Pshaw! we
shall pull through."

"What can have come over the master?" cried Nanon as

she came into the room to light the fire. "First of all, he
says, 'Good morning, great stupid, a happy New Year! Go
upstairs and light a fire in my wife's room; she is feeling
cold.' I thought I must be off my head when I saw him
holding out his hand with a six-franc piece in it that hadn't
been clipped a bit! There! madame, only look at it! Oh!
he is a worthy man, all the same—he is a good man, he is.
There are some as get harder-hearted the older they grow;
but he turns sweeter, like your cordial that improves with
keeping. He is a very good and a very excellent man . . ."

Grandet's speculation had been completely successful; this
was the cause of his high spirits. M. des Grassins—after deducting various amounts which the cooper owed him, partly
for discounting Dutch bills to the amount of a hundred and
fifty thousand francs, and partly for advances of money for
the purchase of a hundred thousand livres worth of consols—
M. des Grassins was sending him, by diligence, thirty thousand francs in crowns, the remainder (after the aforesaid
deductions had been made) of the cooper's half-yearly dividends, and informed Grandet that consols were steadily rising. They stood at eighty-nine at the present moment, and
well-known capitalists were buying for the next account at
the end of January at ninety-two. In two months Grandet
had made twelve per cent on his capital; he had straightened
his accounts; and henceforward he would receive fifty thousand francs every half year, clear of taxes or any outgoing expenses. In short, he had grasped the theory of consols (a
class of investment of which the provincial mind is exceedingly shy), and looking ahead, he beheld himself the master
of six millions of francs in five years' time—six millions,
which would go on accumulating with scarcely any trouble
on his part—six millions of francs! And there was the
value of his landed property to add to this; he saw himself in
a fair way to build up a colossal fortune. The six francs
given to Nanon were perhaps in reality the payment for an
immense service which the girl had unwittingly done her
master.

"Oho! what can Goodman Grandet be after? He is running as if there were a fire somewhere," the shopkeepers said to each other as they took down their shutters that New Year's morning.

A little later when they saw him coming back from the quay followed by a porter from the coach office, who was wheeling a barrow piled up with little bags full of something——

"Ah!" said they, "water always makes for the river, the old boy was hurrying after his crowns."

"They flow in on him from Paris, and Froidfond, and Holland," said one.

"He will buy Saumur before he has done," cried another.

"He does not care a rap for the cold; he is always looking after his business," said a woman to her husband.

"Hi! M. Grandet! if you have more of that than you know what to do with, I can help you to get rid of some of it."

"Eh! they are only coppers," said the vinegrower.

"Silver, he means," said the porter in a low voice.

"Keep a still tongue in your head, if you want me to bear you in mind," said the goodman as he opened the door.

"Oh! the old fox, I thought he was deaf," said the porter to himself, "but it looks as though he could hear well enough in cold weather."

"Here is a franc for a New Year's gift, and keep quiet about this. Off with you! Nanon will bring back the barrow. Nanon!" cried Grandet, "are the women-folk gone to mass?"

"Yes, sir."

"Come, look sharp and lend a hand here, then," he cried, and loaded her with the bags. In another minute the crowns were safely transferred to his room, where he locked himself in.

"Thump on the wall when breakfast is ready," he called through the door, "and take the wheelbarrow back to the coach office."

It was ten o'clock before the family breakfasted.

"Your father will not ask to see your gold now," said Mme. Grandet as they came back from mass; "and if he does, you can shiver and say it is too cold to go upstairs for it. We shall time to make up the money again before your birthday . . ."

Grandet came down the stairs with his head full of schemes for transforming the five-franc pieces just received from Paris into gold coin, which should be neither clipped nor light weight. He thought of his admirably-timed investment in Government stock, and made up his mind that he would continue to put his money into consols until they rose to a hundred francs. Such meditations as these boded ill for Eugénie. As soon as he came in the two women wished him a prosperous New Year, each in her own way; Mme. Grandet was grave and ceremonious, but his daughter put her arms round his neck and kissed him. "Aha! child," he said, kissing her on both cheeks, "I am thinking and working for you, you see! . . . I want you to be happy and if you are to be happy, you must have money; for you won't get anything without it. Look! here is a brand new napoleon, I sent to Paris on purpose for it. *Nom d'un petit bonhomme!* there is not a speck of gold in the house, except yours, you are the one who has the gold. Let me see your gold, little girl."

"Bah! it is too cold, let us have breakfast," Eugénie answered.

"Well, then, after breakfast we will have a look at it, eh? It will be good for our digestions. That great des Grassins sent us this, all the same," he went on, "so get your breakfasts, children, for it costs us nothing. Des Grassins is going on nicely; I am pleased with him; the old fish is doing Charles a service, and all free gratis. Really, he is managing poor dear Grandet's affairs very cleverly. Ououh! ououh!" he cried, with his mouth full, "this is good! Eat away, wife; there is enough here to last us for two days at least."

"I am not hungry. I am very poorly, you know that very well."

"Oh! Ah! but you have a sound constitution; you are a La Bertellière, and you can put away a great deal without any fear of damaging yourself. You may be a trifle sallow, but I have a liking for yellow myself."

The prisoner shrinking from a public and ignominious death could not well await his doom with a more sickening dread than Mme. Grandet and Eugénie felt as they foresaw the end of breakfast and the inevitable sequel. The more boisterously the cooper talked and ate, the lower sank their spirits; but to the girl, in this crisis, a certain support was not lacking, love was strong within her. "I would die a thousand deaths," she thought, "for him, for him!"

She looked at her mother, and courage and defiance shone in her eyes.

By eleven o'clock they had finished breakfast. "Clear everything away," Grandet told Nanon, "but leave us the table. We can look over your little treasure more comfortably so," he said with his eyes on Eugénie. *"Little,* said I? 'Tis not so small, though, upon my word. Your coins altogether are actually worth five thousand nine hundred and fifty-nine francs, then with forty more this morning, that makes six thousand francs all but one. Well, I will give you another franc to make up the sum, because, you see, little girl . . . Well! now, why are you listening to us? Just take yourself off, Nanon, and set about your work!"

Nanon vanished.

"Listen, Eugénie, you must let me have your gold. You will not refuse to let your papa have it? Eh, little daughter?"

Neither of the women spoke.

"I myself have no gold left. I had some once, but I have none now. I will give you six thousand francs in silver for it, and you shall invest it; I will show you how. There is really no need to think of a *dozen.* When you are married (which will be before very long) I will find a husband for you who will give you the handsomest *dozen* that has ever been heard of hereabouts. There is a splendid opportunity just now; you can invest your six thousand francs in Government stock, and every six months, when dividends are due, you will have about two hundred francs coming in, all clear of taxes, and no repairs to pay for, and no frosts nor hail nor bad seasons, none of all the tiresome drawbacks you have to lay your account with if you put your money into land. You don't like to part with your gold, eh? Is that it, little girl? Never mind, let me have it all the same. I will look out for gold coins for you, ducats from Holland, and genovines and Portuguese moidores and rupees, the Mogul's rupees; and what with the coins I shall give you on your birthday and so forth, you will have half your little hoard again in three years' time, besides the three thousand francs in the funds. What do you say, little girl? Look up, child! There! there! bring it here, my pet. You owe me a good kiss for telling you business secrets and mysteries of the life and death of five-franc pieces. Five-franc pieces! Yes, indeed, the coins live and gad about just like men do; they go and come and sweat and multiply."

Eugénie rose and made a few steps towards the door; then she turned abruptly, looked her father full in the face, and said—

"All *my* gold is gone; I have none left."

"All your gold is gone!" echoed Grandet, starting up, as a horse might rear when the cannon thunders not ten paces from him.

"Yes, it is all gone."

"Eugénie! you are dreaming!"

"No."

"By my father's pruning-hook!" Whenever the cooper swore in this fashion, the floors and ceilings trembled.

"Lord have mercy!" cried Nanon; "how white the mistress is!"

"Grandet, you will kill me with your angry fits," said the poor wife.

"Tut, tut, tut; none of your family ever die. Now, Eugénie! what have you done with your money?" he burst out as he turned upon her.

The girl was on her knees beside Mme. Grandet.

"Look! sir," she said, "my mother is very ill . . . do not kill her."

Grandet was alarmed; his wife's dark, sallow complexion had grown so white.

"Nanon, come and help me up to bed," she said in a feeble voice. "This is killing me . . ."

Nanon gave an arm to her mistress, and Eugénie supported her on the other side; but it was only with the greatest difficulty that they reached her room, for the poor mother's strength completely failed her, and she stumbled at every step. Grandet was left alone in the parlor. After a while, however, he came part of the way upstairs, and called out—

"Eugénie! Come down again as soon as your mother is in bed."

"Yes, father."

In no long time she returned to him, after comforting her mother as best she could.

"Now, my daughter," Grandet addressed her, "you will tell me where your money is."

"If I am not perfectly free to do as I like with your presents, father, please take them back again," said Eugénie coldly. She went to the chimney-piece for the napoleon, and gave it to her father.

Grandet pounced upon it, and slipped it into his waistcoat pocket.

"I will never give you anything again, I know," he said, biting his thumb at her. "You look down on your father, do you? You have no confidence in him? Do you know what a father is? If he is not everything to you, he is nothing. *Now;* where is your gold?"

"I do respect you and love you, father, in spite of your anger; but I would very humbly point out to you that I am twenty-two years old. You have told me that I am of age often enough for me to know it. I have done as I liked with my money, and rest assured that it is in good hands——"

"Whose?"

"That is an inviolable secret," she said. "Have you not your secrets?"

"Am I not the head of my family? May I not be allowed to have my own business affairs?"

"This is my own affair."

"It must be something very unsatisfactory, Mlle. Grandet, if you cannot tell your own father about it."

"It is perfectly satisfactory, and I cannot tell my father about it."

"Tell me, at any rate, when you parted with your gold."

Eugénie shook her head.

"You still had it on your birthday, hadn't you? Eh?"

But if greed had made her father crafty, love had taught Eugénie to be wary; she shook her head again.

"Did any one ever hear of such obstinacy, or of such a robbery?" cried Grandet, in a voice which gradually rose till it rang through the house. "What! *here,* in my house, in my own house, some one has taken your gold! Taken all the gold that there was in the place! And I am not to know who it was? Gold is a precious thing. The best of girls go wrong and throw themselves away one way or another; that happens among great folk, and even among decent citizens; but think of throwing gold away! For you gave it to somebody, I suppose, eh?"

Eugénie gave no sign.

"Did any one ever see such a daughter! Can you be a child of mine? If you have parted with your money, you must have a receipt for it——"

"Was I free to do as I wished with it—Yes or No? Was it mine?"

"Why, you are a child."

"I am of age."

At first Grandet was struck dumb by his daughter daring to argue with him, and in this way! He turned pale, stamped, swore, and finding words at last, he shouted—

"Accursed serpent! Miserable girl! Oh! you know well that I love you, and you take advantage of it! You un-

grateful child! She would rob and murder her own father!
Pardieu! you would have thrown all we have at the feet of
that vagabond with the morocco boots. By my father's
pruning-hook, I cannot disinherit you, but *nom d'un tonneau,*
I can curse you; you and your cousin and your children.
Nothing good can come out of this; do you hear? If it was
to Charles that . . . But, no, that is impossible. What
if that miserable puppy should have robbed me?"

He glared at his daughter, who was still silent and un-
moved.

"She does not stir! She does not flinch! She is more of
a Grandet than I am. You did not give your gold away for
nothing, anyhow. Come, now; tell me about it?"

Eugénie looked up at her father; her satirical glance exas-
perated him.

"Eugénie, this is my house; so long as you are under your
father's roof you must do as your father bids you. The
priests command you to obey me."

Eugénie bent her head again.

"You are wounding all my tenderest feelings," he went on.
"Get out of my sight until you are ready to obey me. Go
to your room and stay there until I give you leave to come
out of it. Nanon will bring you bread and water. Do you
hear what I say? Go!"

Eugénie burst into tears, and fled away to her mother.
Grandet took several turns in his garden without heeding the
snow or the cold; then, suspecting that his daughter would
be in his wife's room, and delighted with the idea of catching
them in flagrant disobedience to orders, he climbed the stairs
as stealthily as a cat, and suddenly appeared in Mme. Grandet's room. He was right; she was stroking Eugénie's hair,
and the girl lay with her face hidden in her mother's breast.

"Poor child! Never mind, your father will relent."

"She has no longer a father!" said the cooper. "Is it
really possible, Mme. Grandet, that we have brought such a
disobedient daughter into the world? A pretty bringing up;
and pious, too, above all things! Well! how is it you are

not in your room? Come, off to prison with you; to prison, miss."

"Do you mean to take my daughter away from me, sir?" said Mme. Grandet, as she raised a flushed face and bright, feverish eyes.

"If you want to keep her, take her along with you, and the house will be rid of you both at once. . . . *Tonnerre!* Where is the gold? What has become of the gold?"

Eugénie rose to her feet, looked proudly at her father, and went into her room; the goodman turned the key in the door.

"Nanon!" he shouted, "you can rake out the fire in the parlor;" then he came back and sat down in an easy-chair that stood between the fire and his wife's bedside, saying as he did so, "Of course she gave her gold to that miserable seducer Charles, who only cared for our money."

Mme. Grandet's love for her daughter gave her courage in the face of this danger; to all appearance she was deaf, dumb, and blind to all that was implied by this speech. She turned on her bed so as to avoid the angry glitter of her husband's eyes.

"I knew nothing about all this," she said. "Your anger makes me so ill, that if my forebodings come true I shall only leave this room when they carry me out feet foremost. I think you might have spared me this scene, sir. I, at all events, have never caused you any vexation. Your daughter loves you, and I am sure she is as innocent as a new-born babe; so do not make her miserable, and take back your word. This cold is terribly sharp; it might make her seriously ill."

"I shall neither see her nor speak to her. She shall stop in her room on bread and water until she has done as her father bids her. What the devil! the head of a family ought to know when gold goes out of his house, and where it goes. She had the only rupees that there are in France, for aught I know; then there were genovines besides, and Dutch ducats——"

"Eugénie is our only child, and even if she had flung them into the water——"

"Do you hear what I say?   Go!"

"Into the water!" shouted the worthy cooper. *"Into the water!* Mme. Grandet, you are raving! When I say a thing, I mean it, as you know. If you want to have peace in the house, get her to confess to you, and worm this secret out of her. Women understand each other, and are cleverer at this sort of thing than we are. Whatever she may have done, I certainly shall not eat her. Is she afraid of me? If she had covered her cousin with gold from head to foot, he is safe on the high seas by this time, hein? We cannot run after him——"

"Really, sir . . ." his wife began.

But Mme. Grandet's nature had developed during her daughter's trouble; she felt more keenly, and perhaps her thoughts moved more quickly, or it may be that excitement and the strain upon her over-wrought nerves had sharpened her mental faculties. She saw the wen on her husband's face twitch ominously even as she began to speak, and changed her purpose without changing her voice.

"Really, sir, have I any more authority over her than you have? She has never said a word about it to me She takes after you."

"Goodness! your tongue is hung in the middle this morning! Tut, tut, tut; you are going to fly in my face, I suppose? Perhaps you and she are both in it."

He glared at his wife.

"Really, M. Grandet, if you want to kill me, you have only to keep on as you are doing. I tell you, sir, and if it were to cost me my life, I would say it again—you are too hard on your daughter; she is a great deal more sensible than you are. The money belonged to her; she could only have made a good use of it, and our good works ought to be known to God alone. Sir, I implore you, take Eugénie back into favor. It will lessen the effect of the shock your anger gave me, and perhaps will save my life. My daughter, sir; give me back my daughter!"

"I am off," he said. "It is unbearable here in my house, when a mother and daughter talk and argue as if . . .

Brooouh! Pouah! You have given me bitter New Year's gifts, Eugénie!" he called. "Yes, yes, cry away! You shall repent it, do you hear? What is the good of taking the sacrament six times a quarter if you give your father's gold away on the sly to an idle rascal who will break your heart when you have nothing else left to give him? You will find out what he is, that Charles of yours, with his morocco boots and his stand-off airs. He can have no heart and no conscience either, when he dares to carry off a poor girl's money without the consent of her parents."

As soon as the street-door was shut, Eugénie stole out of her room and came to her mother's bedside.

"You were very brave for your daughter's sake," she said.

"You see where crooked ways lead us, child! . . . You have made me tell a lie."

"Oh! mother, I will pray to God to let all the punishment fall on me."

"Is it true?" asked Nanon, coming upstairs in dismay, "that mademoiselle here is to be put on bread and water for the rest of her life?"

"What does it matter, Nanon?" asked Eugénie calmly.

"Why, before I would eat 'kitchen' while the daughter of the house is eating dry bread, I would . . . no, no, it won't do."

"Don't say a word about it, Nanon," Eugénie warned her.

"It would stick in my throat; but you shall see."

Grandet dined alone for the first time in twenty-four years.

"So you are a widower, sir," said Nanon. "It is a very dismal thing to be a widower when you have a wife and daughter in the house."

"I did not speak to you, did I? Keep a still tongue in your head, or you will have to go. What have you in that saucepan that I can hear boiling away on the stove?"

"Some dripping that I am melting down—— "

"There will be some people here this evening; light the fire."

The Cruchots and their friends, Mme. des Grassins and

her son, all came in about eight o'clock, and to their amazement saw neither Mme. Grandet nor her daughter.

"My wife is not very well to-day, and Eugénie is upstairs with her," replied the old cooper, without a trace of perturbation on his face.

After an hour spent in more or less trivial talk, Mme. des Grassins, who had gone upstairs to see Mme. Grandet, came down again to the dining-room, and was met with a general inquiry of "How is Mme. Grandet?"

"She is very far from well," the lady said gravely. "Her health seems to me to be in a very precarious state. At her time of life you ought to take great care of her, papa Grandet."

"We shall see," said the vinegrower abstractedly, and the whole party took leave of him. As soon as the Cruchots were out in the street and the door was shut behind them, Mme. des Grassins turned to them and said, "Something has happened among the Grandets. The mother is very ill; she herself has no idea how ill she is, and the girl's eyes are red, as if she had been crying for a long while. Are they wanting to marry her against her will?"

That night, when the cooper had gone to bed, Nanon, in list slippers, stole up to Eugénie's room, and displayed a raised pie, which she had managed to bake in a saucepan.

"Here, mademoiselle," said the kind soul, "Cornoiller brought a hare for me. You eat so little that the pie will last you for quite a week, and there is no fear of its spoiling in this frost. You shall not live on dry bread, at any rate; it is not at all good for you."

"Poor Nanon!" said Eugénie, as she pressed the girl's hand.

"I have made it very dainty and nice, and *he* never found out about it. I paid for the lard and the bay-leaves out of my six francs; I can surely do as I like with my own money," and the old servant fled, thinking that she heard Grandet stirring.

Several months went by. The cooper went to see his wife at various times in the day, and never mentioned his daughter's name—never saw her, nor made the slightest allusion to her. Mme. Grandet's health grew worse and worse; she had not once left her room since that terrible January morning. But nothing shook the old cooper's determination; he was hard, cold, and unyielding as a block of granite. He came and went, his manner of life was in nowise altered; but he did not stammer now, and he talked less; perhaps, too, in matters of business, people found him harder than before, but errors crept into his book-keeping.

Something had certainly happened in the Grandet family, both Cruchotins and Grassinistes were agreed on that head; and "What can be the matter with the Grandets?" became a stock question which people asked each other at every social gathering in Saumur.

Eugénie went regularly to church, escorted by Nanon. If Mme. des Grassins spoke to her in the porch as she came out, the girl would answer evasively, and the lady's curiosity remained ungratified. But after two months spent in this fashion it was almost impossible to hide the real state of affairs from Mme. des Grassins or from the Cruchots; a time came when all pretexts were exhausted, and Eugénie's constant absence still demanded an explanation. A little later, though no one could say how or when the secret leaked out, it became common property, and the whole town knew that ever since New Year's Day Mlle. Grandet had been locked up in her room by her father's orders, and that there she lived on bread and water in solitary confinement, and without a fire. Nanon, it was reported, cooked dainties for her, and brought food secretly to her room at night. Further particulars were known. It was even said that only when Grandet was out of the house could the young girl nurse her mother, or indeed see her at all.

People blamed Grandet severely. He was regarded as an outlaw, as it were, by the whole town; all his hardness, his bad faith was remembered against him, and every one shunned him. They whispered and pointed at him as he went by; and as his daughter passed along the crooked street on her way to mass or to vespers, with Nanon at her side, people would hurry to their windows and look curiously at the wealthy heiress' face—a face so sad and so divinely sweet.

The town gossip reached her ears as slowly as it reached her father's. Her imprisonment and her father's displeasure were as nothing to her; had she not her map of the world? And from her window could she not see the little bench, the old wall, and the garden walks? Was not the sweetness of those past kisses still upon her lips? So, sustained by love and by the consciousness of her innocence in the sight of God, she could patiently endure her solitary life and her father's anger; but there was another sorrow, so deep and so overwhelming that Eugénie could not find a refuge from it. The gentle, patient mother was gradually passing away; it seemed as if the beauty of her soul shone out more and more brightly in those dark days as she drew nearer to the tomb. Eugénie often bitterly blamed herself for this illness, telling herself that she had been the innocent cause of the painful malady that was slowly consuming her mother's life; and, in spite of all her mother said to comfort her, this remorseful feeling made her cling more closely to the love she was to lose so soon. Every morning, as soon as her father had left the house, she went to sit at her mother's bedside. Nanon used to bring her breakfast to her there. But for poor Eugénie in her sadness, this suffering was almost more than she could bear; she looked at her mother's face, and then at Nanon, with tears in her eyes, and was dumb; she did not dare to speak of her cousin now. It was always Mme. Grandet who began to talk of him; it was she who was forced to say, "Where is _he_? Why does _he_ not write?"

Neither mother nor daughter had any idea of the distance.

"Let us think of him without talking about him, mother," Eugénie would answer. "You are suffering; you come before every one;" and when she said, "every one," Eugénie meant "_him._"

"I have no wish to live any longer, children," Mme. Grandet used to say. "God in His protecting care has led me to look forward joyfully to death as the end of my sorrows."

Everything that she said was full of Christian piety. For the first few months of the year her husband breakfasted in her room, and always, as he walked restlessly about, he heard the same words from her, uttered with angelic gentleness, but with firmness; the near approach of death had given her the courage which she had lacked all her life.

"Thank you, sir, for the interest which you take in my health," she said in response to the merest formality of an inquiry; "but if you really wish to sweeten the bitterness of my last moments, and to alleviate my sufferings, forgive our daughter, and act like a Christian, a husband, and a father."

At these words Grandet would come and sit down by the bed, much as a man who is threatened by a shower betakes himself resignedly to the nearest sheltering archway. He would say nothing, and his wife might say what she liked. To the most pathetic, loving, and fervent prayers, he would reply, "My poor wife, you are looking a bit pale to-day."

His daughter seemed to have passed entirely out of his mind; the mention of her name brought no change over his stony face and hard-set mouth. He always gave the same vague answers to her pleadings, couched in almost the same words, and did not heed his wife's white face, nor the tears that flowed down her cheeks.

"May God forgive you, as I do, sir," she said. "You will have need of mercy some day."

Since his wife's illness had begun he had not ventured to make use of his formidable "Tut, tut, tut," but his tyranny was not relaxed one whit by his wife's angelic gentleness.

Her plain face was growing almost beautiful now as a beautiful nature showed itself more and more, and her soul grew absolute. It seemed as if the spirit of prayer had purified and refined the homely features—as if they were lit up by some inner light. Which of us has not known such faces as this, and seen their final transfiguration—the triumph of a soul that has dwelt for so long among pure and lofty thoughts that they set their seal unmistakably upon the roughest lineaments at last? The sight of this transformation wrought by the physical suffering which stripped the soul of the rags of humanity that hid it, had a certain effect, however feeble, upon that man of bronze—the old cooper. A stubborn habit of silence had succeeded to his old contemptuous ways, a wish to keep up his dignity as a father of a family was apparently the motive for this course.

The faithful Nanon no sooner showed herself in the market place than people began to rail at her master and to make jokes at his expense; but however loudly public opinion condemned old Grandet, the maid-servant, jealous for the honor of the family, stoutly defended him.

"Well, now," she would say to those who spoke ill of her master, "don't we all grow harder as we grow older? And would you have him different from other people? Just hold your lying tongues. Mademoiselle lives like a queen. She is all by herself no doubt, but she likes it; and my master and mistress have their very good reasons for what they do."

At last, one evening towards the end of spring, Mme. Grandet, feeling that this trouble, even more than her illness, was shortening her days, and that any further attempt on her part to obtain forgiveness for Eugénie was hopeless, confided her troubles to the Cruchots.

"To put a girl of twenty-three on a diet of bread and water! . . ." cried the President de Bonfons, "and without just and sufficient cause! Why, that constitutes legal cruelty; she might lodge a complaint; *in as much as——*"

"Come, nephew," said the notary, "that is enough of your law court jargon. Be easy, madame; I will bring this imprisonment to an end to-morrow."

Eugénie heard, and came out of her room.

"Gentlemen," she said, impelled by a certain pride, "do nothing in this matter, I beg of you. My father is master in his own house, and so long as I live under his roof I ought to obey him. No one has any right to criticise his conduct; he is

answerable to God, and to God alone. If you have any friendly
feeling for me, I entreat you to say nothing whatever about
this. If you expose my father to censure, you would lower
us all in the eyes of the world. I am very thankful to you,
gentlemen, for the interest you have taken in me, and you
will oblige me still further if you will put a stop to the gossip
that is going on in the town. I only heard of it by accident."

"She is right," said Mme. Grandet.

"Mademoiselle, the best possible way to stop people's talk
would be to set you at liberty," said the old notary respect-
fully; he was struck with the beauty which solitude and love
and sadness had brought into Eugénie's face.

"Well, Eugénie, leave it in M. Cruchot's hands, as he seems
to think success is certain. He knows your father, and he
knows, too, how to put the matter before him. You and your
father must be reconciled at all costs, if you want me to be
happy during the little time I have yet to live."

The next morning Grandet went out to take a certain
number of turns round the little garden, a habit that he had
fallen into during Eugénie's incarceration. He chose to
take the air while Eugénie was dressing; and when he had
reached the great walnut tree, he stood behind it for a few
moments and looked at her window. He watched her as she
brushed her long hair, and there was a sharp struggle doubtless, between his natural stubborn will and a longing to take
his daughter in his arms and kiss her.

He would often go to sit on the little worm-eaten bench
where Charles and Eugénie had vowed to love each other forever; and she, his daughter, also watched her father fur-
tively, or looked into her glass and saw him reflected there,
and the garden and the bench. If he rose and began to walk
again, she went to sit in the window. It was pleasant to her
to be there. She studied the bit of old wall, the delicate
sprays of wild flowers that grew in its crevices, the maiden-
hair fern, the morning glories, and a little plant with thick
leaves and white or yellow flowers, a sort of stone-crop that
grows everywhere among the vines at Saumur and Tours.

Old M. Cruchot came early on a bright June morning and found the vinegrower sitting on the little bench with his back against the wall, absorbed in watching his daughter.

"What can I do for you, M. Cruchot?" he asked, as he became aware of the notary's presence.

"I have come about a matter of business."

"Aha! Have you some gold to exchange for crowns?"

"No, no. It is not a question of money this time, but of your daughter Eugénie. Everybody is talking about you and her."

"What business is it of theirs? A man's house is his castle."

"Just so; and a man can kill himself if he has a mind, or he can do worse, he can throw his money out of the windows."

"What?"

"Eh! but your wife is very ill, my friend. You ought even to call in M. Bergerin, her life is in danger. If she were to die for want of proper care, you would hear of it, I am sure."

"Tut, tut, tut! you know what is the matter with her, and when once one of these doctors sets foot in your house, they will come five or six times a day."

"After all, Grandet, you will do as you think best. We are old friends; there is no one in all Saumur who has your interests more at heart than I, so it was only my duty to let you know this. Whatever happens, you are responsible, and you understand your own business, so there it is. Besides, that was not what I came to speak about. There is something else more serious for you, perhaps; for, after all, you do not wish to kill your wife, she is too useful to you. Just think what your position would be if anything happened to Mme. Grandet; you would have your daughter to face. You would have to give an account to Eugénie of her mother's share of your joint estate; and if she chose, your daughter might demand her mother's fortune, for she, and not you, will succeed to it; and in that case, you might have to sell Froidfond."

Cruchot's words were like a bolt from the blue; for much as the worthy cooper knew about business, he knew very little law. The idea of a forced sale had never occurred to him.

"So I should strongly recommend you to treat her kindly," the notary concluded.

"But do you know what she has done, Cruchot?"

"No. What was it?" asked the notary; he felt curious to know the reason of the quarrel, and a confidence from old Grandet was an interesting novelty.

"She has given away her gold."

"Oh! well, it belonged to her, didn't it?"

"That is what they all say!" said the goodman, letting his arms fall with a tragic gesture.

"And for a trifle like that you would not shut yourself out from all hope of any concessions which you will want her to make if her mother dies?"

"Ah! do you call six thousand francs in gold a trifle?"

"Eh! my old friend, have you any idea what it will cost you to have your property valued and divided if Eugénie should compel you to do so?"

"What would it cost?"

"Two, three, or even four thousand francs. How could you know what it is worth unless you put it up to public auction? While if you come to an understanding——"

"By my father's pruning-hook!" cried the vinegrower, sinking back, and turning quite pale. "We will see about this, Cruchot."

After a moment of agony or of dumb bewilderment, the worthy man spoke, with his eyes fixed on his neighbor's face. "Life is very hard!" he said. "It is full of troubles. Cruchot," he went on, earnestly, "you are incapable of deceiving me; give me your word of honor that this ditty of yours has a solid foundation. Let me look at the Code; I want to see the Code!"

"My poor friend," said the notary, "I ought to understand my own profession."

"Then it is really true? I shall be plundered, cheated, robbed, and murdered by my own daughter!"

"She is her mother's heiress."

"Then what is the good of having children? Oh! my wife, I love my wife; luckily she has a sound constitution; she is a La Bertellière."

"She has not a month to live."

The cooper struck his forehead, took a few paces, and then came back again.

"What is to be done?" he demanded of Cruchot, with a tragic expression on his face.

"Well, perhaps Eugénie might simply give up her claims to her mother's property. You do not mean to disinherit her, do you? But do not treat her harshly if you want her to make a concession of that kind. I am speaking against my own interests, my friend. How do I make a living but by drawing up inventories and conveyances and deeds of arrangement and by winding up estates?"

"We shall see, we shall see. Let us say no more about this now, Cruchot. You have wrung my very soul. Have you taken any gold lately?"

"No; but I have some old louis, nine or ten perhaps, which you can have. Look here, my good friend, make it up with Eugénie; all Saumur is pointing a finger at you."

"The rogues!"

"Well, consols have risen to ninety-nine, so you should be satisfied for once in your life."

"At ninety-nine, Cruchot?"

"Yes."

"Hey! hey! ninety-nine!" the old man said, as he went with the notary to the street door. He felt too much agitated by what he had just heard to stay quietly at home; so he went up to his wife's room.

"Come, mother, you may spend the day with your daughter, I am going to Froidfond. Be good, both of you, while I am away. This is our wedding day, dear wife.—Stay! here are ten crowns for you, for the Fête-Dieu procession; you have wanted to give it for long enough. Take a holiday! have some fun, keep up your spirits and get well. *Vive la joie!*"

He threw down ten crowns of six francs each upon the bed, took her face in his hands, and kissed her on the forehead.

"You are feeling better, dear wife, are you not?"

"But how can you think of receiving God, who forgives, into your house, when you have shut your heart against your daughter?" she said, with deep feeling in her voice.

"Tut, tut, tut!" said the father soothingly; "we will see about that."

"Merciful heaven! Eugénie!" called her mother, her face flushed with joy; "Eugénie, come and give your father a kiss, you are forgiven!" But her worthy father had vanished. He fled with all his might in the direction of his vineyards, where he set himself to the task of constructing his new world out of this chaos of strange ideas.

Grandet had just entered upon his sixty-seventh year. Avarice had gained a stronger hold upon him during the past two years of his life; indeed, all lasting passions grow with man's growth; and it had come to pass with him, as with all men whose lives are ruled by one master-idea, that he clung with all the force of his imagination to the symbol which represented that idea for him. Gold—to have gold, that he might see and touch it, had become with him a perfect monomania. His disposition to tyrannize had also grown with his love of money, and it seemed to him to be *monstrous* that he should be called upon to give up the least portion of his property on the death of his wife. Was he to render an account of her fortune, and to have an inventory drawn up of everything he possessed—personalty and real estate, and put it all up to auction?

"That would be stark ruin," he said aloud to himself, as he stood among his vines and examined their stems.

He made up his mind at last, and came back to Saumur at dinner time fully determined on his course. He would humor Eugénie, and coax and cajole her so that he might die royally, keeping the control of his millions in his hands until his latest sigh. It happened that he let himself in with his master key; he crept noiselessly as a wolf up the stairs to his wife's room, which he entered just as Eugénie was setting the dressing-case, in all its golden glory, upon her mother's bed. The two women had stolen a pleasure in Grandet's absence; they were looking at the portraits and tracing out Charles' features in his mother's likeness.

"It is just his forehead and his mouth!" Eugénie was saying, as the vinegrower opened the door.

Mme. Grandet saw how her husband's eyes darted upon the gold. "Oh! God have pity upon us!" she cried.

The vinegrower seized upon the dressing-case as a tiger might spring upon a sleeping child.

"What may this be?" he said, carrying off the treasure to the window, where he ensconced himself with it. "Gold! solid gold!" he cried, "and plenty of it too; there is a couple of pounds' weight here. Aha! so this was what Charles gave you in exchange for your pretty gold pieces! Why did you not tell me? It was a good stroke of business, little girl. You are your father's own daughter, I see. (Eugénie trembled from head to foot.) This belongs to Charles, doesn't it?" the goodman went on.

"Yes, father; it is not mine. That case is a sacred trust."

"Tut, tut, tut! he has gone off with your money; you ought to make good the loss of your little treasure."

"Oh! father! . . ."

The old man had taken out his pocket-knife, with a view to wrenching away a plate of the precious metal, and for the moment had been obliged to lay the case on a chair beside him. Eugénie sprang forward to secure her treasure; but the cooper, who had kept an eye upon his daughter as well as upon the casket, put out his arm to prevent this, and thrust her back so roughly that she fell on to the bed.

"Sir! sir!" cried the mother, rising and sitting upright.

Grandet had drawn out his knife, and was about to insert the blade beneath the plate.

"Father!" cried Eugénie, going down on her knees and dragging herself nearer to him as she knelt; "father, in the name of all the saints, and the Holy Virgin, for the sake of

Christ who died on the cross, for your own soul's salvation, father, if you have any regard for my life, do not touch it! The case is not yours, and it is not mine. It belongs to an unhappy kinsman, who gave it into my keeping, and I ought to give it back to him untouched."

"What do you look at it for if it is a deposit? Looking at it is worse than touching it."

"Do not pull it to pieces, father! You will bring dishonor upon me. Father! do you hear me?"

"For pity's sake, sir!" entreated the mother.

"Father!"

The shrill cry rang through the house and brought the frightened Nanon upstairs. Eugénie caught up a knife that lay within her reach.

"Well?" said Grandet, calmly, with a cold smile on his lips.

"Sir! you are killing me!" said the mother.

"Father, if you cut away a single scrap of gold, I shall stab myself with this knife. It is your doing that my mother is dying, and now my death will also be laid at your door. It shall be wound for wound."

Grandet held his knife suspended above the case, looked at his daughter, and hesitated.

"Would you really do it, Eugénie?" he asked.

"Yes, sir!" said the mother.

"She would do as she says," cried Nanon. "Do be sensible, sir, for once in your life."

The cooper wavered for a moment, looking first at the gold, and then at his daughter.

Mme. Grandet fainted.

"There! sir, you see, the mistress is dying," cried Nanon.

"There! there! child, do not let us fall out about a box. Just take it back!" cried the cooper hastily, throwing the case on to the bed. "And, Nanon, go for M. Bergerin. Come! come! mother," he said, and he kissed his wife's hand; "never mind, there! there! we have made it up, haven't we, little girl? No more dry bread; you shall eat whatever you

like . . . Ah! she is opening her eyes. Well, now, little
mother, dear little mother, don't take on so! Look! I am
going to kiss Eugénie! She loves her cousin, does she? She
shall marry him if she likes; she shall keep his little case for
him. But you must live for a long while yet, my poor wife!
Come! turn your head a little. Listen! you shall have the
finest altar at the Fête-Dieu that has ever been seen in Saumur."

"Oh! *mon Dieu!* how can you treat your wife and daughter in this way!" moaned Mme. Grandet.

"I will never do so again, never again!" cried the cooper.
"You shall see, my poor wife."

He went to his strong room and returned with a handful
of louis d'or, which he scattered on the coverlet.

"There! Eugénie, there! wife, those are for you," he said,
fingering the gold coins as they lay. "Come! cheer up, and
get well, you shall want for nothing, neither you nor Eugénie. There are a hundred louis for her. You will not give
them away, will you, eh, Eugénie?"

Mme. Grandet and her daughter gazed at each other in
amazement.

"Take back the money, father; we want nothing, nothing
but your love."

"Oh! well, just as you like," he said, as he pocketed the
louis, "let us live together like good friends. Let us all go
down to the dining-room and have dinner, and play loto
every evening, and put our two sous into the pool, and be as
merry as the maids. Eh! my wife?"

"Alas! how I wish that I could, if you would like it," said
the dying woman, "but I am not strong enough to get up."

"Poor mother!" said the cooper, "you do not know ·how
much I love you; and you too, child!"

He drew his daughter to him and embraced her with
fervor.

"Oh! how pleasant it is to kiss one's daughter after a
squabble, my little girl! There! mother, do you see? We are
quite at one again now. Just go and lock that away," he said

to Eugénie, as he pointed to the case. "There! there! don't be frightened; I will never say another word to you about it."

M. Bergerin, who was regarded as the cleverest doctor in Saumur, came before very long. He told Grandet plainly after the interview that the patient was very seriously ill; that any excitement might be fatal to her; that with a light diet, perfect tranquillity, and the most constant care, her life might possibly be prolonged until the end of the autumn.

"Will it be an expensive illness?" asked the worthy householder. "Will she want a lot of physic?"

"Not much physic, but very careful nursing," answered the doctor, who could not help smiling.

"After all, M. Bergerin, you are a man of honor," said Grandet uneasily. "I can depend upon you, can I not? Come and see my wife whenever, and as often as you think it really necessary. Preserve her life. My good wife—I am very fond of her, you see, though I may not show it; it is all shut up inside me, and I am one that takes things terribly to heart; I am in trouble too. It all began with my brother's death; I am spending, oh!—heaps of money in Paris for him, —the very eyes out of my head in fact, and it seems as if there were no end to it. Good day, sir. If you can save my wife, save her, even if it takes a hundred, or two hundred francs."

In spite of Grandet's fervent wishes that his wife might be restored to health, for this question of the inheritance was like a foretaste of death for him; in spite of his readiness to fulfil the least wishes of the astonished mother and daughter in every possible way; in spite of Eugénie's tenderest and most devoted care, it was evident that Mme. Grandet's life was rapidly drawing to a close. Day by day she grew weaker, and, as often happens at her time of life, she had no strength to resist the disease that was wasting her away. She seemed to have no more vitality than the autumn leaves; and as the sunlight shining through the leaves turns them to gold, so she seemed to be transformed by the light of heaven. Her death was a fitting close to her life, a death wholly Christian;

is not that saying that it was sublime? Her love for her daughter, her meek virtues, her angelic patience, had never shone more brightly than in that month of October, 1822, when she passed away. All through her illness she had never uttered the slightest complaint, and her spotless soul left earth for heaven with but one regret—for the daughter whose sweet companionship had been the solace of her dreary life, and for whom her dying eyes foresaw troubles and sorrows manifold. She trembled at the thought of this lamb, spotless as she herself was, left alone in the world among selfish beings who sought to despoil her of her fleece, her treasure.

"There is no happiness save in heaven," she said just before she died;'you will know that one day, my child."

On the morrow after her mother's death, it seemed to Eugénie that she had yet one more reason for clinging fondly to the old house where she had been born, and where she had found life so hard of late—it became for her the place where her mother had died. She could not see the old chair set on little blocks of wood, the place by the window where her mother used to sit, without shedding tears. Her father showed her such tenderness, and took such care of her, that she began to think that she had never understood his nature; he used to come to her room and take her down to breakfast on his arm, and sit looking at her for whole hours with something almost like kindness in his eyes, with the same brooding look that he gave his gold. Indeed, the old cooper almost trembled before his daughter, and was altogether so unlike himself, that Nanon and the Cruchotins wondered at these signs of weakness, and set it down to his advanced age; they began to fear that the old man's mind was giving way. But when the day came on which the family began to wear their mourning, M. Cruchot, who alone was in his client's confidence, was invited to dinner, and these mysteries were explained. Grandet waited till the table had been cleared, and the doors carefully shut.

Then he began. "My dear child, you are your mother's heiress, and there are some little matters of business that we must settle between us. Is not that so, eh, Cruchot?"

"Yes."

"Is it really pressing; must it be settled to-day, father?"

"Yes, yes, little girl. I could not endure this suspense any longer, and I am sure that you would not make things hard for me."

"Oh! father——"

"Well, then, everything must be decided to-night."

"Then what do you want me to do?"

"Why, little girl, it is not for me to tell you. You tell her, Cruchot."

"Mademoiselle, your father wants neither to divide nor to sell his property, nor to pay a heavy succession duty upon the ready money he may happen to have just now. So if these complications are to be avoided, there must be no inventory made out, and all the property must remain undivided for the present——"

"Cruchot, are you quite sure of what you are saying that you talk in this way before a child?"

"Let me say what I have to say, Grandet."

"Yes, yes, my friend. Neither you nor my daughter would plunder me. You would not plunder me, would you, little girl?"

"But what am I to do, M. Cruchot?" asked Eugénie, losing patience.

"Well," said the notary, "you must sign this deed, by which you renounce your claims to your mother's property; the property would be secured to you, but your father would have the use of it for his life, and there would be no need to make a division now."

"I understand nothing of all this that you are saying," Eugénie answered; "give me the deed, and show me where I am to sign my name."

Grandet looked from the document to his daughter, and again from his daughter to the document. His agitation was so great that he actually wiped several drops of perspiration from his forehead.

"I would much rather you simply waived all claim to your

poor dear mother's property, little girl," he broke in, "instead of signing that deed. It will cost a lot to register it. I would rather you renounced your claims and trusted to me for the future. I would allow you a good round sum, say a hundred francs every month. You could pay for masses then, you see; you could have masses said for any one that . . . Eh? A hundred francs (in livres) every month?"

"I will do just as you like, father."

"Mademoiselle," said the notary, "it is my duty to point out to you that you are robbing yourself without guarantee——"

"*Eh! mon Dieu!*" she answered. "What does that matter to me?"

"Do be quiet, Cruchot. So it is settled, quite settled!" cried Grandet, taking his daughter's hand and striking his own into it. "You will not go back from your word, Eugénie? You are a good girl, hein!"

"Oh! father——"

In his joy he embraced his daughter, almost suffocating her as he did so.

"There! child, you have given fresh life to your father; but you are only giving him what he gave you, so we are quits. This is how business ought to be conducted, and life is a business transaction. Bless you! You are a good girl, and one that really loves her old father. You can do as you like now. Then good-bye till to-morrow, Cruchot," he added, turning to the horrified notary. "You will see that the deed of renunciation is properly drawn up for the clerk of the court."

By noon next day the declaration was drawn up, and Eugénie herself signed away all her rights to her heritage. Yet a year slipped by, and the cooper had not kept his promise, and Eugénie had not received a sou of the monthly income which was to have been hers; when Eugénie spoke to him about it, half laughingly, he could not help blushing; he hurried up to his room, and when he came down again he handed her about a third of the jewelry which he had purchased of his nephew.

"There! child," he said, with a certain sarcastic ring in his voice; "will you take these for your twelve hundred francs?"

"Oh! father, really? Will you really give them to me?"

"You shall have as much next year again," said he, flinging it into her lap; "and so, before very long, you will have all his trinkets," he added, rubbing his hands. He had made a very good bargain, thanks to his daughter's sentiment about the jewelry, and was in high good humor.

Yet, although the old man was still hale and vigorous, he began to see that he must take his daughter into his confidence, and that she must learn to manage his concerns. So with this end in view he required her to be present while he gave out the daily stores, and for two years he made her receive the portion of the rent which was paid in kind. Gradually she came to know the names of the vineyards and farms; he took her with him when he visited his tenants. By the end of the third year he considered the initiation was complete; and, in truth, she had fallen into his ways unquestioningly, till it had become a matter of habit with her to do as her father had done before her. He had no further doubts, gave over the keys of the storeroom into her keeping, and installed her as mistress of the house.

Five years went by in this way, and no event disturbed their monotonous existence. Eugénie and her father lived a life of methodical routine with the same regularity of movement that characterized the old clock; doing the same things at the same hour day after day, year after year. Every one knew that there had been a profound sorrow in Mlle. Grandet's life; every circle in Saumur had its theories of this secret trouble, and its suspicions as to the state of the heiress' heart, but she never let fall a word that could enlighten any one on either point.

She saw no one but the three Cruchots and a few of their friends, who had gradually been admitted as visitors to the house. Under their instruction she had mastered the game of whist, and they dropped in nearly every evening for a rubber. In the year 1827 her father began to feel the infirmities of age, and was obliged to take her still further into his confidence; she learned the full extent of his landed possessions, and was recommended in all cases of difficulty to refer to the notary Cruchot, whose integrity could be depended upon. Grandet had reached the age of eighty-two, and towards the end of the year had a paralytic seizure, from which he never rallied. M. Bergerin gave him up, and Eugénie realized that very shortly she would be quite alone in the world; the thought drew her more closely to her father; she clung to this last link of affection that bound her to another soul. Love was all the world for her, as it is for all women who love; and Charles had gone out of her world. She nursed her father with sublime devotion; the old man's intellect had grown feeble, but the greed of gold had become an instinct which survived his faculties.

Grandet died as he had lived. Every morning during that slow death he had himself wheeled across his room to a place beside the fire, whence he could keep the door of his cabinet in view; on the other side of the door, no doubt lay his hoarded treasures of gold. He sat there, passive and motionless; but if any one entered the room, he would glance uneasily at the new-comer, and then at the door with its sheathing of iron plates. He would ask the meaning of every sound, however faint, and, to the notary's amazement, the old man heard the dog bark in the yard at the back of the house. He roused from this apparent stupor at the proper hour on the days for receiving his rents and dues, for settling accounts with his vine-dressers, and giving receipts. Then he shifted his armchair round on its casters, until he faced the door of his cabinet, and his daughter was called upon to open it, and to put away the little bags of money in neat piles, one upon the other. He would watch her until it was all over and the door was locked again; and as soon as she had returned the precious key to him, he would turn round noiselessly and take up his old position, putting the key in his waistcoat pocket, where he felt for it from time to time.

His old friend the notary felt sure that it was only a question of time, and that Eugénie must of necessity marry his

nephew the magistrate, unless, indeed, Charles Grandet returned; so he redoubled his attentions. He came every day
to take Grandet's instructions, went at his bidding to Froidfond, to farm and meadow and vineyard; sold vintages, and
exchanged all moneys received for gold, which was secretly
sent to join the piles of bags stored up in the cabinet.

Then death came up close at last, and the vinegrower's
strong frame wrestled with the Destroyer. Even in those days
he would sit as usual by the fire, facing the door of his cabinet. He used to drag off the blankets that they wrapped
round him, and try to fold them, and say to Nanon, "Lock
that up; lock that up, or they will rob me."

So long as he could open his eyes, where the last sparks of
life seemed to linger, they used to turn at once to the door of
the room where all his treasures lay, and he would say to his
daughter, in tones that seemed to thrill with a panic of fear—

"Are they there still?"

"Yes, father."

"Keep watch over the gold!   . . .   Let me see the gold."

Then Eugénie used to spread out the louis on a table before
him, and he would sit for whole hours with his eyes fixed on
the louis in an unseeing stare, like that of a child who begins
to see for the first time; and sometimes a weak infantine smile,
painful to see, would steal across his features.

"That warms me!" he muttered more than once, and his
face expressed a perfect content.

When the curé came to administer the sacrament, all the
life seemed to have died out of the miser's eyes, but they lit
up for the first time for many hours at the sight of the silver
crucifix, the candlesticks, and holy water vessel, all of silver;
he fixed his gaze on the precious metal, and the wen twitched
for the last time.

As the priest held the gilded crucifix above him that the
image of Christ might be laid to his lips, he made a frightful
effort to clutch it—a last effort which cost him his life. He
called to Eugénie, who saw nothing; she was kneeling beside
him, bathing in tears the hand that was growing cold already.

"Give me your blessing, father," she entreated. "Be very careful!" the last words came from him; "one day you will render an account to me of everything here below." Which utterance clearly shows that a miser should adopt Christianity as his religion.

So Eugénie Grandet was alone in the world, and her house was left to her desolate. There was no one but Nanon with whom she could talk over her troubles; she could look into no other eyes and find a response in them; big Nanon was the only human being who loved her for herself. For Eugénie, Nanon was a providence; she was no longer a servant, she was a humble friend.

M. Cruchot informed Eugénie that she had three hundred thousand livres a year, derived from landed property in and around Saumur, besides six millions in the three per cents (invested when the funds were at sixty francs, whereas they now stood at seventy-seven), and in ready money two millions in gold, and a hundred thousand francs in silver, without counting any arrears that were due. Altogether her property amounted to about seventeen million francs.

"Where can my cousin be?" she said to herself.

On the day when M. Cruchot laid these facts before his new client, together with the information that the estate was now clear and free from all outstanding liabilities, Eugénie and Nanon sat on either side of the hearth, in the parlor, now so empty and so full of memories; everything recalled past days, from her mother's chair set on its wooden blocks to the glass tumbler out of which her cousin once drank.

"Nanon, we are alone, you and I."

"Yes, mam'selle; if I only knew where he was, the charming young gentleman, I would set off on foot to find him."

"The sea lies between us," said Eugénie.

While the poor lonely heiress, with her faithful old servant for company, was shedding tears in the cold, dark house, which was all the world she knew, men talked from Orleans to Nantes of nothing but Mlle. Grandet and her seventeen millions. One of her first acts was to settle a pension of twelve hundred francs on Nanon, who, possessing already an income of six hundred francs of her own, at once became a great match. In less than a month she exchanged her condition of spinster for that of wife, at the instance and through the persuasion of Antoine Cornoiller, who was promoted to the position of bailiff and keeper to Mlle. Grandet. Mme. Cornoiller had an immense advantage over her contemporaries; her large features had stood the test of time better than those of many a comelier woman. She might be fifty-nine years of age, but she did not look more than forty; thanks to an almost monastic regimen, she possessed rude health and a high color, time seemed to have no effect on her, and perhaps she had never looked so well in her life as she did on her wedding day. She had the compensating qualities of her style of ugliness; she was tall, stout, and strong; her face wore an indestructible expression of good humor, and Cornoiller's lot seemed an enviable lot to many beholders.

"Fast color," said the draper.

"She might have a family yet," said the drysalter; "she is as well preserved as if she had been kept in brine, asking your pardon."

"She is rich; that fellow Cornoiller has done a good day's work," said another neighbor.

When Nanon left the old house and went down the crooked street on her way to the parish church, she met with nothing but congratulations and good wishes. Nanon was very popular with her neighbors. Eugénie gave her three dozen spoons and forks as a wedding present. Cornoiller, quite overcome with such munificence, spoke of his mistress with tears in his eyes; he would have let himself be cut in pieces for her. Mme. Cornoiller became Eugénie's confidential servant; she was not only married, and had a husband of her own, her dignity was yet further increased, her happiness was doubled. *She* had at last a storeroom and a bunch of keys; *she* too gave out provisions just as her late master used to do. Then she had two subordinates—a cook and a waiting-woman, who took charge of the house linen and made Mlle. Grandet's dresses. As for Cornoiller, he combined the functions of forester and steward. It is needless to say that the cook and the waiting-woman of Nanon's choosing were real domestic *treasures*. The tenants scarcely noticed the death of their late landlord; they were thoroughly broken in to a severe discipline, and M. and Mme. Cornoiller's reign was no whit less rigorous than that of the old régime.

Eugénie was a woman of thirty, and as yet had known none of the happiness of life. All through her joyless, monotonous childhood she had had but one companion, the broken-spirited mother, whose sensitive nature had found little but suffering in a hard life. That mother had joyfully taken leave of existence, pitying the daughter, who must still live on in the world. Eugénie would never lose the sense of her loss, but little of the bitterness of self-reproach mingled with her memories of her mother.

Love, her first and only love, had been a fresh source of suffering for Eugénie. For a few brief days she had seen her lover; she had given her heart to him between two stolen kisses; then he had left her and had set the lands and seas of the world between them. Her father had cursed her for this love; it had nearly cost her her mother's life; it had brought her pain and sorrow and a few faint hopes. She had striven towards her happiness till her own forces had failed her, and another had not come to her aid.

Our souls live by giving and receiving; we have need of another soul; whatever it gives us we make our own, and give back again in overflowing measure. This is as vitally necessary for our inner life as breathing is for our corporeal existence. Without that wonderful physical process we perish; the heart suffers from lack of air, and ceases to beat. Eugénie was beginning to suffer.

She found no solace in her wealth; it could do nothing for her; her love, her religion, her faith in the future made up all her life. Love was teaching her what eternity meant.

Her own heart and the Gospel each spoke to her of a life to come; life was everlasting, and love no less eternal. Night and day she dwelt with these two infinite thoughts, perhaps for her they were but one. She withdrew more and more into herself; she loved, and believed that she was loved.

For seven years her passion had wholly engrossed her.

Her treasures were not those millions left to her by her father, the money that went on accumulating year after year; but the two portraits which hung above her bed, Charles' leather case, the jewels which she had bought back from her father, and which were now proudly set forth on a layer of cotton wool inside the drawer in the old chest, and her aunt's thimble which Mme. Grandet had used; every day Eugénie took up a piece of embroidery, a sort of Penelope's web, which she had only begun that she might wear the golden thimble, endeared to her by so many memories.

It seemed hardly probable that Mlle. Grandet would marry while she was still in mourning. Her sincere piety was well known. So the Cruchot family, coun- selled by the astute old Abbé, was fain to be content with surrounding the heiress with the most affectionate attentions. Her dining-room was filled every evening with the warmest and most devoted Cruchotins, who endeavored to surpass each other in singing the praises of the mistress of the house in every key. She had her physician-in-ordinary, her grand almoner, her chamberlain, her mistress of the robes, her prime minister, and last, but by no means least, her chancellor—a chancellor whose aim it was to keep her informed of every- thing. If the heiress had expressed any wish for a train- bearer, they would have found one for her. She was a queen in fact, and never was queen so adroitly flattered. A great soul never stoops to flattery; it is the resource of little na- tures, who succeed in making themselves smaller still, that they may the better creep into the hearts of those about whom they circle. Flattery, by its very nature, implies an interested motive. So the people who filled Mlle. Grandet's sitting-room every evening (they addressed her and spoke of her among themselves as Mlle. de Froidfond now) heaped their praises upon their hostess in a manner truly marvelous. This chorus of praise embarrassed Eugénie at first; but however gross the flattery might be, she became accustomed to hear her beauty extolled, and if some new-comer had considered her to be plain, she certainly would have winced more under the criticism than she might have done eight years ago. She came at last to welcome their homage, which in her secret heart she laid at the feet of her idol. So also, by degrees, she accepted the position, and allowed herself to be treated as a queen, and saw her little court full every evening.

M. le Président de Bonfons was the hero of the circle; they lauded his talents, his personal appearance, his learning, his amiability; he was an inexhaustible subject of admiring comment. Such an one would call attention to the fact that in seven years the magistrate had largely increased his fortune; Bonfons had at least ten thousand francs a year; and his property, like the lands of all the Cruchots in fact, lay within the compass of the heiress' vast estates.

"Do you know, mademoiselle," another courtier would remark, "that the Cruchots have forty thousand livres a year among them!"

"And they are putting money by," said Mlle. de Gribeaucourt, an old and trusty Cruchotine. "Quite lately a gentleman came from Paris on purpose to offer M. Cruchot two hundred thousand francs for his professional connection. If he could gain an appointment as justice of the peace, he ought to take the offer."

"He means to succeed M. de Bonfons as President, and is taking steps to that end," said Mme. d'Orsonval, "for M. le Président will be Councillor, and then a President of a Court; he is so gifted that he is sure to succeed."

"Yes," said another, "he is a very remarkable man. Do you not think so, mademoiselle?"

M. le Président had striven to act up to the part he wanted to play. He was forty years old, his countenance was dark and ill-favored, he had, moreover, the wizened look which is frequently seen in men of his profession; but he affected the airs of youth, sported a malacca cane, refrained from taking snuff in Mlle. Grandet's house, and went thither arrayed in a white cravat and a shirt with huge frills, which gave him a quaint family resemblance to a turkey-gobbler. He called the fair heiress " our dear Eugénie," and spoke as if he were an intimate friend of the family. In fact, but for the number of those assembled, and the substitution of whist for loto, and the absence of M. and Mme. Grandet, the scene was scarcely changed; it might almost have been that first evening on which this story began.

The pack was still in pursuit of Eugénie's millions; it was a more numerous pack now; they gave tongue together, and hunted down their prey more systematically.

If Charles had come back from the far-off Indies, he would have found the same motives at work and almost the same people. Mme. des Grassins, for whom Eugénie had nothing but kindness and pity, still remained to vex the Cruchots. Eugénie's face still shone out against the dark background, and Charles (though invisible) reigned there supreme as in other days.

Yet some advance had been made. Eugénie's birthday bouquet was never forgotten by the magistrate. Indeed, it had become an institution; every evening he brought the heiress a huge and wonderful bouquet. Mme. Cornoiller ostentatiously placed these offerings in a vase, and promptly flung them into a corner of the yard as soon as the visitors had departed.

In the early spring Mme. des Grassins made a move, and sought to trouble the felicity of the Cruchotins by talking to Eugénie of the Marquis de Froidfond, whose ruined fortunes might be retrieved if the heiress would return his estate to him by a marriage contract. Mme. des Grassins lauded the Marquis and his title to the skies; and, taking Eugénie's quiet smile for consent, she went about saying that M. le Président Cruchot's marriage was not such a settled thing as *some* people imagined.

"M. de Froidfond may be fifty years old," she said, "but he looks no older than M. Cruchot; he is a widower, and has a family, it is true; but he is a marquis, he will be a peer of France one of these days, it is not such a bad match as times go. I know of my own certain knowledge that when old Grandet added his own property to the Froidfond estate he meant to graft his family into the Froidfonds. He often told me as much. Oh! he was a shrewd old man, was Grandet."

"Ah! Nanon," Eugénie said one evening, as she went to bed, "why has he not once written to me in seven years?" . .

While these events were taking place in Saumur, Charles was making his fortune in the East. His first venture was very successful. He had promptly realized the sum of six thousand dollars. Crossing the line had cured him of many early prejudices; he soon saw very clearly that the best and quickest way of making money was the same in the tropics as in Europe—by buying and selling men. He made a descent on the African coasts and bargained for negroes and other goods in demand in various markets. He threw himself heart and soul into the business, and thought of nothing else. He set one clear aim before him, to reappear in Paris, and to dazzle the world there with his wealth, to attain a position even higher than the one from which he had fallen.

By dint of rubbing shoulders with many men, traveling in many lands, coming in contact with various customs and religions, his code had been relaxed, and he had grown sceptical. His notions of right and wrong became less rigid when he found that what was looked upon as a crime in one country was held up to admiration in another. He saw that every one was working for himself, that disinterestedness was rarely to be met with, and grew selfish and suspicious; the hereditary failings of the Grandets came out in him—the hardness, the shiftiness, and the greed of gain. He sold Chinese coolies, negro slaves, swallow-nests, children, artists, anything and everything that brought in money. He became a money lender on a large scale. Long practice in cheating the customs authorities had made him unscrupulous in other ways. He would make the voyage to St. Thomas, buy booty of the pirates there for a low price, and sell the merchandise in the dearest market.

During his first voyage Eugénie's pure and noble face had been with him, like the image of the Virgin which Spanish sailors set on the prows of their vessels; he had attributed his first success to a kind of magical efficacy possessed by her prayers and vows; but as time went on, the women of other countries, negresses, mulattoes, white skins, and yellow skins, orgies and adventures in many lands, completely effaced all recollection of his cousin, of Saumur, of the old house, of the bench, and of the kiss that he had snatched in the passage. He remembered nothing but the little garden shut in by its crumbling walls where he had learned the fate that lay in store for him; but he rejected all connection with the family. His uncle was an old fox who had filched his jewels. Eugénie had no place in his heart; he never gave her a thought; but she occupied a page in his ledger as a creditor for six thousand francs.

Such conduct and such ideas explained Charles Grandet's silence. In the East Indies, at St. Thomas, on the coast of Africa, at Lisbon, in the United States, Charles Grandet the adventurer was known as Carl Sepherd, a pseudonym which he assumed so as not to compromise his real name. Carl Sepherd could be indefatigable, brazen, and greedy of gain; could conduct himself, in short, like a man who resolves to make a fortune *quibuscumque viis,* and makes haste to have done with villainy as soon as possible, in order to live respected for the rest of his days.

With such methods his career of prosperity was rapid and brilliant, and in 1827 he returned to Bordeaux on board the Marie Caroline, a fine brig belonging to a Royalist firm. He had nineteen hundred thousand francs with him in gold dust, carefully secreted in three strong casks; he hoped to sell it to the Paris mint, and to make eight per cent on the transaction. There was also on board the brig a gentleman-in-ordi-

nary to his Majesty Charles X., a M. d'Aubrion, a worthy old
man who had been rash enough to marry a woman of fashion
whose money came from estates in the West India Islands.
Mme. d'Aubrion's reckless extravagance had obliged him to
go out to the Indies to sell her property. M. and Mme.
d'Aubrion, of the house of d'Aubrion de Buch, which had lost
its *captal* or chieftain just before the Revolution, were now in
straitened circumstances. They had a bare twenty thousand
francs of income and a daughter, a very plain girl, whom her
mother made up her mind to marry without a dowry; for life
in Paris is expensive, and, as has been seen, their means were
reduced. It was an enterprise the success of which might have
seemed somewhat problematical to a man of the world, in
spite of the cleverness with which a woman of fashion is generally credited. Perhaps even Mme. d'Aubrion herself, when
she looked at her daughter, was almost ready to despair of
getting rid of her to any one, even to the most besotted wor-
shiper of rank and titles.

Mlle. d'Aubrion was a tall, spare demoiselle, somewhat like
her namesake the insect; she had a disdainful mouth, overshadowed by a long nose, thick at the tip, sallow in its normal
condition, but very red after a meal, an organic change which
was all the more unpleasant by reason of contrast with a
pallid, insipid countenance. From some points of view she
was all that a worldly mother, who was thirty-eight years of
age, and had still some pretensions to beauty, could desire.
But by way of compensating advantages, the Marquise
d'Aubrion's distinguished air had been inherited by her
daughter, and that young lady had been submitted to a Spar-
tan regimen, which for the time being subdued the offending
hue in her feature to a reasonable flesh-tint. Her mother had
taught her how to dress herself. Under the same instructor
she had acquired a charming manner, and had learned to assume that pensive expression which interests a man and leads
him to imagine that here, surely, is the angel for whom he
has hitherto sought in vain. She was carefully drilled in a
certain manœuvre with her foot—to let it peep forth from be-

13

neath her petticoat, and so call attention to its small size—whenever her nose became unseasonably red; indeed, the mother had made the very best of her daughter. By means of large sleeves, stiff skirts, puffs, padding, and high pressure corsets, she had produced a highly curious and interesting result, a specimen of femininity which ought to have been put into a museum for the edification of mothers generally.

Charles became very intimate with Mme. d'Aubrion; the lady had her own reasons for encouraging him. People said that during the time on board she left no stone unturned to secure such a prize for a son-in-law. It is at any rate certain that when they landed at Bordeaux Charles stayed in the same hotel with M., Mme., and Mlle. d'Aubrion, and they all traveled together to Paris. The hôtel d'Aubrion was hampered with mortgages, and Charles was intended to come to the rescue. The mother had gone so far as to say that it would give her great pleasure to establish a son-in-law on the ground floor. She did not share M. d'Aubrion's aristocratic prejudices, and promised Charles Grandet to obtain letters patent from that easy-tempered monarch, Charles X., which should authorize him, Grandet, to bear the name and assume the arms of the d'Aubrions, and (by purchasing the entail) to succeed to the property of Aubrion, which was worth about thirty-six thousand livres a year, to say nothing of the titles of Captal de Buch and Marquis d'Aubrion. They could be very useful to each other, in short; and what with this arrangement of a joint establishment, and one or two posts about the court, the hôtel d'Aubrion might count upon an income of a hundred thousand francs and more.

"And when a man has a hundred thousand francs a year, a name, a family, and a position at Court—for I shall procure an appointment for you as gentleman of the bedchamber—the rest is easy. You can be anything you choose" (so she instructed Charles), "Master of Requests in the Council of State, Prefect, Secretary to an Embassy, the Ambassador himself if you like. Charles X. is much attached to d'Aubrion; they have known each other from childhood."

She fairly turned his head with these ambitious schemes, and during the voyage Charles began to cherish the hopes and ideas which had been so cleverly insinuated in the form of tender confidences. He never doubted but that his uncle had paid his father's creditors; he had been suddenly launched into the society of the Faubourg St. Germain, at that time the goal of social ambition; and beneath the shadow of Mlle. Mathilde's purple nose, he was shortly to appear as the Comte d'Aubrion, very much as the Dreux shone forth transformed into Brézés. He was dazzled by the apparent prosperity of the restored dynasty, which had seemed to be tottering to its fall when he left France; his head was full of wild, ambitious dreams, which began on the voyage, and did not leave him in Paris. He resolved to strain every nerve to reach those pinnacles of glory which his egotistical would-be mother-in-law had pointed out to him. His cousin was only a dim speck in the remote past; she had no place in this brilliant future, no part in his dreams, but he went to see Annette. That experienced woman of the world gave counsel to her old friend; he must by no means let slip such an opportunity for an alliance; she promised to aid him in all his schemes of advancement. In her heart she was delighted to see Charles thus secured to such a plain and uninteresting girl. He had grown very attractive during his stay in the Indies; his complexion had grown darker, he had gained in manliness and self-possession; he spoke in the firm, decided tones of a man who is used to command and to success. Ever since Charles Grandet had discovered that there was a definite part for him to play in Paris, he was himself at once.

Des Grassins, hearing of his return, his approaching marriage, and his large fortune, came to see him, and spoke of the three hundred thousand francs still owing to his father's creditors. He found Charles closeted with a goldsmith, from whom he had ordered jewels for Mlle. d'Aubrion's *corbeille,* and who was submitting designs. Charles himself had brought magnificent diamonds from the Indies; but the cost of setting them, together with the silver plate and jewelry of the new establishment, amounted to more than two hundred thousand francs. He did not recognize des Grassins at first, and treated him with the cool insolence of a young man of fashion who is conscious that he has killed four men in as many duels in the Indies. As M. des Grassins had already called three or four times, Charles vouchsafed to hear him, but it was with bare politeness, and he did not pay the slightest attention to what the banker said.

"My father's debts are not mine," he said coolly. "I am obliged to you, sir, for the trouble you have been good enough to take, but I am none the better for it that I can see. I have not scraped together a couple of millions, earned with the sweat of my brow, to fling it to my father's creditors."

"But suppose that your father were to be declared bankrupt in a few days' time?"

"In a few days' time I shall be the Comte d'Aubrion, sir; so you can see that it is a matter of entire indifference to me. Besides, you know even better than I do that when a man has a hundred thousand livres a year, his father never has been a bankrupt," and he politely edged the deputy des Grassins to the door.

In the early days of the month of August, in that same year, Eugénie was sitting on the little bench in the garden where her cousin had sworn eternal love, and where she often took breakfast in summer mornings. The poor girl was almost happy for a few brief moments; she went over all the great and little events of her love before those catastrophes that followed. The morning was fresh and bright, and the garden was full of sunlight; her eyes wandered over the wall with its moss and flowers; it was full of cracks now, and all but in ruins, but no one was allowed to touch it, though Cornoiller was always prophesying to his wife that the whole thing would come down and crush somebody or other one of these days. The postman knocked at the door, and gave a letter into the hands of Mme. Cornoiller, who hurried into the garden, crying, "Mademoiselle! A letter! Is it *the* letter?" she added, as she handed it to her mistress.

The words rang through Eugénie's heart as the spoken sounds rang from the ramparts and the old garden wall.

"Paris! . . . It is his writing! Then he has come back."

Eugénie's face grew white; for several seconds she kept the seal unbroken, for her heart beat so fast that she could neither move nor see. Big Nanon stood and waited with both hands on her hips; joy seemed to puff like smoke from every wrinkle in her brown face.

"Do read it, mademoiselle!"

"Oh! why does he come back by way of Paris, Nanon, when he went by way of Saumur?"

"Read it; the letter will tell you why."

Eugénie's fingers trembled as she opened the envelope; a cheque on the firm of "Mme. des Grassins et Corret, Saumur," fell out of it and fluttered down. Nanon picked it up.

"MY DEAR COUSIN . . ."

("I am not 'Eugénie' now," she thought, and her heart stood still.) "You . . ."

"He used to say *thou!*" She folded her arms and dreaded to read any further; great tears gathered in her eyes.

"What is it? Is he dead?" asked Nanon.

"If he were, he could not write," said Eugénie, and she read the letter through. It ran as follows:—

"MY DEAR COUSIN,—You will, I am sure, hear with pleasure of the success of my enterprise. You brought me luck; I have come back to France a wealthy man, as my uncle advised. I have just heard of his death, together with that of my aunt, from M. des Grassins. Our parents must die in the course of nature, and we ourselves must follow them. I hope that by this time you are consoled for your loss; time cures all trouble, as I know by experience. Yes, my dear cousin, the day of illusions is gone by for me. I am sorry, but it cannot be helped. I have knocked about the world so much, and seen so much, that I have been led to reflect on life. I

was a child when I went away; I have come back a man, and
I have many things to think about now which I did not even
dream of then. You are free, my cousin, and I too am free
still; there is apparently nothing to hinder the realization'of
our youthful hopes; but I am too straightforward to hide my
present situation from you. I have not for a moment forgotten that I am bound to you; through all my wanderings
I have always remembered the little wooden bench——"

Eugénie started up as if she were sitting on burning coals,
and sat down on one of the broken stone steps in the yard.

——"the little wooden bench where we vowed to love each other
forever; the passage, the gray parlor, my attic room, the night
when in your thoughtfulness and tact you made my future
easier to me. Yes, these memories have been my support; I
have said in my heart that you were always thinking of me
when I thought of you at the hour we had agreed upon. Did
you not look out into the darkness at nine o'clock? Yes, I
am sure you did. I would not prove false to so sacred a friendship; I cannot deal insincerely with you.

"A marriage has been proposed to me, which is in every
way satisfactory to my mind. Love in a marriage is romantic
nonsense. Experience has clearly shown me that in marrying
we must obey social laws and conform to conventional ideas.
There is some difference of age between you and me, which
would perhaps be more likely to affect your future than mine,
and there are other differences of which I need not speak;
your bringing up, your ways of life, and your tastes have not
fitted you for Parisian life, nor would they harmonize with
the future which I have marked out for myself. For instance, it is part of my plan to maintain a great household,
and to see a good deal of society; and you, I am sure, from
my recollections of you, would prefer a quiet, domestic life
and home-keeping ways. No, I will be open with you; I
will abide by your decision; but I must first, however, lay all
the facts of the case before you, that you may the better
judge.

"I possess at the time of writing an income of eighty thousand livres. With this fortune I am able to marry into the d'Aubrion family; I should take their name on my marriage with their only daughter, a girl of nineteen, and secure at the same time a very brilliant position in society, and the post of gentleman-of-the-bedchamber. I will assure you at once, my dear cousin, that I have not the slightest affection for Mlle. d'Aubrion, but by this marriage I shall secure for my children a social rank which will be of inestimable value in the future. Monarchical principles are daily gaining ground. A few years hence my son, the Marquis d'Aubrion, would have an entailed estate and a yearly rental of forty thousand livres; with such advantages there would be no position to which he might not aspire. We ought to live for our children.

"You see, my cousin, how candidly I am laying the state of my heart, my hopes, and my fortunes before you. Perhaps after seven years of separation you may yourself have forgotten our childish love affair, but I have never forgotten your goodness or my promise. A less conscientious, a less upright man, with a heart less youthful than mine, might scarcely feel himself bound by it; but for me a promise, however lightly given, is sacred. When I tell you plainly that my marriage is solely a marriage of suitability, and that I have not forgotten the love of our youthful days, am I not putting myself entirely into your hands, and making you the arbitress of my fate? Is it not implied that if I must renounce my social ambitions, I shall willingly content myself with the simple and pure happiness which is always called up by the thought of you . . .

"Tra-la-la-tan-ta-ti!" sang Charles Grandet to the air of *Non più andrai,* as he signed himself,

"Your devoted cousin,

"CHARLES."

"By Jove! that is acting handsomely," he said to himself. He looked about him for the cheque, slipped it in, and added a postscript.

"*P. S.*—I enclose a cheque on Mme. des Grassins for eight thousand francs, payable in gold to your order, comprising the capital and interest of the sum you were so kind as to advance me. I am expecting a case from Bordeaux which contains a few things which you must allow me to send you as a token of my unceasing gratitude. You can send my dressing-case by the diligence to the Hôtel d'Aubrion, Rue Hillerin-Bertin."

"By the diligence!" cried Eugénie, "when I would have given my life for it a thousand times!"

Terrible and complete shipwreck of hope; the vessel had gone down, there was not a spar, not a plank in the vast ocean. There are women who when their lover forsakes them will drag him from a rival's arms and murder her, and fly for refuge to the ends of the earth, to the scaffold, or the grave. There is a certain grandeur in this, no doubt; there is something so sublime in the passion of indignation which prompts the crime, that man's justice is awed into silence; but there are other women who suffer and bow their heads. They go on their way, submissive and broken-hearted, weeping and forgiving, praying till their last sigh for him whom they never forget. And this no less is love, love such as the angels know, love that bears itself proudly in anguish, that lives by the secret pain of which it dies at last. This was to be Eugénie's love now that she had read that horrible letter.

She raised her eyes to the sky and thought of her mother's prophetic words, uttered in the moment of clear vision that is sometimes given to dying eyes; and as she thought of her mother's life and death, it seemed to her that she was looking out over her own future. There was nothing left to her now but to live prayerfully till the day of her deliverance should come and the soul spread its wings for heaven.

"My mother was right," she said, weeping. "Suffer—and die."

She went slowly from the garden into the house, avoiding the passage; but when she came into the old gray parlor, it was full of memories of her cousin. On the chimney-piece there stood a certain china saucer, which she used every morning, and the old Sèvres sugar basin.

It was to be a memorable and eventful day for Eugénie. Nanon announced the curé of the parish church. He was related to the Cruchots, and therefore in the interests of the President de Bonfons. For some days past, the Abbé had urged the curé to speak seriously to Mlle. Grandet about the duty of marriage from a religious point of view for a woman in her position. Eugénie, seeing her pastor, fancied that he had come for the thousand francs which she gave him every month for the poor of his parish, and sent Nanon for the money; but the curate began with a smile, "To-day, mademoiselle, I have come to take counsel with you about a poor girl in whom all Saumur takes an interest, and who, through lack of charity to herself, is not living as a Christian should."

"Mon Dieu! M. le Curé, just now I can think of nobody but myself. I am very miserable, my only refuge is in the Church; her heart is large enough to hold all human sorrows, her love so inexhaustible that we need never fear to drain it dry."

"Well, mademoiselle, when we speak of this girl, we shall speak of you. Listen! If you would fain work out your salvation, there are but two ways open to you; you must either leave the world, or live in the world and submit to its laws— you must choose between the earthly and the heavenly vocation."

"Ah! your voice speaks to me when I need to hear a voice. Yes, God has sent you to me. I will bid the world farewell, and live for God alone, in silence and seclusion."

"But, my daughter, you should think long and prayerfully before taking so strong a measure. Marriage is life, the veil and the convent is death."

"Yes, death. Ah! if death would only come quickly, M. le Curé," she said, with dreadful eagerness.

"Death? But you have great obligations to fulfil towards society, mademoiselle. There is your family of poor, to whom you give clothes and firing in winter and work in summer. Your great fortune is a loan, of which you must give account one day. You have always looked on it as a sacred trust. It would be selfish to bury yourself in a convent, and you ought not to live alone in the world. In the first place, how can you endure the burden of your vast fortune alone? You might lose it. You will be involved in endless litigation; you will find yourself in difficulties from which you will not be able to extricate yourself. Take your pastor's word, a husband is useful; you ought not to lose what God has given into your charge. I speak to you as to a cherished lamb of my flock. You love God too sincerely to find hindrances to your salvation in the world; you are one of its fairest ornaments, and should remain in it as an example of holiness."

At this point Mme. des Grassins was announced. The banker's wife was smarting under a grievous disappointment, and thirsted for revenge.

"Mademoiselle   .   .   ." she began. "Oh! M. le Curé is here.   .   .   . I will say no more then. I came to speak about some matters of business, but I see you are deep in something else."

"Madame," said the curé, "I leave the field to you."

"Oh! M. le Curé, pray come back again; I stand in great need of your help just now."

"Yes, indeed, my poor child!" said Mme. des Grassins.

"What do you mean?" asked Eugénie and the curé both together.

"Do you suppose that I haven't heard that your cousin has come back and is going to marry Mlle. d'Aubrion? A woman doesn't go about with her wits in her pocket."

Eugénie was silent, there was a red flush on her face, but she made up her mind at once that henceforward no one should learn anything from her, and looked as impenetrable as her father used to do.

"Well, madame," she said, with a tinge of bitterness in her tones, "it seems that I, at any rate, carry my wits in my pocket, for I am quite at a loss to understand you. Speak out and explain yourself; you can speak freely before M. le Curé, he is my director, as you know."

"Well, then, mademoiselle, see for yourself what des Grassins says. Here is the letter."

Eugénie read :—

"MY DEAR WIFE,—Charles Grandet has returned from the Indies, and has been in Paris these two months——"

"Two months!" said Eugénie to herself, and her hand fell to her side. After a moment she went on reading :—

"I had to dance attendance upon him, and called twice before the future Comte d'Aubrion would condescend to see me. All Paris is talking about his marriage, and the banns are published——"

"And he wrote to me after that?" Eugénie said to herself. She did not round off the sentence as a Parisienne would have done, with "Wretch that he is!" but her scorn was not one whit the less because it was unexpressed.

—"but it will be a good while yet before he marries; it is not likely that the Marquis d'Aubrion will give his daughter to the son of a bankrupt wine merchant. I called and told him of all the trouble we had been at, his uncle and I, in the matter of his father's failure, and of our clever dodges that had kept the creditors quiet so far. The insolent puppy had the effrontery to say to me—to *me,* who for five years have toiled day and night in his interest and to save his credit—that *his father's affairs were not his!* A solicitor would have wanted thirty or forty thousand francs of him in fees at the rate of one per cent on the total of the debt! But, patience! There is something that he does owe, however, and that the law shall make him pay, that is to say, twelve hundred thousand francs to his father's creditors, and I shall declare his father bankrupt. I mixed myself up in this affair on the word of that old crocodile of a Grandet, and I have given promises in the name

of the family. M. le Comte d'Aubrion may not care for his
honor, but I care a good deal for mine! So I shall just explain my position to the creditors. Still, I have too much respect for Mlle. Eugénie (with whom, in happier days, we
hoped to be more closely connected) to take any steps before
you have spoken to her——"

There Eugénie paused, and quietly returned the letter.
"I am obliged to you," she said to Mme. des Grassins.
"We shall see——"
"Your voice was exactly like your father's just then," ex-
claimed Mme. des Grassins.
"Madame," put in Nanon, producing Charles' cheque, "you
have eight thousand francs to pay us."
"True. Be so good as to come with me, Mme. Cornoiller."
"M. le Curé," said Eugénie, with a noble composure that
came of the thought which prompted her, "would it be a sin
to remain in a state of virginity after marriage?"
"It is a case of conscience which I cannot solve. If you
care to know what the celebrated Sanchez says in his great
work, *De Matrimonio,* I could inform you to-morrow."
The curé took leave. Mlle. Grandet went up to her
father's room and spent the day there by herself; she would
not even come down to dinner, though Nanon begged and
scolded. She appeared in the evening at the hour when the
usual company began to arrive. The gray parlor in the Grandet's house had never been so well filled as it was that night.
Every soul in the town knew by that time of Charles' return,
and of his faithlessness and ingratitude; but their inquisitive
curiosity was not to be gratified. Eugénie was a little late,
but no one saw any traces of the cruel agitation through
which she had passed; she could smile benignly in reply to the
compassionate looks and words which some of the group
thought fit to bestow on her; she bore her pain behind a mask
of politeness.
About nine o'clock the card-players drew away from the
tables, paid their losses, and criticised the game and the vari-

ous points that had been made. Just as there was a general move in the direction of the door, an unexpected development took place; the news of it rang through Saumur and four prefectures round about for days after.

"Please stay, M. le Président."

There was not a person in the room who did not thrill with excitement at the words; M. de Bonfons, who was about to take his cane, turned quite white, and sat down again.

"The President takes the millions," said Mlle. de Gribeaucourt.

"It is quite clear that President de Bonfons is going to marry Mlle. Grandet," cried Mme. d'Orsonval.

"The best trick of the game!" commented the Abbé.

"A very pretty *slam*," said the notary.

Every one said his say and cut his joke, every one thought of the heiress mounted upon her millions as if she were on a pedestal. Here was the catastrophe of the drama, begun nine years ago, taking place under their eyes. To tell the President in the face of all Saumur to "stay" was as good as announcing at once that she meant to take the magistrate for her husband. Social conventionalities are rigidly observed in little country towns, and such an infraction as this was looked upon as a binding promise.

"M. le Président," Eugénie began in an unsteady voice, as soon as they were alone, "I know what you care about in me. Swear to leave me free till the end of my life, to claim none of the rights which marriage will give you over me, and my hand is yours. Oh!" she said, seeing him about to fall on his knees, "I have not finished yet. I must tell you frankly that there are memories in my heart which can never be effaced; that friendship is all that I can give my husband; I wish neither to affront him nor to be disloyal to my own heart. But you shall only have my hand and fortune at the price of an immense service which I want you to do me."

"Anything, I will do anything," said the president.

"Here are fifteen hundred thousand francs, M. le Président," she said, drawing from her bodice a certificate for a

hundred shares in the Bank of France; "will you set out for
Paris? You must not even wait till the morning, but go at
once, to-night. You must go straight to M. des Grassins, ask
him for a list of my uncle's creditors, call them together, and
discharge all outstanding claims upon Guillaume Grandet's
estate. Let the creditors have capital and interest at five per
cent from the day the debts were contracted to the present
time; and see that in every case a receipt in full is given, and
that it is made out in proper form. You are a magistrate,
you are the only person whom I feel that I can trust in such
a case. You are a gentleman and a man of honor; you have
given me your word, and, protected by your name, I will make
the perilous voyage of life. We shall know how to make allowances for each other, for we have been acquainted for so
long that it is almost as if we were related, and I am sure you
would not wish to make me unhappy."

The president fell on his knees at the feet of the rich heiress
in a paroxysm of joy.

"I will be your slave!" he said.

"When all the receipts are in your possession, sir," she went
on, looking quietly at him, "you must take them, together
with the bills, to my cousin Grandet, and give them to him
with this letter. When you come back, I will keep my word."

The president understood the state of affairs perfectly well.
"She is accepting me out of pique," he thought, and he hastened to do Mlle. Grandet's bidding with all possible speed,
for fear some chance might bring about a reconciliation between the lovers.

As soon as M. de Bonfons left her, Eugénie sank into her
chair and burst into tears. All was over, and *this* was the end.

The president traveled post to Paris and reached his journey's end on the following evening. The next morning he
went to des Grassins, and arranged for a meeting of the creditors in the office of the notary with whom the bills had been
deposited. Every man of them appeared, every man of them
was punctual to a moment—one should give even creditors
their dues.

M. de Bonfons, in Mlle. Grandet's name, paid down the
money in full, both capital and interest. They were paid interest! It was an amazing portent, a nine days' wonder in
the business world of Paris. After the whole affair had been
wound up, and when, by Eugénie's desire, des Grassins had
received fifty thousand francs for his services, the president
betook himself to the Hôtel d'Aubrion, and was lucky enough
to find Charles at home, and in disgrace with his future
father-in-law. The old Marquis had just informed that gentleman that until Guillaume Grandet's creditors were satisfied, a marriage with his daughter was not to be thought of.

To Charles, thus despondent, the president delivered the
following letter:—

"DEAR COUSIN,—M. le Président de Bonfons has undertaken to hand you a discharge of all claims against my uncle's
estate, and to deliver it in person, together with this letter,
so that I may know that it is safely in your hands. I heard
rumors of bankruptcy, and it occurred to me that difficulties
might possibly arise as a consequence in the matter of your
marriage with Mlle. d'Aubrion. Yes, cousin, you are quite
right about my tastes and manners; I have lived, as you say,
so entirely out of the world, that I know nothing of its ways
or its calculations, and my companionship could never make
up to you for the loss of the pleasures that you look to find in
society. I hope that you will be happy according to the social
conventions to which you have sacrificed our early love. The
only thing in my power to give you to complete your happiness is your father's good name. Farewell; you will always
find a faithful friend in your cousin,   "EUGÉNIE."

In spite of himself an exclamation broke from the man of
social ambitions when his eyes fell on the discharge and receipts. The president smiled.

"We can each announce our marriage," said he.

"Oh! you are to marry Eugénie, are you? Well, I am glad
to hear of it; she is a kind-hearted girl. Why!" struck with
a sudden luminous idea, "she must be rich?"

"Four days ago she had about nineteen millions," the president said, with a malicious twinkle in his eyes; "to-day she has only seventeen."

Charles was dumfounded; he stared at the president.

"Seventeen mil——"

"Seventeen millions. Yes, sir; when we are married, Mlle. Grandet and I shall muster seven hundred and fifty thousand livres a year between us."

"My dear cousin," said Charles, with some return of assurance, "we shall be able to push each other's fortunes."

"Certainly," said the president. "There is something else here," he added, "a little case that I was to give only into your hands," and he set down a box containing the dressing-case upon the table.

The door opened, and in came Mme. la Marquise d'Aubrion; the great lady seemed to be unaware of Cruchot's existence. "Look here! dear," she said, "never mind what that absurd M. d'Aubrion has been saying to you; the Duchesse de Chaulieu has quite turned his head. I repeat it, there is nothing to prevent your marriage——"

"Nothing, madame," answered Charles. "The three millions which my father owed were paid yesterday."

"In money?" she asked.

"In full, capital and interest; I mean to rehabilitate his memory."

"What nonsense!" cried his mother-in-law. "Who is this person?" she asked in Charles' ear, as she saw Cruchot for the first time.

"My man of business," he answered in a low voice. The Marquise gave M. de Bonfons a disdainful bow, and left the room.

"We are beginning to push each other's fortunes already," said the president drily, as he took up his hat. "Good day, cousin."

"The old cockatoo from Saumur is laughing at me; I have a great mind to make him swallow six inches of cold steel," thought Charles.

But the president had departed.

Three days later M. de Bonfons was back in Saumur again, and announced his marriage with Eugénie. After about six months he received his appointment as Councillor to the Court-Royal at Angers, and they went thither. But before Eugénie left Saumur she melted down the trinkets that had long been so sacred and so dear a trust, and gave them, together with the eight thousand francs which her cousin had returned to her, to make a reredos for the altar in the parish church whither she had gone so often to pray to God for him. Henceforward her life was spent partly at Angers, partly at Saumur. Her husband's devotion to the government at a political crisis was rewarded; he was made President of the Chamber, and finally First President. Then he awaited a general election with impatience; he had visions of a place in the government; he had dreams of a peerage; and then, and then . . .

"Then he would call cousins with the king, I suppose?" said Nanon, big Nanon, Mme. Cornoiller, wife of a burgess of Saumur, when her mistress told her of these lofty ambitions and high destinies.

Yet, after all, none of these ambitious dreams were to be realized, and the name of M. de Bonfons (he had finally dropped the patronymic Cruchot) was to undergo no further transformation. He died only eight days after his appointment as deputy of Saumur. God, who sees all hearts, and who never strikes without cause, punished him, doubtless, for his presumptuous schemes, and for the lawyer's cunning with which, *accurante Cruchot,* he had drafted his own marriage contract; in which husband and wife, *in case there was no issue of the marriage, bequeathed to each other all their property, both real estate and personalty, without exception or reservation, dispensing even with the formality of an inventory, provided that the omission of the said inventory should not injure their heirs and assigns, it being understood that this deed of gift, etc., etc.,* a clause which may throw some light on the profound respect which the president constantly showed for his wife's desire to live apart. Women cited M. le

14

Premier Président as one of the most delicately considerate
of men, and pitied him, and often went so far as to blame Eugénie for clinging to her passion and her sorrow; mingling,
according to their wont, cruel insinuations with their criti-
cisms of the president's wife.

"If Mme. de Bonfons lives apart from her husband, she must
be in very bad health, poor thing. Is she likely to recover?
What can be the matter with her? Is it cancer or gastritis,
or what is it? Why does she not go to Paris and see some
specialist? She has looked very sallow for a long time past.
How can she not wish to have a child? They say she is very
fond of her husband; why not give him an heir in his position? Do you know, it is really dreadful! If it is only some
notion which she has taken into her head, it is unpardonable.
Poor president!"

There is a certain keen insight and quick apprehensiveness
that is the gift of a lonely and meditative life—and loneliness,
and sorrow, and the discipline of the last few years had given
Eugénie this clairvoyance of the narrow lot. She knew within
herself that the president was anxious for her death that he
might be the sole possessor of the colossal fortune, now still
further increased by the deaths of the abbé and the notary,
whom Providence had lately seen fit to promote from works to
rewards. The poor solitary woman understood and pitied
the president. Unworthy hopes and selfish calculations were
his strongest motives for respecting Eugénie's hopeless passion. To give life to a child would be death to the egotistical
dreams and ambitions that the president hugged within himself; was it for all these things that his career was cut short?
while she must remain in her prison house, and the coveted
gold for which she cared so little was to be heaped upon her.
It was she who was to live, with the thought of heaven always
before her, and holy thoughts for her companions, to give help
and comfort secretly to those who were in distress. Mme. de
Bonfons was left a widow three years after her marriage,
with an income of eight hundred thousand livres.

She is beautiful still, with the beauty of a woman who is

nearly forty years of age. Her face is very pale and quiet now, and there is a tinge of sadness in the low tones of her voice. She has simple manners, all the dignity of one who has passed through great sorrows, and the saintliness of a soul unspotted by the world; and, no less, the rigidness of an old maid, the little penurious ways and narrow ideas of a dull country town.

Although she has eight hundred thousand livres a year, she lives just as she used to do in the days of stinted allowances of fuel and food while she was still Eugénie Grandet; the fire is never lighted in the parlor before or after the dates fixed by her father, all the regulations in force in the days of her girlhood are still adhered to. She dresses as her mother did. That cold, sunless, dreary house, always overshadowed by the dark ramparts, is like her own life.

She looks carefully after her affairs; her wealth accumulates from year to year; perhaps she might even be called parsimonious, if it were not for the noble use she makes of her fortune. Various pious and charitable institutions, almshouses, and orphan asylums, a richly endowed public library, and donations to various churches in Saumur, are a sufficient answer to the charge of avarice which some few people have brought against her.

They sometimes speak of her in joke as *mademoiselle*, but in fact, people stand somewhat in awe of Mme. de Bonfons. It was as if she, whose heart went out so readily to others, was always to be the victim of their interested calculations, and to be cut off from them by a barrier of distrust; as if for all warmth and brightness in her life she was to find only the pale glitter of metal.

"No one loves me but you," she would sometimes say to Nanon.

Yet her hands are always ready to bind the wounds that other eyes do not see, in any house; and her way to heaven is one long succession of kindness and good deeds. The real greatness of her soul has risen above the cramping influences of her early life. And this is the life history of a woman who dwells in the world, yet is not of it, a woman so grandly fitted to be a wife and mother, but who has neither husband nor children nor kindred.

Of late the good folk of Saumur have begun to talk of a second marriage for her. Rumor is busy with her name and that of the Marquis de Froidfond; indeed, his family have begun to surround the rich widow, just as the Cruchots once flocked about Eugénie Grandet. Nanon and Cornoiller, so it is said, are in the interest of the Marquis, but nothing could be more false; for big Nanon and Cornoiller have neither of them wit enough to understand the corruptions of the world.

A STUDY OF WOMAN

Dedicated to the Marquis Jean-Charles di Negro.

THE Marquise de Listomère is a young woman brought up in the spirit of the Restoration. She has principles, she fasts in season, she takes the Sacrament, she goes very much dressed to balls, to the Bouffons, to the Opera; her spiritual director allows her to combine the sacred and the profane. Always on good terms with the Church and the world, she is an incarnation of the present time, and seems to have taken the word *Legality* for her motto. The Marquise's conduct is marked by exactly enough devotion to enable her, under another Maintenon, to achieve the gloomy piety of the last days of Louis XIV., and enough worldliness to adopt the manners and gallantry of the earlier years of his reign, if they ever could return.

Just now she is virtuous from interest, or, perhaps, by taste. Married some seven years since to the Marquis de Listomère, a deputy who expects a peerage, she perhaps thinks that her conduct may promote the ambitions of the family. Some women wait to pass judgment on her till Monsieur de Listomère is made Pair de France, and till she is six-and-thirty— a time of life when most women discover that they are the dupes of social laws.

The Marquis is an insignificant personage; he is in favor at Court; his good qualities, like his faults, are negative; the former can no more give him a reputation for virtue than the latter can give him the sort of brilliancy bestowed by vice. As a deputy he never speaks, but he votes "straight;" and at home, he behaves as he does in the Chamber. He is considered the best husband in France. Though he is incapable of enthusiasms, he never scolds, unless he is kept waiting. His friends nickname him "Cloudy weather;" and, in fact, there is in him no excessively bright light, and no utter darkness. He is exactly like all the Ministers that have succeeded each other in France since the Charter.

A woman with principles could hardly have fallen into better hands. Is it not a great thing for a virtuous woman to have married a man incapable of a folly? Dandies have been known to venture on the impertinence of slightly pressing the Marquise's hand when dancing with her; they met only looks of scorn, and all have experienced that insulting indifference which, like spring frosts, chills the germs of the fairest hopes. Handsome men, witty men, coxcombs, sentimental men who derive nourishment from sucking the knob of their walking-sticks, men of name and men of fame, men of high birth and of low, all have blenched before her. She has won the right of talking as long and as often as she pleases with men whom she thinks intelligent, without being entered in the calendar of scandal. Some coquettes are capable of pursuing this plan for seven years on end, to gratify their fancy at last; but to ascribe such a covert motive to Madame de Listomère would be to calumniate her. I had been so happy as to meet this Phœnix of a Marquise; she talks well, I am a good listener. I pleased her, and I go to her evening parties. This was the object of my ambition.

Neither plain nor pretty, Madame de Listomère has white teeth, a brilliant complexion, and very red lips; she is tall and well made, has a small, slender foot, which she does not display; her eyes, far from being dulled, as most eyes are in Paris, have a soft gleam which becomes magical when by chance she is animated. You feel there is a soul under this ill-defined personality. When she is interested in the conversation, she reveals the grace that lies buried under the prudery of cold demeanor, and then she is charming. She does not crave for success, and she gets it. We always find the thing we do not seek. This statement is too often true not to become a proverb one day. It will be the moral of this tale, which I should not allow myself to relate if it were not at this moment the talk of every drawing-room in Paris.

One evening, about a month since, the Marquise de Listomère danced with a young man as modest as he is heedless, full of good qualities, but showing only his bad ones; he is impassioned, and laughs at passion; he has talent, and hides it; he assumes the *savant* with aristocrats, and affects to be aristocratic with savants.

Eugène de Rastignac is one of those very sensible young men who try everything, and seem to sound other men to discover what the future will bring forth. Pending the age when he will be ambitious, he laughs at everything; he has grace and originality—two qualities which are rare, because they exclude each other. Without aiming at success, he talked to Madame de Listomère for about half an hour. Without following the deviations of a conversation which, beginning with *William Tell,* went on to the duties of woman, he looked at the Marquise more than once in a way to embarrass her; then he left her, and spoke to her no more all the evening. He danced, sat down to *écarté,* lost a little money, and went home to bed. I have the honor of assuring you that this is exactly what happened. I have added, I have omitted nothing.

The next morning Rastignac woke late, remained in bed, where he gave himself up, no doubt, to some of those morning day-dreams in which a young man glides, like a sylph, behind more than one curtain of silk, wool, or cotton. At such moments, the heavier the body is with sleep, the more nimble is the fancy. Finally Rastignac got up without yawning too much, as so many ill-bred people do, rang for his man-servant, ordered some tea, and drank of it immoderately—which will not seem strange to those who like tea; but, to account for this to those persons who only regard tea as a panacea for indigestion, I will add that Eugène was writing; he sat at his ease, and his feet were more often on the fire-dogs than in his foot-muff.

Oh! to sit with your feet on the polished bar that rests on

the two brackets of a fender, and dream of your love affairs while wrapped in your dressing-gown, is so delightful a thing, that I deeply regret having no mistress, no fire-dogs, and no dressing-gown. When I shall have all those good things, I shall not write my experiences, I shall take the benefit of them.

The first letter Eugène had to write was finished in a quarter of an hour. He folded it, sealed it, and left it lying in front of him without any address. The second letter, begun at eleven o'clock, was not finished till noon. The four pages were written all over.

"That woman runs in my head," said he to himself as he folded the second missive, leaving it there, and intending to address it after ending his involuntary reverie. He crossed the fronts of his flowered dressing-gown, put his feet on a stool, stuffed his hands into the pockets of his red cashmere trousers, and threw himself back in a delicious armchair with deep ears, of which the seat and back were set at the comfortable angle of a hundred and twenty degrees. He drank no more tea, but remained passive, his eyes fixed on the little gilt fist which formed the knob of his fire-shovel, without seeing the shovel, or the hand, or the gilding. He did not even make up the fire. This was a great mistake! Is it not an intense pleasure to fidget with the fire when dreaming of women? Our fancy lends speech to the little blue tongues which suddenly burst up and babble on the hearth. We can find a meaning in the sudden and noisy language of a *bourguignon*.

At this word I must pause and insert, for the benefit of the ignorant, an explanation vouchsafed by a very distinguished etymologist, who wishes to remain anonymous. *Bourguignon* is the popular and symbolical name given, ever since the reign of Charles VI., to the loud explosions which result in the ejection on to a rug or a dress of a fragment of charcoal, the germ of a conflagration. The heat, it is said, explodes a bubble of air remaining in the heart of the wood, in the trail of some gnawing grub. *Inde amor, inde Bur-*

gundus. We quake as we see the charred pieces coming down like an avalanche when we had balanced them so industriously between two blazing logs. Oh! making up a wood-fire when you are in love is the material expression of your sentiments.

It was at this moment that I entered Eugène's room; he started violently, and said:

"So there you are, my dear Horace. How long have you been here?"

"I have this moment come."

"Ah!"

He took the two letters, addressed them, and rang for his servant.

"Take these two notes."

And Joseph went without a remark. Excellent servant!

And we proceeded to discuss the expedition to the Morea, in which I wanted to be employed as surgeon. Eugène pointed out that I should lose much by leaving Paris, and we then talked of indifferent things. I do not think that I shall be blamed for omitting our conversation.

When Madame de Listomère rose at about two in the afternoon, her maid Caroline handed her a letter, which she read while Caroline was dressing her hair. (An imprudence committed by a great many young wives.)

"Ah, dear angel of love, my treasure of life and happiness!"—on reading these words, the Marquise was going to throw the letter into the fire; but a fancy flashed through her head, which any virtuous woman will understand to a marvel, namely, to see how a man might end who began in this strain. She read on. When she turned her fourth page, she dropped her arms like a person who is tired.

"Caroline," said she, "go and find out who left this letter for me."

"Madame, I took it from M. le Baron de Rastignac's man-servant."

There was a long silence.

"Will madame dress now?"

"No."

"He must be excessively impertinent!" thought the Marquise.—I may ask any woman to make her own commentary.

Madame de Listomère closed hers with a formal resolution to shut her door on Monsieur Eugène, and, if she should meet him in company, to treat him with more than contempt; for his audacity was not to be compared with any of the other instances which the Marquise had at last forgiven. At first she thought she would keep the letter, but, on due reflection, she burned it.

"Madame has just received such a flaming love-letter, and she read it!" said Caroline to the housemaid.

"I never should have thought it of madame," said the old woman, quite astonished.

That evening the Marquise was at the house of the Marquis de Beauséant, where she would probably meet Rastignac. It was a Saturday. The Marquis de Beauséant was distantly related to Monsieur de Rastignac, so the young man could not fail to appear in the course of the evening. At two in the morning, Madame de Listomère, who had stayed so late solely to crush Eugène by her coldness, had waited in vain. A witty writer, Stendahl, has given the whimsical name of crystallization to the process worked out by the Marquise's mind before, during, and after this evening.

Four days later Eugène was scolding his man-servant.

"Look here, Joseph; I shall be obliged to get rid of you, my good fellow."

"I beg your pardon, sir?"

"You do nothing but blunder. Where did you take the two letters I gave you on Friday?"

Joseph was bewildered. Like a statue in a cathedral porch he stood motionless, wholly absorbed in the travail of his ideas. Suddenly he smiled foolishly, and said:

"Monsieur, one was for Madame la Marquise de Listomère, Rue Saint-Dominique, and the other was for Monsieur's lawyer——"

"Are you sure of what you say?"

Joseph stood dumfounded. I must evidently interfere—happening to be present at the moment.

"Joseph is right," said I. Eugène turned round to me. "I read the addresses quite involuntarily, and——"

"And," said Eugène, interrupting me, "was not one of them for Madame de Nucingen?"

"No, by all the devils! And so I supposed, my dear boy, that your heart had pirouetted from the Rue Saint-Lazare to the Rue Saint-Dominique."

Eugène struck his forehead with the palm of his hand, and began to smile. Joseph saw plainly that the fault was none of his.

Now, there are certain moral reflections on which all young men should meditate. Mistake the first: Eugène thought it amusing to have made Madame de Listomère laugh at the blunder that had put her in possession of a love-letter which was not intended for her. Mistake the second: He did not go to see Madame de Listomère till four days after the misadventure, thus giving the thoughts of a virtuous young woman time to crystallize. And there were a dozen more mistakes which must be passed over in silence to give ladies *ex professo* the pleasure of deducing them for the benefit of those who cannot guess them.

Eugène arrived at the Marquise's door; but as he was going in, the porter stopped him, and told him that Madame de Listomère was out. As he was getting into his carriage again, the Marquis came in.

"Come up, Eugène," said he; "my wife is at home."

Oh! forgive the Marquis. A husband, however admirable, scarcely ever attains to perfection.

Rastignac as he went upstairs discerned the ten fallacies in worldly logic which stood on this page of the fair book of his life.

When Madame de Listomère saw her husband come in with Eugène, she could not help coloring. The young Baron observed the sudden flush. If the most modest of men never quite loses some little dregs of conceit, which he can no more get rid of than a woman can throw off her inevitable vanities, who can blame Eugène for saying to himself, "What! this stronghold too?" and he settled his head in his cravat. Though young men are not very avaricious, they all love to add a head to their collection of medals.

Monsieur de Listomère seized on the *Gazette de France*, which he saw in a corner by the fireplace, and went to the window to form, by the help of the newspaper, an opinion of his own as to the state of France. No woman, not even a prude, is long in embarrassment even in the most difficult situation in which she can find herself; she seems always to carry in her hand the fig-leaf given to her by our mother Eve. And so, when Eugène, having interpreted the orders given to the porter in a sense flattering to his vanity, made his bow to Madame de Listomère with a tolerably deliberate air, she was able to conceal all her thoughts behind one of those feminine smiles, which are more impenetrable than a King's speech.

"Are you unwell, madame? You had closed your door."

"No, monsieur."

"You were going out perhaps?"

"Not at all."

"You are expecting somebody?"

"Nobody."

"If my visit is ill timed, you have only the Marquis to blame. I was obeying your mysterious orders when he himself invited me into the sanctuary."

"Monsieur de Listomère was not in my confidence. There are certain secrets which it is not always prudent to share with one's husband."

The firm, mild tone in which the Marquise spoke these words, and the imposing dignity of her glance, were enough to make Rastignac feel that he had been in too much haste to plume himself.

"I understand, madame," said he, laughing; "I must therefore congratulate myself all the more on having met Monsieur le Marquis; he has procured me an opportunity for offering you an explanation, which would be fraught with danger, but that you are kindness itself."

The Marquise looked at the young Baron with considerable astonishment, but she replied with dignity.

"On your part, monsieur, silence will be the best excuse. On my side I promise you to forget entirely—a forgiveness you scarcely merit."

"Forgiveness is needless, madame, when there has been no offence.—The letter you received," he added in an undertone, "and which you must have thought so unseemly, was not intended for you."

The Marquise smiled in spite of herself; she wished to appear offended.

"Why tell a falsehood?" she replied with an air of disdainful amusement, but in a very friendly tone. "Now that I have scolded you enough, I am quite ready to laugh at a stratagem not devoid of skill. I know some poor women who would be caught by it. 'Good heavens, how he loves me!' they would say." She forced a laugh, and added with an indulgent air, "If we are to remain friends, let me hear nothing more of mistakes of which I cannot be the dupe."

"On my honor, madame, you are far more so than you fancy," Eugène eagerly replied.

"What are you talking about?" asked Monsieur de Listomère, who for a minute had been listening to the conversation, without being able to pierce the darkness of its meaning.

"Oh, nothing that will interest you," said Madame de Listomère.

The Marquis quietly returned to his paper, saying, "I see Madame de Mortsauf is dead; your poor brother is at Clochegourde no doubt."

"Do you know, monsieur," said the Marquise, addressing Eugène, "that you have just made a very impertinent speech?"

"If I did not know the strictness of your principles," he replied simply, "I should fancy you either meant to put ideas into my head which I dare not allow myself, or to wring my secret from me; or perhaps, indeed, you wish to make fun of me."

The Marquise smiled. This smile put Eugène out of patience.

"May you always believe, madame, in the offence I did not commit!" said he. "And I fervently hope that chance may not lead you to discover in society the person who was intended to read that letter——"

"What! Still Madame de Nucingen?" cried Madame de Listomère, more anxious to master the secret than to be revenged on the young man for his retort.

Eugène reddened. A man must be more than five-and-twenty not to redden when he is blamed for the stupid fidelity which women laugh at only to avoid betraying how much they envy its object. However, he said, calmly enough, "Why not, madame?"

These are the blunders we commit at five-and-twenty. This confession agitated Madame de Listomère violently; but Eugène was not yet able to analyze a woman's face as seen in a glimpse, or from one side. Only her lips turned white. She rang to have some wood put on the fire, and so obliged Eugène to rise to take leave. "If that is the case," said the Marquise, stopping Eugène by her cold, precise manner, "you will find it difficult, monsieur, to explain by what chance my name happened to come to your pen. An address written on a letter is not like the first-come crush hat which a man may heedlessly take for his own on leaving a ball."

Eugène, put quite out of countenance, looked at the Marquise with a mingled expression of stupidity and fatuousness; he felt that he was ridiculous, stammered out some schoolboy speech, and left. A few days later Madame de Listomère had indisputable proof of Eugène's veracity.

For more than a fortnight she has not gone into society.

The Marquis tells every one who asks him the reason of this change:

"My wife has a gastric attack."

I, who attend her, and who know her secret, know that she is only suffering from a little nervous crisis, and takes advantage of it to stay quietly at home.

Paris, *February* 1839.

ANOTHER STUDY OF WOMAN

To Léon Gozlan as a Token of Literary Good-fellowship.

AT Paris there are almost always two separate parties going on at every ball and rout. First, an official party, composed of the persons invited, a fashionable and much-bored circle. Each one grimaces for his neighbor's eye; most of the younger women are there for one person only; when each woman has assured herself that for that one she is the handsomest woman in the room, and that the opinion is perhaps shared by a few others, a few insignificant phrases are exchanged, as: "Do you think of going away soon to La Crampade?" "How well Madame de Portenduère sang!" "Who is the little woman with such a load of diamonds?" Or, after firing off some smart epigrams, which give transient pleasure, and leave wounds that rankle long, the groups thin out, the mere lookers on go away, and the waxlights burn down to the sconces.

The mistress of the house then waylays a few artists, amusing people or intimate friends, saying, "Do not go yet; we will have a snug little supper." These collect in some small room. The second, the real party, now begins; a party where, as of old, every one can hear what is said, conversation is general, each one is bound to be witty and to contribute to the amusement of all. Everything is made to tell, honest laughter takes the place of the gloom which in company saddens the prettiest faces. In short, where the rout ends pleasure begins.

The Rout, a cold display of luxury, a review of self-conceits in full dress, is one of those English inventions which tend to *mechanize* other nations. England seems bent on seeing

the whole world as dull as itself, and dull in the same way.
So this second party is, in some French houses, a happy protest on the part of the old spirit of our light-hearted people.
Only, unfortunately, so few houses protest; and the reason
is a simple one. If we no longer have many suppers nowadays, it is because never, under any rule, have there been
fewer men placed, established, and successful than under the
reign of Louis Philippe, when the Revolution began again,
lawfully. Everybody is on the march some whither, or trot-
ting at the heels of Fortune. Time has become the costliest
commodity, so no one can afford the lavish extravagance of
going home to-morrow morning and getting up late. Hence,
there is no second soirée now but at the houses of women rich
enough to entertain, and since July 1830 such women may
be counted in Paris.

In spite of the covert opposition of the Faubourg Saint-
Germain, two or three women, among them Madame
d'Espard and Mademoiselle des Touches, have not chosen to
give up the share of influence they exercised in Paris, and
have not closed their houses.

The salon of Mademoiselle des Touches is noted in Paris
as being the last refuge where the old French wit has found a
home, with its reserved depths, its myriad subtle byways, and
its exquisite politeness. You will there still find grace of
manner notwithstanding the conventionalities of courtesy,
perfect freedom of talk notwithstanding the reserve which
is natural to persons of breeding, and, above all, a liberal
flow of ideas. No one there thinks of keeping his thought for
a play; and no one regards a story as material for a book. In
short, the hideous skeleton of literature at bay never stalks
there, on the prowl for a clever sally or an interesting subject.

The memory of one of these evenings especially dwells with
me, less by reason of a confidence in which the illustrious
de Marsay opened up one of the deepest recesses of woman's
heart, than on account of the reflections to which his narrative
gave rise, as to the changes that have taken place in the
French woman since the fateful revolution of July.

On that evening chance had brought together several persons, whose indisputable merits have won them European reputations. This is not a piece of flattery addressed to France, for there were a good many foreigners present. And, indeed, the men who most shone were not the most famous. Ingenious repartee, acute remarks, admirable banter, pictures sketched with brilliant precision, all sparkled and flowed without elaboration, were poured out without disdain, but without effort, and were exquisitely expressed and delicately appreciated. The men of the world especially were conspicuous for their really artistic grace and spirit.

Elsewhere in Europe you will find elegant manners, cordiality, genial fellowship, and knowledge; but only in Paris, in this drawing-room, and those to which I have alluded, does the particular wit abound which gives an agreeable and changeful unity to all these social qualities, an indescribable river-like flow which makes this profusion of ideas, of definitions, of anecdotes, of historical incidents, meander with ease. Paris, the capital of taste, alone possesses the science which makes conversation a tourney in which each type of wit is condensed into a shaft, each speaker utters his phrase and casts his experience in a word, in which every one finds amusement, relaxation, and exercise. Here, then, alone, will you exchange ideas; here you need not, like the dolphin in the fable, carry a monkey on your shoulders; here you will be understood, and will not risk staking your gold pieces against base metal.

Here, again, secrets neatly betrayed, and talk, light or deep, play and eddy, changing their aspect and hue at every phrase. Eager criticism and crisp anecdotes lead on from one to the next. All eyes are listening, a gesture asks a question, and an expressive look gives the answer. In short, and in a word, everything is wit and mind.

The phenomenon of speech, which, when duly studied and well handled, is the power of the actor and the story-teller, had never so completely bewitched me. Nor was I alone under the influence of its spell; we all spent a delightful evening. The conversation had drifted into anecdote, and brought out in its rushing course some curious confessions, several portraits, and a thousand follies, which make this enchanting improvisation impossible to record; still, by setting these things down in all their natural freshness and abruptness, their elusive divarications, you may perhaps feel the charm of a real French evening, taken at the moment when the most engaging familiarity makes each one forget his own interests, his personal conceit, or, if you like, his pretensions.

At about two in the morning, as supper ended, no one was left sitting round the table but intimate friends, proved by an intercourse of fifteen years, and some persons of great taste and good breeding, who knew the world. By tacit agreement, perfectly carried out, at supper every one renounced his pretensions to importance. Perfect equality set the tone. But indeed there was no one present who was not very proud of being himself.

Mademoiselle des Touches always insists on her guests remaining at table till they leave, having frequently remarked the change which a move produces in the spirit of a party. Between the dining-room and the drawing-room the charm is destroyed. According to Sterne, the ideas of an author after shaving are different from those he had before. If Sterne is right, may it not be boldly asserted that the frame of mind of a party at table is not the same as that of the same persons returned to the drawing-room? The atmosphere is not heady, the eye no longer contemplates the brilliant disorder of the dessert, lost are the happy effects of that laxness of mood, that benevolence which comes over us while we remain in the humor peculiar to the well-filled man, settled comfortably on one of the springy chairs which are made in these days. Perhaps we are not more ready to talk face to face with the dessert and in the society of good wine, during the delightful interval when every one may sit with an elbow on the table and his head resting on his hand. Not only does every one like to talk then, but also to listen. Digestion, which is almost always attent, is loquacious or silent, as characters differ. Then every one finds his opportunity.

Was not this preamble necessary to make you know the charm of the narrative, by which a celebrated man, now dead, depicted the innocent jesuistry of women, painting it with the subtlety peculiar to persons who have seen much of the world, and which makes statesmen such delightful story-tellers when, like Prince Talleyrand and Prince Metternich, they vouchsafe to tell a story?

De Marsay, prime minister for some six months, had already given proofs of superior capabilities. Those who had known him long were not indeed surprised to see him display all the talents and various aptitudes of a statesman; still it might yet be a question whether he would prove to be a solid politician, or had merely been moulded in the fire of circumstance. This question had just been asked by a man whom he had made préfet, a man of wit and observation, who had for a long time been a journalist, and who admired de Marsay without infusing into his admiration that dash of acrid criticism by which, in Paris, one superior man excuses himself from admiring another.

"Was there ever," said he, "in your former life, any event, any thought or wish which told you what your vocation was?" asked Émile Blondet; "for we all, like Newton, have our apple, which falls and leads us to the spot where our faculties develop——"

"Yes," said de Marsay; "I will tell you about it."

Pretty women, political dandies, artists, old men, de Marsay's intimate friends,—all settled themselves comfortably, each in his favorite attitude, to look at the Minister. Need it be said that the servants had left, that the doors were shut, and the curtains drawn over them? The silence was so complete that the murmurs of the coachmen's voices could be heard from the courtyard, and the pawing and champing made by horses when asking to be taken back to their stable.

"The statesman, my friends, exists by one single quality," said the Minister, playing with his gold and mother-of-pearl dessert knife. "To wit: the power of always being master of himself; of profiting more or less, under all circumstances, by every event, however fortuitous; in short, of having within himself a cold and disinterested other self, who looks on as a spectator at all the changes of life, noting our passions and our sentiments, and whispering to us in every case the judgment of a sort of moral ready-reckoner."

"That explains why a statesman is so rare a thing in France," said old Lord Dudley.

"From a sentimental point of view, this is horrible," the Minister went on. "Hence, when such a phenomenon is seen in a young man—Richelieu, who, when warned overnight by a letter of Concini's peril, slept till midday, when his benefactor was killed at ten o'clock—or say Pitt, or Napoleon, he is a monster. I became such a monster at a very early age, thanks to a woman."

"I fancied," said Madame de Montcornet with a smile, "that more politicians were undone by us than we could make."

"The monster of which I speak is a monster just because he withstands you," replied de Marsay, with a little ironical bow.

"If this is a love-story," the Baronne de Nucingen interposed, "I request that it may not be interrupted by any reflections."

"Reflection is so antipathetic to it!" cried Joseph Bridau.

"I was seventeen," de Marsay went on; "the Restoration was being consolidated; my old friends know how impetuous and fervid I was then. I was in love for the first time, and I was—I may say so now—one of the handsomest young fellows in Paris. I had youth and good looks, two advantages due to good fortune, but of which we are all as proud as of a conquest. I must be silent as to the rest.—Like all youths, I was in love with a woman six years older than myself. No one of you here," said he, looking carefully round the table, "can suspect her name or recognize her. Ronquerolles alone, at the time, ever guessed my secret. He has kept it well,

but I should have feared his smile.   However, he is gone,"
said the Minister, looking round.

"He would not stay to supper," said Madame de Nucingen.

"For six months, possessed by my passion," de Marsay
went on, "but incapable of suspecting that it had overmas-
tered me, I had abandoned myself to that rapturous idolatry
which is at once the triumph and the frail joy of the young.
I treasured *her* old gloves; I drank an infusion of the flowers
she had worn; I got out of bed at night to go and gaze at
her window.   All my blood rushed to my heart when I inhaled
the perfume she used.   I was miles away from knowing that
woman is a stove with a marble casing."

"Oh! spare us your terrible verdicts," cried Madame de
Montcornet with a smile.

"I believe I should have crushed with my scorn the philosopher who first uttered this terrible but profoundly true
thought," said de Marsay.   "You are all far too keen-sighted
for me to say any more on that point.   These few words
will remind you of your own follies.

"A great lady if ever there was one, a widow without children—oh! all was perfect—my idol would shut herself up to
mark my linen with her hair; in short, she responded to my
madness by her own.   And how can we fail to believe in passion when it has the guarantee of madness?

"We each devoted all our minds to concealing a love so perfect and so beautiful from the eyes of the world; and we
succeeded.   And what charm we found in our escapades!   Of
her I will say nothing.   She was perfection then, and to this
day is considered one of the most beautiful women in Paris;
but at that time a man would have endured death to win one
of her glances.   She had been left with an amount of fortune
sufficient for a woman who had loved and was adored; but
the Restoration, to which she owed renewed lustre, made it
seem inadequate in comparison with her name.   In my position I was so fatuous as never to dream of a suspicion.
Though my jealousy would have been of a hundred and
twenty Othello-power, that terrible passion slumbered in me

as gold in the nugget. I would have ordered my servant to thrash me if I had been so base as ever to doubt the purity of that angel—so fragile and so strong, so fair, so artless, pure, spotless, and whose blue eye allowed my gaze to sound it to the very depths of her heart with adorable submissiveness. Never was there the slightest hesitancy in her attitude, her look, or word; always white and fresh, and ready for the Beloved like the Oriental Lily of the 'Song of Songs!' Ah! my friends!" sadly exclaimed the Minister, grown young again, "a man must hit his head very hard on the marble to dispel that poem!"

This cry of nature, finding an echo in the listeners, spurred the curiosity he had excited in them with so much skill.

"Every morning, riding Sultan—the fine horse you sent me from England," de Marsay went on, addressing Lord Dudley, "I rode past her open carriage, the horses' pace being intentionally reduced to a walk, and read the order of the day signaled to me by the flowers of her bouquet in case we were unable to exchange a few words. Though we saw each other almost every evening in society, and she wrote to me every day, to deceive the curious and mislead the observant we had adopted a scheme of conduct: never to look at each other; to avoid meeting; to speak ill of each other. Self-admiration, swagger, or playing the disdained swain,—all these old manœuvres are not to compare on either part with a false passion professed for an indifferent person and an air of indifference towards the true idol. If two lovers will only play that game, the world will always be deceived; but then they must be very secure of each other.

"Her stalking-horse was a man in high favor, a courtier, cold and sanctimonious, whom she never received at her own house. This little comedy was performed for the benefit of simpletons and drawing-room circles, who laughed at it. Marriage was never spoken of between us; six years' difference of age might give her pause; she knew nothing of my fortune, of which, on principle, I have always kept the secret. I, on my part, fascinated by her wit and manners, by the extent of her knowledge and her experience of the world, would have married her without a thought. At the same time, her reserve charmed me. If she had been the first to speak of marriage in a certain tone, I might perhaps have noted it as vulgar in that accomplished soul.

"Six months, full and perfect—a diamond of the purest water! That has been my portion of love in this base world.

"One morning, attacked by the feverish stiffness which marks the beginning of a cold, I wrote her a line to put off one of those secret festivals which are buried under the roofs of Paris like pearls in the sea. No sooner was the letter sent than remorse seized me: she will not believe that I am ill! thought I. She was wont to affect jealousy and suspiciousness.—When jealousy is genuine," said de Marsay, interrupting himself, "it is the visible sign of an unique passion."

"Why?" asked the Princesse de Cadignan eagerly.

"Unique and true love," said de Marsay, "produces a sort of corporeal apathy attuned to the contemplation into which one falls. Then the mind complicates everything; it works on itself, pictures its fancies, turns them into reality and torment; and such jealousy is as delightful as it is distressing."

A foreign minister smiled as, by the light of memory, he felt the truth of this remark.

"Besides," de Marsay went on, "I said to myself, why miss a happy hour? Was it not better to go, even though feverish? And, then, if she learns that I am ill, I believe her capable of hurrying here and compromising herself. I made an effort; I wrote a second letter, and carried it myself, for my confidential servant was now gone. The river lay between us. I had to cross Paris; but at last, within a suitable distance of her house, I caught sight of a messenger; I charged him to have the note sent up to her at once, and I had the happy idea of driving past her door in a hackney cab to see whether she might not by chance receive the two letters together. At the moment when I arrived it was two o'clock; the great gate opened to admit a carriage. Whose?—That of the stalking-horse!

"It is fifteen years since—well, even while I tell the tale, I, the exhausted orator, the Minister dried up by the friction of public business, I still feel a surging in my heart and the hot blood about my diaphragm. At the end of an hour I passed once more; the carriage was still in the courtyard! My note no doubt was in the porter's hands. At last, at half-past three, the carriage drove out. I could observe my rival's expression; he was grave, and did not smile; but he was in love, and no doubt there was business in hand.

"I went to keep my appointment; the queen of my heart met me; I saw her calm, pure, serene. And here I must confess that I have always thought that Othello was not only stupid, but showed very bad taste. Only a man who is half a negro could behave so: indeed Shakespeare felt this when he called his play 'The Moor of Venice.' The sight of the woman we love is such a balm to the heart that it must dispel anguish, doubt, and sorrow. All my rage vanished. I could smile again. Hence this cheerfulness, which at my age now would be the most atrocious dissimulation, was the result of my youth and my love. My jealousy once buried, I had the power of observation. My ailing condition was evident; the horrible doubts that had fermented in me increased it. At last I found an opening for putting in these words: 'You have had no one with you this morning?' making a pretext of the uneasiness I had felt in the fear lest she should have disposed of her time after receiving my first note.—'Ah!' she exclaimed, 'only a man could have such ideas! As if I could think of anything but your suffering. Till the moment when I received your second note I could think only of how I could contrive to go to see you.'—'And you were alone?'— 'Alone,' said she, looking at me with a face of innocence so perfect that it must have been his distrust of such a look as that which made the Moor kill Desdemona. As she lived alone in the house, the word was a fearful lie. One single lie destroys the absolute confidence which to some souls is the very foundation of happiness.

"To explain to you what passed in me at that moment it

must be assumed that we have an internal self of which the exterior *I* is but the husk; that this self, as brilliant as light, is as fragile as a shade—well, that beautiful self was in me thenceforth for ever shrouded in crape. Yes; I felt a cold and fleshless hand cast over me the winding-sheet of experience, dooming me to the eternal mourning into which the first betrayal plunges the soul. As I cast my eyes down that, she might not observe my dizziness, this proud thought somewhat restored my strength: 'If she is deceiving you, she is unworthy of you!'

"I ascribed my sudden reddening and the tears which started to my eyes to an attack of pain, and the sweet creature insisted on driving me home with the blinds of the cab drawn. On the way she was full of a solicitude and tenderness that might have deceived the Moor of Venice whom I have taken as a standard of comparison. Indeed, if that great child were to hesitate two seconds longer, every intelligent spectator feels that he would ask Desdemona's forgiveness. Thus, killing the woman is the act of a boy.—She wept as we parted, so much was she distressed at being unable to nurse me herself. She wished she were my valet, in whose happiness she found a cause of envy, and all this was as elegantly expressed, oh! as Clarissa might have written in her happiness. There is always a precious ape in the prettiest and most angelic woman!"

At these words all the women looked down, as if hurt by this brutal truth so brutally stated.

"I will say nothing of the night, nor of the week I spent," de Marsay went on. "I discovered that I was a statesman."

It was so well said that we all uttered an admiring exclamation.

"As I thought over the really cruel vengeance to be taken on a woman," said de Marsay, continuing his story, "with infernal ingenuity—for, as we had loved each other, some terrible and irreparable revenges were possible—I despised myself, I felt how common I was, I insensibly formulated a horrible code—that of Indulgence. In taking vengeance on a woman, do we not in fact admit that there is but one for us, that we cannot do without her? And, then, is revenge the way to win her back? If she is not indispensable, if there are other women in the world, why not grant her the right to change which we assume?

"This, of course, applies only to passion; in any other sense it would be socially wrong. Nothing more clearly proves the necessity for indissoluble marriage than the instability of passion. The two sexes must be chained up, like wild beasts as they are, by inevitable law, deaf and mute. Eliminate revenge, and infidelity in love is nothing. Those who believe that for them there is but one woman in the world must be in favor of vengeance, and then there is but one form of it—that of Othello.

"Mine was different."

The words produced in each of us the imperceptible movement which newspaper writers represent in Parliamentary reports by the words: *great sensation*.

"Cured of my cold, and of my pure, absolute, divine love, I flung myself into an adventure, of which the heroine was charming, and of a style of beauty utterly opposed to that of my deceiving angel. I took care not to quarrel with this clever woman, who was so good an actress, for I doubt whether true love can give such gracious delights as those lavished by such a dexterous fraud. Such refined hypocrisy is as good as virtue.—I am not speaking to you Englishwomen, my lady," said the Minister suavely, addressing Lady Barimore, Lord Dudley's daughter. "I tried to be the same lover.

"I wished to have some of my hair worked up for my new angel, and I went to a skilled artist who at that time dwelt in the Rue Boucher. The man had a monopoly of capillary keepsakes, and I mention his address for the benefit of those who have not much hair; he has plenty of every kind and every color. After I had explained my order, he showed me his work. I then saw achievements of patience surpassing those which the story books ascribe to fairies, or which are executed by prisoners. He brought me up to date as to the caprices and fashions governing the use of hair. 'For the last year,' said he, 'there has been a rage for marking linen with hair; happily I had a fine collection of hair and skilled needlewomen.'—On hearing this a suspicion flashed upon me; I took out my handkerchief and said, 'So this was done in your shop, with false hair?'—He looked at the handkerchief, and said, 'Ay! that lady was very particular, she insisted on verifying the tint of the hair. My wife herself marked those handkerchiefs. You have there, sir, one of the finest pieces of work we have ever executed.' Before this last ray of light I might have believed something—might have taken a woman's word. I left the shop still having faith in pleasure, but where love was concerned I was as atheistical as a mathematician.

"Two months later I was sitting by the side of the ethereal being in her boudoir, on her sofa; I was holding one of her hands—they were very beautiful—and we scaled the Alps of sentiment, culling their sweetest flowers, and pulling off the daisy-petals; there is always a moment when one pulls daisies to pieces, even if it is in a drawing-room and there are no daisies. At the intensest moment of tenderness, and when we are most in love, love is so well aware of its own short duration that we are irresistibly urged to ask, 'Do you love me? Will you love me always?' I seized the elegiac moment, so warm, so flowery, so full-blown, to lead her to tell her most delightful lies, in the enchanting language of rapturous exaggeration and high-flown poetry peculiar to love. Charlotte displayed her choicest allurements: She could not live without me; I was to her the only man in the world; she feared to weary me, because my presence bereft her of all her wits; with me all her faculties were lost in love; she was indeed too tender to escape alarms; for the last six months she had been seeking some way to bind me to her eternally, and God alone knew that secret; in short, I was her god!"

The women who heard de Marsay seemed offended by seeing themselves so well acted, for he seconded the words by airs, and sidelong attitudes, and mincing grimaces which were quite illusory.

"At the very moment when I might have believed these adorable falsehoods, as I still held her right hand in mine, I said to her, 'When are you to marry the Duke?'

"The thrust was so direct, my· gaze met hers so boldly, and her hand lay so tightly in mine, that her start, slight as it was, could not be disguised; her eyes fell before mine, and a faint blush colored her cheeks.—'The Duke! What do you mean?' she said, affecting great astonishment.—'I know everything,' replied I; 'and in my opinion, you should delay no longer; he is rich; he is a duke; but he is more than devout, he is religious! I am sure, therefore, that you have been faithful to me, thanks to his scruples. You cannot imagine how urgently necessary it is that you should compromise him with himself and with God; short of that you will never bring him to the point.'—'Is this a dream?' said she, pushing her hair from her forehead, fifteen years before Malibran, with the gesture which Malibran has made so famous.—'Come, do not be childish, my angel,' said I, trying to take her hands; but she folded them before her with a little prudish and indignant mien.—'Marry him, you have my permission,' said I, replying to this gesture by using the formal *vous* instead of *tu.* 'Nay, better, I beg you to do so.'—'But,' cried she, falling at my knees, 'there is some horrible mistake; I love no one in the world but you; you may demand any proofs you please.'—'Rise, my dear,' said I, 'and do me the honor of being truthful.'—'As before God.'—'Do you doubt my love?'—'No.'—'Nor my fidelity?'—'No.'— 'Well, I have committed the greatest crime,' I went on. 'I have doubted your love and your fidelity. Between two intoxications I looked calmly about me.'—'Calmly!' sighed she. 'That is enough, Henri; you no longer love me.'

"She had at once found, you perceive, a loophole for escape. In scenes like these an adverb is dangerous. But, happily, curiosity made her add: 'And what did you see? Have I ever spoken of the Duke excepting in public? Have

you detected in my eyes——?'—'No,' said I, 'but in his.
And you have eight times made me go to Saint-Thomas
d'Aquin to see you listening to the same mass as he.'—'Ah!'
she exclaimed, 'then I have made you jealous!'—'Oh! I only
wish I could be!' said I, admiring the pliancy of her quick
intelligence, and these acrobatic feats which can only be
successful in the eyes of the blind. 'But by dint of going
to church I have become very incredulous. On the day of
my first cold, and your first treachery, when you thought I
was in bed, you received the Duke, and you told me you had
seen no one.'—'Do you know that your conduct is infamous?'
—'In what respect? I consider your marriage to the Duke
an excellent arrangement; he gives you a great name, the
only rank that suits you, a brilliant and distinguished position. You will be one of the queens of Paris. I should be
doing you a wrong if I placed any obstacle in the way of this
prospect, this distinguished life, this splendid alliance. Ah!
Charlotte, some day you will do me justice by discovering
how unlike my character is to that of other young men. You
would have been compelled to deceive me; yes, you would
have found it very difficult to break with me, for he watches
you. It is time that we should part, for the Duke is rigidly
virtuous. You must turn prude; I advise you to do so. The
Duke is vain; he will be proud of his wife.'—'Oh!' cried she,
bursting into tears, 'Henri, if only you had spoken! Yes,
if you had chosen'—it was I who was to blame, you understand—'we would have gone to live all our days in a corner,
married, happy, and defied the world.'—'Well, it is too late
now,' said I, kissing her hands, and putting on a victimized
air.—'Good God! But I can undo it all!' said she.—'No,
you have gone too far with the Duke. I ought indeed to go
a journey to part us more effectually. We should both have
reason to fear our own affection——'—'Henri, do you think
the Duke has any suspicions?' I was still 'Henri,' but the *tu*
was lost for ever.—'I do not think so,' I replied, assuming the
manner of a friend; 'but be as devout as possible, reconcile
yourself to God, for the Duke waits for proofs; he hesitates,
you must bring him to the point.'

"She rose, and walked twice round the boudoir in real or affected agitation; then she no doubt found an attitude and a look beseeming the new state of affairs, for she stopped in front of me, held out her hand, and said in a voice broken by emotion, 'Well, Henri, you are loyal, noble, and a charming man; I shall never forget you.'

"These were admirable tactics. She was bewitching in this transition of feeling, indispensable to the situation in which she wished to place herself in regard to me. I fell into the attitude, the manners, and the look of a man so deeply distressed, that I saw her too newly assumed dignity giving way; she looked at me, took my hand, drew me along almost, threw me on to the sofa, but quite gently, and said after a moment's silence, 'I am dreadfully unhappy, my dear fellow. Do you love me?'—'Oh! yes.'—'Well, then, what will become of you?'"

At this point the women all looked at each other.

"Though I can still suffer when I recall her perfidy, I still laugh at her expression of entire conviction and sweet satisfaction that I must die, or at any rate sink into perpetual melancholy," de Marsay went on. "Oh! do not laugh yet!" he said to his listeners; "there is better to come. I looked at her very tenderly after a pause, and said to her, 'Yes, that is what I have been wondering.'—'Well, what will you do?'—'I asked myself that the day after my cold.'—'And——?' she asked with eager anxiety.—'And I have made advances to the little lady to whom I was supposed to be attached.'

"Charlotte started up from the sofa like a frightened doe, trembling like a leaf, gave me one of those looks in which women forego all their dignity, all their modesty, their refinement, and even their grace, the sparkling glitter of a hunted viper's eye when driven into a corner, and said, 'And I have loved this man! I have struggled! I have——' On this last thought, which I leave you to guess, she made the most impressive pause I ever heard.—'Good God!' she cried, 'how unhappy are we women! we never can be loved. To you there is nothing serious in the purest feelings. But never mind; when you cheat us you still are our dupes!'—'I see that plainly,' said I, with a stricken air; 'you have far too much wit in your anger for your heart to suffer from it.'—This modest epigram increased her rage; she found some tears of vexation. 'You disgust me with the world and with life,' she said; 'you snatch away all my illusions; you deprave my heart.'

"She said to me all that I had a right to say to her, and with a simple effrontery, an artless audacity, which would certainly have nailed any man but me on the spot.—'What is to become of us poor women in a state of society such as Louis XVIII.'s charter has made it?'—(Imagine how her words had run away from her.)—'Yes, indeed, we are born to suffer. In matters of passion we are always superior to you, and you are beneath all loyalty. There is no honesty in your hearts. To you love is a game in which you always cheat.'—'My dear,' said I, 'to take anything serious in society nowadays would be like making romantic love to an actress.'—'What a shameless betrayal! It was deliberately planned!'—'No, only a rational issue.'—'Good-bye, Monsieur de Marsay,' said she; 'you have deceived me horribly.'—'Surely,' I replied, taking up a submissive attitude, 'Madame la Duchesse will not remember Charlotte's grievances?'—'Certainly,' she answered bitterly.—'Then, in fact, you hate me?'—She bowed, and I said to myself, 'There is something still left!'

"The feeling she had when I parted from her allowed her to believe that she still had something to avenge. Well, my friends, I have carefully studied the lives of men who have had great success with women, but I do not believe that the Maréchal de Richelieu, or Lauzun, or Louis de Valois ever effected a more judicious retreat at the first attempt. As to my mind and heart, they were cast in a mould then and there, once for all, and the power of control I thus acquired over the thoughtless impulses which make us commit so many follies gained me the admirable presence of mind you all know."

16

"How deeply I pity the second!" exclaimed the Baronne de Nucingen.

A scarcely perceptible smile on de Marsay's pale lips made Delphine de Nucingen color.

"How we do forget!" said the Baron de Nucingen.

The great banker's simplicity was so extremely droll, that his wife, who was de Marsay's "second," could not help laughing like every one else.

"You are all ready to condemn the woman," said Lady Dudley. "Well, I quite understand that she did not regard her marriage as an act of inconstancy. Men will never distinguish between constancy and fidelity.—I know the woman whose story Monsieur de Marsay has told us, and she is one of the last of your truly great ladies."

"Alas! my lady, you are right," replied de Marsay. "For very nearly fifty years we have been looking on at the progressive ruin of all social distinctions. We ought to have saved our women from this great wreck, but the Civil Code has swept its leveling influence over their heads. However terrible the words, they must be spoken: Duchesses are vanishing, and marquises too! As to the baronesses—I must apologize to Madame de Nucingen, who will become a countess when her husband is made a peer of France—baronesses have never succeeded in getting people to take them seriously."

"Aristocracy begins with the viscountess," said Blondet with a smile.

"Countesses will survive," said de Marsay. "An elegant woman will be more or less of a countess—a countess of the Empire or of yesterday, a countess of the old block, or, as they say in Italy, a countess by courtesy. But as to the great lady, she died out with the dignified splendor of the last century, with powder, patches, high-heeled slippers, and stiff bodices with a delta stomacher of bows. Duchesses in these days can pass through a door without any need to widen it for their hoops. The Empire saw the last of gowns with trains! I am still puzzled to understand how a sovereign who wished to see his drawing-room swept by ducal satin and velvet did not make indestructible laws. Napoleon never guessed the results of the Code he was so proud of. That man, by creating duchesses, founded the race of our 'ladies' of to-day —the indirect offspring of his legislation."

"It was logic, handled as a hammer by boys just out of school and by obscure journalists, which demolished the splendors of the social state," said the Comte de Vandenesse. "In these days every rogue who can hold his head straight in his collar, cover his manly bosom with half an ell of satin by way of a cuirass, display a brow where apocryphal genius gleams under curling locks, and strut in a pair of patent-leather pumps graced by silk socks which cost six francs, screws his eye-glass into one of his eye-sockets by puckering up his cheek, and whether he be an attorney's clerk, a contractor's son, or a banker's bastard, he stares impertinently at the prettiest duchess, appraises her as she walks downstairs, and says to his friend—dressed by Buisson, as we all are, and mounted in patent-leather like any duke himself—'There, my boy, that is a perfect lady.' "

"You have not known how to form a party," said Lord Dudley; "it will be a long time yet before you have a policy. You talk a great deal in France about organizing labor, and you have not yet organized property. So this is what happens: Any duke—and even in the time of Louis XVIII. and Charles X. there were some left who had two hundred thousand francs a year, a magnificent residence, and a sumptuous train of servants—well, such a duke could live like a great lord. The last of these great gentlemen in France was the Prince de Talleyrand.—This duke leaves four children, two of them girls. Granting that he has great luck in marrying them all well, each of these descendants will have but sixty or eighty thousand francs a year now; each is the father or mother of children, and consequently obliged to live with the strictest economy in a flat on the ground floor or first floor of a large house. Who knows if they may not even be hunting a fortune? Henceforth the eldest son's wife, a duchess in name only, has no carriage, no people, no opera-box, no time to herself. She has not her own rooms in the family mansion, nor her fortune, nor her pretty toys; she is buried in marriage as a wife in the Rue Saint-Denis is buried in trade; she buys socks for her dear little children, nurses them herself, and keeps an eye on her girls, whom she no longer sends to school at a convent. Thus your noblest dames have been turned into worthy brood-hens."

"Alas! it is true," said Joseph Bridau. "In our day we cannot show those beautiful flowers of womanhood which graced the golden ages of the French Monarchy. The great lady's fan is broken. A woman has nothing now to blush for; she need not slander or whisper, hide her face or reveal it. A fan is of no use now but for fanning herself. When once a thing is no more than what it is, it is too useful to be a form of luxury."

"Everything in France has aided and abetted the 'perfect lady,' " said Daniel d'Arthez. "The aristocracy has acknowledged her by retreating to the recesses of its landed estates, where it has hidden itself to die—emigrating inland before the march of ideas, as of old to foreign lands before that of the masses. The women who could have founded European *salons,* could have guided opinion and turned it inside out like a glove, could have ruled the world by ruling the men of art or of intellect who ought to have ruled it, have committed the blunder of abandoning their ground; they were ashamed of having to fight against the citizen class drunk with power, and rushing out on to the stage of the world, there to be cut to pieces perhaps by the barbarians who are at its heels. Hence, where the middle class insist on seeing princesses, these are really only ladylike young women. In these days princes can find no great ladies whom they may compromise; they cannot even confer honor on a woman taken up at random. The Duc de Bourbon was the last prince to avail himself of this privilege."

"And God alone knows how dearly he paid for it," said Lord Dudley.

"Nowadays princes have lady-like wives, obliged to share their opera-box with other ladies; royal favor could not raise them higher by a hair's-breadth; they glide unremarkable between the waters of the citizen class and those of the nobility —not altogether noble nor altogether *bourgeoises*," said the Marquise de Rochegude acridly.

"The press has fallen heir to the Woman," exclaimed Rastignac. "She no longer has the quality of a spoken *feuilleton*—delightful calumnies graced by elegant language. We read *feuilletons* written in a dialect which changes every three years, society papers about as mirthful as an undertaker's mute, and as light as the lead of their type. French conversation is carried on from one end of the country to the other in a revolutionary jargon, through long columns of type printed in old mansions where a press groans in the place where formerly elegant company used to meet."

"The knell of the highest society is tolling," said a Russian Prince. "Do you hear it? And the first stroke is your modern word *lady*."

"You are right, Prince," said de Marsay. "The 'perfect lady,' issuing from the ranks of the nobility, or sprouting from the citizen class, and the product of every soil, even of the provinces is the expression of these times, a last remaining embodiment of good taste, grace, wit, and distinction, all combined, but dwarfed. We shall see no more great ladies in France, but there will be 'ladies' for a long time, elected by public opinion to form an upper chamber of women, and who will be among the fair sex what a 'gentleman' is in England."

"And that they call progress!" exclaimed Mademoiselle des Touches. "I should like to know where the progress lies?"

"Why, in this," said Madame de Nucingen. "Formerly a woman might have the voice of a fish-seller, the walk of a grenadier, the face of an impudent courtesan, her hair too high on her forehead, a large foot, a thick hand—she was a great lady in spite of it all; but in these days, even if she were a Montmorency—if a Montmorency would ever be such a creature—she would not be a lady."

"But what do you mean by a 'perfect lady'?" asked Count Adam Laginski.

"She is a modern product, a deplorable triumph of the elective system as applied to the fair sex," said the Minister. "Every revolution has a word of its own which epitomizes and depicts it."

"You are right," said the Russian, who had come to make a literary reputation in Paris. "The explanation of certain words added from time to time to your beautiful language would make a magnificent history. *Organize,* for instance, is the word of the Empire, and sums up Napoleon completely."

"But all that does not explain what is meant by a lady!" the young Pole exclaimed, with some impatience.

"Well, I will tell you," said Émile Blondet to Count Adam. "One fine morning you go for a saunter in Paris. It is past two, but five has not yet struck. You see a woman coming towards you; your first glance at her is like the preface to a good book, it leads you to expect a world of elegance and refinement. Like a botanist over hill and dale in his pursuit of plants, among the vulgarities of Paris life you have at last found a rare flower. This woman is attended by two very distinguished-looking men, of whom one, at any rate, wears an order; or else a servant out of livery follows her at a distance of ten yards. She displays no gaudy colors, no open-worked stockings, no over-elaborate waist-buckle, no embroidered frills to her drawers fussing round her ankles. You will see that she is shod with prunella shoes, with sandals crossed over extremely fine cotton stockings, or plain gray silk stockings; or perhaps she wears boots of the most exquisite simplicity. You notice that her gown is made of a neat and inexpensive material, but made in a way that surprises more than one woman of the middle class; it is almost always a long pelisse, with bows to fasten it, and neatly bound with fine cord or an imperceptible braid. The Unknown has a way of her own in wrapping herself in her shawl or mantilla; she knows how to draw it round her from her hips to her neck, outlining a carapace, as it were, which would make an ordinary woman look like a turtle, but which in her sets off the most beautiful forms while concealing them. How does she do it? This secret she keeps, though unguarded by any patent.

"As she walks she gives herself a little concentric and harmonious twist, which makes her supple or dangerous slenderness writhe under the stuff, as a snake does under the green gauze of trembling grass. Is it to an angel or a devil that she owes the graceful undulation which plays under her long black silk cape, stirs its lace frill, sheds an airy balm, and what I should like to call the breeze of a Parisienne? You may recognize over her arms, round her waist, about her throat, a science of drapery recalling the antique Mnemosyne.

"Oh! how thoroughly she understands the *cut* of her gait— forgive the expression. Study the way she puts her foot forward, moulding her skirt with such a decent preciseness that the passer-by is filled with admiration, mingled with desire, but subdued by deep respect. When an Englishwoman attempts this step, she looks like a grenadier marching forward to attack a redoubt. The women of Paris have a genius for walking. The municipality really owed them asphalt footwalks.

"Our Unknown jostles no one. If she wants to pass, she waits with proud humility till some one makes way. The distinction peculiar to a well-bred woman betrays itself, especially in the way she holds her shawl or cloak crossed over her bosom. Even as she walks she has a little air of serene dignity, like Raphael's Madonnas in their frames. Her aspect, at once quiet and disdainful, makes the most insolent dandy step aside for her.

"Her bonnet, remarkable for its simplicity, is trimmed with crisp ribbons; there may be flowers in it, but the cleverest of such women wear only bows. Feathers demand a carriage; flowers are too showy. Beneath it you see the fresh unworn face of a woman who, without conceit, is sure of herself; who looks at nothing, and sees everything; whose vanity, satiated by being constantly gratified, stamps her face with an indifference which piques your curiosity. She knows that she is looked at, she knows that everybody, even women, turn round to see her again. And she threads her way through Paris like a gossamer, spotless and pure.

"This delightful species affects the hottest latitudes, the cleanest longitudes of Paris; you will meet her between the 10th and 110th Arcade of the Rue de Rivoli; along the line of the Boulevards from the equator of the Passage des Panoramas, where the products of India flourish, where the warmest creations of industry are displayed, to the Cape of the Madeleine; in the least muddy districts of the citizen quarters, between No. 30 and No. 130 of the Rue du Faubourg Saint-Honoré. During the winter, she haunts the terrace of the Feuillants, but not the asphalt pavement that lies parallel. According to the weather, she may be seen flying in the Avenue of the Champs-Elysées, which is bounded on the east by the Place Louis XV., on the west by the Avenue de Marigny, to the south by the road, to the north by the gardens of the Faubourg Saint-Honoré. Never is this pretty variety of woman to be seen in the hyperborean regions of the Rue Saint-Denis, never in the Kamtschatka of miry, narrow, commercial streets; never anywhere in bad weather. These flowers of Paris, blooming only in Oriental weather, perfume the highways; and after five o'clock fold up like morning-glory flowers. The women you will see later, looking a little like them, trying to ape them, are would-be ladies; while the fair Unknown, your Beatrice of a day, is a 'perfect lady.'

"It is not very easy for a foreigner, my dear Count, to recognize the differences by which the observer *emeritus* distinguishes them—women are such consummate actresses; but they are glaring in the eyes of Parisians: hooks ill fastened, strings showing loops of rusty-white tape through a gaping slit in the back, rubbed shoe-leather, ironed bonnet-strings, an over-full skirt, an over-tight waist. You will see a certain effort in the intentional droop of the eyelid. There is something conventional in the attitude.

"As to the *bourgeoise,* the citizen womankind, she cannot possibly be mistaken for the lady; she is an admirable foil to her, she accounts for the spell cast over you by the Unknown. She is bustling, and goes out in all weathers, trots about, comes, goes, gazes, does not know whether she will or will not go into a shop. Where the lady knows just what she wants and what she is doing, the townswoman is undecided, tucks up her skirts to cross a gutter, dragging a child by the hand, which compels her to look out for the vehicles; she is a mother in public, and talks to her daughter; she carries money in her bag, and has open-work stockings on her feet; in winter, she wears a boa over her fur cloak; in summer, a shawl and a scarf; she is accomplished in the redundancies of dress.

"You will meet the fair Unknown again at the Italiens, at the Opera, at a ball. She will then appear under such a different aspect that you would think them two beings devoid of any analogy. The woman has emerged from those mysterious garments like a butterfly from its silky cocoon. She serves up, like some rare dainty, to your ravished eyes, the forms which her bodice scarcely revealed in the morning. At the theatre she never mounts higher than the second tier, excepting at the Italiens. You can there watch at your leisure the studied deliberateness of her movements. The enchanting deceiver plays off all the little political artifices of her sex so naturally as to exclude all idea of art or premeditation. If she has a royally beautiful hand, the most perspicacious beholder will believe that it is absolutely necessary that she should twist, or refix, or push aside the ringlet or curl she plays with. If she has some dignity of profile, you will be persuaded that she is giving irony or grace to what she says to her neighbor, sitting in such a position as to produce the magical effect of the 'lost profile,' so dear to great painters, by which the cheek catches the high light, the nose is shown in clear outline, the nostrils are transparently rosy, the forehead

squarely modeled, the eye has its spangle of fire, but fixed on
space, and the white roundness of the chin is accentuated
by a line of light. If she has a pretty foot, she will throw
herself on a sofa with the coquettish grace of a cat in the
sunshine, her feet outstretched without your feeling that her
attitude is anything but the most charming model ever given
to a sculptor by lassitude.

"Only the perfect lady is quite at her ease in full dress;
nothing inconveniences her. You will never see her, like
the woman of the citizen class, pulling up a refractory
shoulder-strap, or pushing down a rebellious whalebone, or
looking whether her tucker is doing its office of faithful
guardian to two treasures of dazzling whiteness, or glancing
in the mirrors to see if her head-dress is keeping its place.
Her toilet is always in harmony with her character; she has
had time to study herself, to learn what becomes her, for she
has long known what does not suit her. You will not find
her as you go out; she vanishes before the end of the play.
If by chance she is to be seen, calm and stately, on the stairs,
she is experiencing some violent emotion; she has to bestow
a glance, to receive a promise. Perhaps she goes down so
slowly on purpose to gratify the vanity of a slave whom she
sometimes obeys. If your meeting takes place at a ball or an
evening party, you will gather the honey, natural or affected,
of her insinuating voice; her empty words will enchant you,
and she will know how to give them the value of thought by
her inimitable bearing."

"To be such a woman, is it not necessary to be very clever?"
asked the Polish Count.

"It is necessary to have great taste," replied the Princesse
de Cadignan.

"And in France taste is more than cleverness," said the
Russian.

"This woman's cleverness is the triumph of a purely plastic
art," Blondet went on. "You will not know what she said,
but you will be fascinated. She will toss her head, or gently
shrug her white shoulders; she will gild an insignificant

speech with a charming pout and smile; or throw a Voltairean epigram into an 'Indeed!' an 'Ah!' a 'What then!' A jerk of her head will be her most pertinent form of questioning; she will give meaning to the movement by which she twirls a vinaigrette hanging to her finger by a ring. She gets an artificial grandeur out of superlative trivialities; she simply drops her hand impressively, letting it fall over the arm of her chair as dewdrops hang on the cup of a flower, and all is said—she has pronounced judgment beyond appeal, to the apprehension of the most obtuse. She knows how to listen to you; she gives you the opportunity of shining, and—I ask your modesty—those moments are rare?"

The candid simplicity of the young Pole, to whom Blondet spoke, made all the party shout with laughter.

"Now, you will not talk for half-an-hour with a *bourgeoise* without her alluding to her husband in one way or another," Blondet went on with unperturbed gravity; "whereas, even if you know that your lady is married, she will have the delicacy to conceal her husband so effectually that it will need the enterprise of Christopher Columbus to discover him. Often you will fail in the attempt single-handed. If you have had no opportunity of inquiring, towards the end of the evening you detect her gazing fixedly at a middle-aged man wearing a decoration, who bows and goes out. She has ordered her carriage, and goes.

"You are not the rose, but you have been with the rose, and you go to bed under the golden canopy of a delicious dream, which will last perhaps after Sleep, with his heavy finger, has opened the ivory gates of the temple of dreams.

"The lady, when she is at home, sees no one before four; she is shrewd enough always to keep you waiting. In her house you will find everything in good taste; her luxury is for hourly use, and duly renewed; you will see nothing under glass shades, no rags of wrappings hanging about, and looking like a pantry. You will find the staircase warmed. Flowers on all sides will charm your sight—flowers, the only gift she accepts, and those only from certain people, for nosegays

live but a day; they give pleasure, and must be replaced; to
her they are, as in the East, a symbol and a promise. The
costly toys of fashion lie about, but not so as to suggest a
museum or a curiosity shop. You will find her sitting by
the fire in a low chair, from which she will not rise to greet
you. Her talk will not now be what it was at the ball; there
she was our creditor; in her own home she owes you the
pleasure of her wit. These are the shades of which the lady
is a marvelous mistress. What she likes in you is a man to
swell her circle, an object for the cares and attentions which
such women are now happy to bestow. Therefore, to attract
you to her drawing-room, she will be bewitchingly charming.
This especially is where you feel how isolated women are
nowadays, and why they want a little world of their own,
to which they may seem a constellation. Conversation is
impossible without generalities."

"Yes," said de Marsay, "you have truly hit the fault of
our age. The epigram—a volume in a word—no longer
strikes, as it did in the eighteenth century, at persons or at
things, but at squalid events, and it dies in a day."

"Hence," said Blondet, "the intelligence of the lady, if
she has any, consists in casting doubts on everything, while
the *bourgeoise* uses her to affirm everything. Here lies the
great difference between the two women; the townswoman is
certainly virtuous; the lady does not know yet whether she
is, or whether she always will be; she hesitates and struggles
where the other refuses point-blank and falls full length.
This hesitancy in everything is one of the last graces left
to her by our horrible times. She rarely goes to church,
but she will talk to you of religion; and if you have the good
taste to affect Free-thought, she will try to convert you, for
you will have opened a way for the stereotyped phrases,
the head-shaking and gestures understood by all these women:
'For shame! I thought you had too much sense to attack
religion. Society is tottering, and you deprive it of its support. Why, religion at this moment means you and me;
it is property, and the future of our children! Ah! let us

not be selfish! Individualism is the disease of the age, and
religion is the only remedy; it unites families which your
laws put asunder,' and so forth. Then she plunges into some
neo-Christian speech sprinkled with political notions which is
neither Catholic nor Protestant—but moral? Oh! deuced
moral!—in which you may recognize a fag end of every
material woven by modern doctrines, at loggerheads together."

The women could not help laughing at the airs by which
Blondet illustrated his satire.

"This explanation, dear Count Adam," said Blondet, turning to the Pole, "will have proved to you that the 'perfect
lady' represents the intellectual no less than the political
muddle, just as she is surrounded by the showy and not
very lasting products of an industry which is always aiming
at destroying its work in order to replace it by something
else. When you leave her you say to yourself: She certainly
has superior ideas! And you believe it all the more because
she will have sounded your heart with a delicate touch, and
have asked you your secrets; she affects ignorance, to learn
everything; there are some things she never knows, not even
when she knows them. You alone will be uneasy, you will
know nothing of the state of her heart. The great ladies of
old flaunted their love-affairs, with newspapers and adver-
tisements; in these days the lady has her little passion neatly
ruled like a sheet of music with its crotchets and quavers
and minims, its rests, its pauses, its sharps to sign the key.
A mere weak woman, she is anxious not to compromise her
love, or her husband, or the future of her children. Name,
position, and fortune are no longer flags so respected as to
protect all kinds of merchandise on board. The whole aristocracy no longer advances in a body to screen the lady.
She has not, like the great lady of the past, the demeanor of
lofty antagonism; she can crush nothing under foot, it is
she who would be crushed. Thus she is apt at Jesuitical
mezzo termine, she is a creature of equivocal compromises,
of guarded proprieties, of anonymous passions steered between

two reef-bound shores. She is as much afraid of her servants as an Englishwoman who lives in dread of a trial in the divorce-court. This woman—so free at a ball, so attractive out walking—is a slave at home; she is never independent but in perfect privacy, or theoretically. She must preserve herself in her position as a lady. This is her task.

"For in our day a woman repudiated by her husband, reduced to a meagre allowance, with no carriage, no luxury, no opera-box, none of the divine accessories of the toilet, is no longer a wife, a maid, or a townswoman; she is adrift, and becomes a chattel. The Carmelites will not receive a married woman; it would be bigamy. Would her lover still have anything to say to her? That is the question. Thus your perfect lady may perhaps give occasion to calumny, never to slander."

"It is all horribly true," said the Princesse de Cadignan.

"And so," said Blondet, "our 'perfect lady' lives between English hypocrisy and the delightful frankness of the eighteenth century—a bastard system, symptomatic of an age in which nothing that grows up is at all like the thing that has vanished, in which transition leads nowhere, everything is a matter of degree; all the great figures shrink into the background, and distinction is purely personal. I am fully convinced that it is impossible for a woman, even if she were born close to a throne, to acquire before the age of five-and-twenty the encyclopædic knowledge of trifles, the practice of manœuvring, the important small things, the musical tones and harmony of coloring, the angelic bedevilments and innocent cunning, the speech and the silence, the seriousness and the banter, the wit and the obtuseness, the diplomacy and the ignorance which make up the perfect lady."

"And where, in accordance with the sketch you have drawn," said Mademoiselle des Touches to Émile Blondet, "would you class the female author? Is she a perfect lady, a woman *comme il faut?*"

"When she has no genius, she is a woman *comme il n'en faut pas,*" Blondet replied, emphasizing the words with a stolen glance, which might make them seem praise frankly addressed to Camille Maupin. "This epigram is not mine, but Napoleon's," he added.

"You need not owe Napoleon any grudge on that score," said Canalis, with an emphatic tone and gesture. "It was one of his weaknesses to be jealous of literary genius—for he had his mean points. Who will ever explain, depict, or understand Napoleon? A man represented with his arms folded, and who did everything, who was the greatest force ever known, the most concentrated, the most mordant, the most acid of all forces; a singular genius who carried armed civilization in every direction without fixing it anywhere; a man who could do everything because he willed everything; a prodigious phenomenon of will, conquering an illness by a battle, and yet doomed to die of disease in bed after living in the midst of ball and bullets; a man with a code and a sword in his brain, word and deed; a clear-sighted spirit that foresaw everything but his own fall; a capricious politician who risked men by handfuls out of economy, and who spared three heads—those of Talleyrand, of Pozzo di Borgo, and of Metternich, diplomatists whose death would have saved the French Empire, and who seemed to him of greater weight than thousands of soldiers; a man to whom nature, as a rare privilege, had given a heart in a frame of bronze; mirthful and kind at midnight amid women, and next morning manipulating Europe as a young girl might amuse herself by splashing the water in her bath! Hypocritical and generous; loving tawdriness and simplicity; devoid of taste, but protecting the arts; and in spite of these antitheses, really great in everything by instinct or by temperament; Cæsar at five-and-twenty, Cromwell at thirty; and then, like my grocer buried in Père Lachaise, a good husband and a good father. In short, he improvised public works, empires, kings, codes, verses, a romance—and all with more range than precision. Did he not aim at making all Europe France? And after making us weigh on the earth in such a way as to change the laws of gravitation, he left us poorer than on the day when he

first laid hands on us; while he, who had taken an empire by
his name, lost his name on the frontier of his empire in a sea
of blood and soldiers. A man all thought and all action, who
comprehended Desaix and Fouché."

"All despotism and all justice at the right moments. The
true king!" said de Marsay.

"Ah! vat a pleashre it is to dichest vile you talk," said
Baron de Nucingen.

"But do you suppose that the treat we are giving you is
a common one?" asked Joseph Bridau. "If you had to pay
for the charms of conversation as you do for those of dancing
or of music, your fortune would be inadequate! There is
no second performance of the same flash of wit."

"And are we really so much deteriorated as these gentlemen
think?" said the Princesse de Cadignan, addressing the women with a smile at once sceptical and ironical. "Because,
in these days, under a régime which makes everything small,
you prefer small dishes, small rooms, small pictures, small
articles, small newspapers, small books, does that prove
that women too have grown smaller? Why should the human
heart change because you change your coat? In all ages
the passions will remain the same. I know cases of beautiful
devotion, of sublime sufferings, which lack the publicity—
the glory, if you choose—which formerly gave lustre to the
errors of some women. But though one may not have saved
a King of France, one is not the less an Agnes Sorel. Do you
believe that our dear Marquise d'Espard is not the peer of
Madame Doublet, or Madame du Deffant, in whose rooms
so much evil was spoken and done? Is not Taglioni a
match for Camargo? or Malibran the equal of Saint-Huberti?
Are not our poets superior to those of the eighteenth century? If at this moment, through the fault of the Grocers
who govern us, we have not a style of our own, had not the
Empire its distinguishing stamp as the age of Louis XV. had,
and was not its splendor fabulous? Have the sciences lost
anything?"

"I am quite of your opinion, madame; the women of this

age are truly great," replied the Comte de Vandenesse. "When posterity shall have followed us, will not Madame Récamier appear in proportions as fine as those of the most beautiful women of the past? We have made so much history that historians will be lacking! The age of Louis XIV. had but one Madame de Sévigné; we have a thousand now in Paris who certainly write better than she did, and who do not publish their letters. Whether the Frenchwoman be called 'perfect lady' or great lady, she will always be *the* woman among women.

"Émile Blondet has given us a picture of the fascinations of a woman of the day; but, at need, this creature who bridles or shows off, who chirps out the ideas of Mr. This and Mr. That, would be heroic. And it must be said, your faults, mesdames, are all the more poetical, because they must always and under all circumstances be surrounded by greater perils. I have seen much of the world, I have studied it perhaps too late; but in cases where the illegality of your feelings might be excused, I have always observed the effects of I know not what chance—which you may call Providence—inevitably overwhelming such as we consider light women."

"I hope," said Madame de Vandenesse, "that we can be great in other ways——"

"Oh, let the Comte de Vandenesse preach to us!" exclaimed Madame de Sérizy.

"With all the more reason because he has preached a great deal by example," said the Baronne de Nucingen.

"On my honor!" said General de Montriveau, "in all the dramas—a word you are very fond of," he said, looking at Blondet—"in which the finger of God has been visible, the most frightful I ever knew was very near being by my act——"

"Well, tell us all about it!" cried Lady Barimore; "I love to shudder!"

"It is the taste of a virtuous woman," replied de Marsay, looking at Lord Dudley's lovely daughter.

"During the campaign of 1812," General de Montriveau

17

began, "I was the involuntary cause of a terrible disaster which may be of use to you, Doctor Bianchon," turning to me, "since, while devoting yourself to the human body, you concern yourself a good deal with the mind; it may tend to solve some of the problems of the will.

"I was going through my second campaign; I enjoyed danger, and laughed at everything, like the young and foolish lieutenant of artillery that I was. When we reached the Beresina, the army had, as you know, lost all discipline, and had forgotten military obedience. It was a medley of men of all nations, instinctively making their way from north to south. The soldiers would drive a general in rags and bare-foot away from their fire if he brought neither wood nor victuals. After the passage of this famous river disorder did not diminish. I had come quietly and alone, without food, out of the marshes of Zembin, and was wandering in search of a house where I might be taken in. Finding none, or driven away from those I came across, happily towards evening I perceived a wretched little Polish farm, of which nothing can give you any idea unless you have seen the wooden houses of Lower Normandy, or the poorest farm-buildings of la Beauce. These dwellings consist of a single room, with one end divided off by a wooden partition, the smaller division serving as a store-room for forage.

"In the darkness of twilight I could just see a faint smoke rising above this house. Hoping to find there some comrades more compassionate than those I had hitherto addressed, I boldly walked as far as the farm. On going in, I found the table laid. Several officers, and with them a woman—a common sight enough—were eating potatoes, some horse-flesh broiled over the charcoal, and some frozen beetroots. I recognized among the company two or three artillery captains of the regiment in which I had first served. I was welcomed with a shout of acclamation, which would have amazed me greatly on the other side of the Beresina; but at this moment the cold was less intense; my fellow-officers were resting, they were warm, they had food, and the room, strewn with trusses of straw, gave the promise of a delightful night. We did not ask for so much in those days. My comrades could be philanthropists *gratis*—one of the commonest ways of being philanthropic. I sat down to eat on one of the bundles of straw.

"At the end of the table, by the side of the door opening into the smaller room full of straw and hay, sat my old colonel, one of the most extraordinary men I ever saw among all the mixed collection of men it has been my lot to meet. He was an Italian. Now, whenever human nature is truly fine in the lands of the South, it is really sublime. I do not know whether you have ever observed the extreme fairness of Italians when they are fair. It is exquisite, especially under an artificial light. When I read the fantastical portrait of Colonel Oudet sketched by Charles Nodier, I found my own sensations in every one of his elegant phrases. Italian, then, as were most of the officers of his regiment, which had, in fact, been borrowed by the Emperor from Eugène's army, my colonel was a tall man, at least eight or nine inches above the standard, and admirably proportioned—a little stout perhaps, but prodigiously powerful, active, and clean-limbed as a greyhound. His black hair in abundant curls showed up his complexion, as white as a woman's; he had small hands, a shapely foot, a pleasant mouth, and an aquiline nose delicately formed, of which the tip used to become naturally pinched and white whenever he was angry, as happened often. His irascibility was so far beyond belief that I will tell you nothing about it; you will have the opportunity of judging of it. No one could be calm in his presence. I alone, perhaps, was not afraid of him; he had indeed taken such a singular fancy to me that he thought everything I did right. When he was in a rage his brow was knit and the muscles of the middle of his forehead set in a delta, or, to be more explicit, in Redgauntlet's horseshoe. This mark was, perhaps, even more terrifying than the magnetic flashes of his blue eyes. His whole frame quivered, and his strength, great as it was in his normal state, became almost unbounded.

"He spoke with a strong guttural roll. His voice, at least as powerful as that of Charles Nodier's Oudet, threw an incredible fulness of tone into the syllable or the consonant in which this burr was sounded. Though this faulty pronunciation was at times a grace, when commanding his men, or when he was excited, you cannot imagine, unless you had heard it, what force was expressed by this accent, which at Paris is so common. When the Colonel was quiescent, his blue eyes were angelically sweet, and his smooth brow had a most charming expression. On parade, or with the army of Italy, not a man could compare with him. Indeed, d'Orsay himself, the handsome d'Orsay, was eclipsed by our colonel on the occasion of the last review held by Napoleon before the invasion of Russia.

"Everything was in contrasts in this exceptional man. Passion lives on contrast. Hence you need not ask whether he exerted over women the irresistible influences to which our nature yields"—and the general looked at the Princesse de Cadignan—"as vitreous matter is moulded under the pipe of the glass-blower; still, by a singular fatality—an observer might perhaps explain the phenomenon—the Colonel was not a lady-killer, or was indifferent to such successes.

"To give you an idea of his violence, I will tell you in a few words what I once saw him do in a paroxysm of fury. We were dragging our guns up a very narrow road, bordered by a somewhat high slope on one side, and by thickets on the other. When we were half-way up we met another regiment of artillery, its colonel marching at the head. This colonel wanted to make the captain who was at the head of our foremost battery back down again. The captain, of course, refused; but the colonel of the other regiment signed to his foremost battery to advance, and in spite of the care the driver took to keep among the scrub, the wheel of the first gun struck our captain's right leg and broke it, throwing him over on the near side of his horse. All this was the work of a moment. Our Colonel, who was but a little way off, guessed that there was a quarrel; he galloped up, riding among the

guns at the risk of falling with his horse's four feet in the
air, and reached the spot, face to face with the other colonel,
at the very moment when the captain fell, calling out 'Help!'
No, our Italian colonel was no longer human! Foam like
the froth of champagne rose to his lips; he roared inarticu-
lately like a lion. Incapable of uttering a word, or even a
cry, he made a terrific signal to his antagonist, pointing to
the wood and drawing his sword. The two colonels went
aside. In two seconds we saw our Colonel's opponent
stretched on the ground, his skull split in two. The soldiers
of his regiment backed—yes, by heaven, and pretty quickly
too.

"The captain, who had been so nearly crushed, and who
lay yelping in the puddle where the gun carriage had thrown
him, had an Italian wife, a beautiful Sicilian of Messina,
who was not indifferent to our Colonel. This circumstance
had aggravated his rage. He was pledged to protect the
husband, bound to defend him as he would have defended
the woman herself.

"Now, in the hovel beyond Zembin, where I was so well
received, this captain was sitting opposite to me, and his
wife was at the other end of the table, facing the Colonel.
This Sicilian was a little woman named Rosina, very dark, but
with all the fire of the Southern sun in her black almond-
shaped eyes. At this moment she was deplorably thin; her
face was covered with dust, like fruit exposed to the drought
of a highroad. Scarcely clothed in rags, exhausted by
marches, her hair in disorder, and clinging together under
a piece of a shawl tied close over her head, still she had the
graces of a woman; her movements were engaging, her small
rosy mouth and white teeth, the outline of her features and
figure, charms which misery, cold, and neglect had not altogether defaced, still suggested love to any man who could
think of a woman. Rosina had one of those frames which are
fragile in appearance, but wiry and full of spring. Her
husband, a gentleman of Piedmont, had a face expressive
of ironical simplicity, if it is allowable to ally the two words.

Brave and well informed, he seemed to know nothing of
the connection which had subsisted between his wife and the
Colonel for three years past. I ascribed this unconcern to
Italian manners, or to some domestic secret; yet there was
in the man's countenance one feature which always filled
me with involuntary distrust. His under lip, which was
thin and very restless, turned down at the corners instead of
turning up, and this, as I thought, betrayed a streak of
cruelty in a character which seemed so phlegmatic and indo-
lent.

"As you may suppose the conversation was not very sparkling when I went in. My weary comrades ate in silence; of
course, they asked me some questions, and we related our
misadventures, mingled with reflections on the campaign,
the generals, their mistakes, the Russians, and the cold. A
minute after my arrival the colonel, having finished his
meagre meal, wiped his moustache, bid us good-night, shot a
black look at the Italian woman, saying, 'Rosina?' and then,
without waiting for a reply, went into the little barn full of
hay, to bed. The meaning of the Colonel's utterance was self-
evident. The young wife replied by an indescribable gesture,
expressing all the annoyance she could not but feel at seeing
her thralldom thus flaunted without human decency, and the
offence to her dignity as a woman, and to her husband.
But there was, too, in the rigid setting of her features and
the tight knitting of her brows a sort of presentiment; perhaps she foresaw her fate. Rosina remained quietly in her
place.

"A minute later, and apparently when the Colonel was snug
in his couch of straw or hay, he repeated, 'Rosina?'

"The tone of this second call was even more brutally questioning than the first. The Colonel's strong burr, and the
length which the Italian language allows to be given to
vowels and the final syllable, concentrated all the man's despotism, impatience, and strength of will. Rosina turned
pale, but she rose, passed behind us, and went to the Colonel.

"All the party sat in utter silence; I, unluckily, after

looking at them all, began to laugh, and then the ail laughed too.—'*Tu ridi?*—you laugh?' said the husband.

" 'On my honor, old comrade,' said I, becoming serious again, 'I confess that I was wrong; I ask your pardon a thousand times, and if you are not satisfied by my apologies I am ready to give you satisfaction.'

" 'Oh! it is not you who are wrong, it is I!' he replied coldly.

"Thereupon we all lay down in the room, and before long all were sound asleep.

"Next morning each one, without rousing his neighbor or seeking companionship, set out again on his way, with that selfishness which made our rout one of the most horrible dramas of self-seeking, melancholy, and horror which ever was enacted under heaven. Nevertheless, at about seven or eight hundred paces from our shelter we, most of us, met again and walked on together, like geese led in flocks by a child's wilful tyranny. The same necessity urged us all.

"Having reached a knoll where we could still see the farmhouse where we had spent the night, we heard sounds resembling the roar of lions in the desert, the bellowing of bulls—no, it was a noise which can be compared to no known cry. And yet, mingling with this horrible and ominous roar, we could hear a woman's feeble scream. We all looked round, seized by I know not what impulse of terror; we no longer saw the house, but a huge bonfire. The farmhouse had been barricaded, and was in flames. Swirls of smoke borne on the wind brought us hoarse cries and an indescribable pungent smell. A few yards behind, the captain was quietly approaching to join our caravan; we gazed at him in silence, for no one dared question him; but he, understanding our curiosity, pointed to his breast with the forefinger of his right hand, and, waving the left in the direction of the fire, he said, . '*Son'io.*'

"We all walked on without saying a word to him."

"There is nothing more terrible than the revolt of a sheep," said de Marsay.

"It would be frightful to let us leave with this horrible picture in our memory," said Madame de Montcornet. "I shall dream of it——"

"And what was the punishment of Monsieur de Marsay's 'First'?" said Lord Dudley, smiling.

"When the English are in jest, their foils have the buttons on," said Blondet.

"Monsieur Bianchon can tell us, for he saw her dying," replied de Marsay, turning to me.

"Yes," said I; "and her end was one of the most beautiful I ever saw. The Duke and I had spent the night by the dying woman's pillow; pulmonary consumption, in the last stage, left no hope; she had taken the sacrament the day before. The Duke had fallen asleep. The Duchess, waking at about four in the morning, signed to me in the most touching way, with a friendly smile, to bid me leave him to rest, and she meanwhile was about to die. She had become incredibly thin, but her face had preserved its really sublime outline and features. Her pallor made her skin look like porcelain with a light within. Her bright eyes and color contrasted with this languidly elegant complexion, and her countenance was full of expressive calm. She seemed to pity the Duke, and the feeling had its origin in a lofty tenderness which, as death approached, seemed to know no bounds. The silence was absolute. The room, softly lighted by a lamp, looked like every sickroom at the hour of death.

"At this moment the clock struck. The Duke awoke, and was in despair at having fallen asleep. I did not see the gesture of impatience by which he manifested the regret he felt at having lost sight of his wife for a few of the last minutes vouchsafed to him; but it is quite certain that any one but the dying woman might have misunderstood it. A busy statesman, always thinking of the interests of France, the Duke had a thousand odd ways on the surface, such as often lead to a man of genius being mistaken for a madman, and of which the explanation lies in the exquisiteness and exacting needs of their intellect. He came to seat himself in an armchair by his wife's side, and looked fixedly at her. The dying woman put her hand out a little way, took her husband's and clasped it feebly; and in a low but agitated voice she said, 'My poor dear, who is left to understand you now?' Then she died, looking at him."

"The stories the doctor tells us," said the Comte de Vandenesse, "always leave a deep impression."

"But a sweet one," said Mademoiselle des Touches, rising.

PARIS, *June* 1839-42.

LA GRANDE BRETECHE

(Sequel to "Another Study of Woman.")

"Ah! madame," replied the doctor, "I have some appalling stories in my collection. But each one has its proper hour in a conversation—you know the pretty jest recorded by Chamfort, and said to the Duc de Fronsac: 'Between your sally and the present moment lie ten bottles of champagne.'"

"But it is two in the morning, and the story of Rosina has prepared us," said the mistress of the house.

"Tell us, Monsieur Bianchon!" was the cry on every side.

The obliging doctor bowed, and silence reigned.

"At about a hundred paces from Vendôme, on the banks of the Loir," said he, "stands an old brown house, crowned with very high roofs, and so completely isolated that there is nothing near it, not even a fetid tannery or a squalid tavern, such as are commonly seen outside small towns. In front of this house is a garden down to the river, where the box shrubs, formerly clipped close to edge the walks, now straggle at their own will. A few willows, rooted in the stream, have grown up quickly like an enclosing fence, and half hide the house. The wild plants we call weeds have clothed the bank with their beautiful luxuriance. The fruit-trees, neglected for these ten years past, no longer bear a crop, and their suckers have formed a thicket. The espaliers are like a copse. The paths, once graveled, are overgrown with purslane; but, to be accurate, there is no trace of a path.

"Looking down from the hilltop, to which cling the ruins of the old castle of the Dukes of Vendôme, the only spot whence the eye can see into this enclosure, we think that at a time, difficult now to determine, this spot of earth must have been the joy of some country gentleman devoted to

(267)

roses and tulips, in a word, to horticulture, but above all
a lover of choice fruit. An arbor is visible, or rather the
wreck of an arbor, and under it a table still stands not entirely
destroyed by time. At the aspect of this garden that is no
more, the negative joys of the peaceful life of the provinces
may be divined as we divine the history of a worthy trades-
man when we read the epitaph on his tomb. To complete
the mournful and tender impressions which seize the soul,
on one of the walls there is a sundial graced with this homely
Christian motto, *'Ultimam cogita.'*

"The roof of this house is dreadfully dilapidated; the outside shutters are always closed; the balconies are hung
with swallows' nests; the doors are for ever shut. Strag-
gling grasses have outlined the flagstones of the steps with
green; the ironwork is rusty. Moon and sun, winter, summer, and snow have eaten into the wood, warped the boards,
peeled off the paint. The dreary silence is broken only by
birds and cats, polecats, rats, and mice, free to scamper
round, and fight, and eat each other. An invisible hand has
written over it all: 'Mystery.'

"If, prompted by curiosity, you go to look at this house
from the street, you will see a large gate, with a round-arched
top; the children have made many holes in it. I learned
later that this door had been blocked for ten years. Through
these irregular breaches you will see that the side towards
the courtyard is in perfect harmony with the side towards
the garden. The same ruin prevails. Tufts of weeds outline
the paving-stones; the walls are scored by enormous cracks,
and the blackened coping is laced with a thousand festoons
of pellitory. The stone steps are disjointed; the bell-cord is
rotten; the gutter-spouts broken. What fire from heaven
can have fallen there? By what decree has salt been sown
on this dwelling? Has God been mocked here? Or was
France betrayed? These are the questions we ask ourselves.
Reptiles crawl over it, but give no reply. This empty and
deserted house is a vast enigma of which the answer is
known to none.

"It was formerly a little domain, held in fief, and is known
as La Grande Bretêche. During my stay at Vendôme, where
Despleins had left me in charge of a rich patient, the sight
of this strange dwelling became one of my keenest pleasures.
Was it not far better than a ruin? Certain memories of indisputable authenticity attach themselves to a ruin; but this
house, still standing, though being slowly destroyed by an
avenging hand, contained a secret, an unrevealed thought.
At the very least, it testified to a caprice. More than once
in the evening I boarded the hedge, run wild, which surrounded the enclosure. I braved scratches, I got into this
ownerless garden, this plot which was no longer public or
private; I lingered there for hours gazing at the disorder.
I would not, as the price of the story to which this strange
scene no doubt was due, have asked a single question of any
gossiping native. On that spot I wove delightful romances,
and abandoned myself to little debauches of melancholy
which enchanted me. If I had known the reason—perhaps
quite commonplace—of this neglect, I should have lost the
unwritten poetry which intoxicated me. To me this refuge
represented the most various phases of human life, shadowed
by misfortune; sometimes the calm of a cloister without the
monks; sometimes the peace of the graveyard without the
dead, who speak in the language of epitaphs; one day I saw
in it the home of lepers; another, the house of the Atridæ;
but, above all, I found there provincial life, with its contem-
plative ideas, its hour-glass existence. I often wept there, I
never laughed.

"More than once I felt involuntary terrors as I heard over-
head the dull hum of the wings of some hurrying wood-
pigeon. The earth is dank; you must be on the watch for
lizards, vipers, and frogs, wandering about with the wild
freedom of nature; above all, you must have no fear of cold,
for in a few moments you feel an icy cloak settle on your
shoulders, like the Commendatore's hand on Don Giovanni's
neck.

"One evening I felt a shudder; the wind had turned an

old rusty weathercock, and the creaking sounded like a cry
from the house, at the very moment when I was finishing
a gloomy drama to account for this monumental embodiment of woe. I returned to my inn, lost in gloomy thoughts.
When I had supped, the hostess came into my room with an
air of mystery, and said, 'Monsieur, here is Monsieur
Regnault.'

" 'Who is Monsieur Regnault?'

" 'What, sir, do you not know Monsieur Regnault?—Well,
that's odd,' said she, leaving the room.

"On a sudden I saw a man appear, tall, slim, dressed in
black, hat in hand, who came in like a ram ready to butt his
opponent, showing a receding forehead, a small pointed head,
and a colorless face of the hue of a glass of dirty water.
You would have taken him for an usher. The stranger wore
an old coat, much worn at the seams; but he had a diamond
in his shirt frill, and gold rings in his ears.

" 'Monsieur,' said I, 'whom have I the honor of addressing?'
—He took a chair, placed himself in front of my fire,
put his hat on my table, and answered while he rubbed his
hands: 'Dear me, it is very cold.—Monsieur, I am Monsieur
Regnault.'

"I was encouraging myself by saying to myself, '*Il bondo
cani!* Seek!'

" 'I am,' he went on, 'notary at Vendôme."

" 'I am delighted to hear it, monsieur,' I exclaimed. 'But
I am not in a position to make a will for reasons best known
to myself.'

" 'One moment!' said he, holding up his hand as though
to gain silence. 'Allow me, monsieur, allow me! I am informed that you sometimes go to walk in the garden of la
Grande Bretêche.'

" 'Yes, monsieur.'

" 'One moment!' said he, repeating his gesture. 'That
constitutes a misdemeanor. Monsieur, as executor under the
will of the late Comtesse de Merret, I come in her name to
beg you to discontinue the practice. One moment! I am not

a Turk, and do not wish to make a crime of it. And besides, you are free to be ignorant of the circumstances which
compel me to leave the finest mansion in Vendôme to fall
into ruin. Nevertheless, monsieur, you must be a man of
education, and you should know that the laws forbid, under
heavy penalties, any trespass on enclosed property. A hedge
is the same as a wall. But, the state in which the place is
left may be an excuse for your curiosity. For my part, I
should be quite content to make you free to come and go in
the house; but being bound to respect the will of the testatrix,
I have the honor, monsieur, to beg that you will go into the
garden no more. I myself, monsieur, since the will was
read, have never set foot in the house, which, as I had the
honor of informing you, is part of the estate of the late
Madame de Merret. We have done nothing there but verify
the number of doors and windows to assess the taxes I have
to pay annually out of the funds left for that purpose by the
late Madame de Merret. Ah! my dear sir, her will made a
great commotion in the town.'

"The good man paused to blow his nose. I respected his
volubility, perfectly understanding that the administration
of Madame de Merret's estate had been the most important
event of his life, his reputation, his glory, his Restoration.
As I was forced to bid farewell to my beautiful reveries and
romances, I was to reject learning the truth on official authority.

"'Monsieur,' said I, 'would it be indiscreet if I were to
ask you the reasons for such eccentricity?'

"At these words an expression, which revealed all the pleasure which men feel who are accustomed to ride a hobby,
overspread the lawyer's countenance. He pulled up the collar
of his shirt with an air, took out his snuffbox, opened it,
and offered me a pinch; on my refusing, he took a large one.
He was happy! A man who has no hobby does not know all
the good to be got out of life. A hobby is the happy medium
between a passion and a monomania. At this moment I
understood the whole bearing of Sterne's charming passion,

and had a perfect idea of the delight with which my uncle
Toby, encouraged by Trim, bestrode his hobby-horse.

"'Monsieur,' said Monsieur Regnault, 'I was head-clerk
in Monsieur Roguin's office, in Paris. A first-rate house,
which you may have heard mentioned? No! An unfortunate
bankruptcy made it famous.—Not having money enough to
purchase a practice in Paris at the price to which they were
run up in 1816, I came here and bought my predecessor's business. I had relations in Vendôme; among others, a wealthy
aunt, who allowed me to marry her daughter.—Monsieur,'
he went on after a little pause, 'three months after being
licensed by the Keeper of the Seals, one evening, as I was
going to bed—it was before my marriage—I was sent for
by Madame la Comtesse de Merret, to her Château of Merret.
Her maid, a good girl, who is now a servant in this inn, was
waiting at my door with the Countess' own carriage. Ah!
one moment! I ought to tell you that Monsieur le Comte
de Merret had gone to Paris to die two months before I
came here. He came to a miserable end, flinging himself
into every kind of dissipation. You understand?

"'On the day when he left, Madame la Comtesse had
quitted la Grande Bretêche, having dismantled it. Some
people even say that she had burnt all the furniture, the
hangings—in short, all the chattels and furniture whatever
used in furnishing the premises now let by the said M.—
(Dear! what am I saying? I beg your pardon, I thought
I was dictating a lease.)—In short, that she burnt everything in the meadow at Merret. Have you been to Merret,
monsieur?—No,' said he, answering himself. 'Ah, it is a
very fine place.'

"'For about three months previously,' he went on, with a
jerk of his head, 'the Count and Countess had lived in a
very eccentric way; they admitted no visitors; Madame lived
on the ground-floor, and Monsieur on the first floor. When
the Countess was left alone, she was never seen excepting
at church. Subsequently, at home, at the château, she refused
to see the friends, whether gentlemen or ladies, who went to

call on her. She was already very much altered when she left la Grande Bretêche to go to Merret. That dear lady— I say dear lady, for it was she who gave me this diamond, but indeed I saw her but once—that kind lady was very ill; she had, no doubt, given up all hope, for she died without choosing to send for a doctor; indeed, many of our ladies fancied she was not quite right in her head. Well, sir, my curiosity was strangely excited by hearing that Madame de Merret had need of my services. Nor was I the only person who took an interest in the affair. That very night, though it was already late, all the town knew that I was going to Merret.

" 'The waiting-woman replied but vaguely to the questions I asked her on the way; nevertheless, she told me that her mistress had received the Sacrament in the course of the day at the hands of the Curé of Merret, and seemed unlikely to live through the night. It was about eleven when I reached the château. I went up the great staircase. After crossing some large, lofty, dark rooms, diabolically cold and damp, I reached the state bedroom where the Countess lay. From the rumors that were current concerning this lady (monsieur, I should never end if I were to repeat all the tales that were told about her), I had imagined her a coquette. Imagine, then, that I had great difficulty in seeing her in the great bed where she was lying. To be sure, to light this enormous room, with old-fashioned heavy cornices, and so thick with dust that merely to see it was enough to make you sneeze, she had only an old Argand lamp. Ah! but you have not been to Merret. Well, the bed is one of those old-world beds, with a high tester hung with flowered chintz. A small table stood by the bed, on which I saw an "Imitation of Christ," which, by the way, I bought for my wife, as well as the lamp. There were also a deep armchair for her confidential maid, and two small chairs. There was no fire. That was all the furniture, not enough to fill ten lines in an inventory.

" 'My dear sir, if you had seen, as I then saw, that vast
18

room, papered and hung with brown, you would have felt
yourself transported into a scene of a romance. It was icy,
nay more, funereal,' and he lifted his hand with a theatrical
gesture and paused.

" 'By dint of seeking, as I approached the bed, at last I
saw Madame de Merret, under the glimmer of the lamp,
which fell on the pillows. Her face was as yellow as wax,
and as narrow as two folded hands. The Countess had a
lace cap showing abundant hair, but as white as linen thread.
She was sitting up in bed, and seemed to keep upright with
great difficulty. Her large black eyes, dimmed by fever,
no doubt, and half-dead already, hardly moved under the
bony arch of her eyebrows.—There,' he added, pointing to
his own brow. 'Her forehead was clammy; her fleshless
hands were like bones covered with soft skin; the veins and
muscles were perfectly visible. She must have been very
handsome; but at this moment I was startled into an indescribable emotion at the sight. Never, said those who wrapped
her in her shroud, had any living creature been so emaciated
and lived. In short, it was awful to behold! Sickness had
so consumed that woman, that she was no more than a phan-
tom. Her lips, which were pale violet, seemed to me not to
move when she spoke to me.

" 'Though my profession has familiarized me with such
spectacles, by calling me not infrequently to the bedside of
the dying to record their last wishes, I confess that families
in tears and the agonies I have seen were as nothing in comparison with this lonely and silent woman in her vast château.
I heard not the least sound, I did not perceive the movement
which the sufferer's breathing ought to have given to the
sheets that covered her, and I stood motionless, absorbed in
looking at her in a sort of stupor. In fancy I am there still.
At last her large eyes moved; she tried to raise her right hand,
but it fell back on the bed, and she uttered these words, which
came like a breath, for her voice was no longer a voice: "I
have waited for you with the greatest impatience." A bright
flush rose to her cheeks. It was a great effort to her to speak.

" ' "Madame," I began. She signed to me to be silent. At that moment the old housekeeper rose and said in my ear, "Do not speak; Madame la Comtesse is not in a state to bear the slightest noise, and what you would say might agitate her."

" 'I sat down. A few instants after, Madame de Merret collected all her remaining strength to move her right hand, and slipped it, not without infinite difficulty, under the bolster; she then paused a moment. With a last effort she withdrew her hand; and when she brought out a sealed paper, drops of perspiration rolled from her brow. "I place my will in your hands—Oh! God! Oh!" and that was all. She clutched a crucifix that lay on the bed, lifted it hastily to her lips, and died.

" 'The expression of her eyes still makes me shudder as I think of it. She must have suffered much! There was joy in her last glance, and it remained stamped on her dead eyes.

" 'I brought away the will, and when it was opened I found that Madame de Merret had appointed me her executor. She left the whole of her property to the hospital at Vendôme excepting a few legacies. But these were her instructions as relating to la Grande Bretêche: She ordered me to leave the place, for fifty years counting from the day of her death, in the state in which it might be at the time of her decease, forbidding any one, whoever he might be, to enter the apartments, prohibiting any repairs whatever, and even settling a salary to pay watchmen if it were needful to secure the absolute fulfilment of her intentions. At the expiration of that term, if the will of the testatrix has been duly carried out, the house is to become the property of my heirs, for, as you know, a notary cannot take a bequest. Otherwise la Grande Bretêche reverts to the heirs-at-law, but on condition of fulfilling certain conditions set forth in a codicil to the will, which is not to be opened till the expiration of the said term of fifty years. The will has not been disputed, so——' And without finishing his sentence, the lanky notary looked at me with an air of triumph; I made him quite happy by offering him my congratulations.

"'Monsieur,' I said in conclusion, 'you have so vividly impressed me that I fancy I see the dying woman whiter than her sheets; her glittering eyes frighten me; I shall dream of her to-night.—But you must have formed some idea as to the instructions contained in that extraordinary will.'

"'Monsieur,' said he, with comical reticence, 'I never allow myself to criticise the conduct of a person who honors me with the gift of a diamond.'

"However, I soon loosened the tongue of the discreet notary of Vendôme, who communicated to me, not without long digressions, the opinions of the deep politicians of both sexes whose judgments are law in Vendôme. But these opinions were so contradictory, so diffuse, that I was near falling asleep in spite of the interest I felt in this authentic history. The notary's ponderous voice and monotonous accent, accustomed no doubt to listen to himself and to make himself listened to by his clients or fellow-townsmen, were too much for my curiosity. Happily, he soon went away.

"'Ah, ha, monsieur,' said he on the stairs, 'a good many persons would be glad to live five-and-forty years longer; but —one moment!' and he laid the first finger of his right hand to his nostril with a cunning look, as much as to say, 'Mark my words!—To last as long as that—as long as that,' said he, 'you must not be past sixty now.'

"I closed my door, having been roused from my apathy by this last speech, which the notary thought very funny; then I sat down in my armchair, with my feet on the fire-dogs. I had lost myself in a romance à la Radcliffe, constructed on the juridical base given me by Monsieur Regnault, when the door, opened by a woman's cautious hand, turned on the hinges. I saw my landlady come in, a buxom, florid dame, always good-humored, who had missed her calling in life. She was a Fleming, who ought to have seen the light in a picture by Teniers.

"'Well, monsieur,' said she, 'Monsieur Regnault has no doubt been giving you his history of la Grande Bretêche?'

" 'Yes, Madame Lepas.'

" 'And what did he tell you?'

"I repeated in a few words the creepy and sinister story of Madame de Merret. At each sentence my hostess put her head forward, looking at me with an innkeeper's keen scrutiny, a happy compromise between the instinct of a police constable, the astuteness of a spy, and the cunning of a dealer.

" 'My good Madame Lepas,' said I as I ended, 'you seem to know more about it. Heh? If not, why have you come up to me?'

" 'On my word, as an honest woman——'

" 'Do not swear; your eyes are big with a secret. You knew Monsieur de Merret; what sort of man was he?'

" 'Monsieur de Merret—well, you see he was a man you never could see the top of, he was so tall! A very good gentleman, from Picardy, and who had, as we say, his head close to his cap. He paid for everything down, so as never to have difficulties with any one. He was hot-tempered, you see! All our ladies liked him very much.'

" 'Because he was hot-tempered?' I asked her.

" 'Well, may be,' said she; 'and you may suppose, sir, that a man had to have something to show for a figurehead before he could marry Madame de Merret, who, without any reflection on others, was the handsomest and richest heiress in our parts. She had about twenty thousand francs a year. All the town was at the wedding; the bride was pretty and sweet-looking, quite a gem of a woman. Oh, they were a handsome couple in their day!'

" 'And were they happy together?'

" 'Hm, hm! so-so—so far as can be guessed, for, as you may suppose, we of the common sort were not hail-fellow-well-met with them.—Madame de Merret was a kind woman and very pleasant, who had no doubt sometimes to put up with her husband's tantrums. But though he was rather haughty, we were fond of him. After all, it was his place to behave so. When a man is a born nobleman, you see——'

" 'Still, there must have been some catastrophe for Monsieur and Madame de Merret to part so violently ?'

" 'I did not say there was any catastrophe, sir. I know nothing about it.'

" 'Indeed. Well, now, I am sure you know everything.'

" 'Well, sir, I will tell you the whole story.—When I saw Monsieur Regnault go up to see you, it struck me that he would speak to you about Madame de Merret as having to do with la Grande Bretêche. That put it into my head to ask your advice, sir, seeming to me that you are a man of good judgment and incapable of playing a poor woman like me false—for I never did any one a wrong, and yet I am tormented by my conscience. Up to now I have never dared to say a word to the people of these parts; they are all chattermags, with tongues like knives. And never till now, sir, have I had any traveler here who stayed so long in the inn as you have, and to whom I could tell the history of the fifteen thousand francs——'

" 'My dear Madame Lepas, if there is anything in your story of a nature to compromise me,' I said, interrupting the flow of her words, 'I would not hear it for all the world.'

" 'You need have no fears,' said she; 'you will see.'

"Her eagerness made me suspect that I was not the only person to whom my worthy landlady had communicated the secret of which I was to be sole possessor, but I listened.

" 'Monsieur,' said she, 'when the Emperor sent the Spaniards here, prisoners of war and others, I was required to lodge at the charge of the Government a young Spaniard sent to Vendôme on parole. Notwithstanding his parole, he had to show himself every day to the sub-prefect. He was a Spanish grandee—neither more nor less. He had a name in *os* and *dia,* something like Bagos de Férédia. I wrote his name down in my books, and you may see it if you like. Ah! he was a handsome young fellow for a Spaniard, who are all ugly they say. He was not more than five feet two or three in height, but so well made; and he had little hands that he kept so beautifully! Ah! you should have seen them.

He had as many brushes for his hands as a woman has for her toilet. He had thick, black hair, a flame in his eye, a somewhat coppery complexion, but which I admired all the same. He wore the finest linen I have ever seen, though I have had princesses to lodge here, and, among others, General Bertrand, the Duc and Duchesse d'Abrantés, Monsieur Descazes, and the King of Spain. He did not eat much, but he had such polite and amiable ways that it was impossible to owe him a grudge for that. Oh! I was very fond of him, though he did not say four words to me in a day, and it was impossible to have the least bit of talk with him; if he was spoken to, he did not answer; it is a way, a mania they all have, it would seem.

" 'He read his breviary like a priest, and went to mass and all the services quite regularly. And where did he post himself?—we found this out later.—Within two yards of Madame de Merret's chapel. As he took that place the very first time he entered the church, no one imagined that there was any purpose in it. Besides, he never raised his nose above his book, poor young man! And then, monsieur, of an evening he went for a walk on the hill among the ruins of the old castle. It was his only amusement, poor man; it reminded him of his native land. They say that Spain is all hills!

" 'One evening, a few days after he was sent here, he was out very late. I was rather uneasy when he did not come in till just on the stroke of midnight; but we all got used to his whims; he took the key of the door, and we never sat up for him. He lived in a house belonging to us in the Rue des Casernes. Well, then, one of our stable-boys told us one evening that, going down to wash the horses in the river, he fancied he had seen the Spanish Grandee swimming some little way off, just like a fish. When he came in, I told him to be careful of the weeds, and he seemed put out at having been seen in the water.

" 'At last, monsieur, one day, or rather one morning, we did not find him in his room; he had not come back. By hunting through his things, I found a written paper in the drawer of his table, with fifty pieces of Spanish gold of the kind they call doubloons, worth about five thousand francs; and in a little sealed box ten thousand francs worth of diamonds. The paper said that in case he should not return, he left us this money and these diamonds in trust to found masses to thank God for his escape and for his salvation.

"'At that time I still had my husband, who ran off in search of him. And this is the queer part of the story: he brought back the Spaniard's clothes, which he had found under a big stone on a sort of breakwater along the river bank, nearly opposite la Grande Bretêche. My husband went so early that no one saw him. After reading the letter, he burnt the clothes, and, in obedience to Count Férédia's wish, we announced that he had escaped.

"'The sub-prefect set all the constabulary at his heels; but, pshaw! he was never caught. Lepas believed that the Spaniard had drowned himself. I, sir, have never thought so; I believe, on the contrary, that he had something to do with the business about Madame de Merret, seeing that Rosalie told me that the crucifix her mistress was so fond of that she had it buried with her, was made of ebony and silver; now in the early days of his stay here, Monsieur Férédia had one of ebony and silver which I never saw later.—And now, monsieur, do not you say that I need have no remorse about the Spaniard's fifteen thousand francs? Are they not really and truly mine?'

"'Certainly.—But have you never tried to question Rosalie?' said I.

"'Oh, to be sure I have, sir. But what is to be done? That girl is like a wall. She knows something, but it is impossible to make her talk.'

"After chatting with me for a few minutes, my hostess left me a prey to vague and sinister thoughts, to romantic curiosity, and a religious dread, not unlike the deep emotion which comes upon us when we go into a dark church at night and discern a feeble light glimmering under a lofty vault—a dim figure glides across—the sweep of a gown or of a priest's cassock is audible—and we shiver! La Grande Bretêche, with its rank grasses, its shuttered windows, its rusty iron-work, its locked doors, it deserted rooms, suddenly rose before me in fantastic vividness. I tried to get into the mysterious dwelling to search out the heart of this solemn story, this drama which had killed three persons.

"Rosalie became in my eyes the most interesting being in Vendôme. As I studied her, I detected signs of an inmost thought, in spite of the blooming health that glowed in her dimpled face. There was in her soul some element of ruth or of hope; her manner suggested a secret, like the expression of devout souls who pray in excess, or of a girl who has killed her child and for ever hears its last cry. Nevertheless, she was simple and clumsy in her ways; her vacant smile had nothing criminal in it, and you would have pronounced her innocent only from seeing the large red and blue checked kerchief that covered her stalwart bust, tucked into the tight-laced square bodice of a lilac- and white-striped gown. 'No,' said I to myself, 'I will not quit Vendôme without knowing the whole history of la Grande Bretêche. To achieve this end, I will make love to Rosalie if it proves necessary.'

" 'Rosalie!' said I one evening.

" 'Your servant, sir?'

" 'You are not married?' She started a little.

" 'Oh! there is no lack of men if ever I take a fancy to be miserable!' she replied, laughing. She got over her agitation at once; for every woman, from the highest lady to the inn-servant inclusive, has a native presence of mind.

" 'Yes; you are fresh and good-looking enough never to lack lovers! But tell me, Rosalie, why did you become an inn-servant on leaving Madame de Merret? Did she not leave you some little annuity?'

" 'Oh yes, sir. But my place here is the best in all the town of Vendôme.'

"This reply was such an one as judges and attorneys call evasive. Rosalie, as it seemed to me, held in this romantic affair the place of the middle square of the chess-board; she was at the very centre of the interest and of the truth; she appeared to me to be tied into the knot of it. It was not a case for ordinary love-making; this girl contained the last chapter of a romance, and from that moment all my attentions were devoted to Rosalie. By dint of studying the girl, I observed in her, as in every woman whom we make our ruling thought, a variety of good qualities; she was clean and neat; she was handsome, I need not say; she soon was possessed of every charm that desire can lend to a woman in whatever rank of life. A fortnight after the notary's visit, one evening, or rather one morning, in the small hours, I said to Rosalie:

" 'Come, tell me all you know about Madame de Merret.'

" 'Oh!' she cried in terror, 'do not ask me that, Monsieur Horace!'

"Her handsome features clouded over, her bright coloring grew pale, and her eyes lost their artless, liquid brightness.

" 'Well,' she said, 'I will tell you; but keep the secret carefully.'

" 'All right, my child; I will keep all your secrets with a thief's honor, which is the most loyal known.'

" 'If it is all the same to you,' said she, 'I would rather it should be with your own.'

"Thereupon she set her head-kerchief straight, and settled herself to tell the tale; for there is no doubt a particular attitude of confidence and security is necessary to the telling of a narrative. The best tales are told at a certain hour— just as we are all here at table. No one ever told a story well standing up, or fasting.

"If I were to reproduce exactly Rosalie's diffuse eloquence, a whole volume would scarcely contain it. Now, as the event of which she gave me a confused account stands exactly midway between the notary's gossip and that of Madame Lepas, as precisely as the middle term of a rule-of-three sum stands between the first and third, I have only to relate it in as few words as may be. I shall therefore be brief.

"The room at La Grande Bretêche in which Madame de Merret slept was on the ground floor; a little cupboard in the wall, about four feet deep, served her to hang her dresses in. Three months before the evening of which I have to relate the events, Madame de Merret had been seriously ailing, so much so that her husband had left her to herself, and had his own bedroom on the first floor. By one of those accidents which it is impossible to foresee, he came in that evening two hours later than usual from the club, where he went to read the papers and talk politics with the residents in the, neighborhood. His wife supposed him to have come in, to be in bed and asleep. But the invasion of France had been the subject of a very animated discussion; the game of billiards had waxed vehement; he had lost forty francs, an enormous sum at Vendôme, where everybody is thrifty, and where social habits are restrained within the bounds of a simplicity worthy of all praise, and the foundation perhaps of a form of true happiness which no Parisian would care for.

"For some time past Monsieur de Merret had been satisfied to ask Rosalie whether his wife was in bed; on the girl's replying always in the affirmative, he at once went to his own room, with the good faith that comes of habit and confidence. But this evening, on coming in, he took it into his head to go to see Madame de Merret, to tell her of his ill-luck, and perhaps to find consolation. During dinner he had observed that his wife was very becomingly dressed; he reflected as he came home from the club that his wife was certainly much better, that convalescence had improved her beauty, discovering it, as husbands discover everything, a little too late. Instead of calling Rosalie, who was in the kitchen at the moment watching the cook and the coachman playing a puzzling hand at cards, Monsieur de Merret made his way to his wife's room by the light of his lantern, which he set down on the lowest step of the stairs. His step, easy to recognize, rang under the vaulted passage.

"At the instant when the gentleman turned the key to enter his wife's room, he fancied he heard the door shut of the closet of which I have spoken; but when he went in, Madame de Merret was alone, standing in front of the fireplace. The

unsuspecting husband fancied that Rosalie was in the cupboard; nevertheless, a doubt, ringing in his ears like a peal
of bells, put him on his guard; he looked at his wife, and
read in her eyes an indescribably anxious and haunted expression.

" 'You are very late,' said she.—Her voice, usually so
clear and sweet, struck him as being slightly husky.

"Monsieur de Merret made no reply, for at this moment
Rosalie came in. This was like a thunder-clap. He
walked up and down the room, going from one window to
another at a regular pace, his arms folded.

" 'Have you had bad news, or are you ill?' his wife asked
him timidly, while Rosalie helped her to undress. He made
no reply.

" 'You can go, Rosalie,' said Madame de Merret to her
maid; 'I can put in my curl-papers myself.'—She scented
disaster at the mere aspect of her husband's face, and wished
to be alone with him. As soon as Rosalie was gone, or supposed to be gone, for she lingered a few minutes in the
passage, Monsieur de Merret came and stood facing his
wife, and said coldly, 'Madame, there is some one in your
cupboard!' She looked at her husband calmly, and replied
quite simply, 'No, monsieur.'

"This 'No' wrung Monsieur de Merret's heart; he did not
believe it; and yet his wife had never appeared purer or more
saintly than she seemed to be at this moment. He rose to
go and open the closet door. Madame de Merret took his
hand, stopped him, looked at him sadly, and said in a voice
of strange emotion, 'Remember, if you should find no one
there, everything must be at an end between you and me.'

"The extraordinary dignity of his wife's attitude filled
him with deep esteem for her, and inspired him with one of
those resolves which need only a grander stage to become
immortal.

" 'No, Josephine,' he said, 'I will not open it. In either
event we should be parted for ever. Listen; I know all the
purity of your soul, I know you lead a saintly life, and would
not commit a deadly sin to save your life.'—At these words

Madame de Merret looked at her husband with a haggard stare.—'See, here is your crucifix,' he went on. 'Swear to me before God that there is no one in there; I will believe you— I will never open that door.'

"Madame de Merret took up the crucifix and said, 'I swear it.'

" 'Louder,' said her husband; 'and repeat: "I swear before God that there is nobody in that closet." ' She repeated the words without flinching.

" 'That will do,' said Monsieur de Merret coldly. After a moment's silence: 'You have there a fine piece of work which I never saw before,' said he, examining the crucifix of ebony and silver, very artistically wrought.

" 'I found it at Duvivier's; last year when that troop of Spanish prisoners came through Vendôme, he bought it of a Spanish monk.'

" 'Indeed,' said Monsieur de Merret, hanging the crucifix on its nail; and he rang the bell.

"He had not to wait for Rosalie. Monsieur de Merret went forward quickly to meet her, led her into the bay of the window that looked on to the garden, and said to her in an undertone:

" 'I know that Gorenflot wants to marry you, that poverty alone prevents your setting up house, and that you told him you would not be his wife till he found means to become a master mason.—Well, go and fetch him; tell him to come here with his trowel and tools. Contrive to wake no one in his house but himself. His reward will be beyond your wishes. Above all, go out without saying a word—or else !' and he frowned.

"Rosalie was going, and he called her back. 'Here, take my latch-key,' said he.

" 'Jean !' Monsieur de Merret called in a voice of thunder down the passage. Jean, who was both coachman and confidential servant, left his cards and came.

" 'Go to bed, all of you,' said his master, beckoning him to come close; and the gentleman added in a whisper, 'When they are all asleep—mind, *asleep*—you understand?—come down and tell me.'

"Monsieur de Merret, who had never lost sight of his wife while giving his orders, quietly came back to her at the fireside, and began to tell her the details of the game of billiards and the discussion at the club. When Rosalie returned she found Monsieur and Madame de Merret conversing amiably.

"Not long before this Monsieur de Merret had had new ceilings made to all the reception-rooms on the ground floor. Plaster is very scarce at Vendôme; the price is enhanced by the cost of carriage; the gentleman had therefore had a considerable quantity delivered to him, knowing that he could always find purchasers for what might be left. It was this circumstance which suggested the plan he carried out.

" 'Gorenflot is here, sir,' said Rosalie in a whisper.

" 'Tell him to come in,' said her master aloud.

"Madame de Merret turned paler when she saw the mason.

" 'Gorenflot,' said her husband, 'go and fetch some bricks from the coach-house; bring enough to wall up the door of this cupboard; you can use the plaster that is left for cement.' Then, dragging Rosalie and the workman close to him— 'Listen, Gorenflot,' said he, in a low voice, 'you are to sleep here to-night; but to-morrow morning you shall have a passport to take you abroad to a place I will tell you of. I will give you six thousand francs for your journey. You must live in that town for ten years; if you find you do not like it, you may settle in another, but it must be in the same country. Go through Paris and wait there till I join you. I will there give you an agreement for six thousand francs more, to be paid to you on your return, provided you have carried out the conditions of the bargain. For that price you are to keep perfect silence as to what you have to do this night. To you, Rosalie, I will secure ten thousand francs, which will not be paid to you till your wedding day, and on condition of your marrying Gorenflot; but, to get married, you must hold your tongue. If not, no wedding gift!'

" 'Rosalie,' said Madame de Merret, 'come and brush my hair.'

She fainted away

"Her husband quietly walked up and down the room, keeping an eye on the door, on the mason, and on his wife, but without any insulting display of suspicion. Gorenflot could not help making some noise. Madame de Merret seized a moment when he was unloading some bricks, and when her husband was at the other end of the room, to say to Rosalie: 'My dear child, I will give you a thousand francs a year if only you will tell Gorenflot to leave a crack at the bottom.' Then she added aloud quite coolly: 'You had better help him.'

"Monsieur and Madame de Merret were silent all the time while Gorenflot was walling up the door. This silence was intentional on the husband's part; he did not wish to give his wife the opportunity of saying anything with a double meaning. On Madame de Merret's side it was pride or prudence. When the wall was half built up the cunning mason took advantage of his master's back being turned to break one of the two panes in the top of the door with a blow of his pick. By this Madame de Merret understood that Rosalie had spoken to Gorenflot. They all three then saw the face of a dark, gloomy-looking man, with black hair and flaming eyes.

"Before her husband turned round again the poor woman had nodded to the stranger, to whom the signal was meant to convey, 'Hope.'

"At four o'clock, as day was dawning, for it was the month of September, the work was done. The mason was placed in charge of Jean, and Monsieur de Merret slept in his wife's room.

"Next morning when he got up he said with apparent carelessness, 'Oh, by the way, I must go to the Mairie for the passport.' He put on his hat, took two or three steps towards the door, paused, and took the crucifix. His wife was trembling with joy.

" 'He will go to Duvivier's,' thought she.

"As soon as he had left, Madame de Merret rang for Rosalie, and then in a terrible voice she cried: 'The pick! Bring the pick! and set to work. I saw how Gorenflot did it yesterday; we shall have time to make a gap and build it up again.'

"In an instant Rosalie had brought her mistress a sort of cleaver; she, with a vehemence of which no words can give an idea, set to work to demolish the wall. She had already got out a few bricks, when, turning to deal a stronger blow than before, she saw behind her Monsieur de Merret. She fainted away.

" 'Lay madame on her bed,' said he coldly.

"Foreseeing what would certainly happen in his absence, he had laid this trap for his wife; he had merely written to the Maire and sent for Duvivier. The jeweler arrived just as the disorder in the room had been repaired.

" 'Duvivier,' asked Monsieur de Merret, 'did not you buy some crucifixes of the Spaniards who passed through the town?'

" 'No, monsieur.'

" 'Very good; thank you,' said he, flashing a tiger's glare at his wife. 'Jean,' he added, turning to his confidential valet, 'you can serve my meals here in Madame de Merret's room. She is ill, and I shall not leave her till she recovers.'

"The cruel man remained in his wife's room for twenty days. During the earlier time, when there was some little noise in the closet, and Josephine wanted to intercede for the dying man, he said, without allowing her to utter a word, 'You swore on the Cross that there was no one there.' "

After this story all the ladies rose from table, and thus the spell under which Bianchon had held them was broken. But there were some among them who had almost shivered at the last words.

DOMESTIC PEACE

Dedicated to my dear niece Valentine Surville.

THE incident recorded in this sketch took place towards the end of the month of November 1809, the moment when Napoleon's fugitive empire attained the apogee of its splendor. The trumpet-blasts of Wagram were still sounding an echo in the heart of the Austrian monarchy. Peace was being signed between France and the Coalition. Kings and princes came to perform their orbits, like stars, round Napoleon, who gave himself the pleasure of dragging all Europe in his train —a magnificent experiment in the power he afterwards displayed at Dresden. Never, as contemporaries tell us, did Paris see entertainments more superb than those which preceded and followed the sovereign's marriage with an Austrian archduchess. Never, in the most splendid days of the Monarchy, had so many crowned heads thronged the shores of the Seine, never had the French aristocracy been so rich or so splendid. The diamonds lavishly scattered over the women's dresses, and the gold and silver embroidery on the uniforms contrasted so strongly with the penury of the Republic, that the wealth of the globe seemed to be rolling through the drawing-rooms of Paris. Intoxication seemed to have turned the brains of this Empire of a day. All the military, not excepting their chief, reveled like parvenus in the treasure conquered for them by a million men with worsted epaulettes, whose demands were satisfied by a few yards of red ribbon.

At this time most women affected that lightness of conduct and facility of morals which distinguished the reign of Louis XV. Whether it were in imitation of the tone of the fallen monarchy, or because certain members of the Imperial family had set the example—as certain malcontents of the Faubourg Saint-Germain chose to say—it is certain that men and women alike flung themselves into a life of pleasure with an intrepidity which seemed to forebode the end of the world. But there was at that time another cause for such license. The infatuation of women for the military became a frenzy, and was too consonant to the Emperor's views for him to try to check it. The frequent calls to arms, which gave every treaty concluded between Napoleon and the rest of Europe the character of an armistice, left every passion open to a termination as sudden as the decisions of the Commander-in-chief of all these busbys, pelisses, and aiguillettes, which so fascinated the fair sex. Hearts were as nomadic as the regiments. Between the first and the fifth bulletins from the *Grande Armée* a woman might be in succession mistress, wife, mother, and widow.

Was it the prospect of early widowhood, the hope of a jointure, or that of bearing a name promised to history, which made the soldiers so attractive? Were women drawn to them by the certainty that the secret of their passions would be buried on the field of battle? or may we find the reason of this gentle fanaticism in the noble charm that courage has for a woman? Perhaps all these reasons, which the future historian of the manners of the Empire will no doubt amuse himself by weighing, counted for something in their facile readiness to abandon themselves to love intrigues. Be that as it may, it must here be confessed that at that time laurels hid many errors, women showed an ardent preference for the brave adventurers, whom they regarded as the true fount of honor, wealth, or pleasure; and in the eyes of young girls, an epaulette—the hieroglyphic of a future—signified happiness and liberty.

One feature, and a characteristic one, of this unique period in our history was an unbridled mania for everything glittering. Never were fireworks so much in vogue, never were diamonds so highly prized. The men, as greedy as the women of these translucent pebbles, displayed them no less lavishly.

Possibly the necessity for carrying plunder in the most porta-
ble form made gems the fashion in the army. A man was
not ridiculous then, as he would be now, if his shirt-frill or
his fingers blazed with large diamonds. Murat, an Oriental
by nature, set the example of preposterous luxury to modern
soldiers.

The Comte de Gondreville,. formerly known as Citizen
Malin, whose elevation had made him famous, having become
a Lucullus of the Conservative Senate, which "conserved"
nothing, had postponed an entertainment in honor of the
peace only that he might the better pay his court to Napoleon
by his efforts to eclipse those flatterers who had been beforehand with him. The ambassadors from all the Powers
friendly with France, with an eye to favors to come, the most
important personages of the Empire, and even a few princes,
were at this hour assembled in the wealthy senator's drawing-
rooms. Dancing flagged; every one was watching for the
Emperor, whose presence the Count had promised his guests.
And Napoleon would have kept his word but for the scene
which had broken out that very evening between him and
Josephine—the scene which portended the impending divorce
of the august pair. The report of this incident, at the time
kept very secret, but recorded by history, did not reach the
ears of the courtiers, and had no effect on the gaiety of Comte
de Gondreville's party beyond keeping Napoleon away.

The prettiest women in Paris, eager to be at the Count's
on the strength of mere hearsay, at this moment were a be-
sieging force of luxury, coquettishness, elegance, and beauty.
The financial world, proud of its riches, challenged the
splendor of the generals and high officials of the Empire, so
recently gorged with orders, titles, and honors. These grand
balls were always an opportunity seized upon by wealthy families for introducing their heiresses to Napoleon's Prætorian
Guard, in the foolish hope of exchanging their splendid fortunes for uncertain favors. The women who believed themselves strong enough in their beauty alone came to test their
power. There, as elsewhere, amusement was but a blind. Calm

and smiling faces and placid brows covered sordid interests, expressions of friendship were a lie, and more than one man was less distrustful of his enemies than of his friends.

These remarks are necessary to explain the incidents of the little imbroglio which is the subject of this study, and the picture, softened as it is, of the tone then dominant in Paris drawing-rooms.

"Turn your eyes a little towards the pedestal supporting that candelabrum—do you see a young lady with her hair drawn back *à la Chinoise!*—There, in the corner to the left; she has bluebells in the knot of chestnut curls which fall in clusters on her head. Do not you see her? She is so pale you might fancy she was ill, delicate-looking, and very small; there—now she is turning her head this way; her almond-shaped blue eyes, so delightfully soft, look as if they were made expressly for tears. Look, look! She is bending forward to see Madame de Vaudremont below the crowd of heads in constant motion; the high head-dresses prevent her having a clear view."

"I see her now, my dear fellow. You had only to say that she had the whitest skin of all the women here; I should have known whom you meant. I had noticed her before; she has the loveliest complexion I ever admired. From hence I defy you to see against her throat the pearls between the sapphires of her necklace. But she is a prude or a coquette, for the tucker of her bodice scarcely lets one suspect the beauty of her bust. What shoulders! what lily-whiteness!"

"Who is she?" asked the first speaker.

"Ah! that I do not know."

"Aristocrat!—Do you want to keep them all to yourself, Montcornet?"

"You of all men to banter me!" replied Montcornet, with a smile. "Do you think you have a right to insult a poor general like me because, being a happy rival of Soulanges, you cannot even turn on your heel without alarming Madame de Vaudremont? Or is it because I came only a month ago into the Promised Land? How insolent you can be, you men

in office, who sit glued to your chairs while we are dodging
shot and shell! Come, Monsieur le Maître des Requêtes, allow
us to glean in the field of which you can only have precarious
possession from the moment when we evacuate it. The deuce
is in it! We have all a right to live! My good friend, if
you knew the German women, you would, I believe, do me
a good turn with the Parisian you love best."

"Well, General, since you have vouchsafed to turn your
attention to that lady, whom I never saw till now, have the
charity to tell me if you have seen her dance."

"Why, my dear Martial, where have you dropped from?
If you are ever sent with an embassy, I have small hopes
of your success. Do not you see a triple rank of the most
undaunted coquettes of Paris between her and the swarm
of dancing men that buzz under the chandelier? And was
it not only by the help of your eyeglass that you were able
to discover her at all in the corner by that pillar, where she
seems buried in the gloom, in spite of the candles blazing
above her head? Between her and us there is such a sparkle
of diamonds and glances, so many floating plumes, such a flutter of lace, of flowers and curls, that it would be a real miracle
if any dancer could detect her among those stars. Why, Martial, how is it that you have not understood her to be the
wife of some sous-préfet from Lippe or Dyle, who has come
to try to get her husband promoted?"

"Oh, he will be!" exclaimed the Master of Appeals
quickly.

"I doubt it," replied the Colonel of Cuirassiers, laughing.
"She seems as raw in intrigue as you are in diplomacy. I
dare bet, Martial, that you do not know how she got into that
place."

The lawyer looked at the Colonel of Cuirassiers with an
expression as much of contempt as of curiosity.

"Well," proceeded Montcornet, "she arrived, I have no
doubt, punctually at nine, the first of the company perhaps,
and probably she greatly embarrassed the Comtesse de Gondreville, who cannot put two ideas together. Repulsed by the

mistress of the house, routed from chair to chair by each
newcomer, and driven into the darkness of this little corner,
she allowed herself to be walled in, the victim of the jealousy
of the other ladies, who would gladly have buried that dangerous beauty. She had, of course, no friend to encourage her
to maintain the place she first held in the front rank; then
each of those treacherous fair ones would have enjoined on
the men of her circle on no account to take out our poor friend,
under pain of the severest punishment. That, my dear fellow,
is the way in which those sweet faces, in appearance so tender
and so artless, would have formed a coalition against the
stranger, and that without a word beyond the question, 'Tell
me, dear, do you know that little woman in blue?'—Look here,
Martial, if you care to run the gantlet of more flattering
glances and inviting questions than you will ever again meet
in the whole of your life, just try to get through the triple
rampart which defends that Queen of Dyle, or Lippe, or
Charente. You will see whether the dullest woman of them
all will not be equal to inventing some wile that would hinder
the most determined man from bringing the plaintive stranger
to the light. Does it not strike you that she looks like an
elegy?"

"Do you think so, Montcornet? Then she must be a married woman?"

"Why not a widow?"

"She would be less passive," said the lawyer, laughing.

"She is perhaps the widow of a man who is gambling," replied the handsome Colonel.

"To be sure; since the peace there are so many widows of
that class!" said Martial. "But, my dear Montcornet, we
are a couple of simpletons. That face is still too ingenuous,
there is too much youth and freshness on the brow and tem-
ples for her to be married. What splendid flesh-tints!
Nothing has sunk in the modeling of the nose. Lips, chin,
everything in her face is as fresh as a white rosebud, though
the expression is veiled, as it were, by the clouds of sadness.
Who can it be that makes that young creature weep?"

"Women cry for so little," said the Colonel.

"I do not know," replied Martial; "but she does not cry because she is left there without a partner; her grief is not of to-day. It is evident that she has beautified herself for this evening with intention. I would wager that she is in love already."

"Bah! She is perhaps the daughter of some German prince-ling; no one talks to her," said Montcornet.

"Dear! how unhappy a poor child may be!" Martial went on. "Can there be anything more graceful and refined than our little stranger? Well, not one of those furies who stand round her, and who believe that they can feel, will say a word to her. If she would but speak, we should see if she has fine teeth."

"Bless me, you boil over like milk at the least increase of temperature!" cried the Colonel, a little nettled at so soon finding a rival in his friend.

"What!" exclaimed the lawyer, without heeding the Colonel's question. "Can nobody here tell us the name of this exotic flower?"

"Some lady companion!" said Montcornet.

"What next? A companion! wearing sapphires fit for a queen, and a dress of Malines lace? Tell that to the marines, General. You, too, would not shine in diplomacy if, in the course of your conjectures, you jump in a breath from a German princess to a lady companion."

Montcornet stopped a man by taking his arm—a fat little man, whose iron-gray hair and clever eyes were to be seen at the lintel of every doorway, and who mingled uncere-moniously with the various groups which welcomed him re-spectfully.

"Gondreville, my friend," said Montcornet, "who is that quite charming little woman sitting out there under that huge candelabrum?"

"The candelabrum? Ravrio's work; Isabey made the de-sign."

"Oh, I recognized your lavishness and taste; but the lady?"

"Ah! I do not know. Some friend of my wife's, no doubt."

"Or your mistress, you old rascal."

"No, on my honor. The Comtesse de Gondreville is the only person capable of inviting people whom no one knows."

In spite of this very acrimonious comment, the fat little man's lips did not lose the smile which the Colonel's suggestion had brought to them. Montcornet returned to the lawyer, who had rejoined a neighboring group, intent on asking, but in vain, for information as to the fair unknown. He grasped Martial's arm, and said in his ear:

"My dear Martial, mind what you are about. Madame de Vaudremont has been watching you for some minutes with ominous attentiveness; she is a woman who can guess by the mere movement of your lips what you say to me; our eyes have already told her too much; she has perceived and followed their direction, and I suspect that at this moment she is thinking even more than we are of the little blue lady."

"That is too old a trick in warfare, my dear Montcornet! However, what do I care? Like the Emperor, when I have made a conquest, I keep it."

"Martial, your fatuity cries out for a lesson. What! you, a civilian, and so lucky as to be the husband-designate of Madame de Vaudremont, a widow of two-and-twenty, burdened with four thousand napoleons a year—a woman who slips such a diamond as this on your finger," he added, taking the lawyer's left hand, which the young man complacently allowed; "and, to crown all, you affect the Lovelace, just as if you were a colonel and obliged to keep up the reputation of the military in home quarters! Fie, fie! Only think of all you may lose."

"At any rate, I shall not lose my liberty," replied Martial, with a forced laugh.

He cast a passionate glance at Madame de Vaudremont, who responded only by a smile of some uneasiness, for she had seen the Colonel examining the lawyer's ring.

"Listen to me, Martial. If you flutter round my young stranger, I shall set to work to win Madame de Vaudremont."

"You have my full permission, my dear Cuirassier, but you will not gain this much," and the young Maître des Requêtes put his polished thumb-nail under an upper tooth with a little mocking click.

"Remember that I am unmarried," said the Colonel; "that my sword is my whole fortune; and that such a challenge is setting Tantalus down to a banquet which he will devour."

"Prrr."

This defiant roll of consonants was the only reply to the Colonel's declaration, as Martial looked him from head to foot before turning away.

The fashion of the time required men to wear at a ball white kerseymere breeches and silk stockings. This pretty costume showed to great advantage the perfection of Mont-cornet's fine shape. He was five-and-thirty, and attracted attention by his stalwart height, insisted on for the Cuirassiers of the Imperial Guard whose handsome uniform enhanced the dignity of his figure, still youthful in spite of the stoutness occasioned by living on horseback. A black moustache emphasized the frank expression of a thoroughly soldierly countenance, with a broad, high forehead, an aquiline nose, and bright red lips. Montcornet's manner, stamped with a certain superiority due to the habit of command, might please a woman sensible enough not to aim at making a slave of her husband. The Colonel smiled as he looked at the lawyer, one of his favorite college friends, whose small figure made it necessary for Montcornet to look down a little as he answered his raillery with a friendly glance.

Baron Martial de la Roche-Hugon was a young Provençal patronized by Napoleon; his fate might probably be some splendid embassy. He had won the Emperor by his Italian suppleness and a genius for intrigue, a drawing-room elo-quence, and a knowledge of manners, which are so good a substitute for the higher qualities of a sterling man. Though young and eager, his face had already acquired the rigid brilliancy of tinned iron, one of the indispensable character-istics of diplomatists, which allows them to conceal their emo-

tions and disguise their feelings, unless, indeed, this impassi-
bility indicates an absence of all emotion and the death of
every feeling. The heart of a diplomate may be regarded
as an insoluble problem, for the three most illustrious ambassadors of the time have been distinguished by perdurable
hatreds and most romantic attachments.

Martial, however, was one of those men who are capable
of reckoning on the future in the midst of their intensest
enjoyment; he had already learned to judge the world, and
hid his ambition under the fatuity of a lady-killer, cloaking
his talent under the commonplace of mediocrity as soon as
he observed the rapid advancement of those men who gave the
master little umbrage.

The two friends now had to part with a cordial grasp of
hands. The introductory tune, warning the ladies to form
in squares for a fresh quadrille, cleared the men away from
the space they had filled while talking in the middle of the
large room. This hurried dialogue had taken place during the
usual interval between two dances, in front of the fireplace
of the great drawing-room of Gondreville's mansion. The
questions and answers of this very ordinary ballroom gossip
had been almost whispered by each of the speakers into his
neighbor's ear. At the same time, the chandeliers and the
flambeaux on the chimney-shelf shed such a flood of light
on the two friends that their faces, strongly illuminated,
failed, in spite of their diplomatic discretion, to conceal the
faint expression of their feelings either from the keen-sighted
countess or the artless stranger. This espionage of people's
thoughts is perhaps to idle persons one of the pleasures they
find in society, while numbers of disappointed numskulls are
bored there without daring to own it.

Fully to appreciate the interest of this conversation, it is
necessary to relate an incident which would presently serve
as an invisible bond, drawing together the actors in this
little drama, who were at present scattered through the rooms.

At about eleven o'clock, just as the dancers were returning

to their seats, the company had observed the entrance of the handsomest woman in Paris, the queen of fashion, the only person wanting to this brilliant assembly. She made it a rule never to appear till the moment when a party had reached that pitch of excited movement which does not allow the women to preserve much longer the freshness of their faces or of their dress. This brief hour is, as it were, the springtime of a ball. An hour after, when pleasure falls flat and fatigue is encroaching, everything is spoilt. Madame de Vaudremont never committed the blunder of remaining at a party to be seen with drooping flowers, hair out of curl, tumbled frills, and a face like every other that sleep is courting— not always without success. She took good care not to let her beauty be seen drowsy, as her rivals did; she was so clever as to keep up her reputation for smartness by always leaving a ballroom in brilliant order, as she had entered it. Women whispered to each other with a feeling of envy that she planned and wore as many different dresses as the parties she went to in one evening.

On the present occasion Madame de Vaudremont was not destined to be free to leave when she would the ballroom she had entered in triumph. Pausing for a moment on the threshold, she shot swift but observant glances on the women present, hastily scrutinizing their dresses to assure herself that her own eclipsed them all.

The illustrious beauty presented herself to the admiration of the crowd at the same moment with one of the bravest colonels of the Guards' Artillery and the Emperor's favorite, the Comte de Soulanges. The transient and fortuitous association of these two had about it a certain air of mystery. On hearing the names announced of Monsieur de Soulanges and the Comtesse de Vaudremont, a few women sitting by the wall rose, and men, hurrying in from the side-rooms, pressed forward to the principal doorway. One of the jesters who are always to be found in any large assembly said, as the Countess and her escort came in, that "women had quite as much curiosity about seeing a man who was faithful to his passion as men had in studying a woman who was difficult to enthrall."

Though the Comte de Soulanges, a young man of about two-and-thirty, was endowed with the nervous temperament which in a man gives rise to fine qualities, his slender build and pale complexion were not at first sight attractive; his black eyes betrayed great vivacity, but he was taciturn in company, and there was nothing in his appearance to reveal the gift for oratory which subsequently distinguished him, on the Right, in the legislative assembly under the Restoration.

The Comtesse de Vaudremont, a tall woman, rather fat, with a skin of dazzling whiteness, a small head that she carried well, and the immense advantage of inspiring love by the graciousness of her manner, was one of those beings who keep all the promise of their beauty.

The pair, who for a few minutes were the centre of general observation, did not for long give curiosity an opportunity of exercising itself about them. The Colonel and the Countess seemed perfectly to understand that accident had placed them in an awkward position. Martial, as they came forward, had hastened to join the group of men by the fireplace, that he might watch Madame de Vaudremont with the jealous anxiety of the first flame of passion, from behind the heads which formed a sort of rampart; a secret voice seemed to warn him that the success on which he prided himself might perhaps be precarious. But the coldly polite smile with which the Countess thanked Monsieur de Soulanges, and her little bow of dismissal as she sat down by Madame de Gondreville, relaxed the muscles of his face which jealousy had made rigid. Seeing Soulanges, however, still standing quite near the sofa on which Madame de Vaudremont was seated, not apparently having understood the glance by which the lady had conveyed to him that they were both playing a ridiculous part, the volcanic Provençal again knit the black brows that overshadowed his blue eyes, smoothed his chestnut curls to keep himself in countenance, and without betraying the agitation which made his heart beat, watched the faces of the Countess and of

M. de Soulanges while still chatting with his neighbors. He then took the hand of Colonel Montcornet, who had just renewed their old acquaintance, but he listened to him without hearing him; his mind was elsewhere.

Soulanges was gazing calmly at the women, sitting four ranks deep all round the immense ballroom, admiring this dado of diamonds, rubies, masses of gold and shining hair, of which the lustre almost outshone the blaze of waxlights, the cutglass of the chandeliers, and the gilding. His rival's stolid indifference put the lawyer out of countenance. Quite incapable of controlling his secret transports of impatience, Martial went towards Madame de Vaudremont with a bow. On seeing the Provençal, Soulanges gave him a covert glance, and impertinently turned away his head. Solemn silence now reigned in the room, where curiosity was at the highest pitch. All these eager faces wore the strangest mixed expressions; every one apprehended one of those outbreaks which men of breeding carefully avoid. Suddenly the Count's pale face turned as red as the scarlet facings of his coat, and he fixed his gaze on the floor that the cause of his agitation might not be guessed. On catching sight of the unknown lady humbly seated by the pedestal of the candelabrum, he moved away with a melancholy air, passing in front of the lawyer, and took refuge in one of the cardrooms. Martial and all the company thought that Soulanges had publicly surrendered the post, out of fear of the ridicule which invariably attaches to a discarded lover. The lawyer proudly raised his head and looked at the strange lady; then, as he took his seat at his ease near Madame de Vaudremont, he listened to her so inattentively that he did not catch these words spoken behind her fan:

"Martial, you will oblige me this evening by not wearing that ring that you snatched from me. I have my reasons, and will explain them to you in a moment when we go away. You must give me your arm to go to the Princesse de Wagram's."

"Why did you come in with the Colonel?" asked the Baron.

"I met him in the hall," she replied. "But leave me now; everybody is looki_⌣ at us."

Martial returned to the Colonel of Cuirassiers. Then it was that the little blue lady had become the object of the curiosity which agitated in such various ways the Colonel, Soulanges, Martial, and Madame de Vaudremont.

When the friends parted, after the challenge which closed their conversation, the Baron flew to Madame de Vaudremont, and led her to a place in the most brilliant quadrille. Favored by the sort of intoxication which dancing always produces in a woman, and by the turmoil of a ball, where men appear in all the trickery of dress, which adds no less to their attractions than it does to those of women, Martial thought he might yield with impunity to the charm that attracted his gaze to the fair stranger. Though he succeeded in hiding his first glances towards the lady in blue from the anxious activity of the Countess' eyes, he was ere long caught in the fact; and though he managed to excuse himself once for his absence of mind, he could not justify the unseemly silence with which he presently heard the most insinuating question which a woman can put to a man:

"Do you like me very much this evening?"

And the more dreamy he became, the more the Countess pressed and teased him.

While Martial was dancing, the Colonel moved from group to group, seeking information about the unknown lady. After exhausting the good-humor even of the most indifferent, he had resolved to take advantage of a moment when the Comtesse de Gondreville seemed to be at liberty, to ask her the name of the mysterious lady, when he perceived a little space left clear between the pedestal of the candelabrum and the two sofas, which ended in that corner. The dance had left several of the chairs vacant, which formed rows of fortifications held by mothers or women of middle age; and the Colonel seized the opportunity to make his way through this palisade hung with shawls and wraps. He began by making himself agreeable to the dowagers, and so from one to another, and from compliment to compliment, he at last reached the empty space next the stranger. At the risk of catching on to the gryphons and chimæras of the huge candelabrum, he stood there, braving the glare and dropping of the wax candles, to Martial's extreme annoyance.

The Colonel, far too tactful to speak suddenly to the little blue lady on his right, began by saying to a plain woman who was seated on the left:

"This is a splendid ball, madame! What luxury! What life! On my word, every woman here is pretty! You are not dancing—because you do not care for it, no doubt."

This vapid conversation was solely intended to induce his right-hand neighbor to speak; but she, silent and absent-minded, paid not the least attention. The officer had in store a number of phrases which he intended should lead up to: "And you, madame?"—a question from which he hoped great things. But he was strangely surprised to see tears in the strange lady's eyes, which seemed wholly absorbed in gazing on Madame de Vaudremont.

"You are married, no doubt, madame?" he asked her at length, in hesitating tones.

"Yes, monsieur," replied the lady.

"And your husband is here, of course?"

"Yes, monsieur."

"And why, madame, do you remain in this spot? Is it to attract attention?"

The mournful lady smiled sadly.

"Allow me the honor, madame, of being your partner in the next quadrille, and I will take care not to bring you back here. I see a vacant settee near the fire; come and take it. When so many people are ready to ascend the throne, and Royalty is the mania of the day, I cannot imagine that you will refuse the title of Queen of the Ball which your beauty may claim."

"I do not intend to dance, monsieur."

The curt tone of the lady's replies was so discouraging that the Colonel found himself compelled to raise the siege. Martial, who guessed what the officer's last request had been, and the refusal he had met with, began to smile, and stroked his chin, making the diamond sparkle which he wore on his finger.

"What are you laughing at?" said the Comtesse de Vaudremont.

"At the failure of the poor Colonel, who has just put his foot in it——"

"I begged you to take your ring off," said the Countess, interrupting him.

"I did not hear you."

"If you can hear nothing this evening, at any rate you see everything, Monsieur le Baron," said Madame de Vaudremont, with an air of vexation.

"That young man is displaying a very fine diamond," the stranger remarked to the Colonel.

"Splendid," he replied. "The man is the Baron Martial de la Roche-Hugon, one of my most intimate friends."

"I have to thank you for telling me his name," she went on; "he seems an agreeable man."

"Yes, but he is rather fickle."

"He seems to be on the best terms with the Comtesse de Vaudremont?" said the lady, with an inquiring look at the Colonel.

"On the very best."

The unknown turned pale.

"Hallo!" thought the soldier, "she is in love with that lucky devil Martial."

"I fancied that Madame de Vaudremont had long been devoted to M. de Soulanges," said the lady, recovering a little from the suppressed grief which had clouded the fairness of her face.

"For a week past the Countess has been faithless," replied the Colonel. "But you must have seen poor Soulanges when he came in; he is still trying to disbelieve in his disaster."

"Yes, I saw him," said the lady. Then she added, "Thank

you very much, monsieur," in a tone which signified a dismissal.

At this moment the quadrille was coming to an end. Montcornet had only time to withdraw, saying to himself by way of consolation, "She is married."

"Well, valiant Cuirassier," exclaimed the Baron, drawing the Colonel aside into a window-bay to breathe the fresh air from the garden, "how are you getting on?"

"She is a married woman, my dear fellow."

"What does that matter?"

"Oh, deuce take it! I am a decent sort of man," replied the Colonel. "I have no idea of paying my addresses to a woman I cannot marry. Besides, Martial, she expressly told me that she did not intend to dance."

"Colonel, I will bet a hundred napoleons to your gray horse that she will dance with me this evening."

"Done!" said the Colonel, putting his hand in the coxcomb's. "Meanwhile I am going to look for Soulanges; he perhaps knows the lady, as she seems interested in him."

"You have lost, my good fellow," cried Martial, laughing. "My eyes have met hers, and I know what they mean. My dear friend, you owe me no grudge for dancing with her after she has refused you?"

"No, no. Those who laugh last, laugh longest. But I am an honest gambler and a generous enemy, Martial, and I warn you, she is fond of diamonds."

With these words the friends parted; General Montcornet made his way to the cardroom, where he saw the Comte de Soulanges sitting at a *bouillotte* table. Though there was no friendship between the two soldiers, beyond the superficial comradeship arising from the perils of war and the duties of the service, the Colonel of Cuirassiers was painfully struck by seeing the Colonel of Artillery, whom he knew to be a prudent man, playing at a game which might bring him to ruin. The heaps of gold and notes piled on the fateful cards showed the frenzy of play. A circle of silent men stood round the players at the table. Now and then a few words

20

were spoken—*pass, play, I stop, a thousand louis, taken*—
but, looking at the five motionless men, it seemed as though
they talked only with their eyes. As the Colonel, alarmed
by Soulanges' pallor, went up to him, the Count was winning.
Field-Marshal the Duc d'Isemberg, Keller, and a famous
banker rose from the table completely cleaned out of considerable sums. Soulanges looked gloomier than ever as he
swept up a quantity of gold and notes; he did not even
count it; his lips curled with bitter scorn, he seemed to defy
fortune rather than be grateful for her favors.

"Courage," said the Colonel. "Courage, Soulanges!"
Then, believing he would do him a service by dragging him
from play, he added: "Come with me. I have some good
news for you, but on one condition."

"What is that?" asked Soulanges.

"That you will answer a question I will ask you."

The Comte de Soulanges rose abruptly, placing his win-
nings with reckless indifference in his handkerchief, which
he had been twisting with convulsive nervousness, and his
expression was so savage that none of the players took exception to his walking off with their money. Indeed, every
face seemed to dilate with relief when his morose and
crabbed countenance was no longer to be seen under the circle
of light which a shaded lamp casts on a gaming-table.

"Those fiends of soldiers are always as thick as thieves at a
fair!" said a diplomate who had been looking on, as he took
Soulanges' place. One single pallid and fatigued face turned
to the newcomer, and said with a glance that flashed and
died out like the sparkle of a diamond: "When we say military men, we do not mean civil, Monsieur le Ministre."

"My dear fellow," said Montcornet to Soulanges, leading
him into a corner, "the Emperor spoke warmly in your praise
this morning, and your promotion to be field-marshal is a
certainty."

"The Master does not love the Artillery."

"No, but he adores the nobility, and you are an aristocrat.
The Master said," added Montcornet, "that the men who had

married in Paris during the campaign were not therefore to be considered in disgrace. Well then?"

The Comte de Soulanges looked as if he understood nothing of this speech.

"And now I hope," the Colonel went on, "that you will tell me if you know a charming little woman who is sitting under a huge candelabrum——"

At these words the Count's face lighted up; he violently seized the Colonel's hand: "My dear General," said he, in a perceptibly altered voice, "if any man but you had asked me such a question, I would have cracked his skull with this mass of gold. Leave me, I entreat you. I feel more like blowing out my brains this evening, I assure you, than—— I hate everything I see. And, in fact, I am going. This gaiety, this music, these stupid faces, all laughing, are killing me!"

"My poor friend!" replied Montcornet gently, and giving the Count's hand a friendly pressure, "you are too vehement. What would you say if I told you that Martial is thinking so little of Madame de Vaudremont that he is quite smitten with that little lady?"

"If he says a word to her," cried Soulanges, stammering with rage, "I will thrash him as flat as his own portfolio, even if the coxcomb were in the Emperor's lap!"

And he sank quite overcome on an easy-chair to which Montcornet had led him. The Colonel slowly went away, for he perceived that Soulanges was in a state of fury far too violent for the pleasantries or the attentions of superficial friendship to soothe him.

When Montcornet returned to the ballroom, Madame de Vaudremont was the first person on whom his eyes fell, and he observed on her face, usually so calm, some symptoms of ill-disguised agitation. A chair was vacant near hers, and the Colonel seated himself.

"I dare wager something has vexed you?" said he.

"A mere trifle, General. I want to be gone, for I have promised to go to a ball at the Grand Duchess of Berg's, and I must look in first at the Princesse de Wagram's. Mou- sieur de la Roche-Hugon, who knows this, is amusing him- self by flirting with the dowagers."

"That is not the whole secret of your disturbance, and I will bet a hundred louis that you will remain here the whole evening."

"Impertinent man!"

"Then I have hit the truth?"

"Well, tell me, what am I thinking of?" said the Countess, tapping the Colonel's fingers with her fan. "I might even reward you if you guess rightly."

"I will not accept the challenge; I have too much the ad- vantage of you."

"You are presumptuous."

"You are afraid of seeing Martial at the feet——"

"Of whom?" cried the Countess, affecting surprise.

"Of that candelabrum," replied the Colonel, glancing at the fair stranger, and then looking at the Countess with embarrassing scrutiny.

"You have guessed it," replied the coquette, hiding her face behind her fan, which she began to play with. "Old Madame de Lansac, who is, you know, as malicious as an old monkey," she went on, after a pause, "has just told me that Monsieur de la Roche-Hugon is running into danger by flirting with that stranger, who sits here this evening like a skeleton at a feast. I would rather see a death's head than that face, so cruelly beautiful, and as pale as a ghost. She is my evil genius.— Madame de Lansac," she added, after a flash and gesture of annoyance, "who only goes to a ball to watch everything while pretending to sleep, has made me miserably anxious. Mar- tial shall pay dearly for playing me such a trick. Urge him, meanwhile, since he is your friend, not to make me so un- happy."

"I have just been with a man who promises to blow his brains out, and nothing less, if he speaks to that little lady And he is a man, madame, to keep his word. But then I know Martial; such threats are to him an encouragement.

And, besides, we have wagered——" Here the Colonel lowered his voice.

"Can it be true?" said the Countess.

"On my word of honor."

"Thank you, my dear Colonel," replied Madame de Vaudremont, with a glance full of invitation.

"Will you do me the honor of dancing with me?"

"Yes; but the next quadrille. During this one I want to
find out what will come of this little intrigue, and to ascer-
tain who the little blue lady may be; she looks intelligent."

The Colonel, understanding that Madame de Vaudremont
wished to be alone, retired, well content to have begun his
attack so well.

At most entertainments women are to be met who are
there, like Madame de Lansac, as old sailors gather on the
seashore to watch younger mariners struggling with the
tempest. At this moment Madame de Lansac, who seemed
to be interested in the personages of this drama, could easily
guess the agitation which the Countess was going through.
The lady might fan herself gracefully, smile on the young
men who bowed to her, and bring into play all the arts by
which a woman hides her emotion,—the Dowager, one of the
most clear-sighted and mischief-loving duchesses bequeathed
by the eighteenth century to the nineteenth, could read her
heart and mind through it all.

The old lady seemed to detect the slightest movement that
revealed the impressions of the soul. The imperceptible
frown that furrowed that calm, pure forehead, the faintest
quiver of the cheeks, the curve of the eyebrows, the least
curl of the lips, whose living coral could conceal nothing
from her,—all these were to the Duchess like the print of a
book. From the depths of her large arm-chair, completely
filled by the flow of her dress, the coquette of the past, while
talking to a diplomate who had sought her out to hear the
anecdotes she told so cleverly, was admiring herself in the
younger coquette; she felt kindly to her, seeing how bravely

she disguised her annoyance and grief of heart. Madame
de Vaudremont, in fact, felt as much sorrow as she feigned
cheerfulness; she had believed that she had found in Martial
a man of talent on whose support she could count for adorn-
ing her life with all the enchantment of power; and at this
moment she perceived her mistake, as injurious to her reputation as to her good opinion of herself. In her, as in other
women of that time, the suddenness of their passions increased
their vehemence. Souls which love much and love often,
suffer no less than those which burn themselves out in one
affection. Her liking for Martial was but of yesterday, it is
true, but the least experienced surgeon knows that the pain
caused by the amputation of a healthy limb is more acute
than the removal of a diseased one. There was a future before Madame de Vaudremont's passion for Martial, while her
previous love had been hopeless, and poisoned by Soulanges'
remorse.

The old Duchess, who was watching for an opportunity
of speaking to the Countess, hastened to dismiss her Ambassador; for in comparison with a lover's quarrel every interest pales, even with an old woman. To engage battle,
Madame de Lansac shot at the younger lady a sardonic
glance which made the Countess fear lest her fate was in the
dowager's hands. There are looks between woman and
woman which are like the torches brought on at the climax
of a tragedy. No one who had not known that Duchess could
appreciate the terror which the expression of her countenance
inspired in the Countess.

Madame de Lansac was tall, and her features led people
to say, "That must have been a handsome woman!" She
coated her cheeks so thickly with rouge that the wrinkles
were scarcely visible; but her eyes, far from gaining a facti-
tious brilliancy from this strong carmine, looked all the more
dim. She wore a vast quantity of diamonds, and dressed
with sufficient taste not to make herself ridiculous. Her
sharp nose promised epigram. A well-fitted set of teeth preserved a smile of such irony as recalled that of Voltaire. At

the same time, the exquisite politeness of her manners so effectually softened the mischievous twist in her mind, that it was impossible to accuse her of spitefulness.

The old woman's eyes lighted up, and a triumphant glance, seconded by a smile, which said, "I promised you as much!" shot across the room, and brought a blush of hope to the pale cheeks of the young creature languishing under the great chandelier. The alliance between Madame de Lansac and the stranger could not escape the practised eye of the Comtesse de Vaudremont, who scented a mystery, and was determined to penetrate it.

At this instant the Baron de la Roche-Hugon, after questioning all the dowagers without success as to the blue lady's name, applied in despair to the Comtesse de Gondreville, from whom he reached only this unsatisfactory reply, "A lady whom the 'ancient' Duchesse de Lansac introduced to me."

Turning by chance towards the armchair occupied by the old lady, the lawyer intercepted the glance of intelligence she sent to the stranger; and although he had for some time been on bad terms with her, he determined to speak to her. The "ancient" Duchess, seeing the jaunty Baron prowling round her chair, smiled with sardonic irony, and looked at Madame de Vaudremont with an expression that made Montcornet laugh.

"If the old witch affects to be friendly," thought the Baron, "she is certainly going to play me some spiteful trick.— Madame," he said, "you have, I am told, undertaken the charge of a very precious treasure."

"Do you take me for a dragon?" said the old lady. "But of whom are you speaking?" she added, with a sweetness which revived Martial's hopes.

"Of that little lady, unknown to all, whom the jealousy of all these coquettes has imprisoned in that corner. You, no doubt, know her family?"

"Yes," said the Duchess. "But what concern have you with a provincial heiress, married some time since, a woman of good birth, whom you none of you know, you men; she goes nowhere."

"Why does not she dance, she is such a pretty creature?— May we conclude a treaty of peace? If you will vouchsafe to tell me all I want to know, I promise you that a petition for the restitution of the woods of Navarreins by the Commissioners of Crown Lands shall be strongly urged on the Emperor."

The younger branch of the house of Navarreins bears quarterly with the arms of Navarreins those of Lansac, namely, azure and argent party per pale raguly, between six spear-heads in pale, and the old lady's liaison with Louis XV. had earned her husband the title of duke by royal patent. Now, as the Navarreins had not yet resettled in France, it was sheer trickery that the young lawyer thus proposed to the old lady by suggesting to her that she should petition for an estate belonging to the elder branch of the family.

"Monsieur," said the old woman with deceptive gravity, "bring the Comtesse de Vaudremont across to me. I promise you that I will reveal to her the mystery of the interesting unknown. You see, every man in the room has reached as great a curiosity as your own. All eyes are involuntarily turned towards the corner where my protégée has so modestly placed herself; she is reaping all the homage the women wished to deprive her of. Happy the man she chooses for her partner!" She interrupted herself, fixing her eyes on Madame de Vaudremont with one of those looks which plainly say, "We are talking of you."—Then she added, "I imagine you would rather learn the stranger's name from the lips of your handsome Countess than from mine."

There was such marked defiance in the Duchess' attitude that Madame de Vaudremont rose, came up to her, and took the chair Martial placed for her; then without noticing him she said, "I can guess, madame, that you are talking of me; but I admit my want of perspicacity; I do not know whether it is for good or evil."

Madame de Lansac pressed the young woman's pretty hand

in her own dry and wrinkled fingers, and answered in a low, compassionate tone, "Poor child!"

The women looked at each other. Madame de Vaudremont understood that Martial was in the way, and dismissed him, saying with an imperious expression, "Leave us."

The Baron, ill-pleased at seeing the Countess under the spell of the dangerous sibyl who had drawn her to her side, gave one of those looks which a man can give—potent over a blinded heart, but simply ridiculous in the eyes of a woman who is beginning to criticise the man who has attracted her.

"Do you think you can play the Emperor?" said Madame de Vaudremont, turning three-quarters of her face to fix an ironical sidelong gaze on the lawyer.

Martial was too much a man of the world, and had too much wit and acumen, to risk breaking with a woman who was in favor at Court, and whom the Emperor wished to see married. He counted, too, on the jealousy he intended to provoke in her as the surest means of discovering the secret of her coolness, and withdrew all the more willingly, because at this moment a new quadrille was putting everybody in motion.

With an air of making room for the dancing, the Baron leaned back against the marble slab of a console, folded his arms, and stood absorbed in watching the two ladies talking. From time to time he followed the glances which both frequently directed to the stranger. Then, comparing the Countess with the new beauty, made so attractive by a touch of mystery, the Baron fell a prey to the detestable self-interest common to adventurous lady-killers; he hesitated between a fortune within his grasp and the indulgence of his caprice. The blaze of light gave such strong relief to his anxious and sullen face, against the hangings of white silk moreen brushed by his black hair, that he might have been compared to an evil genius. Even from a distance more than one observer no doubt said to himself, "There is another poor wretch who seems to be enjoying himself!"

The Colonel, meanwhile, with one shoulder leaning lightly

against the side-post of the doorway between the ballroom
and the cardroom, could laugh undetected under his ample
moustache; it amused him to look on at the turmoil of the
dance; he could see a hundred pretty heads turning about
in obedience to the figures; he could read in some faces, as
in those of the Countess and his friend Martial, the secrets
of their agitation; and then, looking round, he wondered
what connection there could be between the gloomy looks of
the Comte de Soulanges, still seated on the sofa, and the
plaintive expression of the fair unknown, on whose features
the joys of hope and the anguish of involuntary dread were
alternately legible.   Montcornet stood like the king of the
feast.   In this moving picture he saw a complete presentment
of the world, and he laughed at it as he found himself the
object of inviting smiles from a hundred beautiful and elegant
women.   A Colonel of the Imperial Guard, a position equal
to that of a Brigadier-General, was undoubtedly one of the
best matches in the army.

It was now nearly midnight.   The conversation, the gambling, the dancing, the flirtations, interests, petty rivalries,
and scheming had all reached the pitch of ardor which makes
a young man exclaim involuntarily, "A fine ball!"

"My sweet little angel," said Madame de Lansac to the
Countess, "you are now at an age when in my day I made
many mistakes.   Seeing you just now enduring a thousand
deaths, it occurred to me that I might give you some
charitable advice.   To go wrong at two-and-twenty means
spoiling your future; is it not tearing the gown you must
wear?   My dear, it is not till much later that we learn to
go about in it without crumpling it.   Go on, sweetheart,
making clever enemies, and friends who have no sense of
conduct, and you will see what a pleasant life you will some
day be leading!"

"Oh, madame, it is very hard for a woman to be happy,
do not you think?" the Countess eagerly exclaimed.

"My child, at your age you must learn to choose between
pleasure and happiness.   You want to marry Martial, who

is not fool enough to make a good husband, nor passionate enough to remain a lover. He is in debt, my dear; he is the man to run through your fortune; still, that would be nothing if he could make you happy.—Do not you see how aged he is? The man must have been often ill; he is making the most of what is left him. In three years he will be a wreck. Then he will be ambitious; perhaps he may succeed. I do not think so.—What is he? A man of intrigue, who may have the business faculty to perfection, and be able to gossip agreeably; but he is too presumptuous to have any sterling merit; he will not go far. Besides—only look at him. Is it not written on his brow that, at this very moment, what he sees in you is not a young and pretty woman, but the two million francs you possess? He does not love you, my dear; he is reckoning you up as if you were an investment. If you are bent on marrying, find an older man who has an assured position and is half-way on his career. A widow's marriage ought not to be a trivial love affair. Is a mouse to be caught a second time in the same trap? A new alliance ought now to be a good speculation on your part, and in marrying again you ought at least to have a hope of being some day addressed as Madame la Maréchale!"

As she spoke, both women naturally fixed their eyes on Colonel Montcornet's handsome face.

"If you would rather play the delicate part of a flirt and not marry again," the Duchess went on, with blunt good-nature; "well! my poor child, you, better than any woman, will know how to raise the storm-clouds and disperse them again. But, I beseech you, never make it your pleasure to disturb the peace of families, to destroy unions, and ruin the happiness of happy wives. I, my dear, have played that perilous game. Dear heaven! for a triumph of vanity some poor virtuous soul is murdered—for there really are virtuous women, child,—and we may make ourselves mortally hated. I learned, a little too late, that, as the Duc d'Albe once said, one salmon is worth a thousand frogs! A genuine affection certainly brings a thousand times more happiness than the transient passions we may inspire.—Well, I came here on purpose to preach to you; yes, you are the cause of my appearance in this house, which stinks of the lower class. Have I not just seen actors here? Formerly, my dear, we received them in our boudoir; but in the drawing-room— never!—Why do you look at me with so much amazement? Listen to me. If you want to play with men, do not try to wring the hearts of any but those whose life is not yet settled, who have no duties to fulfil; the others do not forgive us for the errors that have made them happy. Profit by this maxim, founded on my long experience.—That luckless Soulanges, for instance, whose head you have turned, whom you have intoxicated for these fifteen months past, God knows how! Do you know at what you have struck?—At his whole life. He has been married these two years; he is worshiped by a charming wife, whom he loves, but neglects; she lives in tears and embittered silence. Soulanges has had hours of remorse more terrible than his pleasure has been sweet. And you, you artful little thing, have deserted him.—Well, come and see your work."

The old lady took Madame de Vaudremont's hand, and they rose.

"There," said Madame de Lansac, and her eyes showed her the stranger, sitting pale and tremulous under the glare of the candles, "that is my grandniece, the Comtesse de Soulanges; to-day she yielded at last to my persuasion, and consented to leave the sorrowful room, where the sight of her child gives her but little consolation. You see her? You think her charming? Then imagine, dear Beauty, what she must have been when happiness and love shed their glory on that face now blighted."

The Countess looked away in silence, and seemed lost in sad reflections.

The Duchess led her to the door into the card-room; then, after looking round the room as if in search of some one— "And there is Soulanges!" she said in deep tones.

The Countess shuddered as she saw, in the least brilliantly

lighted corner, the pale, set face of Soulanges stretched in an easy-chair. The indifference of his attitude and the rigidity of his brow betrayed his suffering. The players passed him to and fro, without paying any more attention to him than if he had been dead. The picture of the wife in tears, and the dejected, morose husband, separated in the midst of this festivity like the two halves of a tree blasted by lightning, had perhaps a prophetic significance for the Countess. She dreaded lest she here saw an image of the revenges the future might have in store for her. Her heart has not yet so dried up that feeling and generosity were entirely excluded, and she pressed the Duchess' hand, while thanking her by one of those smiles which have a certain childlike grace.

"My dear child," the old lady said in her ear, "remember henceforth that we are just as capable of repelling a man's attentions as of attracting them."

"She is yours if you are not a simpleton." These words were whispered into Colonel Montcornet's ear by Madame de Lansac, while the handsome Countess was still absorbed in compassion at the sight of Soulanges, for she still loved him truly enough to wish to restore him to happiness, and was promising herself in her own mind that she would exert the irresistible power her charms still had over him to make him return to his wife.

"Oh! I will talk to him!" said she to Madame de Lansac.

"Do nothing of the kind, my dear!" cried the old lady, as she went back to her armchair. "Choose a good husband, and shut your door to my nephew. Believe me, my child, a wife cannot accept her husband's heart as the gift of another woman; she is a hundred times happier in the belief that she has reconquered it. By bringing my niece here I believe I have given her an excellent chance of regaining her husband's affection. All the assistance I need of you is to play the Colonel." She pointed to the Baron's friend, and the Countess smiled.

"Well, madame, do you at last know the name of the unknown?" asked Martial, with an air of pique, to the Countess
when he saw her alone.

"Yes," said Madame de Vaudremont, looking him in the
face.

Her features expressed as much roguery as fun. The smile
which gave life to her lips and cheeks, the liquid brightness
of her eyes, were like the will-o'-the-wisp which leads travelers
astray. Martial, who believed that she still loved him, assumed the coquetting graces in which a man is so ready to lull
himself in the presence of the woman he loves. He said with
a fatuous air:

"And will you be annoyed with me if I seem to attach
great importance to your telling me that name?"

"Will you be annoyed with me," answered Madame de Vaudremont, "if a remnant of affection prevents my telling you;
and if I forbid you to make the smallest advances to that
young lady? It would be at the risk of your life perhaps."

"To lose your good graces, madame, would be worse than
to lose my life."

"Martial," said the Countess severely, "she is Madame de
Soulanges. Her husband would blow your brains out—if,
indeed, you have any——"

"Ha! ha!" laughed the coxcomb. "What! the Colonel can
leave the man in peace who has robbed him of your love,
and then would fight for his wife! What a subversion of
principles!—I beg of you to allow me to dance with the little
lady. You will then be able to judge how little love that
heart of ice could feel for you; for, if the Colonel disapproves
of my dancing with his wife after allowing me to——"

"But she loves her husband."

"A still further obstacle that I shall have the pleasure of
conquering."

"But she is married."

"A whimsical objection!"

"Ah!" said the Countess, with a bitter smile, "you punish
us alike for our faults and our repentance!"

"Do not be angry!" exclaimed Martial eagerly. "Oh, forgive me, I beseech you. There, I will think no more of Madame de Soulanges."

"You deserve that I should send you to her."

"I am off then," said the Baron, laughing, "and I shall return more devoted to you than ever. You will see that the prettiest woman in the world cannot capture the heart that is yours."

"That is to say, that you want to win Colonel Montcornet's horse?"

"Ah! Traitor!" said he, threatening his friend with his finger. The Colonel smiled and joined them; the Baron gave him the seat near the Countess, saying to her with a sardonic accent:

"Here, madame, is a man who boasted that he could win your good graces in one evening."

He went away, thinking himself clever to have piqued the Countess' pride and done Montcornet an ill turn; but, in spite of his habitual keenness, he had not appreciated the irony underlying Madame de Vaudremont's speech, and did not perceive that she had come as far to meet his friend as his friend towards her, though both were unconscious of it.

At the moment when the lawyer went fluttering up to the candelabrum by which Madame de Soulanges sat, pale, timid, and apparently alive only in her eyes, her husband came to the door of the ballroom, his eyes flashing with anger. The old Duchess, watchful of everything, flew to her nephew, begged him to give her his arm and find her carriage, affecting to be mortally bored, and hoping thus to prevent a vexatious outbreak. Before going she fired a singular glance of intelligence at her niece, indicating the enterprising knight who was about to address her, and this signal seemed to say, "There he is, avenge yourself!"

Madame de Vaudremont caught these looks of the aunt and niece; a sudden light dawned on her mind; she was frightened lest she was the dupe of this old woman, so cunning and so practised in intrigue.

"That perfidious Duchess," said she to herself, "has perhaps been amusing herself by preaching morality to me while playing me some spiteful trick of her own."

At this thought Madame de Vaudremont's pride was perhaps more roused than her curiosity to disentangle the thread of this intrigue. In the absorption of mind to which she was a prey she was no longer mistress of herself. The Colonel, interpreting to his own advantage the embarrassment evident in the Countess' manner and speech, became more ardent and pressing. The old blasé diplomates, amusing themselves by watching the play of faces, had never found so many intrigues at once to watch or guess at. The passions agitating the two couples were to be seen with variations at every step in the crowded rooms, and reflected with different shades in other countenances. The spectacle of so many vivid passions, of all these lovers' quarrels, these pleasing revenges, these cruel favors, these flaming glances, of all this ardent life diffused around them, only made them feel their impotence more keenly.

At last the Baron had found a seat by Madame de Soulanges. His eyes stole a long look at her neck, as fresh as dew and as fragrant as field flowers. He admired close at hand the beauty which had amazed him from afar. He could see a small, well-shod foot, and measure with his eye a slender and graceful shape. At that time women wore their sash tied close under the bosom, in imitation of Greek statues, a pitiless fashion for those whose bust was faulty. As he cast furtive glances at the Countess' figure, Martial was enchanted with its perfection.

"You have not danced once this evening, madame," said he in soft and flattering tones. "Not, I should suppose, for lack of a partner?"

"I never go to parties; I am quite unknown," replied Madame de Soulanges coldly, not having understood the look by which her aunt had just conveyed to her that she was to attract the Baron.

Martial, to give himself countenance, twisted the diamond

he wore on his left hand; the rainbow fires of the gem seemed to flash a sudden light on the young Countess' mind; she blushed and looked at the Baron with an undefinable expression.

"Do you like dancing?" asked the Provençal, to reopen the conversation.

"Yes, very much, monsieur."

At this strange reply their eyes met. The young man, surprised by the earnest accent, which aroused a vague hope in his heart, had suddenly questioned the lady's eyes.

"Then, madame, am I not overbold in offering myself to be your partner for the next quadrille?"

Artless confusion colored the Countess' white cheeks.

"But, monsieur, I have already refused one partner—a military man——"

"Was it that tall cavalry colonel whom you see over there?"

"Precisely so."

"Oh! he is a friend of mine; feel no alarm. Will you grant me the favor I dare hope for?"

"Yes, monsieur."

Her tone betrayed an emotion so new and so deep that the lawyer's world-worn soul was touched. He was overcome by shyness like a schoolboy's, lost his confidence, and his southern brain caught fire; he tried to talk, but his phrases struck him as graceless in comparison with Madame de Soulanges' bright and subtle replies. It was lucky for him that the quadrille was forming. Standing by his beautiful partner, he felt more at ease. To many men dancing is a phase of being; they think that they can more powerfully influence the heart of woman by displaying the graces of their bodies than by their intellect. Martial wished, no doubt, at this moment to put forth all his most effective seductions, to judge by the pretentiousness of his movements and gestures.

He led his conquest to the quadrille in which the most brilliant women in the room made it a point of chimerical importance to dance in preference to any other. While the orchestra played the introductory bars to the first figure,

21

the Baron felt it an incredible gratification to his pride to perceive, as he reviewed the ladies forming the lines of that formidable square, that Madame de Soulanges' dress might challenge that even of Madame de Vaudremont, who, by a chance not perhaps unsought, was standing with Montcornet *vis-à-vis* to himself and the lady in blue. All eyes were for a moment turned on Madame de Soulanges; a flattering murmur showed that she was the subject of every man's conversation with his partner. Looks of admiration and envy centered on her, with so much eagerness that the young creature, abashed by a triumph she seemed to disclaim, modestly looked down, blushed, and was all the more charming. When she raised her white eyelids it was to look at her ravished partner as though she wished to transfer the glory of this admiration to him, and to say that she cared more for his than for all the rest. She threw her innocence into her vanity; or rather she seemed to give herself up to the guileless admiration which is the beginning of love, with the good faith found only in youthful hearts. As she danced, the lookers-on might easily believe that she displayed her grace for Martial alone; and though she was modest, and new to the trickery of the ballroom, she knew as well as the most accomplished coquette how to raise her eyes to his at the right moment and drop their lids with assumed modesty.

When the movement of a new figure, invented by a dancer named Trénis, and named after him, brought Martial face to face with the Colonel—"I have won your horse," said he, laughing.

"Yes, but you have lost eighty thousand francs a year!" retorted Montcornet, glancing at Madame de Vaudremont.

"What do I care?" replied Martial. "Madame de Soulanges is worth millions!"

At the end of the quadrille more than one whisper was poured into more than one ear. The less pretty women made moral speeches to their partners, commenting on the budding *liaison* between Martial and the Comtesse de Soulanges. The handsomest wondered at her easy surrender. The men could

not understand such luck as the Baron's, not regarding him
as particularly fascinating. A few indulgent women said it
was not fair to judge the Countess too hastily; young wives
would be in a very hapless plight if an expressive look or a few
graceful dancing steps were enough to compromise a woman.

Martial alone knew the extent of his happiness. During
the last figure, when the ladies had to form the *moulinet,*
his fingers clasped those of the Countess, and he fancied that,
through the thin perfumed kid of her gloves, the young wife's
grasp responded to his amorous appeal.

"Madame," said he, as the quadrille ended, "do not go back
to the odious corner where you have been burying your face
and your dress until now. Is admiration the only benefit
you can obtain from the jewels that adorn your white neck
and beautifully dressed hair? Come and take a turn through
the rooms to enjoy the scene and yourself."

Madame de Soulanges yielded to her seducer, who thought
she would be his all the more surely if he could only show
her off. Side by side they walked two or three times amid
the groups who crowded the rooms. The Comtesse de Soulanges, evidently uneasy, paused for an instant at each door
before entering, only doing so after stretching her neck to
look at all the men there. This alarm, which crowned the
Baron's satisfaction, did not seem to be removed till he said
to her, "Make yourself easy; *he* is not here."

They thus made their way to an immense picture gallery
in a wing of the mansion, where their eyes could feast in
anticipation on the splendid display of a collation prepared
for three hundred persons. As supper was about to begin,
Martial led the Countess to an oval boudoir looking on to the
garden, where the rarest flowers and a few shrubs made a
scented bower under bright blue hangings. The murmurs
of the festivity here died away. The Countess, at first
startled, refused firmly to follow the young man; but, glancing in a mirror, she no doubt assured herself that they could
be seen, for she seated herself on an ottoman with a fairly
good grace.

"'This room is charming," said she, admiring the sky-blue hangings looped with pearls.

"All here is love and delight!" said the Baron, with deep emotion.

In the mysterious light which prevailed he looked at the Countess, and detected on her gently agitated face an expression of uneasiness, modesty, and eagerness which enchanted him. The young lady smiled, and this smile seemed to put an end to the struggle of feeling surging in her heart; in the most insinuating way she took her adorer's left hand, and drew from his finger the ring on which she had fixed her eyes.

"What a fine diamond!" she exclaimed in the artless tone of a young girl betraying the incitement of a first temptation.

Martial, troubled by the Countess' involuntary but intoxicating touch, like a caress, as she drew off the ring, looked at her with eyes as glittering as the gem.

"Wear it," he said, "in memory of this hour, and for the love of——"

She was looking at him with such rapture that he did not end the sentence; he kissed her hand.

"You give it me?" she said, looking much astonished.

"I wish I had the whole world to offer you!"

"You are not joking?" she went on, in a voice husky with too great satisfaction.

"Will you accept only my diamond?"

"You will never take it back?" she insisted.

"Never."

She put the ring on her finger. Martial, confident of coming happiness, was about to put his hand round her waist, but she suddenly rose, and said in a clear voice, without any agitation:

"I accept the diamond, monsieur, with the less scruple because it belongs to me."

The Baron was speechless.

"Monsieur de Soulanges took it lately from my dressing-table, and told me he had lost it."

"You are mistaken, madame," said Martial, nettled. "It was given me by Madame de Vaudremont."

"Precisely so," she said with a smile. "My husband borrowed this ring of me, he gave it to her, she made it a present to you; my ring has made a little journey, that is all. This ring will perhaps tell me all I do not know, and teach me the secret of always pleasing.—Monsieur," she went on, "if it had not been my own, you may be sure I should not have risked paying so dear for it; for a young woman, it is said, is in danger with you. But, you see," and she touched a spring within the ring, "here is M. de Soulanges' hair."

She fled into the crowded rooms so swiftly, that it seemed useless to try to follow her; besides, Martial, utterly confounded, was in no mood to carry the adventure further. The Countess' laugh found an echo in the boudoir, where the young coxcomb now perceived, between two shrubs, the Colonel and Madame de Vaudremont, both laughing heartily.

"Will you have my horse, to ride after your prize?" said the Colonel.

The Baron took the banter poured upon him by Madame de Vaudremont and Montcornet with a good grace, which secured their silence as to the events of the evening, when his friend exchanged his charger for a rich and pretty young wife.

As the Comtesse de Soulanges drove across Paris from the Chaussée d'Antin to the Faubourg Saint-Germain, where she lived, her soul was a prey to many alarms. Before leaving the Hôtel Gondreville she went through all the rooms, but found neither her aunt nor her husband, who had gone away without her. Frightful suspicions then tortured her ingenuous mind. A silent witness of her husband's torments since the day when Madame de Vaudremont had chained him to her car, she had confidently hoped that repentance would ere long restore her husband to her. It was with unspeakable repugnance that she had consented to the scheme plotted by

her aunt, Madame de Lansac, and at this moment she feared
she had made a mistake.

The evening's experience had saddened her innocent soul.
Alarmed at first by the Count's look of suffering and dejec-
tion, she had become more so on seeing her rival's beauty,
and the corruption of society had gripped her heart. As she
crossed the Pont Royal she threw away the desecrated hair
at the back of the diamond, given to her once as a token of
the purest affection. She wept as she remembered the bitter
grief to which she had so long been a victim, and shuddered
more than once as she reflected that the duty of a woman,
who wishes for peace in her home, compels her to bury sufferings so keen as hers at the bottom of her heart, and without
a complaint.

"Alas!" thought she, "what can women do when they do
not love? What is the fount of their indulgence? I cannot believe that, as my aunt tells me, reason is all-sufficient
to maintain them in such devotion."

She was still sighing when her man-servant let down the
handsome carriage-step down which she flew into the hall
of her house. She rushed precipitately upstairs, and when
she reached her room was startled by seeing her husband sitting by the fire.

"How long is it, my dear, since you have gone to balls
without telling me beforehand?" he asked in a broken voice.
"You must know that a woman is always out of place without her husband. You compromised yourself strangely by
remaining in the dark corner where you had ensconced yourself."

"Oh, my dear, good Léon," said she in a coaxing tone, "I
could not resist the happiness of seeing you without your
seeing me. My aunt took me to this ball, and I was very
happy there!"

This speech disarmed the Count's looks of their assumed
severity, for he had been blaming himself while dreading his
wife's return, no doubt fully informed at the ball of an infidelity he had hoped to hide from her; and, as is the way

of lovers conscious of their guilt, he tried, by being the first
to find fault, to escape her just anger. Happy in seeing her
husband smile, and in finding him at this hour in a room
whither of late he had come more rarely, the Countess looked
at him so tenderly that she blushed and cast down her eyes.
Her clemency enraptured Soulanges all the more, because this
scene followed on the misery he had endured at the ball. He
seized his wife's hand and kissed it gratefully. Is not gratitude often a part of love?

"Hortense, what is that on your finger that has hurt my lip
so much?" asked he, laughing.

"It is my diamond which you said you had lost, and which
I have found.

General Montcornet did not marry Madame de Vaudremont, in spite of the mutual understanding in which they had
lived for a few minutes, for she was one of the victims of
the terrible fire which sealed the fame of the ball given by
the Austrian ambassador on the occasion of Napoleon's marriage with the daughter of the Emperor Joseph II.

July 1829.

THE IMAGINARY MISTRESS

Dedicated to the Comtesse Clara Maffei.

In the month of September 1835, one of the richest heiresses
of the Faubourg Saint-Germain, Mademoiselle du Rouvre,
the only child of the Marquis du Rouvre, married Count
Adam Mitgislas Laginski, a young Polish exile.

I allow myself to spell the names as they are pronounced,
to spare the reader the sight of the fortifications of consonants by which, in the Slav languages, the vowels are protected, no doubt to secure them against loss, seeing how few
they are.

The Marquis du Rouvre had dissipated almost the whole of
one of the finest fortunes of the nobility, to which he had
formerly owed his alliance with a Mademoiselle de Ronquerolles. Hence Clémentine had for her uncle, on her
mother's side, the Marquis de Ronquerolles, and for her aunt
Madame de Sérizy. On her father's side she possessed another uncle in the eccentric person of the Chevalier du
Rouvre, the younger son of the house, an old bachelor who
had grown rich by speculations in lands and houses.

The Marquis de Ronquerolles was so unhappy as to lose
both his children during the visitation of cholera. Madame
de Sérizy's only son, a young officer of the highest promise,
was killed in Africa at the fight by the Macta. In these
days rich families run the risk of ruining their children if
they have too many, or of becoming extinct if they have but
one or two, a singular result of the Civil Code not foreseen
by Napoleon. Thus, by accident, and in spite of Monsieur du
Rouvre's reckless extravagances for Florine, one of the most
charming of Paris actresses, Clémentine had become an

heiress. The Marquis de Ronquerolles, one of the most accomplished diplomates of the new dynasty, his sister, Madame de Sérizy, and the Chevalier du Rouvre agreed that, to rescue their fortunes from the Marquis' clutches, they would leave them to their niece, to whom they each promised ten thousand francs a year on her marriage.

It is quite unnecessary to say that the Pole, though a refugee, cost the French Government absolutely nothing. Count Adam belonged to one of the oldest and most illustrious families of Poland, connected with most of the princely houses of Germany, with the Sapiéhas, the Radziwills, the Mniszechs, the Rzewuskis, the Czartoryskis, the Leszinskis, the Lubomirskis, in short, all the great Sarmatian *skis*. But a knowledge of heraldry is not a strong point in France under Louis Philippe, and such nobility could be no recommendation to the *bourgeoisie* then in power. Besides, when, in 1833, Adam made his appearance on the Boulevard des Italiens, at Frascati's, at the Jockey Club, he led the life of a man who, having lost his political prospects, falls back on his vices and his love of pleasure. He was taken for a student.

The Polish nationality, as the result of an odious Government reaction, had fallen as low as the Republicans had tried to think it high. The strange struggle of Movement against Resistance—two words which thirty years hence will be inexplicable—made a farce of what ought to have been so worthy: the name, that is, of a vanquished nation to which France gave hospitality, for which entertainments were devised, for which every one danced or sang by subscription; a nation, in short, which at the time when, in 1796, Europe was fighting France, had offered her six thousand men, and such men!

Do not conclude from this that I mean to represent the Emperor Nicholas as being in the wrong as regards Poland, or Poland as regards the Emperor Nicholas. In the first place, it would be a silly thing enough to slip a political discussion into a tale which ought to interest or to amuse. Besides, Russia and Poland were equally right: one for aiming at unity of Empire, the other for desiring to be free again. It may be said, in passing, that Poland might have conquered Russia by the influence of manners instead of beating her with weapons; thus imitating the Chinese, who at last Chinesified the Tartars, and who, it is to be hoped, will do the same by the English. Poland ought to have *polished* the Russians; Poniatowski had tried it in the least temperate district of the Empire. But that gentleman was a misunderstood king—all the more so because he did not perhaps understand himself.

How was it possible not to hate the poor people who were the cause of the horrible deceit committed on the occasion of the review when all Paris was eager to rescue Poland? People affected to regard the Poles as allies of the Republican party, forgetting that Poland was an aristocratic republic. Thenceforth the party of wealth poured ignoble contempt on the Pole, who had been deified but a few days since. The wind of a riot has always blown the Parisians round from north to south under every form of government. This weathercock temper of Paris opinion must be remembered if we would understand how, in 1835, the name of Pole was a word of ridicule among the race who believe themselves to be the wittiest and politest in the world, and its central luminary, in a city which, at this day, wields the sceptre of art and literature.

There are, alas! two types of Polish refugees—the republican Pole, the son of Lelewel, and the noble Pole, of the party led 'by Prince Czartoryski. These two kinds of Pole are as fire and water, but why blame them? Are not such divisions always to be observed among refugees whatever nation they belong to, and no matter what country they go to? They carry their country and their hatreds with them. At Brussels two French émigré priests expressed the greatest aversion for each other; and when one of them was asked his reasons, he replied, pointing to his companion in misery, "He is a Jansenist!" Dante, in his exile, would gladly have stabbed any adversary of the *Bianchi*. In this lies the rea-

son of the attacks made on the venerable Prince Adam
Czartoryski by the French radicals, and that of the disap-
proval shown to a section of the Polish emigrants by the
Cæsars of the counter and the Alexanders by letters patent.

In 1834 Adam Mitgislas Laginski was the butt of Parisian
witticisms.—"He is a nice fellow though he is a Pole," said
Rastignac.—"All the Poles are great lords," said Maxime
de Trailles, "but this one pays his gambling debts; I begin
to think that he must have had an estate."

And without offence to the exiles, it may be remarked that
the levity, the recklessness, the fluidity of the Sarmatian character justified the calumnies of the Parisians, who, indeed,
in similar circumstances, would be exactly like the Poles.
The French aristocracy, so admirably supported by the Polish
aristocracy during the Revolution, certainly made no equiva-
lent return to those who were forced to emigrate in 1832.
We must have the melancholy courage to say that, in this,
the Faubourg Saint-Germain remains Poland's debtor.

Was Count Adam rich, was he poor, was he an adventurer?
The problem long remained unsolved. Diplomatic circles,
faithful to their instructions, imitated the silence observed
by the Emperor Nicholas, who at that time counted every
Polish émigré as dead. The Tuileries, and most of those who
took their cue from thence, gave an odious proof of this
characteristic policy dignified by the name of prudence. A
Russian prince, with whom they had smoked many cigars at
the time of the emigration, was ignored because, as it seemed,
he had fallen into disgrace with the Emperor Nicholas.

Thus placed between the prudence of the Court and that
of diplomatic circles, Poles of good family lived in the Bib-
lical solitude of *Super flumina Babylonis,* or frequented certain drawing-rooms which served as neutral territory for
every variety of opinion. In a city of pleasure like Paris,
where amusement is to be had in every rank, Polish recklessness found twice as many pretexts as it needed for leading a
dissipated bachelor life. Besides, it must be said, Adam
had against him at first both his appearance and his manners.

There are two types of Pole, as there are two types of Englishwoman. When an Englishwoman is not a beauty, she is horribly ugly—and Count Adam belongs to the second category. His face is small, somewhat sour, and looks as if it had been squeezed in a vise. His short nose, fair hair, red moustaches and beard, give him the expression of a goat; all the more so because he is short and thin, and his eyes, tinged with dingy yellow, startle you by the oblique leer which Virgil's line has made famous. How is it that, in spite of such unfavorable conditions, he has such exquisite manners and style? The solution of this mystery is given by his dress, that of a finished dandy, and by the education he owes to his mother, a Radziwill. If his courage carries him to the point of rashness, his mind is not above the current and trivial pleasantries of Paris conversation; still, he does not often find a young fellow who is his superior among men of fashion. These young men nowadays talk far too much of horses, income, taxes, and deputies, for French conversation to be what once it was. Wit needs leisure, and certain inequalities of position. Conversation is better perhaps at Petersburg and at Vienna than it is in Paris. Equals need no subtleties; they tell each other everything straight out, just as it is. Hence the ironical laughers of Paris could scarcely discern a man of family in a light-hearted student, as he seemed, who in talking passed carelessly from one subject to another, who pursued amusement with all the more frenzy because he had just escaped from great perils, and who, having left the country where his family was known, thought himself at liberty to lead an irresponsible life without risking a loss of consideration.

One fine day in 1834, Adam bought a large house in the Rue de la Pépinière. Six months later it was on as handsome a footing as the richest houses in Paris. Just at the time when Laginski was beginning to be taken seriously, he saw Clémentine at the Italian opera, and fell in love with her. A year later, he married her. Madame d'Espard's circle set the fashion of approval. Mothers of families then learned, too late, that ever since the year 900, the Laginskis had ranked with the most illustrious families of the North. By a stroke of prudence, most unlike a Pole, the young Count's mother had, at the beginning of the rebellion, mortgaged her estates for an immense sum advanced by two Jewish houses, and invested in the French funds. Count Adam Laginski had an income of more than eighty thousand francs. This put an end to the astonishment expressed in some drawing-rooms at the rashness of Madame de Sérizy, of old de Ronquerolles, and of the Chevalier du Rouvre in yielding to their niece's mad passion.

As usual, the world rushed from one extreme to the other. During the winter of 1836, Count Adam became the fashion, and Clémentine Laginski one of the queens of Paris. Madame de Laginski, at the present time, is one of the charming group of young married women among whom shine Mesdames de Lestorade, de Portenduère, Marie de Vandenesse, du Guénic, and de Maufrigneuse, the very flower of Paris society, who live high above the parvenus, bourgeois, and wire-pullers of recent politics.

This preamble was needful to define the sphere in which was carried through one of those sublime efforts, less rare than the detractors of the present time imagine,—pearls hidden in rough shells, and lost in the depths of that abyss, that ocean, that never-resting tide called the World—the Age —Paris, London, or Petersburg—whichever you will.

If ever the truth that architecture is the expression of the manners of a race was fully demonstrated, is it not since the revolution of 1830, under the reign of the House of Orleans? Great fortunes have shrunk in France, and the majestic mansions of our fathers are constantly being demolished and replaced by a sort of tenement houses, in which a peer of France of July dwells on the third floor, over some newly-enriched empiric. Styles are mingled in confusion. As there is no longer any Court, any nobility to set a "tone," no harmony is to be seen in the productions of art. On the other hand, architecture has never found more economical tricks for imitating what is genuine and thorough, never displayed more ingenuity and resource in arrangement. Ask an artist to deal with a strip of the garden of an old "hôtel" now destroyed, and he will build you a little Louvre crushed under its ornamentation; he will give you a courtyard, stables, and, if you insist, a garden; inside he contrives such a number of little rooms and corridors, and cheats the eye so effectually, that you fancy yourself comfortable; in fact, there are so many bedrooms, that a ducal retinue can live and move in what was only the bake-house of a president of a law court.

The Comtesse Laginski's house is one of these modern structures, with a courtyard in front and a garden behind. To the right of the courtyard are the servants' quarters, balanced on the left by the stables and coach-houses. The porter's lodge stands between two handsome gates. The chief luxury of this house consists in a delightful conservatory at the end of a boudoir on the ground floor, where all the beautiful reception rooms are. It was a philanthropist driven out of England who built this architectural gem, constructed the conservatory, planned the garden, varnished the doors, paved the outbuildings with brick, filled the windows with green glass, and realized a vision like that—in due proportion—of George IV. at Brighton. The inventive, industrious, and ready Paris artisan had carved his doors and window-frames; his ceilings were imitated from those of the Middle Ages or of Venetian palaces, and there was a lavish outlay of marble slabs in external paneling. Steinbock and François Souchet had carved the cornices of the doors and chimney-shelves; Schinner had painted the ceilings with the brush of a master. The wonders of the stairs—marble as white as a woman's arm—defied those of the Hôtel Rothschild.

In consequence of the disturbances, the price of this folly was not more than eleven hundred thousand francs. For an Englishman this was giving it away. All this splendor, called princely by people who do not know what a real prince is, stood in the garden of a contractor—a Crœsus of the Revolution, who had died at Brussels, a bankrupt after a sudden convulsion of the Bourse. The Englishman died at Paris —died of Paris—for to many people Paris is a disease; sometimes it is several diseases. His widow, a Methodist, had a perfect horror of the nabob's little house—this philanthropist had been a dealer in opium. The virtuous widow ordered that the scandalous property should be sold just at the time when the disturbances made peace doubtful on any terms. Count Adam took advantage of the opportunity; and you shall be told how it happened, for nothing could be less consonant with his lordly habits.

Behind this house, built of stone fretted like a melon, spreads the green velvet of an English lawn, shaded at the further end by an elegant clump of exotic trees, among which rises a Chinese pavilion with its mute bells and pendent gilt eggs. The greenhouse and its fantastic decorations screen the outer wall on the south side. The other wall, opposite the greenhouse, is hung with creepers grown in arcades over poles and cross-beams painted green. This meadow, this realm of flowers, these graveled paths, this mimic forest, these aerial trellises cover an area of about twenty-five square perches, of which the present value would be four hundred thousand francs, as much as a real forest. In the heart of this silence won from Paris, birds sing; there are blackbirds, nightingales, bullfinches, chaffinches, and numbers of sparrows. The conservatory is a vast flower-bed, where the air is loaded with perfume, and where you may walk in winter as though summer was blazing with all its fires. The means by which an atmosphere is produced at will of the tropics, China or Italy, are ingeniously concealed from view. The pipes in which the boiling water circulates—the steam, hot air, what not— are covered with soil, and look like garlands of growing flowers.

The boudoir is spacious. On a small plot of ground the miracle wrought by the Paris fairy called Architecture is to produce everything on a large scale. The young Countess' boudoir was the pride of the artist to whom Count Adam intrusted the task of redecorating the house. To sin there would be impossible, there are too many pretty trifles. Love would not know where to alight amid work-tables of Chinese carving, where the eye can find thousands of droll little figures wrought in the ivory—the outcome of the toil of two families of Chinese artists; vases of burnt topaz mounted on filigree stands; mosaics that invite to theft; Dutch pictures, such as Schinner now paints again; angels imagined as Steinbock conceives of them (but does not always work them out himself); statuettes executed by geniuses pursued by creditors (the true interpretation of the Arab myths); sublime first sketches by our greatest artists; fronts of carved chests let into the wainscot, and alternating with the inventions of Indian embroidery; gold-colored curtains draped over the doors from an architrave of black oak wrought with the swarming figures of a hunting scene; chairs and tables worthy of Madame de Pompadour; a Persian carpet, and so forth. And finally, as a crowning touch, all this splendor, seen under a softened light filtering in through lace curtains, looks all the more beautiful. On a marble slab, among some antiques, a lady's whip, with a handle carved by Mademoiselle de Fauveau, shows that the Countess is fond of riding.

Such is a boudoir in 1837, a display of property to divert the eye, as though ennui threatened to invade the most restless and unresting society in the world. Why is there nothing individual, intimate, nothing to invite reverie and repose?—Why?—Because no one is sure of the morrow, and every one enjoys life as a prodigal spends a life interest.

One morning Clémentine affected a meditative air, as she lounged on one of those deep siesta chairs from which we cannot bear to rise, so cleverly has the upholsterer who invented them contrived to fit them to the curves of laziness and the comfort of the *Dolce far niente*. The doors to the conservatory were open, admitting the scent of vegetation and the perfumes of the tropics. The young wife watched Adam, who was smoking an elegant narghileh, the only form

22

of pipe she allowed in this room. Over the other door, curtains, caught back by handsome ropes, showed two magnificent rooms beyond: one in white and gold, resembling that
of the Hôtel Forbin-Janson, the other in the taste of the
Renaissance. The dining-room, unrivaled in Paris by any
but that of the Baron de Nucingen, is at the end of a corridor, with a ceiling and walls decorated in a mediæval style.
This corridor is reached, on the courtyard front, through a
large ante-room, through whose glass door the splendor of the
stairs is seen.

The Count and Countess had just breakfasted; the sky was
a sheet of blue without a cloud; the month of April was drawing to a close. The household had already known two years
of happiness, and now, only two days since, Clémentine had
discovered in her home something resembling a secret, a
mystery. A Pole, let it be repeated to his honor, is generally
weak in the presence of a woman; he is so full of tenderness
that, in Poland, he becomes her inferior; and though Polish
women are admirable creatures, a Pole is even more quickly
routed by a Parisienne. Hence, Count Adam, pressed hard
with questions, had not enough artless cunning to sell his
secret dear to his wife. With a woman there is always something to be got for a secret; and she likes you the better for
it, as a rogue respects an honest man whom he has failed to
take in. The Count, more ready with his sword than with
his tongue, only stipulated that he should not be required to
answer till he had finished his narghileh full of *tombaki*.

"When we were traveling," said she, "you replied to every
difficulty by saying, 'Paz will see to that!' You never wrote
to anybody but Paz. On my return, every one refers me to
the Captain. I want to go out.—The Captain! Is there a
bill to be paid?—The Captain. If my horse's pace is rough,
they will speak to Captain Paz. In short, here I feel as if
it were a game of dominoes; everywhere Paz! I hear no
one talked of but Paz, but I can never see Paz. What is Paz?
Let our Paz be brought to see me."

"Then is not everything as it ought to be?" said the
Count, relinquishing the mouthpiece of his narghileh.

"Everything is so quite what it ought to be, that if we had two hundred thousand francs a year, we should be ruined by living in the way we do with a hundred and ten thousand," said she. She pulled the bell-handle embroidered in tent-stitch, a marvel of skill. A man-servant dressed like a Minister at once appeared.

"Tell Monsieur le Capitaine Paz that I wish to speak to him," said she.

"If you fancy you will find anything out in that way——," said Count Adam with a smile.

It may be useful to say that Adam and Clémentine, married in December 1835, after spending the winter in Paris, had during 1836 traveled in Italy, Switzerland, and Germany. They returned home in November, and during the winter just past the Countess had for the first time received her friends, and then had discovered the existence—the almost speechless and unacknowledged, but most useful presence—of a factotum whose person seemed to be invisible—this Captain Paz or Paç.

"Monsieur le Capitaine Paz begs Madame le Comtesse to excuse him; he is round at the stables, and in a dress which does not allow of his coming at this minute. But as soon as he is dressed Count Paz will come," said the man-servant.

"Why, what was he doing?"

"He was showing Constantine how to groom the Countess' horse; the man did not do it to his mind," replied the servant.

The Countess looked at the man; he was quite serious, and took good care not to imply by a smile that comment which inferiors so often allow themselves on a superior who seems to have descended to their level.

"Ah, he was brushing down Cora?"

"You are not riding out this morning, madame?" said the servant; but he got no answer, and went.

"Is he a Pole?" asked Clémentine of her husband, who bowed affirmatively.

Clémentine lay silent, examining Adam. Her feet, almost

at full length on a cushion, her head in the attitude of a
bird listening on the edge of its nest to the sounds of the
grove, she would have seemed charming to the most blasé of
men. Fair and slight, her hair curled à l'Anglaise, she looked
like one of the almost fabulous figures in Keepsakes, especially
as she was wrapped in a morning gown of Persian silk, of
which the thick folds did not so effectually disguise the
graces of her figure and the slenderness of her waist, as that
they could not be admired through the thick covering of
flowers and embroidery. As she crossed the brightly colored
stuff over her chest, the hollow of her throat remained visible,
the white skin contrasting in tone with the handsome lace
trimming over the shoulders. Her eyes, fringed with black
lashes, emphasized the expression of curiosity that puckered
a pretty mouth. On her well-formed brow were traced the
characteristic curves of the Paris woman, wilful, light-hearted,
well-educated, but invulnerable to vulgar temptations. Her
hands, almost transparent, hung from each arm of her deep
chair; the taper fingers, curved at the tips, showed nails like
pink almonds that caught the light.

Adam smiled at his wife's impatience, gazing at her with
a look which conjugal satiety had not yet made lukewarm.
This slim little Countess had known how to be mistress in
her own house, for she scarcely acknowledged Adam's admiration. In the glances she stole at him there was perhaps a
dawning consciousness of the superiority of a Parisienne to
this spruce, lean, and red-haired Pole.

"Here comes Paz," said the Count, hearing a step that rang
in the corridor.

The Countess saw a tall, handsome man come in, well built,
bearing in his features the marks of the grief which comes
of strength and misfortune. Paz had dressed hastily in
one of those tightly-fitting coats, fastened by braid straps
and oval buttons, which used to be called polonaises. Thick,
black hair, but ill-kempt, covered his squarely-shaped head,
and Clémentine could see his broad forehead as shiny as a
piece of marble, for he held his peaked cap in his hand. That

hand was like the hand of the Hercules carrying the infant
Mercury. Robust health bloomed in a face equally divided
by a large Roman nose, which reminded Clémentine of the
handsome Trasteverini. A black silk stock put a finishing
touch of martial appearance to this mystery of near six feet
high, with jet-black eyes as lustrous as an Italian's The width
of his full trousers, hiding all but the toes of his boots,
showed that Paz still was faithful to the fashions of Poland.
Certainly, to a romantic woman, there must have been something burlesque in the violent contrast observable between
the Captain and the Count, between the little Pole with his
narrow frame and this fine soldier, between the carpet-knight
and the knight servitor.

"Good-morning, Adam," he said to the Count with familiarity.

Then he bowed gracefully, asking Clémentine in what way
he could serve her.

"Then you are Laginski's friend?" asked the lady.

"For life and death," replied Paz, on whom the young
Count shed his most affectionate smile, as he exhaled his last
fragrant puff of smoke.

"Well, then, why do you not eat with us? Why did you
not accompany us to Italy and to Switzerland? Why do
you hide yourself so as to avoid the thanks I owe you for the
constant services you do us?" said the young Countess, with
a sort of irritation, but without the slightest feeling.

In fact, she detected a kind of volunteer slavery on the
part of Paz. At that time such an idea was inseparable from
a certain disdain for a socially amphibious creature, a being
at once secretary and bailiff, neither wholly bailiff nor wholly
secretary, some poor relation—inconvenient as a friend.

"The fact is, Countess," he replied with some freedom,
"that no thanks are owing to me. I am Adam's friend, and
I find my pleasure in taking charge of his interests."

"And is it for your pleasure too that you remain standing?" said Count Adam.

Paz sat down in an armchair near the doorway.

"I remember having seen you on the occasion of our marriage, and sometimes in the courtyard," said the lady; "but why do you, a friend of Adam's, place yourself in a position of inferiority?"

"The opinion of the Paris world is to me a matter of indifference," said he. "I live for myself, or, if you choose, for you two."

"But the opinion of the world as regards my husband's friend cannot be a matter of indifference to me——"

"Oh, madame, the world is easily satisfied by one word: Eccentric—say that."

After a short pause he asked, "Do you purpose going out?"

"Will you come to the Bois?" said the Countess.

"With pleasure," and so saying Paz bowed and went out.

"What a good soul! He is as simple as a child," said Adam.

"Tell me now how you became friends," said Clémentine.

"Paz, my dearest, is of a family as old, as noble, and as illustrious as our own. At the time of the fall of the Pazzi a member of that family escaped from Florence into Poland, where he settled with some little fortune, and founded the family of the Paz, on which the title of count was conferred.

"This family, having distinguished itself in the days of our royal republic, grew rich. The cutting from the tree felled in Italy grew with such vigor that there are several branches of the house of the Counts Paz. It will not, therefore, surprise you to be told that there are rich and poor members of the family. Our Paz is the son of a poor branch. As an orphan, with no fortune but his sword, he served under the Grand Duke Constantine at the time of our Revolution. Carried away by the Polish party, he fought like a Pole, like a patriot, like a man who has nothing—three reasons for fighting well. In the last skirmish, believing his men were following him, he rushed on a Russian battery, and was taken prisoner. I was there. This feat of courage roused my blood. 'Let us go and fetch him!' cried I to my horsemen. We charged the battery like freebooters, and I rescued Paz, I being the seventh. We were twenty when we set out, and eight when we came back, including Paz.

"When Warsaw was betrayed we had to think of escaping from the Russians. By a singular chance Paz and I found ourselves together at the same hour and in the same place on the other side of the Vistula. I saw the poor Captain arrested by some Prussians, who at that time had made themselves bloodhounds for the Russians. When one has fished a man out of the Styx, one gets attached to him. This new danger threatening Paz distressed me so much that I allowed myself to be taken with him, intending to be of service to him. Two men can sometimes escape when one alone is lost. Thanks to my name and some family connection with those on whom our fate depended—for we were then in the power of the Prussians—my flight was winked at. I got my dear Captain through as a common soldier and a servant of my house, and we succeeded in reaching Dantzic. We stowed ourselves in a Dutch vessel sailing for England, where we landed two months later.

"My mother had fallen ill in England, and awaited me there; Paz and I nursed her till her death, which was accelerated by the disasters to our cause.

"We then left England, and I brought Paz to France; in such adversities two men become brothers. When I found myself in Paris with sixty odd thousand francs a year, not to mention the remains of a sum derived from the sale of my mother's diamonds and the family pictures, I wished to secure a living to Paz before giving myself up to the dissipations of Paris life. I had discerned some sadness in the Captain's eyes, sometimes even a suppressed tear floated there. I had had opportunities of appreciating his soul, which is thoroughly noble, lofty, and generous. Perhaps it was painful to him to find himself bound by benefits to a man six years younger than himself without being able to repay him. I, careless and light-hearted as a boy, might ruin myself at play, or let myself be ensnared by some woman; Paz and I might some day be sundered. Though I promised myself that I would always provide for all his needs, I foresaw many chances of forgetting, or being unable to pay Paz an allowance. In short, my angel, I wished to spare him the discomfort, the humiliation, the shame of having to ask me for money, or of seeking in vain for his comrade in some day of necessity. *Dunque,* one morning after breakfast, with our feet on the fire-dogs, each smoking his pipe, after many blushes, and with many precautions, till I saw he was looking at me quite anxiously, I held out to him a bond to bearer producing two thousand four hundred francs interest yearly——"

Clémentine rose, seated herself on Adam's knees, and putting her arm round his neck, kissed him on the brow, saying:

"Dear heart, how noble I think you! And what did Paz say?"

"Thaddeus?" said the Count; "he turned pale and said nothing."

"Thaddeus—is that his name?"

"Yes.—Thaddeus folded up the paper and returned it to me, saying, 'I thought, Adam, that we were as one in life and death, and that we should never part; do you wish to see no more of me?'—'Oh,' said I, 'is that the way you take it? Well, then, say no more about it. If I am ruined, you will be ruined.'—Said he, 'You are not rich enough to live as a Laginski should; and do you not need a friend to take care of your concerns, who will be father and brother to you, and a trusted confidant?' My dear girl, Paz, as he uttered the words, spoke with a calmness of tone and look which covered a motherly feeling, but which betrayed the gratitude of an Arab, the devotion of a dog, and the friendship of a savage, always ready and always unassuming. On my honor! I took him in our Polish fashion, laying my hand on his shoulder, and I kissed him on the lips. 'For life and death, then,' said I. 'All I have is yours, do just as you will.'

"It was he who found me this house for almost nothing. He sold my shares when they were high, and bought when they were low, and we purchased this hovel out of the difference.

He is a connoisseur in horses, and deals in them so well that my stable has cost me very little, and yet I have the finest beasts and the prettiest turnout in Paris. Our servants, old Polish soldiers whom he found, would pass through the fire for us. While I seem to be ruining myself, Paz keeps my house with such perfect order and economy that he has even made good some losses at play, the follies of a young man. My Thaddeus is as cunning as two Genoese, as keen for profit as a Polish Jew, as cautious as a good housekeeper. I have never been able to persuade him to live as I did when I was a bachelor. Sometimes it has needed the gentle violence of friendship to induce him to come to the play when I was going alone, or to one of the dinners I was giving at an eating-house to a party of congenial companions. He does not like the life of drawing-rooms."

"Then what does he like?" asked Clémentine.

"He loves Poland, and weeps over her. His only extravagance has been money sent, more in my name than his own, to some of our poor exiles."

"Dear, how fond I shall be of that good fellow," said the Countess. "He seems to me as simple as everything that is truly great."

"All the pretty things you see here," said Adam, praising his friend with the most generous security, "have been found by Paz; he has bought them at sales, or by some chance. Oh! he is keener at a bargain than a trader. If you see him rubbing his hands in the courtyard, it is because he has exchanged a good horse for a better. He lives in me; his delight is to see me well dressed in a dazzlingly smart carriage. He performs all the duties he imposes on himself without fuss or display. One night I had lost twenty thousand francs at whist. 'What will Paz say?' thought I to myself as I reached home. Paz gave me the sum, not without a sigh; but he did not blame me even by a look. This sigh checked me more than all the remonstrances of uncles, wives, or mothers in similar circumstances. 'You regret the money?' I asked him.—'Oh, not for you, nor for myself; no, I was only thinking that twenty poor relations of mine could have lived on it for a year.'

"The family of Paz, you understand, is quite equal to that of Laginski, and I have never regarded my dear Paz as an inferior. I have tried to be as magnanimous in my degree as he in his. I never go out or come in without going to Paz, as if he were my father. My fortune is his. In short, Thaddeus knows that at this day I would rush into danger to rescue him, as I have done twice before."

"That is not a small thing to say, my dear," remarked the Countess. "Devotion is a lightning-flash. Men devote themselves in war, but they no longer devote themselves in Paris."

"Well, then," said Adam, "for Paz I am always in war. Our two natures have preserved their asperities and their faults, but the mutual intimacy of our souls has tightened the bonds, already so close, of our friendship. A man may save his comrade's life, and kill him afterwards if he finds him a bad companion; but we have gone through what makes friendship indissoluble. There is between us that constant exchange of pleasing impressions on both sides which makes friendship, from that point of view, a richer joy, perhaps, than love."

A pretty little hand shut the Count's mouth so suddenly that the movement was almost a blow.

"Yes, indeed, my darling," said he. "Friendship knows nothing of the bankruptcy of sentiment, the insolvency of pleasures. Love, after giving more than it has, ends by giving less than it receives."

"On both sides alike then," said Clémentine, smiling.

"Yes," said Adam. "While friendship can but increase. You need not pout. We, my angel, are as much friends as lovers; we, at least, I hope, have combined the two feelings in our happy marriage."

"I will explain to you what has made you two such good friends," said Clémentine. "The difference in your love arises from a difference in your tastes, and not from compulsory choice; from preference, and not from the necessity of position. So far as a man can be judged from a glimpse, and from what you tell me, in this instance the subaltern may at times be the superior."

"Oh! Paz is really my superior," replied Adam simply. "I have no advantage over him but that of luck."

His wife kissed him for this generous avowal.

"The perfect skill with which he conceals the loftiness of his soul is an immense superiority," the Count went on. "I say to him, 'You are a sly fellow; you have vast domains in your mind to which you retire.' He has a right to the title of Count Paz; in Paris he will only be called Captain."

"In short, a Florentine of the Middle Ages has resuscitated after three centuries," said the Countess. "There is something of Dante in him, and something of Michael Angelo."

"Indeed, you are right; he is at heart a poet," replied Adam.

"And so I am married to two Poles," said the young Countess, with a gesture resembling that of a genius on the stage.

"Darling child!" said Adam, clasping Clémentine to him, "you would have distressed me very much if you had not liked my friend. We were both afraid of that, though he was delighted at my marrying. You will make him very happy by telling him that you love him—oh! as an old friend."

"Then I will go to dress; it is fine, we will all three go out," said Clémentine, ringing for her maid.

Paz led such an underground life that all the fashion of Paris wondered who it was that accompanied Clémentine Laginski when they saw her driving to the Bois and back between him and her husband. During the drive Clémentine had insisted that Thaddeus was to dine with her. This whim of a despotic sovereign compelled the Captain to make an unwonted toilet. On returning from her drive Clémentine dressed with some coquettish care, in such a way as to produce as effect even on Adam as she entered the room where the two friends were awaiting her.

"Count Paz," said she, "we will go to the opera together."

It was said in the tone which from a woman conveys, "If you refuse, we shall quarrel."

"With pleasure, madame," replied the Captain. "But as I have not a Count's fortune, call me Captain."

"Well, then, Captain, give me your arm," said she, taking it and leading him into the dining-room with a suggestion of the caressing familiarity which enraptures a lover.

The Countess placed the Captain next her, and he sat like a poor sub-lieutenant dining with a wealthy general. Paz left it to Clémentine to talk, listening to her with all the air of deference to a superior, contradicting her in nothing, and waiting for a positive question before making any reply. In short, to the Countess he seemed almost stupid, and her graces all fell flat before this icy gravity and diplomatic dignity. In vain did Adam try to rouse him by saying, "Come, cheer up, Captain. It might be supposed that you were not at home. You must have laid a bet that you would disconcert Clémentine?" Thaddeus remained heavy and half asleep.

When the three were alone at dessert the Captain explained that his life was planned diametrically unlike that of other people; he went to bed at eight o'clock, and rose at daybreak; and he thus excused himself, saying he was very sleepy.

"My intention in taking you to the opera was only to amuse you, Captain; but do just as you please," said Clémentine, a little nettled.

"I will go," said Paz.

"Duprez is singing in *William Tell*," said Adam. "Would you prefer the *Variétés?*"

The Captain smiled and rang the bell; the man-servant appeared. "Tell Constantine," said Paz, "to take out the large carriage instead of the coupé.—We cannot sit comfortably in it," he added, turning to the Count.

"A Frenchman would not have thought of that," said Clémentine, smiling.

"Ah, but we are Florentines transplanted to the North,"

replied Thaddeus, with a meaning and an expression which showed that his dulness at dinner had been assumed.

But by a very conceivable want of judgment, there was too great a contrast between the involuntary self-betrayal of this speech and the Captain's attitude during dinner. Clémentine examined him with one of those keen flashes by which a woman reveals at once her surprise and her observancy. Thus, during the few minutes while they were taking their coffee in the drawing-room, silence reigned—an uncomfortable silence for Adam, who could not divine its cause. Clémentine no longer disturbed Thaddeus. The Captain, for his part, retired again into military rigidity, and came out of it no more, either on the way, or in the box, where he affected to be asleep.

"You see, madame, that I am very dull company," said he, during the ballet in the last act of *William Tell*. "Was I not right to 'stick to my last,' as the proverb says?"

"On my word, my dear Captain, you are neither a coxcomb nor a chatterbox; you are perhaps a Pole."

"Leave me then to watch over your pleasures," he replied, "to take care of your fortune and your house; that is all I am good for."

"Tartufe! begone!" cried Adam, smiling. "My dear, he is full of heart, well informed—he could, if he chose, hold his own in any drawing-room. Clémentine, do not believe what his modesty tells you."

"Good-night, Countess. I have proved my willingness, and now will avail myself of your carriage to go to bed at once. I will send it back for you."

Clémentine bowed slightly, and let him go without replying.

"What a bear!" said she to the Count. "You are much, much nicer."

Adam pressed his wife's hand unseen.

"Poor, dear Thaddeus, he has endeavored to be a foil when many men would have tried to seem more attractive than I."

"Oh!" said she, "I am not sure that was not intentional; his behavior would have mystified an ordinary woman."

Half an hour later, while Boleslas the groom was calling "Gate," and the coachman, having turned the carriage to drive in, was waiting for the gates to be opened, Clémentine said to the Count:

"Where does the Captain roost?"

"Up there," said Adam, pointing to an elegantly con-structed attic extending on both sides of the gateway with a window looking on to the street. "His rooms are over the coach-houses."

"And who lives in the other half?"

"No one as yet," replied Adam. "The other little suite, over the stables, will do for our children and their tutor."

"He is not in bed," said the Countess, seeing a light in the Captain's room when the carriage was under the pillared portico—copied from that at the Tuileries, and taking the place of the ordinary zinc awning painted to imitate striped ticking.

Paz, in his dressing-gown, and pipe in hand, was watching Clémentine as she disappeared into the hall. The day had been a cruel one to him. And this is the reason: Thaddeus had felt a fearful shock to his heart on the day when, Adam having taken him to the opera to pronounce his opinion, he first saw Mademoiselle du Rouvre; and again, when he saw her in the Maire's office and at Saint-Thomas d'Aquin, and recognized in her the woman whom a man must love to the exclusion of all others—for Don Juan himself preferred one among the *mille e tre!*

Hence Paz had strongly advocated the classical bridal tour after the wedding. Fairly easy all the time while Clémentine was absent, his tortures began again on the return of the happy couple. And this was what he was thinking as he in-haled his latakia from a cherry-stem pipe, six feet long, a gift from Adam: "Only I and God, who will reward me for suffering in silence, may ever know how I love her! But how can I manage to avoid alike her love or her hatred?"

And he sat thinking, thinking, over this problem of the strategy of love.

It must not be supposed that Thaddeus lived bereft of all joy in the midst of his pain. The triumphant cunning of this day was a source of secret satisfaction. Since the Count's return with his wife, day by day he felt ineffable happiness in seeing that he was necessary to the couple, who, but for him, would have rushed inevitably into ruin. What fortune can hold out against the extravagance of Paris life? Clémentine, brought up by a reckless father, knew nothing of household management, which nowadays the richest women and the highest in rank are obliged to undertake themselves. Who in these days can afford to keep a steward? Adam, on his part, as the son of one of the great Polish nobles who allowed themselves to be devoured by the Jews, and who was incapable of husbanding the remains of one of the most enormous fortunes in Poland—where fortunes were enormous—was not of a temper to restrict either his own fancies or his wife's. If he had been alone, he would probably have ruined himself before his marriage. Paz had kept him from gambling on the Bourse, and does not that say all?

Consequently, when he found that, in spite of himself, he was in love with Clémentine, Paz had not the choice of leaving the house and traveling to forget his passion. Gratitude, the clue of the mystery of his life, held him to the house where he alone could act as man of business to this heedless couple. Their long absence made him hope for a calmer spirit; but the Countess came back more than ever lovely, having acquired that freedom of thought which marriage confers on the Paris woman, and displaying all the charms of a young wife, with the indefinable something which comes of happiness or of the independence allowed her by a man as trusting, as chivalrous, and as much in love as Adam was.

The consciousness of being the working hub of this magnificent house, the sight of Clémentine stepping out of her carriage on her return from a party, or setting out in the morning for the Bois de Boulogne, a glimpse of her on the Boulevards in her pretty carriage, like a flower in its nest of leaves, filled poor Thaddeus with deep, mysterious ecstasies which blossomed at the bottom of his heart without the slightest trace appearing in his features. How, during these five months, should the Countess ever have seen the Captain? He hid from her, concealing the care he took to keep out of her way.

Nothing is so near divine love as a hopeless love. Must not a man have some depth of soul thus to devote himself in silence and obscurity? This depth, where lurks the pride of a father—or of God—enshrines the worship of love for love's sake, as power for power's sake was the watchword of the Jesuits; a sublime kind of avarice, since it is perennially generous, and modeled indeed on the mysterious Being of the first principles of the world. Is not their result Nature? And Nature is an enchantress; she belongs to man, to the poet, the painter, the lover; but is not the Cause superior to Nature in the sight of certain privileged souls, and some stupendous thinkers? The Cause is God. In that sphere of Causes dwelt the spirits of Newton, of Laplace, of Kepler, of Descartes, Malebranche, Spinoza, Buffon, of the true poets and saints of the second century of our era, of Saint Theresa of Spain and the sublime mystics. Every human emotion contains some analogy with the frame of mind in which the Effect is neglected in favor of the Cause, and Thaddeus has risen to the height whence all things look different. Abandoned to the unspeakable joys of creative energy, Thaddeus was, in love, what we recognize as greatest in the records of genius.

"No, she is not altogether deceived," thought he, as he watched the smoke curl from his pipe. "She might involve me in an irremediable quarrel with Adam if she spited me; and if she should flirt to torment me, what would become of me?"

The fatuity of this hypothesis was so unlike the Captain's modest nature, and his somewhat German shyness, that he was vexed with himself for its having occurred to him, and went to bed determined to await events before taking any decisive steps.

Next morning Clémentine breakfasted very well without Thaddeus, and made no remark on his disobedience. That day, as it happened, was her day for being "at home," and this, with her, demanded a royal display. She did not observe the absence of Captain Paz, on whom devolved all the arrangements for these great occasions.

"Well and good!" said Paz to himself, as he heard the carriages rumble out at two in the morning; "the Countess was only prompted by a Parisian's whim or curiosity."

So the Captain fell back into his regular routine, disturbed for a day by this incident. Clémentine, diverted by the details of life in Paris, seemed to have forgotten Paz. For do you suppose that it is a mere trifle to reign over this inconstant city? Do you imagine, by any chance, that a woman risks nothing but her fortune at that absorbing game?

The winter is to a woman of fashion what, of yore, a campaign was to the soldiers of the Empire. What a work of art—of genius—is a costume or a head-dress created to make a sensation! A fragile, delicate woman wears her hard and dazzling armor of flowers and diamonds, silk and steel, from nine in the evening till two or often three in the morning. She eats little, to attract the eye by her slender shape; she cheats the hunger that attacks her during the evening with debilitating cups of tea, sweet cakes, heating ices, or heavy slices of pastry. The stomach must submit to the commands of vanity. She awakes late, and thus everything is in contradiction to the laws of Nature, and Nature is ruthless.

No sooner is she up than the woman of fashion begins to dress for the morning, planning her dress for the afternoon. Must she not receive and pay visits, and go to the Bois on horseback or in her carriage? Must she not always be practising the drill of smiles, and fatigue her brain in inventing compliments which shall seem neither stale nor studied? And it is not every woman who succeeds. And then you are surprised, when you see a young woman, whom the world has welcomed in her freshness, faded and blighted at the end of three years. Six months spent in the country are

23

barely enough to heal the wounds inflicted by the winter. We hear nothing talked of but dyspepsia and strange maladies, unknown to women who devote themselves to their household. Formerly a woman was sometimes seen; now she is perpetually on the stage.

Clémentine had to fight her way; she was beginning to be quoted, and amid the cares of this struggle between her and her rivals there was hardly a place for love of her husband! Thaddeus might well be forgotten. However, a month later, in May, a few days before her departure to stay at Ronquerolles in Burgundy, as she was returning from her drive she saw Thaddeus in a side alley of the Champs-Elysées,—Thaddeus, carefully dressed, and in raptures at seeing his Countess so beautiful in her phaeton, with champing horses, splendid liveries; in short, the dear people he admired so much.

"There is the Captain," said she to Adam.

"Happy fellow!" said the Count. "These are his great treats. There is not a smarter turnout than ours, and he delights in seeing everybody envying us our happiness. You have never noticed him before, but he is there almost every day."

"What can he be thinking of?" said Clémentine.

"He is thinking at this moment that the winter has cost a great deal, and that we shall save a little by staying with your old uncle Ronquerolles," said Adam.

The Countess had the carriage stopped in front of Paz, and desired him to take the seat by her side in the carriage. Thaddeus turned as red as a cherry.

"I shall poison you," he said; "I have just been smoking cigars."

"And does not Adam poison me?" she replied quickly.,

"Yes, but he is Adam," replied the Captain.

"And why should not Thaddeus enjoy the same privilege?" said the Countess with a smile.

This heavenly smile had a power which was too much for his heroic resolutions; he gazed at Clémentine with all the fire

of his soul in his eyes, but tempered by the angelic expression
of his gratitude—that of a man who lived solely by gratitude.
The Countess folded her arms in her shawl, leaned back pensively against the cushions, crumpling the feathers of her
handsome bonnet, and gazed out at the passers-by. This
flash from a soul so noble, and hitherto so resigned, appealed
to her feelings. What, after all, was Adam's great merit?
Was it not natural that he should be brave and generous?
But the Captain!—Thaddeus possessed, or seemed to possess,
an immense superiority over Adam. What sinister thoughts
distressed the Countess when she once more observed the
contrast between the fine, complete physical nature which
distinguished Thaddeus and the frail constitution which, in
her husband, betrayed the inevitable degeneration of aristocratic families which are so mad as to persist in intermarry-
ing! But the Devil alone knew these thoughts, for the
young wife sat with vague meditation in her eyes, saying
nothing till they reached home.

"You must dine with us, or I shall be angry with you for
having disobeyed me," said she as she went in. "You are
Thaddeus to me, as you are to Adam. I know the obligations
you feel to him, but I also know all we owe to you. In return
for two impulses of generosity which are so natural, you are
generous at all hours and day after day.—My father is coming
to dine with us, as well as my uncle Ronquerolles and my
aunt de Sérizy; dress at once," she said, pressing the hand
he offered to help her out of the carriage.

Thaddeus went to his room to dress, his heart at once re-
joicing and oppressed by an agonizing flutter. He came down
at the last moment, and all through dinner played his part
of a soldier fit for nothing but to fulfil the duties of a steward.
But this time Clémentine was not his dupe. His look had
enlightened her. Ronquerolles, the cleverest of ambassadors
next to Talleyrand, and who served de Marsay so well during
his short ministry, was informed by his niece of the high
merits of Count Paz, who so modestly made himself his
friend's steward.

"And how is it that this is the first time I have ever seen Count Paz?" asked the Marquis de Ronquerolles.

"Eh! he is very sly and underhand," replied Clémentine, with a look at Paz to desire him to change his demeanor.

Alas! it must be owned, at the risk of making the Captain less interesting to the reader, Paz, though superior to his friend Adam, was not a man of strong temper. He owed his apparent superiority to his misfortunes. In his days of poverty and isolation at Warsaw he had read and educated himself, had compared and thought much; but the creative power which makes a great man he did not possess—can it ever be acquired? Paz was great only through his feelings, and there could rise to the sublime; but in the sphere of sentiment, being a man of action rather than of ideas, he kept his thoughts to himself. His thoughts, then, did nothing but eat his heart out.

And what, after all, is an unuttered thought?

At Clémentine's speech the Marquis de Ronquerolles and his sister exchanged glances, with a side look at their niece, Count Adam, and Paz. It was one of those swift dramas which are played only in Italy or in Paris. Only in these two parts of the world—excepting at all courts—can the eyes say as much. To infuse into the eye all the power of the soul, to give it the full value of speech and throw a poem or a drama into a single flash, excessive servitude or excessive liberty is needed.

Adam, the Marquis du Rouvre, and the Countess did not perceive this flash of observation between a past coquette and an old diplomatist; but Paz, like a faithful dog, understood its forecast. It was, you must remember, an affair of two seconds. To describe the hurricane that ravaged the Captain's heart would be too elaborate for these days.

"What! the uncle and aunt already fancy that she perhaps loves me?" said he to himself. "My happiness then depends only on my own audacity.—And Adam! . . ."

Ideal love and mere desire, both quite as potent as friendship and gratitude, rent his soul, and for a moment love had the upper hand. This poor heroic lover longed to have his day! Paz became witty; he intended to please, and in answer to some question from Monsieur de Ronquerolles he sketched in grand outlines the Polish rebellion. Thus, at dessert, Paz saw Clémentine hanging on his lips, regarding him as a hero, and forgetting that Adam, after sacrificing a third of his immense fortune, had taken the risks of exile. At nine o'clock, having taken coffee, Madame de Sérizy kissed her niece on the forehead and took leave, carrying off Count Adam with an assertion of authority, and leaving the Marquis du Rouvre and M. de Ronquerolles, who withdrew ten minutes later. Paz and Clémentine were left together.

"I will bid you good-night, madame," said Thaddeus; "you will join them at the opera."

"No," replied she. "I do not care for dancing, and they are giving an odious ballet this evening, *The Revolt of the Seraglio.*"

There was a moment's silence.

"Two years ago Adam would not have gone without me," she went on, without looking at Paz.

"He loves you to distraction——" Thaddeus began.

"Oh! it is because he loves me to distraction that by to-morrow he will perhaps have ceased to love me!" exclaimed the Countess.

"The women of Paris are inexplicable," said Thaddeus. "When they are loved to distraction, they want to be loved rationally; when they are loved rationally, they accuse a man of not knowing how to love."

"And they are always right, Thaddeus," she replied with a smile. "I know Adam well; I owe him no grudge for it; he is fickle, and, above all, a great gentleman; he will always be pleased to have me for his wife, and will never thwart me in any of my tastes; but——"

"What marriage was ever without a but?" said Thaddeus gently, trying to give the Countess' thoughts another direction.

The least conceited man would perhaps have had the

thought which nearly drove this lover mad: "If I do not tell her that I love her," said he to himself, "I am an idiot!"

There was silence between these two, one of those terrible pauses which seem bursting with thoughts. The Countess fixed a covert gaze on Paz, and Paz watched her in a mirror. Sitting back in his armchair, like a man given up to digestion, in the attitude of an old man or an indifferent husband, the Captain clasped his hands over his stomach, and mechanically twirled his thumbs, looking stupidly at their rapid movement.

"But say something good about Adam!" exclaimed Clémentine. "Tell me that he is not fickle, you who know him so well."

The appeal was sublime.

"This is the opportunity for raising an insurmountable barrier between us," thought the unhappy Paz, devising a heroic lie.—"Something good?" he said aloud. "I love him too well, you would not believe me. I am incapable of telling you any evil of him. . . . And so . . . Madame, I have a hard part to play between you two."

Clémentine looked down, fixing her eyes on his patent leather shoes.

"You northerners have mere physical courage, you have no constancy in your decisions," said she in a low tone.

"What are you going to do alone, madame?" replied Paz, with a perfectly ingenuous expression.

"You are not going to keep me company?"

"Forgive me for leaving you."

"Why! where are you going?"

"I am going to the circus; it is the first night, in the Champs-Elysées, and I must not fail to be there . . ."

"Why not?" asked Clémentine, with a half-angry flash.

"Must I lay bare my heart?" he replied, coloring, "and confide to you what I conceal from my dear Adam, who believes that I love Poland alone?"

"What! our dear, noble Captain has a secret?"

"A disgrace which you will understand, and for which you can comfort me."

"A disgrace!—You? . . ."

"Yes, I—Count Paz, am madly in love with a girl who was touring round France with the Bouthor family, people who have a circus after the pattern of Franconi's, but who only perform at fairs! I got her an engagement from the manager of the Cirque-Olympique."

"Is she handsome?" asked the Countess.

"In my eyes," he replied sadly. "Malaga, that is her name to the public, is strong, nimble, and supple. Why do I prefer her to every other woman in the world?—Indeed, I cannot tell you. When I see her with her black hair tied back with blue ribbons that float over her bare olive-tinted shoulders, dressed in a white tunic with a gilt border, and silk tights which make her appear a living Greek statue, her feet in frayed satin slippers, flourishing flags in her hand to the sound of a military band, and flying through an enormous hoop covered with paper which crashes in the air—when her horse rushes round at a gallop, and she gracefully drops on to him again, applauded, honestly applauded, by a whole people—well, it excites me."

"More than a woman at a ball?" said Clémentine, with insinuating surprise.

"Yes," said Paz in a choked voice. "This splendid agility, this unfailing grace in constant peril, seem to me the greatest triumph of woman. Yes, madame, Cinti and Malibran, Grisi and Taglioni, Pasta and Ellsler, all who reign or ever reigned on the boards, seem to me unworthy to untie Malaga's shoe strings—Malaga, who can mount or dismount a horse at a mad gallop, who slips under him from the left to reappear on the right, who flutters about the most fiery steed like a white will-o'-the-wisp, who can stand on the tip of one toe and then drop, sitting with her feet hanging, on a horse still galloping round, and who finally stands on his back without any reins, knitting a stocking, beating eggs, or stirring an omelette, to the intense admiration of the people, the true people, the peasantry and soldiers. During the walk round, madame, that enchanting Columbine used to carry chairs

balanced on the tip of her nose, the prettiest Greek nose I
ever saw. Malaga is dexterity personified. Her strength is
Herculean; with her tiny fist or her little foot she can shake
off three or four men. She is the goddess of athletics."

"She must be stupid."

"Oh!" cried Paz, "she is as amusing as the heroine of *Peveril of the Peak*. As heedless as a gypsy, she says everything
that comes into her head; she cares no more for the future
than you care for the halfpence you throw to a beggar, and
she lets out really sublime things. Nothing will ever convince
her that an old diplomate is a handsome young man, and a
million of francs would not make her change her opinion.
Her love for a man is a perpetual flattery. Enjoying really
insolent health, her teeth are two-and-thirty Oriental pearls
set in coral. Her 'snout'—so she calls the lower part of her
face—is, as Shakespeare has it, as fresh and sweet as a heifer's
muzzle. And it can give bitter pain! She respects fine men,
strong men—an Adolphus, an Augustus, an Alexander—
acrobats and tumblers. Her teacher, a horrible Cassandro,
thrashed her unmercifully; it cost thousands of blows to give
her such agility, grace, and intrepidity."

"You are drunk with Malaga!" said the Countess.

"Her name is Malaga only on the posters," said Paz, with
a look of annoyance. "She lives in the Rue Saint-Lazare,
in a little apartment on the third floor, in velvet and silk,
like a princess. She leads two lives—one as a dancer, and
one as a pretty woman."

"And does she love you?"

"She loves me—you will laugh—solely because I am a
Pole. She sees in every Pole a Poniatowski, as he is shown
in the print, jumping into the Elster; for to every Frenchman
the Elster, in which it is impossible to drown, is a foaming
torrent which swallowed up Poniatowski.—And with all this
I am very unhappy, madame——"

Clémentine was touched by a tear of rage in the Captain's
eye.

"You love the extraordinary, you men," said she.

"And you?" asked Thaddeus.

"I know Adam so well that I know he could forget me for some acrobatic tumbler like your Malaga. But where did you find her?"

"At Saint-Cloud, last September, at the fair. She was standing in a corner of the platform covered with canvas, where the performers walk round. Her comrades, all dressed as Poles, were making a terrific Babel. I saw her silent and dreamy, and fancied I could guess that her thoughts were melancholy. Was there not enough to make her so—a girl of twenty? That was what touched me."

The Countess was leaning in a bewitching attitude, pensive, almost sad.

"Poor, poor Thaddeus!" she exclaimed. And with the good-fellowship of a really great lady, she added, not without a meaning smile, "Go; go to the circus!"

Thaddeus took her hand and kissed it, dropping a hot tear, and then went out. After having invented a passion for a circus-rider, he must give it some reality. Of his whole story nothing had been true but the minute's attention he had given to the famous Malaga, the rider of the Bouthor troupe at Saint-Cloud; her name had just caught his eye on an advertisement of the circus. The clown, bribed by a single five-franc piece, had told Paz that the girl was a foundling, or had perhaps been stolen.

Thaddeus now went to the circus and saw the handsome horsewoman again. For ten francs, a groom—they fill the place of dressers at a circus—informed him that Malaga's name was Marguerite Turquet, and that she lived at the Rue des Fossés-du-Temple, on a fifth floor.

Next day, with death in his soul, Paz found his way to that quarter, and asked for Mademoiselle Turquet, in summer the understudy of the principal rider at the cirque, and in winter "a super" in a Boulevard theatre.

"Malaga!" shouted the doorkeeper, rushing into the attic, "here is a fine gentleman for you! He is asking Chapuzot all about you; and Chapuzot is cramming him to give me time to let you know."

"Thank you, M'ame Chapuzot; but what will he say to find me ironing my gown?"

"Pooh, stuff! When a man is in love, he loves everything about you."

"Is he an Englishman? They are fond of horses."

"No. He looks to me like a Spaniard."

"So much the worse. The Spaniards are down in the market they say.—Stay here, Madame Chapuzot, I shall not look so left to myself."

"Who were you wanting, monsieur?" said the woman, opening the door to Thaddeus.

"Mademoiselle Turquet."

"My child," said the porter's wife, wrapping her shawl round her, "here is somebody asking for you."

A rope on which some linen was airing knocked off the Captain's hat.

"What is your business, monsieur?" asked Malaga, picking it up.

"I saw you at the circus; you remind me, mademoiselle, of a daughter I lost; and out of affection for my Héloïse, whom you are so wonderfully like, I should wish to be of use to you if you will allow me."

"Well, to be sure! But sit down, Monsieur le Général," said Madame Chapuzot. "You cannot say fairer—nor handsomer."

"I am not by way of love-making, my good lady," said Paz. "I am a father in deep distress, eager to be cheated by a likeness."

"And so I am to pass as your daughter?" said Malaga, very roguishly, and without suspecting the absolute truth of the statement.

"Yes," said Paz. "I will come sometimes to see you; and that the illusion may be perfect, I will place you in handsome lodgings, nicely furnished——"

"I shall have furniture of my own?" said Malaga, looking at Madame Chapuzot.

"And servants," Paz went on; "and live quite at your ease."

Malaga looked at the stranger from under her brows.

"From what country are you, monsieur?"

"I am a Pole."

"Then I accept," said she.

Paz went away, promising to call again.

"That is a tough one!" said Marguerite Turquet, looking at Madame Chapuzot. "But I am afraid this man is wheedling me to humor some fancy. Well, I will risk it."

A month after this whimsical scene, the fair circus-rider was established in rooms charmingly furnished by Count Adam's upholsterer, for Paz wished that his folly should be talked about in the Laginski household. Malaga, to whom the adventure was like an Arabian Nights' dream, was waited on by the Chapuzot couple—at once her servants and her confidants. The Chapuzots and Marguerite Turquet expected some startling climax; but at the end of three months, neither Malaga nor the Chapuzots could account for the Polish Count's fancy. Paz would spend about an hour there once a week, during which he sat in the drawing-room, never choosing to go either into Malaga's boudoir nor into her bedroom, which, in fact, he never entered in spite of the cleverest manœuvring on her part and on that of the Chapuzots. The Count inquired about the little incidents that varied the horsewoman's life, and on going away he always left two forty-franc pieces on the chimney-shelf.

"He looks dreadfully bored," said Madame Chapuzot.

"Yes," replied Malaga, "that man is as cold as frost after a thaw."

"He is a jolly good fellow, all the same," cried Chapuzot, delighted to see himself dressed in blue Elbeuf cloth, and as smart as a Minister's office-messenger.

Paz, by his periodical tribute, made Marguerite Turquet an allowance of three hundred and twenty francs a month. This sum, added to her small earnings at the circus, secured her a splendid existence as compared with her past squalor. Strange tales were current among the performers at the circus as to Malaga's good fortune. The girl's vanity allowed her rent to be stated at sixty thousand francs, instead of the modest six thousand which her rooms cost the prudent Captain. According to the clowns and supers, Malaga ate off silver plate; and she certainly came to the circus in pretty burnouses, in shawls, and elegant scarfs. And, to crown all, the Pole was the best fellow a circus-rider could come across; never tiresome, never jealous, leaving Malaga perfect freedom.

"Some women are so lucky!" said Malaga's rival. "Such a thing would never happen to me, though I bring in a third of the receipts."

Malaga wore smart "coal-scuttles," and sometimes gave herself airs in a carriage in the Bois de Boulogne, where the youth of fashion began to observe her. In short, Malaga was talked about in the flash world of equivocal women, and her good fortune was attacked by calumny. She was reported to be a somnambulist, and the Pole was said to be a magnetizer in search of the Philosopher's Stone. Other comments of a far more venomous taint made Malaga more inquisitive than Psyche; she reported them, with tears, to Paz.

"When I owe a woman a grudge," said she to conclude, "I do not calumniate her, I do not say that a man magnetizes her to find stones. I say that she is a bad lot, and I prove it. Why do you get me into trouble?"

Paz was cruelly speechless.

Madame Chapuzot succeeded at last in discovering his name and title. Then, at the Hôtel Laginski, she ascertained some positive facts: Thaddeus was unmarried, he was not known to have a dead daughter either in Poland or France. Malaga could not help feeling a thrill of terror.

"My dear child," said Madame Chapuzot, "that monster——"

A man who was satisfied with gazing at a beautiful creature like Malaga—gazing at her by stealth—from under his brows —not daring to come to any decision—without any confidence; such a man, in Madame Chapuzot's mind, must be a monster. "That monster is breaking you in, to lead you on to something illegal or criminal. God above us! if you were to be brought up at the Assizes—and it makes me shudder from head to foot to think of it, I quake only to speak of it—or in the Criminal Court, and your name was in the newspapers! . . . Do you know what I should do in your place? Well, in your place, to make all safe, I should warn the police."

One day, when mad notions were fermenting in Malaga's brain, Paz having laid his gold pieces on the velvet chimney-shelf, she snatched up the money and flung it in his face, saying, "I will not take stolen money!"

The Captain gave the gold to the Chapuzots, and came no more.

Clémentine was spending the summer on the estate of her uncle, the Marquis de Ronquerolles, in Burgundy.

When the troupe at the circus no longer saw Thaddeus in his seat, there was a great talk among the artists. Malaga's magnanimity was regarded as folly by some, as cunning by others. The Pole's behavior, as explained to the most experienced of the women, seemed inexplicable. In the course of a single week, Thaddeus received thirty-seven letters from women of the town. Happily for him, his singular reserve gave rise to no curiosity in fashionable circles, and remained the subject of discussion in the flash set only.

Two months later, the handsome rider, swamped in debt, wrote to Count Paz the following letter, which the dandies of the day regarded as a masterpiece:—

"You, whom I still venture to call my friend, will you not take pity on me after what passed between us, which you took so ill? My heart disowns everything that could hurt your feelings. If I was so happy as to make you feel some charm when you sat near me, as you used to do, come again . . . otherwise, I shall sink into despair. Poverty has come upon me already, and you do not know what stupid things it brings with it. Yesterday I lived on a herring for two sous and one sou's worth of bread. Is that a breakfast for the woman you love? The Chapuzots have left me after

seeming so devoted to me. Your absence has shown me the
shallowness of human attachment. A bailiff, who turned a
deaf ear to me, has seized everything on behalf of the landlord, who has no pity, and of the jeweler, who will not wait
even ten days; for with you men, credit vanishes with confidence. What a position for a woman who has nothing to reproach herself for but a little amusement! My dear friend,
I have taken everything of any value to my uncle's; I have
nothing left but my memory of you, and the hard weather
is coming on. All through the winter I shall have no fire,
since nothing but melodrama is played at the Boulevard,
in which I have nothing to do but tiny parts, which do not
show a woman off. How could you misunderstand my noble
feelings towards you, for, after all, we have not two ways of
expressing our gratitude? How is it that you, who seemed
so pleased to see me comfortable, could leave me in misery?
Oh, my only friend on earth, before I go back to travel from
fair to fair with the Bouthors—for so, at any rate, I can
make my living—forgive me for wanting to know if I have
really lost you for ever. If I should happen to think of you
just as I was jumping through the hoop, I might break my
legs by missing time. Come what may, I am yours for life.

"MARGUERITE TURQUET."

"This letter," exclaimed Thaddeus, shouting with laughter,
"is well worth my ten thousand francs."

Clémentine came home on the following day, and Paz saw
her once more, lovelier and more gracious than ever. During
dinner the Countess preserved an air of perfect indifference
towards Thaddeus, but a scene took place between the Count
and his wife after their friend had left. Thaddeus, with
an affectation of asking Adam's advice, had left Malaga's
letter in his hands, as if by accident.

"Poor Thaddeus!" said Adam to his wife, after seeing Paz
make his escape. "What a misfortune for a man of his
superior stamp to be the plaything of a ballet-girl of the
lowest class! He will love anything; he will degrade himself;

he will be unrecognizable before long. Here, my dear, read that," and he handed her Malaga's letter.

Clémentine read the note, which smelt of tobacco, and tossed it away with disgust.

"However thick the bandage over his eyes may be, he must have found something out. Malaga must have played him some faithless trick."

"And he is going back to her!" cried Clémentine. "He will forgive her! You men can have no pity for any but those horrible women."

"They want it so badly!" said Adam.

"Thaddeus did himself justice—by keeping to himself!" said she.

"Oh, my dearest, you go too far," said the Count, who, though he was at first delighted to lower his friend in his wife's eyes, would not the death of the sinner.

Thaddeus, who knew Adam well, had begged for absolute secrecy; he had only spoken, he said, as an excuse for his dissipations, and to beg his friend to allow him to have a thousand crowns for Malaga.

"He is a man of great pride," Adam went on.

"What do you mean?"

"Well, to have spent no more than ten thousand francs on her, and to wait for such a letter as that to rouse him before taking her the money to pay her debts! For a Pole, on my honor! . . ."

"But he may ruin you!" said Clémentine in the acrid tone of a Parisian woman when she expresses her cat-like distrustfulness.

"Oh! I know him," said Adam. "He would sacrifice Malaga to us."

"We shall see," replied the Countess.

"If it were needful for his happiness, I should not hesitate to ask him to give her up. Constantine tells me that during the time when he was seeing her, Paz, usually so sober, sometimes came in quite fuddled. If he allowed himself to take to drink, I should be as much grieved as if he were my son."

"Do not tell me any more!" cried the Countess with another gesture of disgust.

Two days later the Captain could see in her manner, in the tone of her voice, in her eyes, the terrible results of Adam's betrayal. Scorn had opened gulfs between him and this charming woman. And he fell forthwith into deep melancholy, devoured by this thought, "You have made yourself unworthy of her." Life became a burden to him; the bright sunshine was gloomy in his eyes. Nevertheless, under these floods of bitter thought, he had some happy moments: he could now give himself up without danger to his admiration for the Countess, who never paid him the slightest attention when, at a party, hidden in a corner, mute, all eyes and all heart, he did not lose one of her movements, not a note of her song when she sang. He lived in this enchanting life: he might himself groom the horse that she was to ride, and devote himself to the management of her splendid house with redoubled care for its interests.

These unspoken joys were buried in his heart like those of a mother, whose child never knows anything of his mother's heart: for is it knowledge so long as even one thing remains unknown? Was not this finer than Petrarch's chaste passion for Laura, which, after all, was well repaid by a wealth of glory, and by the triumph of the poetry she had inspired? Was not the emotion which Assas felt in dying, in truth a whole life? This emotion Paz felt every day without dying, but also without the guerdon of immortality.

What is there in love, that Paz, notwithstanding these secret delights, was consumed by sorrow? The Catholic religion has so elevated love that she has married it inseparably, so to speak, to esteem and generosity. Love does not exist apart from the fine qualities of which man is proud, and so rarely are we loved if we are contemned, that Thaddeus was perishing of his self-inflicted wounds. Only to hear her say that she could have loved him, and then to die! The hapless lover would have thought his life well paid for. The torments of his previous position seemed to him preferable

to living close to her, loading her with his generosity without
being appreciated or understood. In short, he wanted the
price of his virtue.

He grew thin and yellow, and fell so thoroughly ill, consumed by low fever, that during the month of January he
kept his bed, though refusing to see a physician. Count
Adam grew extremely uneasy about his poor Thaddeus. The
Countess then was so cruel as to say, when they were together
one day, "Let him alone; do not you see that he has some
Olympian remorse?"

This speech stung Thaddeus to the courage of despair; he
got up, went out, tried some amusement, and recovered his
health.

In the month of February Adam lost a rather considerable
sum at the Jockey Club, and, being afraid of his wife, he
begged Thaddeus to place this sum to the account of his extravagance for Malaga.

"What is there strange in the notion that the ballet-girl
should have cost you twenty thousand francs? It concerns
on one but me. Whereas, if the Countess should know that
I had lost it at play, I should fall in her esteem, and she would
be in alarm for the future."

"This to crown all!" cried Thaddeus, with a deep sigh.

"Ah! Thaddeus, this service would make us quits if I
were not already the debtor."

"Adam, you may have children. Give up gambling," said
his friend.

"Twenty thousand francs more that Malaga has cost us!"
exclaimed the Countess some days after, on discovering
Adam's generosity to Paz. "And ten thousand before—that
is thirty thousand in all! Fifteen hundred francs a year,
the price of my box at the Italian opera, a whole fortune to
many people. . . . Oh! you Poles are incomprehensi-
ble!" cried she, as she picked some flowers in her beautiful
conservatory. "You care no more than that!"

"Poor Paz——"

"Poor Paz, poor Paz!" she echoed, interrupting him.

24

"What good does he do us? I will manage the house my-self! Give him the hundred louis a year that he refused, and let him make his own arrangements with the Olympic Circus."

"He is of the greatest use to us; he has saved us at least forty thousand francs this year. In short, my dearest, he has placed a hundred thousand francs for us in Nucingen's bank, and a steward would have netted them."

Clémentine was softened, but she was not the less hard on Thaddeus.

Some days after she desired Paz to come to her in her boudoir, where, a year since, she had been startled by com-paring him with the Count. This time she received him alone, without any suspicion of danger.

"My dear Paz," said she, with the careless familiarity of fine folks to their inferiors, "if you love Adam as you say you do, you will do one thing which he will never ask, but which I, as his wife, do not hesitate to require of you——"

"It is about Malaga?" said Thaddeus with deep irony.

"Well, yes, it is," she said. "If you want to end your days with us, if you wish that we should remain friends, give her up. How can an old soldier——"

"I am but five-and-thirty, and have not a gray hair!"

"You look as if you had," said she, "and that is the same thing. How can a man so capable of putting two and two together, so superior . . ."

What was horrible was that she spoke the word with such an evident intention of rousing in him the nobleness of soul which she believed to be dead.

"So superior as you are," she went on, after a little pause, which a gesture from Paz forced from her, "allow yourself to be entrapped like a boy. Your affair with her has made Malaga famous.—Well! My uncle wanted to see her, My uncle is not the only one; Malaga is very ready to receive all these gentlemen.—I believed you to be high-minded.— Take shame to yourself! Come, would she be an irreparable loss to you?"

"Madame, if I knew of any sacrifice by which I might recover your esteem, it would soon be made; but to give up Malaga is not a sacrifice——"

"In your place that is what I should say if I were a man," replied Clémentine. "Well, but if I take it as a great sacrifice, there is nothing to be angry at."

Paz went away, fearing he might do some mad act; he felt his brain invaded by crazy notions. He went out for a walk, lightly dressed in spite of the cold, but failed to cool the burning of his face and brow. "I believed you to be high-minded!" He heard the words again and again. "And scarcely a year ago," said he to himself, "to hear Clémentine, I had beaten the Russians single-handed!" He thought of quitting the Laginski household, of asking to be sent on service in the Spahi regiment, and getting himself killed in Africa; but a dreadful fear checked him: "What would become of them without me? They would soon be ruined. Poor Countess, what a horrible life it would be for her to be reduced even to thirty thousand francs a year! Come," said he to himself, "since she can never be yours, courage, finish your work!"

As all the world knows, since 1830 the Carnival in Paris has grown to prodigious proportions, making it European, and burlesque, and animated to a far greater degree than the departed carnivals of Venice. Is this because, since fortunes have so enormously diminished, Parisians have thought of amusing themselves collectively, just as in their clubs they have a drawing-room without any mistress of the house, without politeness, and quite cheap? Be this as it may, the month of March was prodigal of those balls, where dancing, farce, coarse fun, delirium, grotesque figures, and banter made keen by Paris wit, achieved gigantic results. This madness had its Pandemonium at that time in the Rue Saint-Honoré, and its Napoleon in Musard, a little man born to rule an orchestra as tremendous as the rampant mob, and to conduct a galop—that whirl of witches at their Sabbath, and one of Auber's triumphs, for the galop derived its form and its poetry from the famous galop in *Gustavus*. May not this vehement finale serve as a symbol of an age when, for fifty years, everything has rushed on with the swiftness of a dream?

Now, our grave Thaddeus, bearing an immaculate image in his heart, went to Malaga to invite her, the queen of carnival dancing, to spend an evening at Musard's as soon as he learned that the Countess, disguised to the teeth, was intending to come with two other young ladies, escorted by their husbands, to see the curious spectacle of one of these monster balls. On Shrove Tuesday night, in the year of grace 1838, at four o'clock in the morning, the Countess, wrapped in a black domino, and seated on a bench of one of the amphitheatres of the Babylonian hall where Valentino has since given his concerts, saw Thaddeus, dressed as Robert Macaire, leading the circus-rider in the costume of a savage, her head dressed with nodding plumes like a horse at a coronation, and leaping among the groups like a perfect Jack-o'-lantern.

"Oh!" exclaimed Clémentine to her husband, "you Poles are not men of character. Who would not have felt sure of Thaddeus? He gave me his word, not knowing that I should be here and see all without being seen."

Some days after this she invited Paz to dinner. After dinner, Adam left them together, and Clémentine scolded Thaddeus in such a way as to make him feel that she would no longer have him about the house.

"Indeed, madame," said Thaddeus humbly, "you are quite right. I am a wretch; I had pledged my word. But what can I do? I put off the parting with Malaga till after the Carnival. . . . And I will be honest with you; the woman has so much power over me . . ."

"A woman who gets herself turned out of Musard's by the police, and for such dancing?"

"I admit it; I sit condemned; I will quit your house. But you know Adam. If I hand over to you the conduct of your affairs, you will have to exert great energy. Though

I have the vice of Malaga, I know how to keep an eye on
your concerns, how to manage your household, and superin-
tend the smallest details. Allow me then to remain till I
have seen you qualified to continue my system of management. You have now been married three years, and are safe
from the first follies consequent on the honeymoon. The
ladies of Paris society, even with the highest titles, understand very well in these days how to control a fortune and
a household. . . . Well, as soon as I am assured, not of
your capacity, but of your firmness, I will leave Paris."

"It is Thaddeus of Warsaw that speaks, not Thaddeus of
the circus. Come back to us cured."

"Cured?—Never!" said Paz, his eyes fixed on Clémentine's pretty feet. "You cannot know, Countess, all the spice,
the unexpectedness there is in that woman's wit." And feeling his courage fail him, he added: "There is not a single
woman of fashion, with her prim airs, who is worth that
frank young animal nature."

"In fact, I should not choose to have anything in me of
the animal!" said the Countess, with a flashing look like an
adder in a rage.

After that day Count Paz explained to Clémentine all her
affairs, made himself her tutor, taught her the difficulties of
managing her property, the real cost of things, and the way
to avoid being too extensively robbed by her people. She
might trust Constantine, and make him her major-domo.
Thaddeus had trained Constantine. By the month of May he
thought the Countess perfectly capable of administering her
fortune; for Clémentine was one of those clear-sighted women
whose instincts are alert, with an inborn genius for household
rule.

The situation thus naturally brought about by Thaddeus
took a sudden turn most distressing for him, for his sufferings
were not so light as he made them seen. The hapless lover
had not reckoned with accident. Adam fell very seriously
ill. Thaddeus, instead of leaving, installed himself as his

friend's sick-nurse. His devotedness was indefatigablc. A woman who had had an interest in looking through the telescope of foresight would have seen in the Captain's heroism the sort of punishment which noble souls inflict on themselves to subdue their involuntary thoughts of sin; but women see everything or nothing, according to their frame of mind; love is their sole luminary.

For forty-five days Paz watched and nursed Mitgislas without seeming to have a thought of Malaga, for the excellent reason that he never did think of her. Clémentine, seeing Adam at death's door, and yet not dead, had a consultation of the most famous doctors.

"If he gets through this," said the most learned of the physicians, "it can only be by an effort of nature. It lies with those who nurse him to watch for the moment and aid nature. The Count's life is in the hands of his attendants."

Thaddeus went to communicate this verdict to Clémentine, who was sitting in the Chinese pavilion, as much to rest after her fatigues as to leave the field free for the doctors, and not to be in their way. As he trod the graveled paths leading from the boudoir to the rockery on which the Chinese summer house was built, Clémentine's lover felt as though he were in one of the gulfs described by Alighieri. The unhappy man had never foreseen the chance of becoming Clémentine's husband, and he had bogged himself in a swamp of mud. When he reached her his face was set, sublime in its despair. Like Medusa's head, it communicated terror.

"He is dead?" said Clémentine.

"They have given no hope; at least, they leave it to nature. Do not go in just yet. They are still there, and Bianchon himself is examining him."

"Poor fellow!—I wonder whether I have ever worried him," she said.

"You have made him very happy; be quite easy on that point," said Thaddeus; "and you have been indulgent to him——"

"The loss will be irreparable."

"But, dear lady, supposing the Count should die, had you not formed your opinion of him?"

"I do not love him blindly," she said; "but I loved as a wife ought to love her husband."

"Then," said Thaddeus, in a voice new to Clémentine's experience of him, "you ought to feel less regret than if you were losing one of those men who are a woman's pride, her love, her whole life! You may be frank with such a friend as I am. . . . I shall regret him—I! Long before your marriage I had made him my child, and I have devoted my life to him. I shall have no interest left on earth. But life still has charms for a widow of four-and-twenty."

"Why, you know very well that I love no one," said she, with the roughness of sorrow.

"You do not know yet what it is to love," said Thaddeus.

"Oh! husband for husband, I have sense enough to prefer a child like my poor Adam to a superior man. For nearly a month now we have been asking ourselves, 'Will he live?' These fluctuations have prepared me, as they have you, for this end. I may be frank with you?—Well, then, I would give part of my life to save Adam's. Does not independence for a woman, here in Paris,. mean liberty to be gulled by the pretence of love in men who are ruined or profligate? I have prayed God to spare me my husband—so gentle, such a good fellow, so little fractious, and who was beginning to be a little afraid of me."

"You are honest, and I like you the better for it," said Thaddeus, taking Clémentine's hands, which she allowed him to kiss. "In such a solemn moment there is indescribable satisfaction in finding a woman devoid of hypocrisy. It is possible to talk to you.—Consider the future; supposing God should not listen to you—and I am one of those who are most ready to cry to Him: Spare my friend!—for these fifty nights past have not made my eyes heavy, and if thirty days' and thirty nights' more care are needed, you, madame, may sleep while I watch. I will snatch him from death, if, as they say, he can be saved by care. But if, in spite of you, in spite of me, the Count is dead. Well, then, if you were loved, or worshiped, by a man whose heart and character were worthy of yours——"

"I have perhaps madly wished to be loved, but I have never met——"

"Supposing you were mistaken."

Clémentine looked steadily at Thaddeus, suspecting him less of loving her than of a covetous dream; she poured contempt on him by a glance, measuring him from head to foot, and crushed him with two words, "Poor Malaga!" pronounced in those tones such as fine ladies alone can find in the gamut of their contempt.

She rose and left Thaddeus fainting, for she did not turn round, but walked with great dignity back to her boudoir, and thence up to her husband's room.

An hour later Paz returned to the sick man's bedside, and gave all his care to the Count, as though he had not received his own death-blow.

From that dreadful moment he became silent; he had a duel to fight with disease, and he carried it through in a way that excited the admiration of the doctors. At any hour his eyes were always beaming like two lamps. Without showing the slightest resentment towards Clémentine, he listened to her thanks without accepting them; he seemed deaf. He had said to himself, "She shall owe Adam's life to me!" and these words he had, as it were, written in letters of fire in the sick man's room.

At the end of a fortnight Clémentine was obliged to give up some of the nursing, or risk falling ill from so much fatigue. Paz was inexhaustible. At last, about the end of August, Bianchon, the family doctor, answered for the Count's life:

"Ah, madame," said he to Clémentine, "you are under not the slightest obligation to me. But for his friend we could not have saved him!"

On the day after the terrible scene in the Chinese pavilion, the Marquis de Ronquerolles had come to see his nephew, for he was setting out for Russia with a secret mission; and Paz, overwhelmed by the previous evening, had spoken a few words to the diplomate.

On the very day when Count Adam and his wife went out for the first time for a drive, at the moment when the carriage was turning from the steps, an orderly came into the courtyard and asked for Count Paz. Thaddeus, who was sitting with his back to the horses, turned round to take a letter bearing the stamp of the Minister for Foreign Affairs, and put it into the side-pocket of his coat, with a decision which precluded any questions on the part of Clémentine or Adam. It cannot be denied that persons of good breeding are masters of the language that uses no speech. Nevertheless, as they reached the Porte Maillot, Adam, assuming the privilege of a convalescent whose whims must be indulged, said to Thaddeus:

"There can be no indiscretions between two brothers who love each other as you and I do; you know what is in that letter; tell me, I am in a fever of curiosity."

Clémentine looked at Thaddeus as an angry woman can, and said to her husband, "He has been so sulky with me these two months, that I shall take good care not to press him."

"Oh dear me!" replied Thaddeus, "as I cannot hinder the newspapers from publishing it, I may very well reveal the secret. The Emperor Nicholas does me the favor of appointing me Captain on service in a regiment starting with the Khiva Expedition."

"And you are going?" cried Adam.

"I shall go, my dear fellow. I came as Captain, and as Captain I return. Malaga might lead me to make a fool of myself. We shall dine together to-morrow for the last time. If I did not set out in September for St. Petersburg, I should have to travel overland, and I am not rich. I must leave Malaga her little independence. How can I fail to provide for the future of the only woman who has understood me? Malaga thinks me a great man! Malaga thinks me handsome! Malaga may perhaps be faithless, but she would go through——"

"Through a hoop for you, and fall on her feet on horseback!" said Clémentine, sharply.

"Oh, you do not know Malaga," said the Captain, with deep bitterness, and an ironical look which made Clémentine uneasy and silent.

"Farewell to the young trees of this lovely Bois de Boulogne, where Parisian ladies drive, and the exiles wander who have found a home here. I know that my eyes will never again see the green trees of the Allée de Mademoiselle, or of the Route des Dames, nor the acacias, nor the cedar at the Ronds-points.

"On the Asiatic frontier, obedient to the schemes of the great Emperor I have chosen to be my master, promoted perhaps to command an army, for sheer courage, for constantly risking my life, I may indeed regret the Champs-Elysées where you, once, made me take a place in the carriage, by your side.—Finally, I shall never cease to regret the severity of Malaga—of the Malaga I am at this moment thinking of."

This was said in a tone that made Clémentine shiver.

"Then you love Malaga very truly?" she said.

"I have sacrificed for her the honor we never sacrifice——"

"Which?"

"That which we would fain preserve at any cost in the eyes of the idol we worship."

After this speech Thaddeus kept impenetrable silence; he broke it only when, as they drove down the Champs-Elysées, he pointed to a wooden structure and said, "There is the circus!"

Before their last dinner he went to the Russian Embassy for a few minutes, and from thence to the Ministry for Foreign Affairs, and he started for le Havre next morning before the Countess and Adam were up.

"I have lost a friend," said Adam, with tears in his eyes,

as he learned that Count Paz was gone, "a friend in the truest sense of the word, and I cannot think what has made him flee from my house as if it were the plague. We are not the sort of friends to quarrel over a woman," he went on, looking full at Clémentine, "and yet all he said yesterday about Malaga—But he never laid the tip of his finger on the girl."

"How do you know?" asked Clémentine.

"Well, I was naturally curious to see Mademoiselle Turquet, and the poor girl cannot account for Thaddeus' extraordinary reserve——"

"That is enough," said the Countess, going off to her own room, and saying to herself, "I have surely been the victim of some sublime hoax."

She had scarcely made the reflection, when Constantine placed in her hands the following letter, which Thaddeus had scrawled in the night:—

"COUNTESS,—To go to be killed in the Caucasus, and to bear the burden of your scorn, is too much; a man should die unmutilated. I loved you from the first time I saw you, as a man loves the woman he will love for ever, even when she is faithless—I, under obligations to Adam, whom you chose and married—I, so poor, the volunteer steward, devoted to your household. In this dreadful catastrophe I found a delightful existence. To be an indispensable wheel in the machine, to know myself useful to your luxury and comfort, was a source of joy to me; and if that joy had been keen when Adam alone was my care, think what it must have been when the woman I worshiped was at once the cause and the effect! I have known all the joys of motherhood in my love; and I accepted life on those terms. Like the beggars on the highroads, I built myself a hut of stones on the skirts of your beautiful home, but without holding out my hand for alms. I, poor and unhappy, but. blinded by Adam's happiness, I was the donor. Yes, you were hedged in by a love as pure as that of a guardian angel; it watched while you slept; it caressed you with a look as you passed by; it was glad merely to exist; in short, you were the sunshine of home to the hapless exile who is now writing to you, with tears in his eyes, as he recalls the happiness of those early days.

"At the age of eighteen, with no one to love me, I had chosen as an ideal mistress a charming woman at Warsaw, to whom I referred all my thoughts and my wishes, the queen of my days and nights. This woman knew nothing of it, but why inform her? For my part, what I loved was love.

"You may fancy, from this adventure of my boyhood, how happy I was, living within the sphere of your influence, grooming your horse, picking out new gold pieces for your purse, superintending the splendor of your table and your entertainments, seeing you eclipse fortunes greater than your own by my good management. With what zeal did I not rush round Paris when Adam said to me, 'Thaddeus, *She* wants this or that!' It was one of those joys for which there are no words. You have now and again wished for some trifle within a certain time which has compelled me to feats of expedition, driving for six or seven hours in a cab; and what happiness it has been to walk in your service. When I have watched you smiling in the midst of your flowers without being seen by you, I have forgotten that no one loved me— in short, at such moments I was but eighteen again.

"Sometimes, when my happiness turned my brain, I would go at night and kiss the spot where your feet had left, for me, a luminous trace, just as of old I had stolen, with a thief's miraculous skill, to kiss a key which Countess Ladislas had touched on opening a door. The air you breathed was embalmed; to me it was fresh life to breathe it; and I felt, as they say is the case in the tropics, overwhelmed by an atmosphere surcharged with creative elements. I must tell you all these things to account for the strange fatuity of my involuntary thoughts. I would have died sooner than divulge my secret.

"You may remember those few days when you were curious, when you wanted to see the worker of the wonders which had at last struck you with surprise. I believed—forgive me, madame—I believed that you would love me. Your kindliness, your looks—interpreted by a lover—seemed fraught with so much danger to me that I took up Malaga, knowing that there are *liaisons* which no woman can forgive; I took the girl up at the moment when I saw that my love was inevitably infectious. Overwhelm me now with the scorn which you poured upon me so freely when I did not deserve it; but I think I may be quite sure that if, on the evening when your aunt took the Count out, I had said what I have here written, having once said it I should have been like the tame tiger who has at last set his teeth in living flesh, and who scents warm blood. . . .

Midnight.

"I could write no more, the memory of that evening was too vivid! Yes, I was then in a delirium! I saw expectancy in your eyes; victory and its crimson banners may have burned in mine and fascinated yours. My crime was to think such things—and perhaps wrongly. You alone can be judge of that fearful scene when I succeeded in crushing love, desire, the most stupendous forces of manhood under the icy hand of gratitude which must be eternal. Your terrible scorn punished me. You have showed me that neither disgust nor contempt can ever be got over. I love you like a madman. I must have gone away if Adam had died. There is all the more reason since Adam is saved. I did not snatch my friend from the grave to betray him. And, indeed, my departure is the due punishment for the thought that came to me that I would let him die when the physicians said his life depended on his attendants.

"Farewell, madame; in leaving Paris I lose everything, but you lose nothing in parting with yours most faithfully,

"THADDEUS PAZ."

"If my poor Adam says he has lost a friend, what have I lost?" thought Clémentine, sitting dejected, with her eyes fixed on a flower in the carpet.

This is the note which Constantine delivered privately to his master:—

"MY DEAR MITGISLAS,—Malaga has told me all. For the sake of your happiness, never let a word escape you in Clémentine's presence as to your visits to the circus-rider; let her still believe that Malaga cost me a hundred thousand francs. With the Countess' character she will not forgive you either your losses at play or your visits to Malaga.—I am not going to Khiva, but to the Caucasus. I have a fit of spleen, and at the pace I mean to go, in three months I shall be Prince Paz, or dead. Farewell; though I have drawn sixty thousand francs out of Nucingen's, we are quits.

"THADDEUS."

"Idiot that I am! I very nearly betrayed myself just now by speaking of the circus-rider!" said Adam to himself.

Thaddeus has been gone three years, and the papers do not as yet mention any Prince Paz. Countess Laginski takes a keen interest in the Emperor Nicholas' expeditions; she is a Russian at heart, and reads with avidity all the news from that country. Once or twice a year she says to the Ambassador, with an affectation of indifference, "Do you know what has become of our poor friend Paz?"

Alas! most Parisian women, keen-eyed and subtle as they are supposed to be, pass by—and always will pass by—such an one as Paz without observing him. Yes, more than one Paz remains misunderstood; but, fearful thought! some are misunderstood even when they are loved. The simplest woman in the world requires some little coxcombry in the greatest man; and the most heroic love counts for nothing if it is uncut; it needs the arts of the polisher and the jeweler.

In the month of January 1842 Countess Laginski, beautified by gentle melancholy, inspired a mad passion in the

Comte de la Palférine, one of the most audacious bucks of Paris at this day. La Palférine understood the difficulty of conquering a woman guarded by a chimera; to triumph over this bewitching woman, he trusted to a surprise, and to the assistance of a woman who, being a little jealous of Clémentine, would lend herself to plot the chances of the adventure.

Clémentine, incapable with all her wit of suspecting such treachery, was so imprudent as to go with this false friend to the masked ball at the opera. At about three in the morning, carried away by the excitement of the ball, Clémentine, for whom La Palférine had exhausted himself in attentions, consented to sup with him, and was getting into the lady's carriage. At this critical moment she was seized by a strong arm, and in spite of her cries placed in her own carriage, which was standing with the door open, though she did not know that it was waiting.

"He has not left Paris!" she exclaimed, recognizing Thaddeus, who ran off when he saw the carriage drive away with the Countess.

Had ever another woman such a romance in her life?

Clémentine is always hoping to see Paz again.

PARIS, *January 1842.*